The
Seventh
Gate

Bantam Spectra Books
by Margaret Weis and Tracy Hickman

THE DARKSWORD TRILOGY
Forging the Darksword
Doom of the Darksword
Triumph of the Darksword

DARKSWORD ADVENTURES

ROSE OF THE PROPHET
The Will of the Wanderer
The Paladin of the Night
The Prophet of Akhran

THE DEATH GATE CYCLE
Dragon Wing
Elven Star
Fire Sea
Serpent Mage
The Hand of Chaos
Into the Labyrinth
The Seventh Gate

and by Margaret Weis

STAR OF THE GUARDIANS
The Lost King
King's Test
King's Sacrifice
Ghost Legion

A DEATH GATE NOVEL

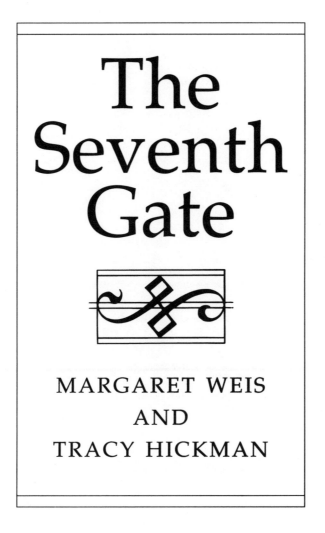

The Seventh Gate

MARGARET WEIS
AND
TRACY HICKMAN

SPECTRA ™

BANTAM BOOKS
NEW YORK   TORONTO   LONDON   SYDNEY   AUCKLAND

THE SEVENTH GATE

A Bantam Spectra Book / September 1994

SPECTRA *and the portrayal of a boxed "s" are trademarks of Bantam Books,*
a division of Bantam Doubleday Dell Publishing Group, Inc.

Library of Congress Cataloging-in-Publication Data

Weis, Margaret.
The seventh gate : a Death Gate novel / Margaret Weis and Tracy Hickman.
p.   cm. — (The Death Gate cycle ; v. 7)
ISBN 0-553-09647-8
I. Hickman, Tracy.   II. Title.   III. Series: Weis, Margaret.
Death Gate cycle ; v. 7.
PS3573.E3978S48   1994
813'.54—dc20   94-2573
CIP

Published simultaneously in the United States and Canada

Bantam Books are published by Bantam Books, a division of Bantam Doubleday Dell Publishing Group, Inc. Its trademark,
consisting of the words "Bantam Books" and the portrayal of a rooster, is Registered in U.S. Patent and Trademark Office and in
other countries. Marca Registrada. Bantam Books, 1540 Broadway, New York, New York 10036.

PRINTED IN THE UNITED STATES OF AMERICA

BVG   0 9 8 7 6 5 4 3 2 1

To

DR. "JAY" SELDARA,
Lake Geneva, Wisconsin

and

DR. JOHN HANSON, Jr.,
Milwaukee, Wisconsin

for hope.

Margaret Weis

◆

To

LYNN ALLEY, BARRY BOUNOUS,
ROB MUIR, and HARRY NILES RISING III.

Somehow, we have lived to tell the tale.

Tracy Hickman

And into that gate they shall enter,
and in that house they shall dwell,
where there shall be no Cloud nor
Sun, no darkness nor dazzling, but
one equal light, no noise nor silence,
but one equal music, no fears nor
hopes, but one equal possession, no
foes nor friends, but one equal
communion and identity, no ends nor
beginnings, but one equal eternity.

◆

John Donne, *XXVI Sermons*

The
Seventh
Gate

CHAPTER ◆ 1

ABRI

THE LABYRINTH

◆

VASU STOOD ON THE WALL ABOVE THE GATES OF THE CITY OF ABRI, STOOD SILENT and thoughtful as the gates boomed shut beneath his feet. It was dawn, which meant, in the Labyrinth, nothing more than a graying of night's black. But this dawn was different than most. It was more glorious than most . . . and more terrifying. It was brightened by hope, darkened by fear.

It was a dawn which saw the city of Abri, in the very center of the Labyrinth, still standing, victorious, after a terrible battle with its most implacable enemies.

It was a dawn smudged with the smoke of funeral pyres; a dawn in which the living could draw a tremulous breath and dare to hope life might be better.

It was a dawn lit by a lurid red glow on the far distant horizon, a red glow that was brightening, strengthening. Those Patryns who guarded the city walls turned their eyes to that strange and unnatural glow, shook their heads, spoke of it in low and ominous tones.

"It bodes nothing good," they said grimly.

Who could blame them for their dark outlook? Not Vasu. Certainly not Vasu, who knew what was transpiring. He would have to tell them soon, destroy the joy of this dawning.

"That glow is the fire of battle," he would have to say to his people. "A battle raging for control of the Final Gate. The dragon-

◆ 1 ◆

snakes who attacked us were not defeated, as you thought. Yes, we killed four of them. But for every four that die, eight are born. Now they are attacking the Final Gate, seeking to shut it, seeking to trap us all in this dread prison.

"Our brothers, those who live in the Nexus and those near the Final Gate, are fighting this evil—so we have reason to believe. But they are few in number and the evil is vast and powerful.

"We are too far away to come to their aid. Too far. By the time we reached them—if we ever did reach them, alive—it would be too late. It may already be too late.

"And when the Final Gate is shut, the evil in the Labyrinth will grow strong. Our fear and our hatred will grow stronger to match and the evil will feed off that fear and that hatred and grow stronger still."

It is hopeless, Vasu told himself, and so he must tell the people. Logic, reason said to him it was hopeless. Yet why, standing on the wall, staring at that red glow in the sky, did he feel hopeful?

It made no sense. He sighed and shook his head.

A hand touched his arm.

"Look, Headman. They have made it safely to the river."

One of the Patryns, standing beside Vasu, had obviously mistaken his sigh, thought it indicated fear for the two who had left the city in the dark hour before the dawn. They were embarking on a dangerous and probably futile search for the green and golden dragon who had fought for them in the skies above Abri. The green and golden dragon was the Serpent Mage, who was also the bumbling Sartan with the mensch name, Alfred.

Certainly Vasu was afraid for them, but he was also hopeful for them. That same illogical, irrational hope.

Vasu was not a man of action. He was a man of thought, of imagination. He had only to look at his soft and pudgy Sartan body, tattooed with Patryn runes, to know that. He must give thought to what his people should do next. He should make plans, he should decide how they must prepare for the inevitable. He should tell them the truth, give his speech of despair.

But he didn't do any of that. He stood on the walls, watching the mensch known as Hugh the Hand and the Patryn woman Marit.

He told himself he would never see them again. They were venturing out into the Labyrinth, dangerous at any time but doubly dangerous now that their defeated enemies skulked about in anger and waited for revenge. The two were going on a foolhardy and hopeless mission. He would never see them again, nor Alfred, the Serpent Mage, the green and golden dragon, for whom they searched.

Vasu stood on the wall and waited—hopefully—for their return.

The River of Anger, which flowed beneath the city walls of Abri, was frozen. Its water had been frozen by their enemies, by spells cast on it. The hideous dragon-snakes had turned the river to ice in order that their troops could cross more easily.

Clambering down the rock-strewn sides of the riverbank, Marit smiled grimly. The tactics of her enemy would serve her.

There was just one small problem.

"You say this was done by magic?" Hugh the Hand, sliding down the bank behind her, skidded to a halt beside the black ice floe. He jabbed at it with the toe of his boot. "How long will the spell last?"

That was the problem.

"I don't know," Marit was forced to admit.

"Yeah." Hugh grunted. "I thought as much. It might end when we're standing in the middle."

"It might." Marit shrugged. If that happened, they would be lost. The rushing black water would suck them down, chill their blood, grind their bodies against the sharp rocks, fill their lungs with the black and now blood-tinged water.

"There's no other way?" Hugh the Hand was looking at her, at the blue sigla tattooed on her body.

He meant, of course, her magic.

"I might be able to get myself across," she told him. Then

again, she might not. She was weakened in body from yesterday's battle, weakened in her spirit from yesterday's confrontation with Lord Xar. "But I'd never be able to manage you."

She set foot on the ice, felt its cold strike through to the very marrow of her bones. Clamping her teeth together to keep them from chattering, she stared at the far shore and said, "Only a short run. It won't take us long."

Hugh the Hand said nothing. He was staring—not at the shore, but at the ice.

And then Marit remembered. This man, a professional assassin, afraid of nothing in *his* world, had come across something in another world he did fear—water.

"What are you scared of?" Marit jeered, hoping to bolster his courage by shaming him. "You can't die."

"I *can* die," he corrected her. "I just don't stay dead. And, lady, I don't mind telling you, this sort of dying doesn't appeal to me."

"It doesn't appeal to me either," she said snappishly back at him, but she noticed she wasn't going anywhere, had hurriedly snatched her foot back off the ice.

She drew in a deep breath. "You can follow or not, as you please."

"I'm of little use to you anyway," he said bitterly, hands clenching and unclenching. "I can't protect you, defend you. I can't even protect or defend myself."

He couldn't be killed. He couldn't kill. Every arrow he fired missed its mark, every blow he aimed fell short, every slash of his sword went wide.

"I can defend myself," Marit answered. "I can defend you, too, for that matter. I need you because you know Alfred better than I do—"

"No, I don't," Hugh returned. "I don't think anyone knew Alfred. Not even Alfred knew Alfred. Haplo did, maybe, but that's not much help to us now."

Marit said nothing, bit her lip.

"But you're right to remind me, lady," Hugh the Hand continued. "If I don't find Alfred, this curse on me will never end. Come on. Let's get it over with."

He set foot on the ice, began to walk across it. His swift and impetuous move took Marit by surprise. She was hurrying after him before she quite knew what she was doing.

The ice was slippery and treacherous. The bone-numbing cold shot through her; she began shivering uncontrollably. She and Hugh clung to each other for support, his arm saving her from more than one sliding fall, her arm steadying him.

Halfway across, an eardrum-shattering crack split the ice, almost beneath their feet. A fur-covered clawed hand and arm shot up from the gurgling water, tried to grab hold of Marit. She grappled for the hilt of her sword.

Hugh the Hand stopped her.

"It's only a corpse," he said.

Marit, looking more closely, saw he was right. The arm was flaccid, sucked down by the current almost immediately.

"The spell's ending," she said, irritated at herself. "We have to hurry."

She continued across. But a thin layer of water was now seeping over the ice, making it even more slippery. Her feet slid out from underneath her. She grabbed at Hugh, but he, too, had lost his footing. They both fell. Landing on her hands and knees, she stared into the horribly grinning mouth and bulging eyes of a dead wolfen.

The black ice split right between her hands. The wolfen popped out, lunged straight at her. Involuntarily, Marit shrank backward. Hugh the Hand caught hold of her.

"The ice is breaking apart," he yelled. "Hurry!"

They were at least two body lengths from the shoreline.

Marit scrambled toward the shore, crawling since she could not stand. Her arms and legs ached with the cold; the pain was intense. Hugh the Hand slithered along beside her. His face was livid, his jaw clenched so tight it resembled the ice. His eyes were wide and staring. For him—born and raised on a waterless world —drowning was the worst possible death imaginable. Terror had very nearly robbed him of his senses.

They were close to the bank, close to safety.

The Labyrinth was intelligent evil, cunning malevolence. It permitted you to hope, let you imagine that you could make it to safety.

Marit's numb hand clutched at a large rock, one of several lining the riverbank. She struggled to grip it with unfeeling fingers, pull herself up.

The ice gave way beneath her. She plunged to her waist in frothing black water. Her hand slid off the rock. The current was carrying her down . . .

A terrific boost from strong arms propelled Marit up and onto the bank. She landed hard, the breath knocked from her body. She lay, gasping, until a gurgle and a wild yell caused her to turn around.

Standing precariously on an ice floe, Hugh clung with one hand to the trunk of a scrub tree growing out of the bank. He had thrown her to safety, then managed to grab hold of the tree.

But the rushing water was tearing the ice floe out from under him. The current was strong. His tenuous hold on the tree was slipping.

Marit flung herself bodily on Hugh just as he lost his grasp. Her numb fingers clutching at the back of his leather vest, she fought to pull him from the river. She was on her knees; the water was rising. If she failed, they would both go under. Desperately she held onto his vest, pulled it up nearly over his head. Digging her knees into the mud, she dragged the man's heavy body backward. Hugh was strong; he gave her what help he could. He kicked with his feet, sought purchase with his flailing legs, and, finally, managed to squirm his way onto the bank.

He lay still, gasping and shivering with cold and terror. Hearing a rumbling sound, Marit looked upriver. A wall of black water tinged with red foam, pushing huge chunks of ice in its path, thundered downstream.

"Hugh!" she cried.

He raised his head, saw the rushing floodwaters. He staggered to his feet, began scrambling up the bank. Marit was past helping him; she could barely make it herself. She collapsed onto firm, level ground; was dimly aware of Hugh the Hand falling somewhere near her.

The river roared in rage at losing its prey; or perhaps that was only her imagination. She stilled her rapid breathing, calmed the wild beating of her heart. Letting the rune-magic warm her, she banished the terrible cold.

But she couldn't lie here long. The enemy—chaodyn, wolfen, tiger-men—must be hiding in the woods, perhaps watching them even now. She glanced at the sigla tattooed on her skin; the glow of the runes would warn her of approaching danger. Her skin was slightly blue, but that was with cold. The sigla were dark.

This should have been reassuring, but it wasn't. It was illogical. Certainly some of those who had attacked the city with such fury yesterday must still be lurking outside the city walls, waiting for a chance to pick off a scouting party.

But the runes did not glimmer, except perhaps very, very faintly. If any of the enemy were about, they were far away and not interested. Marit couldn't understand it and she didn't like it. This uncanny absence of the foe frightened her more than the sight of a pack of wolfen.

Hope. When the Labyrinth offers you hope, it means that it is just about to snatch that hope away.

She pushed herself to a crouching position, alert and wary. Hugh the Hand lay huddled on the ground. He was shivering uncontrollably, his body racked by chills. His lips were blue, his teeth chattering so violently he'd bitten his tongue. Blood dribbled from his mouth.

Marit didn't know much about mensch. Could he die of the cold? Perhaps not, but he might fall sick, slow her up. Moving about, walking, would warm his blood, but she had to get him on his feet first. She recalled hearing from Haplo that rune-magic would work to heal mensch. Crawling over to Hugh, she clasped her hands over his wrists, let the magic flow from her body to his.

His shaking ceased. Slowly, a tinge of color returned to his pallid face. At length, he sighed, fell back on the ground, closed his eyes, letting the blissful warmth spread through his body.

"Don't fall asleep!" Marit warned.

Touching his tender tongue to his teeth, he groaned, grunted. "Back on Arianus, I used to dream that when I was a wealthy man,

I'd wallow in water. Have a big barrel of it outside my house and I'd jump in it, splash it over my head. Now"—he grimaced—"may the ancestors take me if I so much as drink a sip of the cursed stuff!"

Marit stood up. "We can't stay here, out in the open like this. If you're feeling up to it, we have to move."

Hugh was on his feet immediately. "Why? What is it?"

He looked at the runes on her hands and arms; he'd been around Haplo long enough to know the signs. Seeing the sigla dark, he glanced up at her questioningly.

"I don't know," she answered, staring hard into the forest. "There's nothing close, seemingly. But . . ." Unable to explain her uneasiness, she shook her head.

"Which way?" Hugh asked.

Marit considered. Vasu had pointed out the site where the green and golden dragon—Alfred—had last been seen. That was to the gateward side of the city, the side facing the next gate.[1] She and Vasu had judged the distance to be within half a day's walk.

Marit gnawed her lip. She could enter the woods, which would give them shelter but would also make them more vulnerable to their enemies, who—if they were out there—were undoubtedly using the woods to conceal their own movements. Or she could keep to the riverbank, keep in view of the city. For a short distance, any foe who attacked her would be in range of the magical weapons held by the guards on the city walls.

Marit decided to stay near the river, at least until the city could offer no more protection. Perhaps by then she would have picked up a trail that would lead her to Alfred.

What that trail might be, she didn't like to think.

◆

---

[1] Directions in the Labyrinth are based on the "gates," those markers which indicate how far one has progressed through the Labyrinth. The first gate is the Vortex. The city of Abri is between the first and second gates. Since the Labyrinth's innumerable gates are scattered around randomly, directions are based on where one is at the time in relation to the next gate.

She and Hugh moved cautiously along the river's shoreline. The black water churned and fumed in its banks, brooding over the indignities it had suffered. The two took care to keep clear of the slippery bank on one side and avoid the forest shadows on the other.

The woods were silent, strangely silent. It was as if every living being had gone away . . .

Marit halted, sick with realization, understanding.

"That's why no one's around," she said aloud.

"What? Why? What are you talking about?" Hugh the Hand demanded, alarmed by her sudden stop.

Marit pointed to the ominous red glow in the sky. "They've all gone to the Final Gate. To join the fight against my people."

"Good riddance, then," said Hugh the Hand.

Marit shook her head.

"What's wrong?" Hugh continued. "So they've left. Vasu said the Final Gate was a long way from here. Not even those tiger-men could reach it anytime soon."

"You don't understand," Marit replied, overwhelmed by despair. "The Labyrinth could transport them there. It could move them in the blink of an eye, if it wanted. All our enemies, all the evil creatures of the Labyrinth . . . joined together, fighting against my people. How can we survive?"

She was ready to give up. Her task seemed futile. Even if she found Alfred alive, what good could he do? He was only one man, after all. A powerful mage, but only one.

Find Alfred! Haplo had told her. But he couldn't know how great the odds were against them. And now Haplo was gone, perhaps dead. And Lord Xar was gone, too.

Her lord, her liege lord. Marit put her hand to her forehead. The sigil he had tattooed on her skin, the sigil that had been a sign of her love and trust, burned with a dull and aching pain. Xar had betrayed her. Worse, it seemed he had betrayed his people.

He was powerful enough to withstand the onslaught of evil beings. His presence would inspire his people, his magic and his cunning give them a chance for victory.

But Xar had turned his back on them . . .

Shaking the wet hair out of her eyes, Marit resolutely put everything out of her mind except the immediate problem. She'd forgotten an important lesson. Never look too far ahead. What you see could be a mirage. Keep your eyes on the trail on the ground.

And there it was. The sign.

Marit cursed herself. She'd been so preoccupied, she had almost missed what she'd been searching for. Kneeling down, she carefully picked up an object, held it out for Hugh the Hand to see.

It was a green, glittering scale. One of several scales—green and gold—lying on the ground.

Surrounding it were large dollops of fresh blood.

CHAPTER 2

THE LABYRINTH

◆

"According to vasu, the last time he saw alfred—the dragon Alfred—he was falling from the skies. Wounded, bleeding." Marit turned the green scale over and over in her hand.

"There were lots of dragons fighting," Hugh protested.

"But the Labyrinth dragons are red-scaled. Not green. No, this has to be Alfred."

"Whatever you say, lady. I don't believe it myself. A man changing himself into a dragon!" He snorted.

"The same man who brought you back from the dead," Marit said crisply. "Let's go."

The trail of blood—pitiably easy to follow—led into the forest. Marit found glimmering drops on the grass and splattered on the leaves of the trees. Occasionally she and Hugh were forced to make a detour around some impassable tangle of bramble bushes or thick undergrowth, but they could always pick the trail up easily; too easily. The dragon had lost a lot of blood.

"If the dragon *was* Alfred, he was flying *away* from the city," Hugh the Hand observed, crawling over a fallen log. "I wonder why? If he was hurt this badly, you'd think he would have come back to the city for help."

"In the Labyrinth, a mother will often run away from safety to lure the enemy from her child. I think that's what Alfred was doing. That's why he didn't fly toward the city. He was being pursued and so he deliberately led his enemy away from us. Careful. Don't go near that!"

Marit caught hold of Hugh, stopped him from stepping into an innocent-looking tangle of green leaves. "That's a choke vine. It'll tighten around your ankle, cut right through the bone. You won't have a foot left."

"Nice place you've got here, lady," Hugh muttered, falling back. "The damn weed is all over! There's no way around it."

"We'll have to climb." Marit pulled herself up into a tree, began crawling from branch to branch.

Hugh the Hand followed more clumsily and more slowly, his dangling feet barely clearing the choke vine. Its green leaves and tiny white blossoms stirred and rustled beneath him.

Marit pointed grimly to streaks of blood running down the tree trunk. Hugh grunted, said nothing.

Across the vine-patch, Marit slid back down to the ground. She scratched at her skin. The sigla had begun to itch and glow faintly, warning her of danger. Apparently, not all their enemies had rushed to do battle at the Final Gate. She pushed forward with greater urgency, greater caution.

Emerging from a dense thicket, she stepped suddenly and unexpectedly into a cleared space.

"Would you look at this!" Hugh the Hand gave a low whistle.

Marit stared, amazed.

A wide swath of destruction had been cut into the forest. Small trees lay broken on the ground. Their limbs, snapped and twisted, hung from scarred trunks. The undergrowth had been flattened into the mud. The ground was littered with twigs and leaves. Green and golden scales were scattered around, sparkling like jewels in the gray dawn.

Some enormous green-scaled body had fallen from the sky, crashed down among the trees. Alfred, without doubt.

Yet where was he now?

"Could something have carried—" Marit began.

"Hsst!" Hugh the Hand emphasized his warning with a crushing grip on her wrist, dragged her down into the underbrush.

Marit crouched, held perfectly still. She strained to hear whatever sound had caught the Hand's attention.

The silence of the forest was broken now and again by the fall of a branch, but she heard nothing else. Quiet. Too damn quiet. She looked at Hugh questioningly.

"Voices!" He leaned over, whispered into her ear. "I swear I heard something that could have been a voice. It stopped talking when you spoke."

Marit nodded. She hadn't been talking all that loudly. Whatever it was must be close, with sharp hearing.

Patience. She counseled herself to keep still, wait for whatever was out there to reveal itself. Hardly breathing, she and Hugh waited and listened.

They heard the voice then. It spoke with a grating sound, horrible to hear, as if jagged edges of broken bones were grinding against each other. Marit shuddered and even Hugh the Hand blenched. His face twisted in revulsion.

"What the—"

"A dragon!" Marit whispered, cold with dread.

That was why Alfred hadn't flown back to the city. He was being pursued, probably attacked, by the most fearsome creature in the Labyrinth.

The runes on her body glowed. She fought the impulse to turn and flee.

One of the laws of the Labyrinth: never fight a red dragon unless it has you cornered and escape is impossible. Then you fight only to force the dragon to kill you swiftly.

"What's it talking about?" Hugh asked. "Can you understand?"

Marit nodded, sickened.

The dragon was speaking the Patryn language. Marit translated for Hugh's benefit.

"I don't know what you are, man-wyrm," the dragon was saying. "I've never seen anything like you. But I plan to find out. I must have leisure to study you. Take you apart."

"Damn!" Hugh the Hand muttered. "The very sound of the

thing makes me want to piss my pants. Is it talking to Alfred, do you think?"

Marit nodded. Her lips compressed to a thin line. She knew what she had to do; she only wanted the courage to do it. Rubbing her burning arm, the sigla flaring red and blue, she ignored their warning and began creeping forward toward the voice, using its rumbling as cover for her own movement through the brush. Hugh the Hand followed her.

They were downwind of the dragon. It shouldn't be able to pick up their scent. Marit only wanted to get the creature in sight, to see if it had truly captured Alfred. If not—and she was hoping desperately it had not—then she could follow common sense and run.

No shame in running from such a powerful foe. Lord Xar was the only Patryn Marit had ever known who had fought a Labyrinth dragon and survived. And he never spoke of the battle; his face would darken whenever it was mentioned.

"The ancestors have mercy!" Hugh the Hand breathed.

Marit squeezed Hugh's hand, cautioned him to keep quiet.

They could see the dragon easily now. Marit's hope was dashed.

Standing propped up against the bole of a shattered tree was a tall and gangling man with a bald head—smeared with blood—dressed in the tattered remnants of what had once been breeches and a velvet frock coat. He had been in dragon form when they saw him during the battle. Certainly—by the destruction in the forest—he must have been in dragon form when he crashed headlong into the woods.

He was not in dragon form now. Either he was too weak to sustain the magical transformation or, perhaps, his enemy had used its own magic to reveal the Sartan's true appearance.

Surprisingly, considering that his first reaction to any sort of danger was to faint dead away, Alfred was conscious. He was even managing to face this terrible foe with a certain amount of dignity, though this was rather impaired by the fact that he was nursing a broken arm and his face was gray and drawn with pain.

The dragon towered over its prey. Its head was huge, blunt-nosed and rounded, with rows of razor-sharp teeth protruding from the lower jaw. The head was attached to a neck that seemed too thin to support it. The head swung back and forth—such constant oscillating motion could sometimes hypnotize hapless victims. Two small and cunning eyes, on either side of the head, moved independently of each other. The eyes could rotate in any direction, focus forward or backward as required, allowing the dragon to see everything around it.

Its two front legs were strong and powerful, with claw-like "hands," which could lift and carry objects in flight. Enormous wings sprouted from the shoulders. The hind legs were muscular, used to push the dragon off the ground and into the air.

The tail was the deadliest part of the creature, however. The red dragon's tail curled up and over the body. On the end was a bulbous stinger that injected venom into the victim, venom that could either kill or, in small doses, paralyze.

The tail flicked out near Alfred.

"This may burn a little," the dragon said, "but it will keep you docile during our trip back to my cave."

The tip of the stinger grazed Alfred on the cheek. He screamed; his body jerked. Marit clenched her hands tight, dug the nails into her flesh. Beside her, she could hear Hugh the Hand breathing hard, gulping for air.

"What do we do?" His face was covered with sweat. He wiped his mouth with the back of his hand.

Marit looked at the dragon. A limp and unresisting Alfred dangled from the creature's front claws. The dragon carried the man carelessly, as a small child might carry a rag doll.

Unfortunately, the wretched Sartan was still conscious, his eyes open and wide with fear. That was the worst part of the dragon's venom. It kept the victim paralyzed but conscious; feeling, knowing everything.

"Nothing," Marit answered quietly.

Hugh the Hand glowered. "But we have to do something! We can't let it fly off—"

Marit put her hand over the man's mouth. He hadn't spoken above a whisper, yet the dragon's huge head was shifting swiftly toward them, its roving eyes searching the forest.

The baleful gaze raked across them, passed on. The dragon continued its search a bit longer; then, losing interest perhaps, it began to move.

It was walking.

Marit's hopes rose.

The dragon was walking, not flying. It had begun to lumber through the forest, carrying Alfred in its claws. And now that the creature had turned toward her, Marit could see that it was injured. Not critically, but enough to keep it grounded. The membrane of one wing was torn, a gaping hole sliced through it.

Score one for Alfred, Marit said silently, then sighed. That wound would only make the dragon all the more furious. It would keep Alfred alive for a long, long time.

And he wouldn't like it much.

She stood unmoving, silent, until the dragon was well out of eyesight and earshot. Every time Hugh the Hand would have spoken, Marit frowned, shook her head. When she could no longer hear any sound of the dragon crashing through the forest, she turned to Hugh.

"The dragons have excellent hearing. Remember that. You nearly got us killed."

"Why didn't we attack it?" he demanded. "The damn thing is hurt! With your magic—" He waved his hand, too angry to finish.

"With my magic, I could have done exactly nothing," Marit retorted. "These dragons have their own magic, far more powerful than mine. Which it probably wouldn't have even bothered to use! You saw its tail. That stinger moves fast, strikes like lightning. One touch and you're paralyzed, helpless, just like Alfred."

"So that's it." Hugh eyed her grimly. "We give up?"

"No, we don't," Marit said.

She turned her back on him so that he couldn't see her face, couldn't see how wonderful the words "give up" sounded. Resolutely, she began to make her way through the twisted trees, the flattened undergrowth.

"We'll track it. The dragon said it was taking Alfred back to its cave. If we can find the dragon's lair, we can rescue the Sartan."

"What if it kills Alfred on the way?"

"It won't," Marit said. This was one thing she knew for a certainty. "Labyrinth dragons don't kill their prey right off. They keep them for sport."

The dragon's trail was easy to follow. It mowed down everything in its path, never deviating from a straight route through the forest. Giant trees were uprooted with a blow from the massive tail. Scrub trees and brush were crushed beneath the large hind feet. Choke vines, trying to wrap their cutting tendrils around the dragon, realized too late what they had caught. The vines lay black and smoldering on the ground.

Hugh and Marit trudged along in the dragon's devastating wake. The way had been made easier for them; the dragon cleared the path quite effectively. But they moved cautiously, at Marit's insistence, although Hugh protested that with all the noise the dragon was making it wouldn't be likely to hear them. And when the creature changed direction, began traveling upwind of them, Marit stopped to coat her body in foul-smelling mud from a bog. She forced Hugh to do the same.

"I saw a dragon destroy a Squatters' village once," Marit said, dabbing mud on her thighs, smearing it over her legs. "The beast was clever. It could have attacked the village, burned it, killed the inhabitants. But what sport is there in that? Instead, it captured two men alive—young men, strong. Then the dragon proceeded to torture them.

"We heard their screams—terrible screams. The screaming went on for two days. The headman decided to attack the dragon, rescue his people—or at least put them out of their misery. Haplo was with me," she added softly. "We knew about the red dragons. We told the headman he was a fool, but he wouldn't listen to us. Armed with weapons enhanced by magic, the warriors marched on the dragon's lair.

"The dragon came out of its cave, carrying the still living bodies of its two victims—one in each clawed hand. The warriors fired rune-sped arrows at the dragon, arrows that cannot possibly miss their target. The dragon distorted the runes with its own magic. It didn't stop the arrows; it simply slowed them down. The dragon caught the arrows—with the bodies of the two men.

"When they were dead, the dragon tossed the bodies back to their companions. By this time, a few of the arrows had found their mark. The dragon was wounded, beginning to get annoyed. It lashed out with its tail, moving so fast the warriors couldn't escape. It would sting one, then another, then another, darting here and there among the ranks. Each time, the person screamed in horrible pain. His body convulsing, he fell helpless, writhing on the ground.

"The dragon plucked up his victims, tossed them into the cave. More sport. The dragon always chose the young and the strong. The headman was forced to pull his forces back. In trying to save two, he'd lost more than twenty. Haplo advised him to pack up, move his people away. But the headman was half insane by this time, vowed to rescue those the dragon had taken. Turn around," Marit ordered abruptly. "I'll coat your back."

Hugh turned, allowed Marit to slather mud on his back and shoulders. "What happened then?" he asked gruffly.

Marit shrugged. "Haplo and I decided it was time to leave. Later, we came across one of the Squatters, one of the few to survive. He said the dragon kept up the game for a week—coming out of its cave to fight, snatching up new victims, spending the nights torturing them to death. At last, when there was no one left except those too sick or too young to provide any amusement, the dragon razed the village.

"There, now, do you understand?" Marit asked him. "An army of Patryn warriors could not defeat *one* of these dragons. Do you see what we are up against?"

Hugh did not immediately answer. He was slathering mud on his arms and hands. "What's *your* plan, then?" he asked when he was finished.

"The dragon has to eat, which means it will have to go out and hunt—"

"Unless it decides to eat Alfred."

Marit shook her head. "Red dragons don't eat their victims. That would be a waste of good sport. Besides, this one is trying to figure out what Alfred is. The dragon's never seen a Sartan before. No, it will keep Alfred alive, probably longer than he wants. When the dragon leaves the cave to feed, we'll slip in and rescue Alfred."

"If there's anything left to rescue," Hugh muttered.

Marit made no reply.

They pushed on, following the dragon's trail. It led them through the forest, heading away from the city, in the direction of the next gate. The ground began to rise; they were in the foothills of the mountains. They had been traveling all day, pausing only to eat enough to keep up their strength, and to drink whenever they came across clear water.

The gray light of day was dwindling. Clouds filled the sky. Rain began to fall, which Hugh counted as a blessing. He was sick of the stench of the mud.

The rain was fortunate in another way. They had left the thick forest behind, and were climbing up a barren hillside dotted by rocks and boulders. They were out in the open; the rain provided cover.

The dragon's trail was still relatively easy to track—so long as they had light enough to see by. Its feet tore up the ground, gouging out great chunks of dirt and rock. But night was coming.

Would the dragon hole up for the night, perhaps in some cave in the mountains? Or would it press on until it reached its lair? And should they press on, even after dark?

The two discussed it.

"If we stop and the dragon doesn't, it'll be a long way ahead of us by morning," Hugh argued.

"I know." Marit stood, irresolute, thinking.

Hugh the Hand waited for her to continue. When it was obvious she wasn't going to, he shrugged, spoke.

"I've done my share of tracking. I've been in this situation before. Usually I rely on what I know of my mark, try to put myself in his place, figure out what he'd do. But I'm used to tracking men, not beasts. I leave this up to you, lady."

"We'll go," she decided. "Track it by my rune-light." The glow of the runes on her skin faintly illuminated the ground. "But we'll have to move slowly. We have to be careful that we don't accidentally stumble across its lair in the darkness. If the dragon hears us coming . . ." She shook her head. "I remember once, Haplo and I—"

Marit stopped. Why did she keep talking about Haplo? The pain was like a dragon's claw in her heart.

Hugh settled down to rest and eat, chewing on strips of dried meat. Marit nibbled at hers without appetite. When she realized she couldn't swallow the soggy, tasteless mass, she spat it out. She shouldn't keep thinking about Haplo, shouldn't speak his name. It was like speaking the runes; she conjured up his image, a distraction when she needed to concentrate all her faculties on the problem at hand.

Haplo had been dying when Xar took him away. Closing her eyes, Marit saw the lethal wound, the heart-rune ripped open. Xar could save him. Surely, Xar would save him! Xar would not let him die . . .

Marit's hand went to the torn sigil on her forehead. She knew what Xar would do. No use fooling herself. She remembered Haplo's face, the astonishment, the pain when he had known she and Xar were joined. In that moment, he had given up. His wounds were too deep for him to survive. He'd left all he had— their people—in her care.

A hand closed over hers.

"Haplo will be all right, lady." Hugh the Hand spoke awkwardly, not used to offering comfort. "He's tough, that one."

Marit blinked back her tears, angry that he'd caught her in this weakness.

"We should get moving," she said coldly. Standing up, she walked off, assuming he would follow.

◆

The rain had stopped for the moment, but the lowering clouds, obliterating the tops of the mountains, meant that more was coming. A hard rain would wash out the dragon's tracks completely.

Marit climbed onto a boulder, peered up the mountainside, hoping to catch a glimpse of the dragon before darkness fell. Her attention was caught, shifted to the sullen red glow lighting the skyline on the horizon. She watched it in terrible fascination.

What was the glow? Was it a great conflagration, started by the dragon-snakes, meant to act as a beacon fire to lure all evil creatures to the battle? Was the city of the Nexus itself burning? Or was it, perhaps, some type of magical defense thrown up by the Patryns? A ring of fire to protect them from their enemies?

If the Gate fell, they'd be trapped. Trapped inside the Labyrinth with creatures worse than the red dragons, creatures whose evil power would grow stronger and stronger.

Haplo was dying, thinking she didn't love him.

"Marit."

Startled, she turned too swiftly, almost fell from the boulder.

Hugh the Hand steadied her. "Look!" He pointed upward.

She looked, couldn't see anything.

"Wait. Let the clouds pass. There it is! See!"

The clouds lifted momentarily. Marit saw the dragon, moving across the mountainside, heading for a large dark opening in the cliff face.

And then the clouds dropped down again, obscuring the dragon from view. When they lifted, the creature was nowhere in sight.

They had found the dragon's lair.

CHAPTER ◆ 3

THE LABYRINTH

◆

THEY SPENT THE NIGHT CLIMBING THE HILLSIDE, LISTENING TO ALFRED SCREAM.

The screaming was not constant. The dragon apparently allowed its victim time to rest, recuperate. During such lulls, the dragon's voice could be heard, rumbling from the cave, its words only partially discernible. It was describing to its victim, in lurid detail, exactly what torment it planned to inflict on him next. Worse still, it was destroying hope, robbing him of his will to survive.

"Abri . . . rubble," was some of what the red dragon was saying. "Its people . . . slaughtered . . . wolfen, tiger-men overrun . . ."

"No," Marit said softly. "No, it's not true, Alfred. Don't believe the creature. Hold on . . . hold on."

At one point, Alfred's silence lasted longer than usual. The dragon sounded irritated, as might someone attempting to wake a sound sleeper.

"He's dead," Hugh the Hand whispered.

Marit said nothing. She continued climbing. Just when Alfred's silence had lasted long enough to almost convince her that Hugh was right, she heard a low and pleading moan—the victim begging for mercy—that rose to a high-pitched cry of torment, a cry punctuated by the cruel, triumphant voice of the dragon. Listening again to Alfred's screams, the two pushed on.

A narrow path wound along the hillside, leading up toward the cave, which had undoubtedly been used for shelter by a great many of the Labyrinth's population over the years—until the dragon moved in. The path was not difficult to climb, even in the steadily pouring rain, and Marit need not have worried about losing the dragon's trail in the darkness. In its eagerness to reach its lair, the injured dragon dislodged trees and boulders. The beast's gigantic feet dug deep gouges into the soil, forming crude steps.

Marit didn't particularly like all this "help." She had the distinct impression that the dragon knew it was being followed and was quite pleased to do what it could to lure new victims to torment.

She had no choice but to go on. And if ever once she despaired, thought of giving up and turning back, the red glow on the horizon reflected off the storm clouds, drove her forward.

At about midnight, she called a halt. The two were as near the lair as Marit deemed safe. Finding a shallow depression in the rock that would at least offer them some shelter from the rain, she crawled into it, motioned Hugh to follow her.

He did not. He remained crouched on the narrow ledge that led up the hill to the gaping darkness of the dragon's lair. Marit could see, by her rune-light, the mensch's face twisted with hatred and ferocity. One of those terrible, ominous silences had just fallen, after a particularly long session of torture.

"Hugh, we can't go on!" Marit warned him. "It's too dangerous. We *have* to wait until the dragon leaves!"

A fine plan, except that Alfred's cries were weakening.

Hugh didn't hear her. He stared with narrowed eyes up the cliff face. "I'd live this wretched existence forever," he whispered passionately, reverently, "if I could just, this once, have the power to kill!"

Hatred. Marit knew the feeling well, and she knew how dangerous it could be. Reaching out, she grabbed hold of the man and dragged him bodily inside.

"Listen to me, mensch!" she said, arguing as much with herself as with him. "You're feeling exactly what the dragon wants you to feel! Don't you remember anything of what I told you? The dragon's doing this on purpose, torturing us as well as Alfred. It *wants* us to rush in and attack mindlessly. And that's why we won't. We're going to sit right here until it leaves or we think of something else."

Hugh glowered at her and for a moment Marit thought he was going to defy her. She could stop him, of course. He was a strong man, but he was a mensch, without magic and therefore weak, compared to her. She didn't want to have to fight him, however. A magical battle would alert the dragon to their presence—if it didn't already know—and then again there was that cursed Sartan knife Hugh carried . . .

Marit sucked in a breath. Her hold on Hugh the Hand eased.

Hugh wedged his body into the narrow space beside her. "What? You've thought of something?"

"I might just let you rush in mindlessly, after all. That Cursed Blade. Do you still have it?"

"Yes, I've got the damn thing. It's like this cursed life of mine— I can't seem to get rid of either . . ." Hugh paused, the same idea occurring to him. "The blade would save Alfred!"

"Maybe." Marit gnawed her lip. "It's a powerful weapon, but I'm not sure even such a magical object could stand up against a red dragon. Still, the Cursed Blade could at least buy us time, provide a diversion."

"The blade has to believe that Alfred's in danger. No, belay that," Hugh said, thinking swiftly. "It only has to believe that *I'm* in danger."

"You charge in. The dragon will attack you. The Cursed Blade will attack the dragon. I'll find Alfred, use my magic to cure him enough to get him on his feet, and we'll leave."

"Just one problem, lady. The blade could go for you, too."

Marit shrugged. "You've heard Alfred's cries. He's growing weaker. Maybe the dragon's tiring of its sport or maybe, since Alfred's a Sartan, the dragon doesn't know how to keep him alive. Whatever . . . Alfred's dying. If we wait any longer, it may be too late."

Perhaps *now* was too late. The words hung between them, un-spoken. They had heard nothing from Alfred, not even a moan, in all the moments they'd been crouched in the narrow cave. The dragon, too, was strangely silent.

Hugh the Hand fumbled about in his belt, produced the crude, ugly Sartan knife—the Cursed Blade, as he had named it. He eyed it narrowly, held it gingerly.

"Ugh," he grunted, grimacing in disgust. "The damn thing wriggles in my hand like a snake. Let's get on with this. I'd as soon face that dragon as hold on to this knife much longer."

Crafted by the Sartan, the Cursed Blade was intended to be used by mensch to defend their "superiors"—the Sartan—in bat-tle. The blade was sentient; would, of its own accord, assume a form necessary to defeat its foe. It needed Hugh, or any mensch, merely as a means of transport. It did not need his direction to fight. The blade would defend him as its carrier. It would defend any Sartan in danger. Unfortunately, as Hugh had pointed out, the blade had been designed to battle the Sartan's ancient enemy—the Patryns. The blade was just as likely (perhaps *more* likely) to attack Marit as it was to attack the dragon.

"At least now I know how to control the damn thing," he told her. "If it goes for you, I can—"

"—rescue Alfred." Marit cut him off. "Take him back to Abri, to the healers. Don't stop to try to help me, Hugh," she added, as he opened his mouth to protest. "At least the blade will kill me quickly."

He regarded her intently, not meaning to argue with her, but taking her measure, trying to decide if she was all talk or if she had the courage to back her words.

Marit gazed back at him, unblinking.

Nodding once, Hugh slid out of the rock depression. Marit crawled after him. As luck—or the Labyrinth—would have it, the rain that had concealed their movement now stopped. A gentle breeze stirred the trees, producing miniature rainstorms when the water fell from the leaves. The two stood on the ledge, hardly daring to breathe.

Not a whimper, not a moan . . . and the cave's entrance was

only a hundred steps away. Both could see it clearly, a gaping black hole against the white glimmer of the rock. In the distance, the red glow in the sky seemed to burn brighter.

"Perhaps the dragon's asleep!" Hugh the Hand hissed into her ear.

Marit conceded the possibility with a nod and a shrug. She found little comfort in the idea. The dragon would wake soon enough when it smelled fresh sport.

Hugh the Hand took the lead. He trod softly, testing each step, padding along the path with a skill and ease Marit deemed impressive. She crept after him, making no noise at all. Yet Marit had the uneasy feeling that the dragon could hear them coming, that it was lying in wait.

They reached the cavern's entrance. Hugh flattened himself back against the rock wall, wormed his way along the cliff face, hoping to be able to peer inside, see without being seen. Marit waited at a distance, hiding behind a bush, keeping the entrance to the cave in plain sight.

Still no sound. Not an indrawn breath, nor the grating noise of a large body rubbing against stone, nor the rustle of a damaged wing scraping along a rock floor. The rain had washed the mud from her body, and now the runes on Marit's skin glowed brilliantly. The dragon had only to glance outside to know it had company. The light would make her a tempting target when she entered the cave, but it would also give her the chance to find Alfred in the darkness, and so she did not attempt to conceal the glow.

Hugh twisted his body, peered around the rock wall, tried to see inside the cavern. He stared for long moments, head cocked, listening as much as looking. With a wave of his hand, he motioned Marit to join him. Keeping her eye on the cave entrance, she darted across the path, flattened herself next to him.

He leaned over, spoke in her ear. "Dark as an elf's heart in there. Can't see a damn thing. But I thought I heard a gasping breath coming from your right, as you face the cave. It could be Alfred."

Which meant he was still alive. A tiny surge of relief warmed Marit; hope added fuel to her courage.

"Any sign of the dragon?"

"Other than the stench?" he asked, wrinkling his nose in disgust. "No, I didn't see anything of the beast."

The smell was horrible—decayed, rotting flesh. Marit didn't like to think of what they'd find in there. If Vasu had been missing any of his people lately—the shepherd picked off while guarding the flocks, the child who had wandered too far from his mother, the scout who had never come home—the remains were probably in this cave.

Marit hadn't seen the dragon leave. And surely she could have heard it if it were still inside. Perhaps the cavern extended far beneath the hills. Perhaps the dragon had a back way out. Perhaps it *didn't* know they were here. Perhaps the dragon's injury was worse than Marit had thought. Perhaps the wounded creature had crawled far back in its lair to sleep. Perhaps . . . perhaps . . .

Few events in Marit's life had ever worked to her advantage. She always made the wrong decision, ended up in the wrong place, did or said the wrong thing. She had made the mistake of staying with Haplo; then she had made the mistake of leaving him. She had made the mistake of abandoning their child. She had made the mistake of trusting Xar. Finding Haplo again, she had made the mistake of loving him again, only to lose him again.

Surely, now, something in her life must go right! Surely, she was owed this much!

For the dragon to be asleep.

She asked only for the dragon to be asleep.

The two slipped, wary and silent, inside the cave.

Marit's runes illuminated the cavern. The entrance was not very wide or high—the dragon must have a tight fit to squeeze inside, as was evidenced by a crust-like coating of glittering red scales lining the top and sides of the rock.

The entry tunnel opened, expanding upward and outward to form a large, roughly circular room. Marit's bluish-red rune-light reflected off damp walls, lit most of the chamber except the top— which disappeared into darkness—and an opening in the very back. She drew Hugh's attention to that opening. It was big enough for the dragon to use. And apparently, that was what it had done, because the chamber in which they stood was empty.

Empty, except for the dragon's gruesome trophies.

Corpses in various states of decomposition hung from chains on the walls. Men and women and children—all having obviously died in pain and torment. Hugh the Hand, who had lived with death, seen it in all its forms during his life, was sickened. He doubled over and retched.

The sheer brutality, the wanton cruelty overwhelmed even Marit. The horror of it and the attendant rage at the creature that could so callously commit such heinous acts combined to nearly rob her of her senses. The cavern began to swim in her sight. She was lightheaded, dizzy.

Afraid she was about to pass out, she lurched forward, hoping movement would stir her blood.

"Alfred!" Hugh wiped his mouth with the back of his hand. He pointed.

Marit peered through the rune-lit darkness, found Alfred. She concentrated on him, banished everything else from her mind, and felt better. He was alive, though just barely, by the looks of him.

"Go to him," Hugh said, his voice harsh from vomiting. "I'll keep watch." He held the Cursed Blade, drawn and ready. It had begun to glow with an ugly, greenish light.

Marit hurried to Alfred's side.

Like the countless other victims, the Sartan hung from chains. His wrists were manacled to the wall above his head. His feet dangled near the floor, the toes barely touching. His head was bowed down. He might have been dead but for the sound of rasping breath which Hugh had heard outside the cavern. His gasping breaths were much louder in here.

Marit touched him as gently as she could, hoping to rouse him without frightening him. But at the brush of her fingers against his cheek, Alfred moaned, his body convulsed, his heels clattered against the rock wall.

Marit clapped her hand over his mouth, forced his head up,

made him look at her. She dared not say anything aloud, and a whisper would probably mean little to him in his state.

He stared at her with wild, bulging eyes in which there was no recognition, only fear and pain. He struggled instinctively against her, but he was far too weak to break free. His clothes were soaked with blood. Blood spread in pools beneath his feet, yet his flesh— as far as Marit could tell—was whole and undamaged.

The dragon had slashed and torn his flesh, then healed him back up. Probably many times. Even the broken arm had been healed. But the true damage was in the mind. Alfred was very far gone.

"Hugh!" Marit had to risk calling, and though it was no more than a loud whisper, the name echoed eerily through the cavern. She flinched, did not dare repeat it.

Hugh edged his way toward her, never taking his eyes from the back of the cave. "I thought I heard something move inside there. Better make this quick."

Just exactly what she couldn't do!

"If I don't heal him," she said softly, "he'll never make it out of the cave alive. He doesn't even recognize me."

Hugh glanced at Alfred, then at Marit. Hugh had seen the Patryn healers at work; he knew what it entailed. Marit would have to concentrate all her magical power on Alfred. She would have to draw his injuries into herself, release her life-giving energy to him. For long moments, she would be as incapacitated as he was. When the healing process was concluded, both of them would be weak.

Hugh gave a brief nod to show he understood; then he returned to his post.

Marit reached up, touched the manacles that held Alfred, softly spoke the runes. Blue fire twined from her arm; the manacles released. Alfred sagged to the cavern floor, lay sprawled in his own blood. He had lost consciousness.

Swiftly, Marit knelt beside him. Clasping his hands in hers— right in left, left in right—she joined the circle of their beings, called on the magic to heal him.

A series of fantastic, beautiful, wonderful, and frightening im-

ages flooded Marit's mind. She was above Abri, far above Abri—
not just on the city walls, but as if she stood on the top of a mountain, looking down on the city below. And then she leapt from the
mountain and fell—but she was not falling. She was soaring in the
sky, gliding on unseen currents as she might have glided on water.
She was flying.

The experience was terrifying until she grew accustomed to it.
And then it was thrilling. She had enormous, powerful wings, taloned front claws, a long and graceful neck, tearing teeth. She was
huge and awe-inspiring, and when she swooped down upon her
enemies, they fled in shrieking terror. She was Alfred, the Serpent
Mage.

She hovered protectively over Abri, scattered its enemies,
threw down those bold enough to fight. She saw Lord Xar and
Haplo—small and insignificant creatures—and she felt Alfred's
fear for his friends, his determination to help . . .

And then a shadow glimpsed from the corner of the eye . . . a
desperate swerve in midair . . . too late. Something struck her
side, sent her rolling, out of control. She was tumbling, spiraling
downward. Frantically, she beat her wings, clawed her way back
up. She could see her enemy now, a red dragon.

Taloned feet extended, the dragon plunged through the sky,
aiming for her . . .

Confused images of falling, crashing to the ground. Marit shuddered in pain, bit her lip to keep from crying out. Part of her was
Alfred, part of her was flowing into Alfred, but part of her was still
in the dragon's cavern, still very much aware of the danger.

And she could see Hugh, tense and alert, staring into the blackness in the back of the cavern, his face gone rigid. He turned
toward her, gesturing, mouthing something. She couldn't hear, but
then she didn't need to hear.

The dragon was coming.

"Alfred!" Marit pleaded, clasping the man's wrists more
tightly. "Alfred, come back!"

He stirred and groaned. His eyelids fluttered. He caught hold
of her, held on to her.

Horrid images slammed into Marit—a bulbous tail inflicting searing, paralyzing, numbing pain; swirling hot darkness; waking to torment and agony. Marit could no longer hold back the screams.

The dragon slid into the cavern.

CHAPTER ◆ 4

THE LABYRINTH

◆

THE DRAGON HAD BEEN CONCEALED IN THE SHADOWS OF ITS BACK EXIT ALL along, watching the two would-be saviors, waiting for the precise moment when they were weakest, most vulnerable, to attack. It had first heard the two in the forest, guessed that they had come in search of their friend. The dragon would have attacked them then and there, since it knew by experience that few Patryns would attempt such a hopeless rescue. But the dragon quite simply didn't feel up to such a fight and so it had, with regret, contented itself with one toy.

To the dragon's delight, however, these two had decided to follow it. Patryns weren't often this stupid, but the dragon sensed something odd about these two. One of them had a strange smell, unlike anything the dragon had previously encountered in the Labyrinth. The other one the dragon understood well. She was a Patryn and she was desperate. The desperate were often careless.

Once back in its lair, the dragon took its time torturing the Thing it had captured, the Thing that had been a dragon and had then transformed itself back into a man. The Thing was powerful in magic; it was not a Patryn, yet it was like a Patryn. The dragon was intrigued by it, but not intrigued enough to waste time investigating. The Thing had not proved as amusing as the dragon had hoped. It gave up too easily and actually seemed on the verge of dying.

Becoming bored with tormenting the wretched Thing, and feeling weak from its injury, the dragon had crawled back into the inner part of the cavern to heal its wounds and wait for prey that might prove more entertaining.

The two were better than the dragon had hoped. The Patryn female was actually healing the Thing, which was fine with the dragon. Saved it time and trouble, gave it a stronger victim, one who might now live until next nightfall. As for the Patryn, she was young and defiant. She would last a long time. The male the dragon was unsure about. He was the one with the peculiar smell and no magic about him whatsoever. More like an animal, a deer, for example. Not much sport to him, but he was large and well fleshed. The dragon would have no need to go out in search of a meal this day.

The dragon waited until it saw the Patryn's rune-magic wholly consumed by the healing process. Then it moved.

The dragon crawled slowly out of the darkness of the cavern. The tunnel seemed large to Hugh, but it was small for the dragon, which had to duck its head to creep beneath the overhang. Hugh stood his ground, assuming that the dragon would wait until its entire body, including the stinging tail, was out in the open before it would attack. The Sartan knife squirmed in Hugh's grip.

He held it up in challenge, willed it to change form to fight the dragon.

If it had been possible, he would have sworn that the knife seemed ill at ease, unsure. Hugh wished he understood more about the Cursed Blade, tried frantically to recall everything either Haplo or Alfred had said in regard to it. All he could come up with at the moment was that the blade was Sartan-made. And at that moment it occurred to him that the Labyrinth and the creatures in it—including this dragon—had also been made by the Sartan.

The blade was confused. It recognized the same magic inherent in itself, but it also recognized threat. If the dragon had remained patient, gone after Marit, the Sartan blade would not have altered form. But the dragon was hungry. It planned to catch and devour Hugh; then, with a comfortably full stomach, it could go after the other, more difficult prey. Most of the dragon's body was still inside the back part of the cavern; it could not yet use its tail in the attack. But the dragon didn't think it would need such an advantage. Almost lazily, it swiped out a clawed forefoot, intending to impale Hugh the Hand and eat him while his flesh was still warm.

The move caught Hugh by surprise. He ducked and flung himself backward. A giant claw raked across his stomach, tearing the leather armor as if it had been finest silk, slashing through flesh and muscle.

At the attack, the Sartan blade was quick to respond. It wrenched itself free of Hugh's grasp.

A gigantic sweeping tail knocked him aside. Hugh rolled across the cavern floor, bumped up against Marit and Alfred. The two looked terrible—Marit now almost as bad as Alfred. Both seemed dazed, barely conscious. The Hand regained his feet quickly, prepared to defend himself and his helpless companions. He stopped, frozen, staring.

Two dragons were inside the cavern.

The second dragon—actually the Cursed Blade—was a gorgeous creature. Long and slender, this dragon was wingless; its scales sparkled and gleamed like myriad tiny suns, shining in a blue-green sky. It dove for its victim before the Labyrinth dragon had time to fully assimilate what was happening. The blue-green dragon's head darted in close, jaws opened and snapped shut on the Labyrinth dragon's neck.

Shrieking in fury and pain, the red dragon twisted out of its captor's grasp, freeing itself but leaving a bloody chunk of flesh in its enemy's mouth. The red dragon heaved its body from beneath the overhang, its tremendous strength literally bearing back the attacker. The bulbous tail struck out, stinging the blue-green dragon again and again.

Hugh had seen enough. The dragons were fighting each other, but he and his friends were in peril of being smashed by the flailing, struggling bodies.

"Marit!" He shook her.

She was still holding fast to Alfred; her face was gray and drawn, but she was now alert, staring at the two dragons in astonishment. Alfred was conscious, but he obviously had no idea where he was, who was with him, or what was going on. He was gazing about in dazed perplexity.

"Marit, we've got to get out of here!" Hugh shouted.

"Where did that other dragon—" she began.

"The Cursed Blade," Hugh answered shortly. He bent over Alfred. "Grab his other arm!"

Hugh instructed her needlessly. Marit had already taken hold. Between the two of them, they dragged Alfred to a semistanding position and—half dragging, half carrying him—headed for the cave opening.

The going was difficult. Their way was blocked by reptile bodies that twisted and grappled. Slashing clawed feet tore up the dirt floor. Enormous heads cracked into the cavern ceiling; rock shards and dust drifted down on top of them. Magical attacks flared and burst around them.

Half blind, choking, fearful of being trampled to death or caught in a magical fire-storm, the three staggered out of the cavern entrance. Once in the clear, they fled down the narrow pathway, kept going until Alfred collapsed. Hugh and Marit paused, gasping for breath. Behind them, the dragons roared in pain and rage.

"You're hurt!" Marit looked concerned at the sight of the gaping wound across Hugh's stomach.

"It'll heal," he said grimly. "Won't it, Alfred? I'll carry him."

Hugh started to lift Alfred bodily, but the Sartan pushed him away.

"I can make it," he said, struggling to regain his feet. A fierce shriek of fury caused him to blench, glance back at the cavern. "What—"

"No time to explain! Run!" Marit ordered. Grabbing hold of Alfred, she shoved him along ahead of her.

Alfred stumbled, managed to regain his feet and followed orders.

Hugh twisted around. "Where?"

"Down!" Marit answered. "You help Alfred. I'll keep watch behind."

The ground shook with the ferocity of the battle being waged inside the cavern. Hugh moved swiftly down the path, slipping and sliding on the rain-wet rock. Marit followed more slowly, keeping one eye on the path, the other on the cavern. She scrambled down the hillside, often losing her footing in the loose soil. Alfred tumbled head over heels, was well on his way to rolling down the hill when he came up hard against a boulder. By the time they reached the bottom, they were all scratched, bruised, and bleeding.

"Listen!" Marit called a halt.

All was quiet now. Very quiet. The battle had ended.

"I wonder who won?" Hugh asked.

"I can live without knowing," Marit answered.

"If we're lucky, they killed each other," Hugh commented. "I wouldn't care if I never saw that damn blade again."

The silence continued; it had an ominous feel to it. Marit wanted to be farther away, much farther.

"How are you?" she asked, including both Hugh and Alfred.

Hugh grunted, pointed. His wound had almost closed; the rent in his armor was the only indication of where it had been. In explanation, he pulled aside his shirt, revealing a single Sartan sigil, gleaming faintly on his chest. Alfred, at the sight, flushed bright red and averted his gaze.

Suddenly, an explosion rocked the ground, coming from the direction of the cave. They stared at each other, tense, fearful, wondering at the portent.

Then, once again, all was silent.

"We better push on," Marit said, keeping her voice low.

Alfred nodded befuddled agreement. Taking a step, he

stumbled over his own feet, lurched headlong into a tree.

Marit, sighing, reached out to take hold of his arm. Hugh the Hand, on Alfred's other side, moved to do the same.

"Hugh!" Marit pointed at the bloodstained leather belt around his waist.

Hanging from it, wrapped snugly in its sheath, was the Cursed Blade.

CHAPTER ◆ 5

THE LABYRINTH

◆

"I CAN'T . . . GO ON." ALFRED PITCHED FORWARD, LAY VERY STILL.

Marit eyed him, frustrated. They were wasting time. Yet, though she didn't like to admit it, she could not go much farther. Thinking back, she couldn't remember how long it had been since she'd slept.

"You can rest," she said curtly, sitting on a tree stump. "But only a few moments, till we catch our breath."

Alfred lay with his eyes closed, his face half buried in the mud. He looked old—old and shrunken. Marit found it difficult to believe that this gangling, frail Sartan had once been a creature as beautiful and powerful as the green and golden dragon she'd seen soaring above Abri.

"What's the matter with him now?" Hugh the Hand demanded, entering the small clearing where they had stopped. The Hand had been following some distance behind, keeping watch to make certain nothing was tracking them.

Marit shrugged, too tired to respond. She knew what was wrong with Alfred: the same thing that was wrong with her. What was the use? Why bother to keep struggling?

"I found some water," Hugh said, gesturing. "Not far from here . . ."

Marit shook her head. Alfred made no move.

Hugh sat down, nervous, ill at ease. He sat with what patience he could for a few moments, then was on his feet again. "We'll be safer in Abri—"

"For how long?" Marit returned bitterly. "Look. Look up there."

Hugh peered through the tangled branches of the trees. The sky, which had been gray, was now tinged with a faint pinkish-orange glow.

The runes on her skin barely tingled at all. No enemy was near them. Yet that red fire in the sky seemed to be burning up her hope.

She closed her eyes wearily.

And she saw, once again, the world from the dragon's eyes. She was flying above Abri, and saw its buildings and its people, saw its sheltering walls, the arms of the land reaching out to encircle the land's children.

Her children. Her child. Hers and Haplo's.

A girl-child. Her name—Rue. She was eight gates now, or around there. Marit could see her—skinny and wiry, tall for her age, with chestnut hair like her mother and her father's quiet smile.

Marit could see it all so clearly.

"We taught Rue how to snare small game, how to skin a rabbit, how to catch fish with her hands," Marit was telling Headman Vasu, who had inexplicably appeared out of nowhere. "She's old enough to be of some help to us now. I'm glad we decided to keep her with us, instead of leaving her with the Squatters."

Rue could run fast, when need arose, and she could fight if cornered. She had her own rune-covered dagger—a gift from her mother.

"I taught her how to use it," Marit was saying to the headman. "Not long ago, Rue faced down a snog with it. She held the creature at bay until her father and I could rescue her. She wasn't afraid, she said, though she shook in my arms afterward. Then Haplo came and teased her and made her laugh and we were all three of us laughing . . ."

"Hey!"

Marit jerked to sudden wakefulness. Hugh's hand was on her shoulder. He'd caught her just as she was about to topple over.

She flushed deeply. "I'm sorry. I must have fallen asleep."

Rubbing her burning eyes, she stood up. The temptation to slip back into that sweet dream was too strong. For an instant she let herself believe, superstitiously, that the dream held meaning for her. Haplo was alive. He would come back to her. Together, they would find their lost child.

The warmth of that dream lingered in her; she felt surrounded by love and caring . . .

Angrily, she banished it.

A dream, she told herself coldly, firmly. Nothing more. Nothing I can ever attain. I threw it all away.

"What?" Alfred sat up. "What did you say? Something about Haplo?"

Marit didn't think she had spoken aloud, but then she was so tired she didn't know what she was doing anymore.

"We better get going," she said, avoiding the subject.

Alfred staggered to his feet, continued to stare at her with a strange, sad intensity.

"Where is Haplo? I saw him with Lord Xar. Are they in Abri?"

Marit turned away from him. "They left for Abarrach."

"Abarrach . . . the necromancy." Alfred sank down despondently on the trunk of a fallen tree. "The necromancy." He sighed. "Then Haplo is dead."

"He isn't!" Marit cried, rounding on Alfred viciously. "My lord would not let him die!"

"Like hell!" Hugh the Hand snorted. "You tried to kill Haplo— on your lord's orders!"

"That was when he thought Haplo was a traitor!" Marit flared. "My lord knows better now! He knows Haplo was telling him the truth about the dragon-snakes. My lord won't let Haplo die! He won't . . . he won't . . ."

She was so tired, she began to sob like a frightened child. Embarrassed, ashamed, she tried to stop crying, but the pain inside was too great. The emptiness she had nurtured and cherished for so long was gone, filled by a terrible, burning ache only tears seemed to ease. She heard Alfred take a step toward her. Blindly, she turned from him, made it clear she wanted to be left alone.

His footsteps stopped.

When at last Marit was more composed, she wiped her nose, brushed away her tears. Her stomach hurt from sobbing; the muscles in her throat constricted spasmodically. She gulped, coughed.

Hugh the Hand was staring grimly at nothing, kicking moodily at a clump of weeds. Alfred sat hunched over, shoulders stooped, gangling arms dangling between his bony knees. His gaze was abstracted; he appeared deep in thought.

"I'm sorry," Marit said, trying to sound brisk. "I didn't mean to fall apart. I'm tired, that's all. We better get back to Abri—"

"Marit," Alfred interrupted timidly, "how did Lord Xar enter the Labyrinth?"

"I don't know. He didn't say. What does it matter?"

"He must have come through the Vortex," Alfred reasoned. "He knew we entered from that direction. I assume you told him that?"

Marit's skin burned. She lifted her hand involuntarily to touch the sigil on her forehead, the sigil that Xar had rent open, the sigil that had once linked her and her lord together. Seeing Alfred watching her, she snatched her hand away.

"But the Vortex was destroyed—"

"It can never be destroyed," Alfred corrected. "The mountain fell on it. Entering would not be easy, but it could be done. However . . ." He paused, thoughtful.

"He couldn't leave that way!" Marit cried. " 'The Gate swings in only one direction.' You said that to Haplo!"

"If what Alfred said was true," Hugh the Hand growled. "Remember, *he* was the one who didn't want to leave."

"I told you the truth," Alfred said, blushing. "It makes sense, if you stop to think about it. If the Gate swung in both directions, all the Patryns sent into the Labyrinth would have been able to escape back the way they came."

Marit was no longer tired. Renewed energy surged through her. "Xar would have to leave through the Final Gate! That's the only way out. Once he was there, he would see our danger! Our people would cry to him for help. He couldn't leave them to fight alone. We'll find my lord there, at the Final Gate. And Haplo will be with him."

"Perhaps," said Alfred. And now it was his turn to avoid her eyes.

"Of course he will be," Marit said resolutely. "Now we must get there. Quickly. I could use my magic. It will take me to—"

She had been about to say *to Xar*, but then she remembered— the wound on her forehead. She forbore to touch it, though it had begun to burn painfully.

"To the Final Gate," she finished lamely. "I've been there. I can see it in my mind."

"You could go," said Alfred. "But you couldn't take us with you."

"What does it matter?" Marit said, alive with hope. "What do I need with you now, Sartan? My lord will battle his foes and emerge triumphant. And Haplo will be healed . . ."

She made ready to draw the rune-circle, to step inside. Alfred was on his feet, babbling, apparently going to try to stop her. Marit ignored him. If he came too close, she would . . .

"Could I be of assistance, sir, madam?"

A gentleman—imposing, dressed all in black: black breeches, black velvet coat, black silk stockings; white hair, tied in back with a black ribbon—stepped out of the forest. He was accompanied by an old man, with flowing beard and hair, wearing mouse-colored robes, all topped by a shabby and sorry-looking pointed hat.

The old man was singing.

" 'One is one . . . and all alone . . . and ever more shall be so.' " He smiled gently, sadly, sighed, and began again. " 'I'll give you one-o, every day I grow, ei-o. What is your one-o? One is one . . .' "

"Excuse me, sir," said the gentleman in a low voice, "but we are not alone."

"Eh!" The old man gave a violent start. His hat fell off his head. He eyed the three astonished people facing him with deep suspicion. "What are you doing here? Get out!"

The gentleman in black sighed a long-suffering sigh. "I don't believe that would be at all wise. These are the people we came to find, sir."

"You sure?" The old man appeared dubious.

Marit stared. "I know you! In Abarrach. You're a Sartan, a prisoner of my lord."

Marit recalled his rambling, nonsensical conversation in the cells of Abarrach. She had thought him mad.

"Now I wonder if I am," she muttered.

Did the old man truly exist? Or had he leapt into being from her own exhausted mind? People who went without sleep too long began to see things that weren't there. She looked at Hugh the Hand, was relieved to see him staring at the old man, as was Alfred. Either they had all fallen under some extraordinary spell, or the old man was really standing in front of her.

Marit drew her sword.

The old man was regarding them with equal perplexity. "What does this remind me of? Three desperate-looking characters wandering around lost in a forest. No, don't tell me. I'll get it. Great Auntie Em's ghost! The Scarecrow." Rushing forward, the old man grabbed Alfred's hand and shook it heartily.

The old man turned to Hugh. "And the Lion. How do you do, sir? And the Tin Man!" He lunged toward Marit, who lifted the point of her sword to the old man's throat.

"Stay away from me, old fool. How did you get here?"

"Ah." The old man fell back a step, gave her a cunning look. "Not been to Oz, yet, I see. Hearts are free there, my dear. Of course you *do* have to open yourself up to put the heart inside. Some find that rather an inconvenience. Still—"

Marit made a threatening motion with the sword. "Who are you? How did you get here?"

"As to who I am . . ." The old man was thoughtful. "Good point. If you're the Scarecrow, you the Lion, and you the Tin Man, then that must make me . . . Dorothy!"

The old man simpered, gave a curtsey, extended his hand. "My name is Dorothy. A small-town girl from a small town west of Topeka. Like my shoes?"

"Excuse me, sir," the gentleman interrupted. "But you are not—"

"And this," the old man cried triumphantly, flinging his arms around the gentleman in black, "is my little dog Toto!"

The gentleman appeared extremely pained at this suggestion. "I'm afraid *not*, sir." He attempted to extricate himself from the old man's embrace. "Forgive me, sirs, madam," he added. "This is all my fault. I should have been watching him."

"I know! You're Zifnab!" cried Alfred.

"Bless you," the old man returned politely. "Need a hankie?"

"He means you, sir," the gentleman said in resigned tones.

"Does he?" The old man was considerably astonished.

"Yes, sir. You are Zifnab today."

"Not Dorothy?"

"No, sir. And I must say, sir, I never cared for that one," the gentleman added with some asperity.

"He's not referring, perhaps, to Mr. Bond?"

"I am afraid not, sir. Not today. You are Zifnab, sir. A great and powerful wizard."

"Well, of course I am! Pay no attention to the man behind the shower curtain. He's just awakened from a bad dream. Takes a great and powerful wizard to come to the Labyrinth, doesn't it? And I—Why, there, there, old chap. It's nice to see you, too."

Alfred was shaking hands with Zifnab solemnly. "I am so pleased to make your acquaintance, sir. Haplo told me about meeting you. On Pryan, wasn't it?"

"Yes, that was it! I remember!" Zifnab beamed; then his face darkened. He grew sad. "Haplo. Yes, I do remember." He sighed. "I'm so sorry—"

"That will be quite enough, sir," interrupted the gentleman in stern tones.

"What does he mean?" Marit demanded. "What about Haplo?"

"He means nothing," said the gentleman. "Do you, sir?"

"Uh, no. That's right. Nothing. *Nada.* Zip." Zifnab began toying nervously with his beard.

"We overheard you speaking of going to the Final Gate," the

gentleman continued. "I believe that I and my brethren might be of assistance. We are traveling there ourselves."

He glanced skyward. Marit looked up, following his gaze distrustfully. A shadow flowed over her. Another and another. She stared, dazzled and dazed, at hundreds of dragons, blue-green as the sky of Pryan, scales gleaming bright as Pryan's four suns.

And now, towering over her, its great bulk blotting out the gray sun of the Labyrinth, was a huge dragon. Blue-green scales glistened. The gentleman in black was gone.

Marit trembled with fear, but not for her safety or well-being. She was afraid because suddenly her world, her universe, had been ripped asunder, as her lord had ripped open the sigil on her skin. Through the rent, she caught a glimpse of radiant light, suddenly overwhelmed by terrible darkness. She saw the gray sky of the Labyrinth, the Nexus in flames, her people—small, fragile creatures, trapped between the darkness and the light—fighting a last desperate battle.

She struck out at the dragon with her sword, barely knowing what she was attacking or why, only knowing that she was consumed with despair.

"Wait!" Alfred caught hold of her arm. "Don't fight!" He peered up at the dragon. "These dragons are here to help us, Marit. To help your people. They are the enemies of the serpents. Isn't that true?"

"The Wave acts to correct itself," said the Pryan dragon. "So it has been, since the beginning of time. We can take you to the Final Gate. We are taking others."

Patryns rode on the backs of the dragons. Men and women, carrying weapons in their hands. Marit recognized Headman Vasu in the vanguard, and she understood. Her people were leaving the safety of their walled city, going to fight the enemy at the Final Gate.

Hugh the Hand had already mounted the dragon's broad back, was now assisting Alfred—with some difficulty—to climb on behind.

Marit hesitated, preferring to trust in her magic. Then she realized that she might not make it. She was tired. So very tired.

She would need all her strength once they reached the Final Gate.

Marit clambered up on the dragon, sat on the great broad back of the beast, between the shoulder blades where sprouted the enormous, powerful wings.[1] The wings began to beat on the air.

Zifnab, who had been directing operations, completely oblivious to the fact that no one was paying any attention to him, suddenly gave a strangled cry. "Wait! Where am I going to sit?"

"You're not going, sir," said the dragon. "It would be too dangerous for you."

"But I just got here!" Zifnab whined.

"And done far more damage than I would have thought possible in such a short period of time," the dragon remarked gloomily. "But there is that other little matter we spoke about. In Chelestra. I assume you can handle *that* without incident?"

"Mr. Bond could," said Zifnab craftily.

"Out of the question!" The dragon flicked its tail in annoyance.

Zifnab shrugged, twiddled his hat. "On the other hand, I could be Dorothy." He clicked his heels together. " 'There's no place like home. There's no place—' "

"Oh, very well," the dragon snapped. "If nothing else will suit you. Try *not* to make a pig's breakfast of this one, will you?"

"You have my word," said Zifnab solemnly, saluting, "as a member of Her Majesty's Secret Service."

The dragon heaved a sigh. It waved a claw, and Zifnab disappeared.

Wings beat, raising clouds of dust, obscuring Marit's sight. She clasped hold tightly of gleaming scales that were hard as metal to the touch. The dragon soared into the sky. The treetops fell away beneath her. Light—warm and bright as the beacon fire—touched her face.

"What is that light?" she cried fearfully.

---

[1] Those familiar with the dragons of Pryan will recall that they are described as wingless. One can only guess that, like their enemies the dragon-snakes, the Pryan dragons can assume whatever form suits their needs.

"Sunlight," said Alfred, awed.

"Where does the light come from?" she asked, staring all around. "There is no sun in the Labyrinth."

"The citadels," Alfred answered. Tears glimmered in his eyes. "The light beams from the citadel of Pryan. There is hope, Marit. There *is* hope!"

"Keep that in your heart," said the dragon grimly. "For if all hope dies, then we die."

Turning their faces from the light, they flew toward the red-tinged darkness.

CHAPTER ◆ 6

THE CHALICE

CHELESTRA

◆

THE WORLD OF CHELESTRA IS A GLOBE OF WATER, HANGING IN THE COLD BLACK-ness of space. Its outside is ice; its inside—warmed by Chelestra's free-floating sun—is water, warm, breathable as air, destructive of Sartan and Patryn magic. The mensch of Chelestra, brought here by the Sartan, dwell on seamoons—living organisms that drift through the water, following Chelestra's erratic sun. The seamoons make their own atmosphere, surrounding themselves with a bub-ble of air. On these moons, the mensch build cities, raise crops, and sail the water in their magical submersibles.

On Chelestra, unlike the worlds of Arianus and Pryan, the mensch live together in peace. Their world and their lives had remained undisturbed for centuries, until the arrival of Alfred through Death's Gate.[1] He accidentally waked a group of Sartan—the very ones who had sundered the world—from a stasis sleep.

---

[1] Alfred writes: Looking at the recent history of the four worlds, it is instruc-tive to note that the events which were to play such significant roles in the worlds' future all took place near the same time—the time when Haplo first entered Death's Gate.

At this time, the evil dragon-snakes, long held prisoners in Chelestra by the ice, first felt the warmth of the sun. On Arianus, King Stephen hired an assas-sin to kill the changeling Bane. On Abarrach, Prince Edmund led his people to the doomed city of Necropolis. On Pryan, the tytans began their murderous rampage. The good dragons, sensing the awakening of their evil cousins, left their underground homes and prepared to enter the worlds. I do not believe we can consider such timing coincidence. It is, as we are beginning to learn, the Wave correcting itself.

Once considered demigods by the mensch, the Sartan attempted again to rule over those believed to be inferior.

Led by Samah, Head of the Council—the man who had ordered the Sundering—the Sartan were angered and amazed to find that these mensch not only refused to bow down and worship, but actually had the temerity to defy the so-called gods and wall the Sartan up in their own city, keeping them prisoners by flooding that city with the magic-destroying seawater.

Also living on Chelestra were the manifestation of evil in the worlds. Taking the form of enormous serpents, the evil dragon-snakes, as the dwarves named them, had long been seeking a way off Chelestra and into the other three worlds. Samah inadvertently provided it. Enraged at the mensch, fearful, no longer able to control men or events, Samah fell unwitting victim to the dragon-snakes. Despite the fact that he had been warned against it, the Sartan opened Death's Gate.[2] Thus the evil dragon-snakes were able to enter the other worlds, where they worked to foment the chaos and discord that are their meat and drink.

Secretly appalled at what he had done, Samah left Chelestra, intending to travel to Abarrach. Here, as he had learned from Alfred, the Sartan were practicing the ancient and forbidden art of necromancy.

"If," Samah reasoned, "I could bring the dead back to life, we would have a force strong enough to defeat the dragon-snakes, and once again rule the four worlds."

Samah never lived to learn the art of raising the dead. He was captured, along with a strange old Sartan who called himself

---

[2] Some confusion has arisen over this term. If Death's Gate has not previously been open, how have Haplo and Alfred traveled through it? Imagine a room with seven doors leading out of it. On his first journey, Haplo opens the door from the Nexus, shuts it behind him, travels across the room to the door of Arianus, enters. The door shuts behind him. Thus he travels from one place to another, but all other doors remain closed.

Samah, entering the room, causes the doors to open wide, and they remain open, providing ease of travel between the worlds, but also giving access to those who might otherwise have found it difficult or impossible to gain access. The only way to shut the doors now is through the Seventh Gate.

Zifnab, by their ancient enemy the Patryns, who had accompanied their lord Xar to Abarrach. Xar was there also to learn the art of necromancy. He ordered Samah executed, then attempted to raise the Sartan's body through magical means.

Xar's plan was thwarted. Samah's soul was freed by an undead Sartan named Jonathon, of whom the prophecy says, "He will bring life to the dead, hope to the living, and for him the Gate will open."

Following the departure of Samah from Chelestra, the other Sartan remaining on the Chalice—the only stable piece of land in the water-bound world—have been waiting impatiently, and with growing anxiety, for his return.

"The Councillor has been gone well past the time he himself set. We can no longer function leaderless. I urge you, Ramu, to accept your father's position of Head of the Council of Seven."

Ramu glanced around at each of the other six members. "Is this what you all think? Are you all of one mind?"

"We are." They spoke in nods and words.[3]

Ramu had been carved from the same cold stone as Samah, his father. Not much could warm either man. Hard and unyielding, Ramu would shatter before he would bend. It was never twilight in Ramu's vision—it was day or night. The sun shone brightly or darkness engulfed his world. And even when the sun shone, it cast shadows.

But he was basically a good man, honorable, a devoted father,

---

[3] The leadership of the Council is not hereditary, just as membership on the Council is not hereditary. The seven chosen to serve on the Council, the governing body of the Sartan, elect one of themselves to serve as leader. Just how the seven themselves were chosen in those early days is not known, was kept secret by the Sartan, who undoubtedly feared some Patryn might attempt to influence the decision.

Ramu was servitor to the Council—a position required before one can become a member. Either Ramu was promoted to full Council member during the emergency period when the mensch flooded the city or he took over his exiled mother's Council post.

friend, and husband. And if his worry over his own father's disappearance was not etched on the rock-hard surface of his face, it had been burned deep within.

"Then I accept," Ramu said. Glancing around the group again, he added, "until such time as my father returns."

All on the Council gave agreement. To do otherwise would have been to disparage Samah.

Rising to his feet, his white robes brushing softly against the surface of the floor—a surface that was still cold and damp to the touch, despite the fact that the flood-waters had receded—Ramu moved from his seat at the end of the table to take his place in the chair in the center.

The other members of the Council of Seven rearranged themselves to suit, three sitting on Ramu's left and three on his right.

"What business is brought before the Council this day?" Ramu asked.

One of the members stood up. "The mensch have returned a third time to sue for peace, Councillor. They have asked to meet with the Council."

"We have no need to meet with them. For a peaceful settlement, they must meet our terms, as given to them by my father. They know what those are, I believe?"

"Yes, Councillor. The mensch either move off the Chalice, move off our lands which they usurped by force, or they agree to swear fealty to us, to permit themselves to be governed by us."

"And what is their answer to these terms?"

"They will not leave the lands they have taken, Councillor. To be quite fair, they have nowhere else to go. Their former homelands, the seamoons, are now locked in ice."

"They could climb in those boats of theirs and sail after the sun, go search for new homelands."

"They see no need for such a traumatic upheaval in their lives, Councillor. There is land enough for all here on the Chalice. They cannot understand why they cannot settle it."

The Sartan's tone implied that he could not quite understand it, either. Ramu frowned, but at that moment, another Council member rose, asked leave to speak.

"To be fair to the mensch, Councillor," she said deferentially, "they are ashamed of their past actions and are quite willing to ask our forgiveness and be friends. They have made improvements to the land, begun to build homes, establish businesses. I've seen these myself."

"Indeed, Sister?" Ramu's face darkened. "You have traveled among them?"

"Yes, Councillor. It was at their invitation. I saw no harm and the other members agreed with me. You were not available—"

"What's done is done, Sister." Ramu coldly ended the discussion. "Please continue. What have the mensch done to *our* land?"

No one missed the emphasis on the pronoun.

The Sartan nervously cleared her throat. "The elves have settled near the seashore. Their cities are going to be extraordinarily beautiful, Councillor, with dwellings made of coral. The humans have settled farther inland, in the forests which they love, but with access to the sea, granted them by the elves. The dwarves have moved into caverns in the mountains in the interior. They are mining the minerals, raising goats and sheep. They have set up forges—"

"Enough!" Ramu's face was livid with anger. "I've heard enough. They have set up forges, you say. Forges to make weapons of steel which they will use to attack either us or their neighbors. The peace of our lives will be shattered, just as it was long ago. The mensch are quarrelsome, violent children who need our direction and control."

The Council member was inclined to argue. "But they appear to be living quite peacefully—"

Ramu waved his hand, brushed her words away. "The mensch may get along for a time, particularly if they have some new toy to keep them occupied. But their own history shows that they cannot be trusted. They will either agree to live by our rules, under our laws, or they can depart."

The Sartan glanced uncertainly around the Council. The other members indicated with nods that she was to continue. "Then . . . uh . . . the mensch have given me their terms for peace, Councillor."

"Their terms!" Ramu was amazed. "Why should we bother to listen to their terms?"

"They consider that they won a victory over us, Councillor," said the Sartan. She flushed beneath Ramu's baleful gaze. "And it must be admitted that they could do the very same thing to us again. They control the floodgates. They could open them at any time, flood us out. The seawater is devastating to our magic. Some of us have only just recently regained complete use of our power. Without our magic, we are more helpless than the mensch—"

"Mind what you say, Sister!" Ramu warned.

"I speak the truth, Councillor," the Sartan returned quietly. "You cannot deny it."

Ramu did not argue. His hands, lying flat on the table, drew inward; the fingers curled over nothing. The stone table was cold, smelled wet and musty. "What about my father's suggestion? Have we made any attempt to destroy these floodgates, seal them shut?"

"The floodgates are far below water level, Councillor. We cannot reach them, and even if we could, our magic would be rendered powerless by the water itself. Besides"—her voice lowered —"who knows but that the evil dragon-snakes are down there still, lying in wait."

"Perhaps," Ramu said, but would add nothing further. He knew, because his father had told him before he left, that the dragon-snakes had entered Death's Gate, had left Chelestra, taken their evil to other worlds . . .

. . . "This is my fault, my son," Samah said. "One reason I travel to Abarrach is in hopes of making reparation, of finding the means to destroy the dread serpents. I begin to think"—he hesitated, glanced at his son from beneath lowered eyelids—"I begin to think that Alfred was right all along. The true evil *is* here. We created it."

His father placed his hand over his own heart.

Ramu did not understand. "Father, how can you say that? Look at what you created! It is not evil."

Ramu gestured, a broad and sweeping motion that included not only the buildings and ground and trees and gardens of the Chalice, but the world of water itself, and beyond that, the worlds of air and fire and stone.

Samah looked where his son had pointed. "I see only what we destroyed," he said.

Those were his last words, before he walked through Death's Gate.

"Farewell, my father," Ramu called after him. "When you return triumphant, with legions marching behind you, your spirits will lift." . . .

But Samah had not returned. And there had been no word of him.

And now, though Ramu was loath to admit it, the mensch had —to all intents and purposes—conquered the gods. Conquered us! Their superiors! Ramu could see no way out of the present difficulty. Since the floodgates were under the magic-nullifying water, the Sartan could not destroy the floodgates with magic. We might resort to mechanical means. In the Sartan library are books which tell how, in ancient days, men manufactured powerful explosive devices.

But Ramu could not fool himself. He lifted his hands, turned them palm up, stared at them. The palms were soft and smooth, the fingers long and shapely. A conjurer's hands, taught to handle the insubstantial. Not a craftsman's. The clumsiest dwarf could manufacture in an eyeblink what it would take Ramu long hours of toil to produce with nothing but his hands.

"We might, after cycles and cycles, produce something mechanical capable of closing or blocking off the floodgates. But at that point we have become mensch," Ramu said to himself. "Better to just open the floodgates and let the water rush in!"

It was then that the thought occurred to him. Perhaps we should leave. Let the mensch have this world. Let them look after themselves. Let them destroy each other, as—so Alfred had reported—the mensch were doing on other worlds.

Let the unruly and ungrateful children come home to find that their long-suffering parents have gone.

He was suddenly conscious of the other Council members exchanging glances, their expressions anxious, worried. He realized, too late, that his dark thoughts had been reflected on his face. His expression hardened. To leave now was to give up, surrender, admit defeat. He would sooner drown in that blue-green water.

"Either the mensch abandon the Chalice or agree to place themselves under our control. Those are their only two options. I assume the rest of the Council agrees with me?" Ramu glanced around.

The rest of the Council did agree, at least by voice. Any disagreement or dissent was not spoken aloud. This was no time for disunity.

"If the mensch refuse to meet these terms," Ramu continued, frowning, speaking slowly and distinctly, his gaze fixing in turn on each person in the room, "there will be consequences. Dire consequences. You may tell them that."

The Council members appeared more hopeful, relieved. Obviously, their Councillor had a plan. They delegated one of their number to speak to the mensch, then moved on to other business, such as cleaning up damage left by the floodwaters. When there were no other matters left to consider, the Council voted to adjourn. Most of them went about their business, but a few lingered behind, talking with Ramu, hoping to discover some hint of what the Councillor had in mind.

Ramu was expert at keeping his own counsel. He gave away nothing, and the other Council members at length departed. Ramu remained seated at the table, glad to be alone with his thoughts, when he suddenly realized he wasn't alone.

A strange Sartan had entered the room.

The man looked familiar, but was not immediately recognizable. Ramu regarded him intently, trying to place him. Several hundred Sartan lived on the Chalice. A good politician, Ramu knew them all by sight and could generally put a name to a face. It disturbed him that he couldn't remember this one. Yet he was positive he'd seen this man before.

Ramu rose politely to his feet. "Good day, sir. If you have come to present a petition to the Council, you are too late. We have adjourned."

The Sartan smiled and shook his head. He was a man of middle age, handsome, with a receding hairline, strong jaw and nose, sad and thoughtful eyes.

"I come in time, then," the Sartan said, "for I have come to talk to you, Councillor. If you are Ramu, son of Samah and Orlah?"

Ramu frowned, annoyed by this reference to his mother. She had been exiled for crimes against the people; her name was never to be spoken. He was about to make some comment on this when it occurred to him that perhaps the strange Sartan (what *was* his name!) did not know of Orlah's exile to the Labyrinth, in the company of the heretic Alfred. Gossip had undoubtedly spread the word, but, Ramu was forced to admit, this dignified stranger did not look the type to indulge in whispers over the back fence.

Ramu bit back his irritation, made no comment. He answered the question with a slight emphasis that should have given the stranger a clue. "I am Ramu, son of *Samah*."

At that point, Ramu was faced with a problem. Asking the man's name was not a politic move, would reveal that Ramu did not remember him. There were diplomatic ways around this, but— being generally a blunt and forthright man—Ramu could think of none at the moment.

The strange Sartan, however, settled the matter. "You don't remember me, do you, Ramu?"

Ramu flushed, was about to make some polite reply, but the Sartan went on.

"Not surprising. We met long, long, long ago. Before the Sundering. I was a member of the original Council. A good friend of your father's."

Ramu's mouth sagged open. He did remember now . . . in a way. He remembered something disquieting in regard to this man. But what was of more immediate interest was the fact that this Sartan was obviously not a citizen of Chelestra. Which meant he had come from another world.

"Arianus," said the Sartan with a smile. "World of air. Stasis sleep. Much like you and your people, I believe."

"I am pleased to know you again, sir," Ramu said, trying to clear his confusion, recall what he knew about this man, and, at the same time, revel in the newfound hope the stranger brought. There *were* Sartan alive on Arianus!

"I trust you will not be insulted, but it has been, as you say, a long time. Your name . . ."

"You may call me James," said the Sartan.

Ramu eyed him distrustfully. "James is not a Sartan name."

"No, you're right. But as a compatriot of mine must have told you, we on Arianus are not accustomed to using our true Sartan names. I believe you have met Alfred?"

"The heretic? Yes, I've met him." Ramu was grim. "I think it only fair to warn you that he was exiled . . ."

Something stirred in Ramu, a distant memory, not of Alfred. Further back, much further back in time.

He had almost grasped it, but before he could lay hands on the memory, the strange Sartan unraveled it.

James was nodding gravely. "Always a troublemaker, was Alfred. I'm not surprised to hear of his downfall. But I didn't come to speak of him. I came on a far sadder mission. I am the bearer of unhappy news and evil tidings."

"My father," Ramu said, forgetting everything else. "You come with news of my father."

"I am sorry to have to tell you this." James drew near to Ramu, placed a firm hand on the younger man's arm. "Your father is dead."

Ramu bowed his head. He didn't for a moment doubt the stranger's words. He'd known, deep inside, for some time.

"How did he die?"

The Sartan grew more grave, troubled. "He died in the dungeons of Abarrach, at the hands of one who calls himself Xar, Lord of the Patryns."

Ramu went rigid. He could not speak for long moments; then he asked, in a low voice, "How do you know this?"

"I was with him," James said softly, now intently regarding the young man. "I was myself captured by Lord Xar."

"And you escaped? But not my father?" Ramu glowered.

"I am sorry, Councillor. A friend assisted me to escape. Help came too late for your father. By the time we reached him . . ." James sighed.

Ramu was overcome by darkness. But anger soon burned away his grief—anger and hatred and the desire for revenge.

"A friend helped you. Then there *are* Sartan living on Abarrach?"

"Oh, yes," James replied, with a cunning look. "Many Sartan on Abarrach. Their leader is called Balthazar. I know that is not a Sartan name," he added quickly, "but you must remember that these Sartan are twelfth-generation. They have lost or forgotten many of the old ways."

"Yes, of course," Ramu muttered, not giving the matter further thought. "And you say that this Lord Xar is also living on Abarrach. This can only mean one thing."

James nodded gravely. "The Patryns are attempting to break out of the Labyrinth—such are the evil tidings I bear. They have launched an assault on the Final Gate."

Ramu was appalled. "But there must be thousands of them . . ."

"At least," James replied complacently. "It will take all your people, plus the Sartan of Abarrach—"

"—to stop this evil!" Ramu concluded, fist clenched.

"To stop this evil," James repeated, adding solemnly, "You must go at once to the Labyrinth. It's what your father would have wanted, I think."

"Certainly." Ramu's mind was racing ahead. He forgot all about where he might have met this man, under what circumstances. "And this time, we will not be merciful to our enemy. That was my father's mistake."

"Samah has paid for his mistakes," James said quietly, "and he has been forgiven."

Ramu paid no attention. "This time, we will *not* shut the

Patryns up in a prison. This time, we will destroy them—utterly."

He turned on his heel, was about to leave, when he remembered his manners. He faced the elder Sartan. "I thank you, sir, for bringing this news. You may rest assured my father's death will be avenged. I must go now, to discuss this with the other members of the Council, but I will send one of the servitors to you. You will be a guest in my house. Is there anything else I can do to make you comfortable—"

"Not necessary," said James, with a wave of his hand. "Go along to the Labyrinth. I'll manage on my own."

Ramu felt again that same sense of unease and disquiet. He did not doubt the information the strange Sartan had brought to him. One Sartan cannot lie to another. But there was something not quite right . . . What was it about this man?

James stood unmoving, smiling beneath Ramu's scrutiny.

Ramu gave up trying to remember. It was probably nothing, after all. Nothing important. Besides, it had all happened long ago. Now he had more urgent, more immediate problems. Bowing, he left the Council Chamber.

The strange Sartan remained standing in the room, staring after the departed man. "Yes, you remember me, Ramu. You were among the guards who came to arrest me that day, the day of the Sundering. You came to drag me to the Seventh Gate. I told Samah I was going to stop him, you see. He was afraid of me. Not surprising. He was afraid of everything by then."

James sighed.

Walking over to the stone table, he traced his finger through the dust. Despite the recent flood, the dust continued to drift down from the ceiling, coating every object in the Chalice with a thin, fine, white powder.

"But I was gone when you arrived, Ramu. I chose to stay behind. I couldn't stop the Sundering, and so I tried to protect those you left behind. But I couldn't do anything to help them. There were too many dying. I wasn't of much use to anyone then.

"But I am now."

The Sartan's aspect changed, altered. The handsome middle-aged man evolved, transformed in an instant into an old man with a long, scraggly beard, wearing mouse-colored robes and a battered, shapeless hat. The old man stroked his beard, looked extremely proud of himself.

"Pig's breakfast, indeed! Just wait till you hear what I've done now! I handled that just exactly right. Did exactly what you told me, you elongated toad of a dragon . . .

"That is"—Zifnab thoughtfully tugged at his beard—"I *believe* I did what you said. 'At all costs, get Ramu to the Labyrinth.' Yes, those were your exact words . . .

"I think those were the exact words. Um, now that I recall . . ." The old man began to twist his beard into knots. "Perhaps it was 'At all costs, keep Ramu *away* from the Labyrinth'? . . .

"I've got the 'at all costs' bit down pat." Zifnab appeared to take some comfort from this fact. "It's the part that comes after I'm a bit muddled on. Maybe . . . Maybe I just better pop back and check the script."

Mumbling to himself, the old man walked into a wall and vanished.

A Sartan, happening to enter the Council Chamber at that moment, was startled to hear a grim voice saying gloomily, "What *have* you done now, sir?"

CHAPTER 7

THE LABYRINTH

◆

Tʜᴇ ʙʟᴜᴇ-ɢʀᴇᴇɴ ᴅʀᴀɢᴏɴ ᴏꜰ ᴘʀʏᴀɴ ʀᴏsᴇ ʜɪɢʜ ᴀʙᴏᴠᴇ ᴛʜᴇ ᴛʀᴇᴇᴛᴏᴘs. ᴀʟꜰʀᴇᴅ glanced down at the ground once, shuddered, and resolved to look anywhere except that direction. Somehow, flying had been different when *he'd* been the one with the wings. He gripped the dragon's scales more tightly. Trying to take his mind off the fact that he was perched precariously and unsteadily on the back of a dragon, soaring far, far above solid ground, Alfred searched for the source of the wondrous sunlight. He knew it shone from the citadels, but those were located on Pryan. How was the light shining into the Labyrinth? Turning slowly and carefully, he risked peering back tentatively over his shoulder.

"The light shines from the Vortex," Vasu shouted. The headman was flying on another dragon. "Look, look toward the ruined mountain."

Sitting up as tall as he dared, clinging nervously to the dragon, Alfred stared in the direction indicated. He gasped in awe.

It was as if a sun burned deep within the mountain's heart. Shafts of brilliant light beamed from every crack, every crevice, illuminated the sky, poured over the land. The light touched Abri's gray walls, causing them to glisten silver. The trees that had lived so long in the gray day of the Labyrinth seemed to lift their twisted limbs to this new dawn, as an aged man reaches aching fingers to a warm fire.

But, Alfred saw sadly, the light did not penetrate far into the Labyrinth. It was a tiny candle flame in the vast darkness; nothing more. And soon the darkness consumed it.

Alfred watched for as long as he could, until the light was blotted out by mountains, rising jagged and sharp, like bony hands thrust into his face to prohibit hope. He sighed, turned away, and saw the fiery red glow on the horizon ahead.

"What is that?" he called. "Do you know?"

Vasu shook his head. "It began the night after the attack on Abri. In that direction lies the Final Gate."

"I saw the elves burn a walled city on the Volkaran Islands," Hugh the Hand said, dark eyes squinting to see. "Flames leapt from house to house. The heat was so intense, some buildings exploded before the fire even reached them. At night, the blaze lit up the sky. It looked very much like that."

"It is undoubtedly magical fire, created by my lord to drive off the dragon-snakes," Marit said coolly.

Alfred sighed. How could she continue to have faith in Lord Xar? Her hair was gummed together with her own blood, drawn by Xar when he obliterated the sigil which had joined them together. Perhaps that was the reason. She and Xar had been in communication. She was the one who had betrayed them to Xar, had told him their location. Perhaps, somehow, Xar continued to exert his influence over her.

"I should have stopped her at the very beginning," he said to himself. "I saw that sigil when I brought her into the Vortex. I knew what it meant. I should have warned Haplo she would betray him."

And then, as usual, Alfred began to argue with himself. "But Marit saved Haplo's life in Chelestra. It was obvious she loved him. And he loved her. They brought love into a prison house of hate. How could I slam shut the door against it? Yet maybe if I had told him, he could have protected himself . . . I don't know." Alfred sighed bleakly. "I don't know . . . I did what I thought was best . . . And who can say? Perhaps her faith in her lord will be justified."

The blue-green dragons of Pryan flew on through the Labyrinth, circling around the tall mountains, diving through the passes. As they drew nearer the Final Gate, they dipped low, barely skimming the treetops, hiding as best they could from watchful eyes. The darkness grew deeper, an unnatural darkness, for nightfall was some hours distant. This darkness affected not only the eyes, but the heart and the mind as well. An evil, magical darkness, cast by the dragon-snakes, it brought with it the ages-old fear of night we first know as children. It spoke of unknown, hideous things lurking just beyond sight, ready to leap out and drag us off.

Marit's face, bathed in the light of her own warning rune-glow, was pale and strained. The blood on her forehead looked black by contrast. Hugh the Hand constantly turned to stare around.

"We're being watched," he warned.

Alfred cringed at the words, which seemed to bounce back from the darkness in laughing, mocking echoes. Crouching, trying to hide behind the dragon's neck, Alfred grew faint—his preferred form of defense. He knew the signs, and he fought against them: lightheaded, his stomach crawling, his forehead beaded with sweat. He pressed his face against the dragon's cool scales and closed his eyes.

But being blind was worse than seeing, because suddenly Alfred had the vivid memory of falling from the air, spiraling downward, too weak and wounded to stop his descent. The ground spun crazily, soared up to meet him . . .

A hand shook him.

Alfred gasped, jerked upright.

"You damn near fell off," Hugh the Hand told him. "You aren't planning to faint, are you?"

"No-no," Alfred murmured.

"Good thing," the Hand said. "Take a look ahead."

Alfred sat up, wiped the chill sweat from his face. It took a moment for the fog of dizziness to clear from his eyes, and at first he had no idea what it was he was seeing. The darkness was so intense, and now it was mingled with a choking smoke . . .

Smoke. Alfred stared, all things coming into terrible focus.

The city of the Nexus, the beautiful city built by the Sartan for their enemies, was ablaze.

The dragons of Pryan were not affected by the dragon-snakes' magical darkness. They flew through it unerringly, keeping to their destination, whatever that might be. Alfred had no idea where he was being taken, nor did he much care. It would be horrible, wherever it was. Sick at heart, terrified, he longed to turn around, flee back to the bright light shining from the mountain.

"It is a good thing I am riding on the back of this dragon," Vasu said somberly, his voice coming out of the darkness. The runes on his skin glimmered brightly, red and blue. "Otherwise, I would not have had the courage to come this far."

"It shames me to say it, Headman," Marit said in a low voice, "but I feel the same."

"No shame," said the dragon. "The fear grows from seeds planted within you by the serpents. Fear's roots seek out every dark part of you, every memory, every nightmare, and, once found, the roots sink into those dark parts and drink deep. Fear's evil plant flourishes."

"How can I destroy it?" Alfred quavered.

"You cannot," said the dragon. "Fear is a part of you. The serpents know this and that is why they use it. Don't let fear overwhelm you. Don't become afraid of the fear."

"Just what I've been all my life!" Alfred said miserably.

"Not *all* your life," the dragon said—and it might have been Alfred's imagination, but he thought he could see the dragon smile.

Marit gazed down at the buildings of the Nexus, their walls and pillars, towers and spires now black skeletons, lit from within by the devouring flames. The buildings were made of stone, but the support beams and floors and walls within were wood. The stone was protected by runes, wrought by the Sartan, strengthened by the Patryns. Marit wondered at first how the city could have fallen; then she remembered the walls of Abri. They, too, had been

protected by the rune-magic. The serpents had thrown themselves
bodily against the walls, causing small cracks to form, cracks that
widened and spread until they broke apart the runes, tore apart
the magic.

The Nexus. Marit had never considered the city beautiful. She
had always thought of it in terms of practicality, as did most Patryns. Its walls were thick and sound, its streets well laid and
smooth, its buildings strong and solid and sturdy. Now, by the
light of the fire that was destroying it, she noticed its beauty, the
grace and delicacy of its tall spires, the harmonious simplicity of its
design. Even as she watched, one of the spires toppled and fell,
sending up a shower of sparks and a cloud of smoke.

Marit despaired. Her lord could not have let this happen. He
could not be here. Or if he was, he must now be dead. All her
people must now be dead.

"Look!" Vasu cried suddenly. "The Final Gate! It's still open!
We're holding it!"

Marit dragged her gaze from the burning city, stared through
the smoke and darkness, trying to see. The dragons tipped their
wings, turned, started to descend from the sky in large spirals.

Patryns on the ground below lifted their faces upward. Marit
was too far away to see their expressions, but she guessed by their
actions what thoughts were running through their minds. The arrival of a vast army of winged beasts could only mean one thing—
defeat. The death blow.

Understanding their fear, Vasu began to sing; his voice—using
Sartan rune-language—carried clearly through the smoke and the
flame-lit darkness.

Marit couldn't understand the words; she had the feeling they
weren't meant to be understood. But they lifted her heart. The
horrible terror that had almost suffocated her in its choking grasp
shriveled and lost some of its strength.

The Patryns on the ground below stared up in wonder. Vasu's
song was echoed by Patryn voices, shouting encouragement and
war chants. The dragons flew low, allowing their passengers to
jump off. Then the dragons returned to the skies, some circling,
keeping watch, others departing, scouring the area for the enemy

or flying back to the interior of the Labyrinth, to bring more Patryns to the battlefield.

Between the Labyrinth and the Nexus stood a wall covered with Sartan runes—runes strong enough to kill anything that touched them. The wall was immense, stretching from one mountain range to another in an irregular gigantic semicircle. Barren plains extended from the wall on both sides. The city of the Nexus offered life on one side; the dark forests of the Labyrinth offered death on the other.

Those in the Labyrinth who came within sight of the Final Gate faced their most terrible challenge in trying to reach it. The plains were a no-man's-land, bare of any cover, providing an enemy a clear view of anyone attempting to cross. Here was the Labyrinth's last chance to hang on to its victims. Here, on this plain, Marit had nearly died. Here her lord had rescued her.

Flying over the ground that had been churned up and blasted by magic and battle, Marit searched the crowd of weary, bloodied Patryns, looking for Xar. He must be here. He must! The wall stood, the Gate held. Only her lord could have performed such powerful magic.

But if he was in the crowd, she couldn't find him.

The dragon settled to the ground, the Patryns giving it a wide berth, regarding it with dark looks, wary suspicion. The dragon carrying Vasu also landed, both dragons remaining, while the rest returned to the skies and their duties.

The howls of wolfen reverberated from the forests, punctuated by the unnerving clicking sounds made by the chaodyn before a fight. Numerous red dragons flew through the smoke, their scales reflected in the flames of the burning city, but they didn't attack. To her astonishment, Marit saw no sign of the serpents.

But she knew they were near; the sigla on her skin flared almost as brightly as the fire.

The Abri Patryns banded together, waited silently for orders from their headman. Vasu had gone to make himself known to the Patryns at the Gate. Marit accompanied him, still searching for Lord Xar. They passed by Alfred, who was gazing sadly at the wall, wringing his hands.

"We built this monstrous prison," he was lamenting softly. "We built this!" He shook his head. "We have much for which to answer. Much."

"Yes, but not now!" Marit chided him. "I don't want to have to explain to my people what a Sartan is doing here. Not that my people would likely give me much chance to explain before they ripped you apart. You and Hugh keep out of sight, as much as possible."

"I understand," Alfred said unhappily.

"Hugh, keep an eye on him," Marit ordered. "And for all our sakes, keep control of that cursed knife!"

The Hand nodded in silence. His gaze was taking in everything about his surroundings, revealing nothing of his thoughts. He put his hand over the Cursed Blade, as if endeavoring to restrain it.

Vasu strode across the burned and blasted plains, his people remaining silently behind him, showing him respect and support. A woman left the group of Patryns guarding the Gate, walked to meet him.

Marit's heart lurched. She knew this woman! They had lived near each other in the Nexus. Marit was tempted to rush forward, demand to know where Xar was, demand to know where he had taken the wounded Haplo.

She choked back her need. To speak to the woman before Vasu would be a serious discourtesy. The woman, rightly, would rebuff Marit, would refuse to answer her questions. Containing herself, Marit kept as close to Vasu as possible. She glanced back worriedly at Alfred, fearful he would give himself away. He remained on the fringes of the crowd, Hugh the Hand beside him. Nearby, alone, stood the gentleman dressed in black. The blue-green dragon of Pryan had disappeared.

"I am Headman Vasu of the village of Abri." Vasu touched his heart-rune. "A village several gates from here. These are my people."

"You and your people are welcome, Headman Vasu, though you come here only to die," said the woman.

"We will die in good company," Vasu responded politely.

"I am Usha," the woman said, touching her heart-rune. "Our

headman is dead. More than one are dead," she added, her voice grim, her gaze going to the Gate. "The people have turned to me to lead them."[1]

Usha had many gates, as the saying went. Her hair was streaked with gray, her skin wrinkled. But she was strong, in far better physical condition than Vasu. She was, in fact, regarding him with drawn brows and a doubtful look.

"What beasts are these you have brought with you?" she demanded, her gaze going to the dragons wheeling in the sky above them. "I have never seen their like in the Labyrinth before."

"You have obviously never been to our part of the Labyrinth before, Usha," Vasu said.

She frowned, recognizing the answer as evasive. Marit had been wondering how Vasu was going to explain the dragons. One Patryn could not lie outright to another, but certain truths could be kept concealed. It would take a long time to explain the presence of the dragons of Pryan, even if he could.

"You are saying that these creatures come from your part of the Labyrinth, Headman?"

"They do now," Vasu answered gravely. "You need not worry about them, Usha. They are under our control. They are immensely powerful and will aid us in our battle. In fact, these dragons may very well save us."

Usha crossed her arms over her chest. She did not appear convinced, but to argue further would be to challenge Vasu's authority, perhaps might be taken as a challenge to his right to rule. With several hundred Patryns backing him, obviously supporting him loyally, to do such a thing during this time of turmoil would be foolish.

Her stern expression relaxed. "I say again, you are welcome, Headman Vasu. You and your people and—" She hesitated, then said with a grudging smile, "these you call your dragons. As for

[1] If a headman dies during battle, another member of the tribe may take over for the duration of the emergency. Usha is technically headman, but may not lay claim to the title, which can only be awarded by the tribal council. At that time, any challenges to the new headman's rule are accepted.

saving us . . ." Her smile vanished. She sighed, glanced back at
the fire raging in the Nexus. "I do not think there is much hope of
that."

"What is your situation?" Vasu asked.

The two leaders withdrew to talk. At this point, the tribes were
free to mingle with each other. The Patryns of Abri advanced. They
had brought with them weapons, food, water, and other supplies.
They offered their own healing strength, to renew those in need.

Marit cast another worried glance at Alfred. He was, fortunately, keeping to himself and out of trouble. She noticed that
Hugh had a firm grip on the Sartan's arm. The gentleman in black
was no longer anywhere in sight. Her mind at ease about Alfred,
Marit trailed after Usha and Vasu, anxious to hear what they said.

". . . serpents attacked us at dawn," Usha was saying. "Their
numbers were immense. They struck the city of the Nexus first.
Their intent was to trap us in the city, destroy us there, then, when
we were dead, they would seal shut the Final Gate. They made no
secret of their plans, but told us, laughing, what they plotted. How
they would trap our people in the Labyrinth, how the evil would
grow . . ." Usha shuddered. "Their threats were terrible to hear."

"They want your fear," said Vasu. "It feeds them, makes them
strong. What happened after that?"

"We fought them. The battle was hopeless. Our magical weapons are useless against such a powerful foe. The serpents hurled
themselves bodily at the city walls, broke the runes, swarmed inside." Usha glanced back at the burning buildings. "They could
have destroyed us then, every one of us. But they didn't. They let
most of us live. At first, we couldn't understand why. Why didn't
they kill us, when they had the chance?"

"They wanted you inside the Labyrinth," Vasu guessed.

Usha nodded, her face grim. "We fled the city. The serpents
drove us in this direction, murdering any who tried to elude them.
We were caught between the terror of the Labyrinth and the terror
of the serpents. Some of the people were half mad with fear. The
serpents laughed and ringed us around, driving us closer and
closer to the Gate. They picked off victims at random, increasing
the terror and chaos.

"We entered the Gate. What choice did we have? Most of the people found the courage. Those who did not . . ." Usha fell silent. Lowering her head, she blinked her eyes rapidly, swallowed before she could speak again. "We heard them screaming for a long time."

Vasu was slow to reply, his own anger and pity choking his voice. Marit could remain silent no longer.

"Usha," she said desperately. "What of Lord Xar? He is here, isn't he?"

"He *was* here," replied Usha.

"Where has he gone? Was . . . was anyone with him?" Marit faltered, her skin flushing.

Usha eyed her, her expression dark. "As to where he has gone, I neither know nor care. He left us! Left us to die!" She spat on the ground. "That for Lord Xar!"

"No!" Marit murmured. "It's not possible."

"Was anyone with him? I don't know. I couldn't tell." Usha's lip curled. "Lord Xar was riding on a ship, a ship that flew in the air. And it was covered with those markings." She cast a scathing glance at the wall, the Gate. "The runes of our enemy!"

"Sartan runes?" Marit said, in sudden realization. "Then it couldn't have been Lord Xar you saw! It must have been a trick of the serpents! He would never fly a ship with Sartan runes. This proves it couldn't have been Xar!"

"On the contrary," said a voice. "I am afraid it proves it *was* Lord Xar."

Angry, Marit turned to face this new accusation. She was somewhat daunted to find the gentleman in black standing near her. He was regarding her with deep sorrow.

"Lord Xar left Pryan on just such a ship. It was of Sartan make and design—a vessel formed in the likeness of a dragon, with sails for wings?" The gentleman glanced questioningly at Usha.

She confirmed his description with an abrupt nod.

"It can't be!" Marit cried angrily. "My lord couldn't have gone off and left his people! Not when he saw what was happening! Not when he saw that the serpents had betrayed him! Did he say anything?"

"He said he would be back!" Usha snapped the words off bitterly. "And that our deaths would be avenged!"

Her eyes flashed; she glared distrustfully at Marit.

"This may help explain, Usha," said Vasu. Brushing Marit's tangled, blood-encrusted hair from her face, Vasu revealed the torn mark on her forehead.

Usha gazed at it; her expression softened.

"I see," she said. "I am sorry for you."

Turning away from Marit, Usha continued her conversation with Vasu.

"At my suggestion, our people—now caught inside the Labyrinth again—have concentrated their magic on defending the Final Gate. We are attempting to keep it open. If it shuts—" She shook her head grimly.

"That will be the end for us," Vasu agreed.

"The Sartan death-runes on the walls—so long a curse—now prove to be a blessing. After they drove us in here, the serpents discovered that they could not come through the Final Gate or even get near it. They attacked the wall, but the runes were one magic they could not destroy. Whenever they touch the runes, blue light crackles around them. They bellow in pain and back off. It does not kill them, but it seems to weaken them.

"Seeing this, we wove the same blue fire across the Final Gate. We cannot get out, but neither can the serpents seal shut the Gate. Frustrated, the serpents roamed for a while outside the walls. Then, suddenly, they mysteriously departed.

"And now the scouts report that other enemies—all the creatures of the Labyrinth—are massing in the forest behind us. Thousands of them."

"They'll attack from both directions, then," Vasu said. "Pin us against the wall."

"Crush us," said Usha.

"Perhaps not," said Vasu. "What if we . . ."

The two continued talking strategy, defense. Marit ceased to listen, wandered away. What did it all matter anyway? She had been so certain of Xar, so sure . . .

"What is happening?" Alfred asked worriedly. He had waited

until she was alone to come talk to her. "What's going on? Where's Lord Xar?"

Marit said nothing. Instead, the gentleman in black answered. "Lord Xar has gone to Abarrach, as he said he would."

"And Haplo is with him?" Alfred's voice quivered.

"Yes, Haplo is with him," replied the gentleman softly.

"My lord has taken Haplo to Abarrach to heal him!" Marit glared at them, daring them to refute her.

Alfred was silent a moment; then he said quietly, "My way is clear. I will go to Abarrach. Perhaps I can . . ." He glanced at Marit. "Perhaps I can help," he finished lamely.

Marit knew all too well what he was thinking. She, too, saw the living corpses of Abarrach. Dead bodies transformed into mindless slaves. She remembered the torment in the unseeing eyes, the trapped soul peering out through its prison of rotting flesh . . . She saw Haplo . . .

She couldn't breathe. A yellow-tinged blackness blinded her. Gentle arms caught hold of her, steadied her. She gave in to their support, so long as the darkness lasted. When it began to recede, she pushed Alfred away from her.

"Leave me alone. I'm all right now," she muttered, ashamed of her weakness. "And if you're going to Abarrach, so am I."

She turned to the gentleman. "How do we travel there? We don't have a ship."

"You will find a vessel near Lord Xar's dwelling place," said the gentleman. "Or rather—his former dwelling place. The serpents burned it."

"But they left a ship intact?" Marit was suspicious. "That doesn't make sense."

"Perhaps it does—to them," the gentleman replied. "If you are resolved, you must leave quickly, before the serpents return. If they discover the Serpent Mage, and catch him out in the open, they will not hesitate to attack him."

"Where are the dragon-snakes?" Alfred asked nervously.

"They are leading the Patryn's enemies: wolfen, snogs, chaodyn, dragons. The armies of the Labyrinth are massing for a final assault."

"There aren't that many of us left to fight them." Marit wavered in her decision to leave, looking at her people, thinking of the vast numbers of the enemy.

"Reinforcements are already on the way," the gentleman said, with a reassuring smile. "And our serpent cousins won't be expecting to find *us* here. We will come as a nasty surprise to them. Between us, we can hold them off for a long time. As long as it takes," he added with a peculiar look at Alfred.

"What does that mean?" Alfred asked.

The gentleman rested his hand on Alfred's wrist, gazed at him intently. The dragon's eyes were blue-green as Pryan sky, as Chelestra's magic-ending water. "Remember, Coren, hope's light now shines into the Labyrinth. And it will continue to shine, though the Gate is shut."

"You're trying to tell me something, aren't you? Riddles, prophecies! I'm not good at this!" Alfred was sweating. "Why don't you just come out and say it? Tell me what I'm supposed to do!"

"So few people follow instructions these days," the gentleman said, shaking his head gloomily. "Even simple ones."

He patted Alfred's hand. "Still, we do what we can with what we have. Trust to your instincts."

"My instinct is usually to faint!" Alfred protested. "You expect me to do something grand and heroic. But I'm not the type. I'm only going to Abarrach to help a friend."

"Of course you are," said the gentleman softly, and he sighed and turned away.

Marit heard the sigh echo inside her, reminding her of the echo of the trapped souls of Abarrach's living dead.

CHAPTER ◆ 8

NECROPOLIS

ABARRACH

◆

ABARRACH—WORLD OF FIRE, WORLD OF STONE. WORLD OF THE DEAD. AND OF the dying.

In the dungeons of Necropolis, dead city of a dead world, Haplo lay dying.

He lay on a stone bed, his head pillowed on stone. It was not comfortable, but Haplo was past the need for comfort. He had been in terrible pain, but the worst of the pain was gone now. He could feel nothing except the burning pull of every ragged breath, each breath more difficult to draw in than the previous. He was a little afraid of that last breath, the final spasmodic gasp that would not sustain his life; the choke, the rattle. He imagined it, feared it would be similar to the time on Chelestra when he had thought he was drowning.

Then he had drawn water into his lungs and the water had been life-giving. Now he would draw in nothing. He would struggle to keep away the darkness, a struggle terrifying, but mercifully brief.

And his lord was here beside him. Haplo was not alone.

"This is not easy for me, my son," Xar said.

He was not being sarcastic, or ironic. He was truly grieving. He sat beside Haplo's hard bed and the lord's shoulders were stooped, his head bowed. He looked far older than his many, many years. His eyes, watching Haplo die, shimmered with unshed tears.

Xar could have killed Haplo, but he didn't.

Xar could have saved Haplo's life, but he wasn't doing that either.

"You must die, my son," Xar said. "I dare not let you live. I cannot trust you. You are more valuable to me dead than you are alive. And so I must let you die. But I cannot kill you. I gave you life. Yes, I suppose that this makes it my right to take that life away. But I cannot. You were one of the best. And I loved you. I still love you. I would save you if only . . . if only . . ."

Xar did not finish.

Haplo said nothing, made no argument, no plea for his life. He knew the pain this must cause his lord and he knew that if there were any way, Xar would spare him. But there wasn't. Xar was right. The Lord of the Nexus could no longer trust his "son." Haplo would fight him and continue to fight until, as now, he had no more strength left.

Xar would be a fool to give Haplo back that strength. Once Haplo was dead, his corpse—poor mindless, soulless shell—would be at Xar's command. Haplo—the living, breathing, thinking Haplo—would not.

"There is no other way," Xar said, his thoughts running parallel with Haplo's, as they often did. "I must let you die. You understand, my son. I know you do. You will serve me in death, as you did in life. Only better. Only better."

The Lord of the Nexus sighed. "But this is still not easy for me. You understand that, too, don't you, my son?"

"Yes," Haplo whispered. "I understand."

And so the two remained together in the darkness of the dungeon. It was quiet; very, very quiet. Xar had ordered all the other Patryns to leave them alone. The only sounds were Haplo's shuddering breaths; Xar's occasional question; Haplo's whispered answers.

"Do you mind talking?" Xar asked. "If it pains you, I will not press you."

"No, Lord. I don't feel any pain. Not anymore."

"A sip of water, to ease the dryness."

"Yes, Lord. Thank you."

Xar's touch was cool. His hand smoothed back Haplo's sweat-damp hair from his feverish forehead. He lifted Haplo's head, held a cup of water to the dying man's lips. Gently, the lord laid Haplo back down on the stone.

"That city in which I found you, the city of Abri. A city in the Labyrinth. And I never knew it was there. Not surprising, of course, since it was in the very heart of the Labyrinth. Abri has been there a long, long time, I assume, judging by its size."

Haplo nodded. He was very tired, but it was comforting to hear his lord's voice. Haplo had a dim recollection of being a boy riding on his father's back. The boy's small arms wrapped around muscular shoulders, small head drooping. He could hear his father's voice and feel it at the same time, feel it resonate in his chest. He could hear his lord's voice and feel it at the same time—an odd sensation, as if it were coming to him through the cold hard stone.

"Our people are not city-builders," Xar commented.

"The Sartan," Haplo whispered.

"Yes, so I judged. The Sartan who, long ago, defied Samah and the Council of Seven. They were punished for their defiance, sent to the Labyrinth with their enemies. And we did not turn on them and kill them. I find that strange."

"Not so strange," said Haplo, thinking of Alfred.

Not when two people have to fight to survive in a terrible land that is intent on destroying them both. He and Alfred had survived only by helping each other. Now Alfred was in the Labyrinth, in Abri, perhaps helping Haplo's people to survive.

"This Vasu, the leader of Abri, a Sartan, isn't he?" Xar continued. "Part Sartan, at least. Yes, I thought so. I did not meet him, but I saw him on the fringes of my mind. Very powerful, very capable. A good leader. But ambitious, certainly. Especially now that he knows the world is not bounded by Abri's walls. He will want his share, I am afraid. Perhaps the whole of it. That is the Sartan in him. I can't permit it. He must be eradicated. And there may be more like him. All those of our people whose blood has been tainted by the Sartan. I am afraid they will seek to overthrow my rule."

I am afraid . . .

You are wrong, Lord, Haplo said silently. Vasu cares only for his people, not for power. He is *not* afraid. He is what you were, Lord. He will not become what you are—afraid. You will rid yourself of Vasu, because you fear him. Then you will destroy all those Patryns who have Sartan ancestry. Then you will destroy the Patryns who were friends of those who have been destroyed. And at the end, there will be no one left but yourself—the person you fear most.

"The end is the beginning," Haplo murmured.

"What?" Xar leaned forward, sharp, intent. "What did you say, my son?"

Haplo had no recollection. He was in Chelestra, world of water, drifting in the seawater, sinking slowly beneath the waves, as he had done once before. Except that now he was no longer afraid. He was only a little sad, a little regretful. Leaving matters undone, unfinished.

But others were left to pick up what he had been forced to let fall. Alfred, bumbling, clumsy . . . golden, soaring dragon. Marit, beloved, strong. Their child . . . unknown. No, that was not quite true. He knew her. He'd seen her face . . . faces of his children . . . in the Labyrinth. All of these . . . drifting on the waves.

The wave bore him up, cradled him, rocked him. But he saw it as it had once been—a tidal wave, rising, rising to a fearful promontory, crashing down to engulf, deluge the world, split it apart.

Samah.

And then the ebb. Debris, wreckage, floating on the water. The survivors clinging to fragments until they found safe haven on strange shores. They flourished, for a time. But the wave must correct itself.

Slowly, slowly, the wave built again, in the opposite direction. A vast mountain of water, threatening to again crash down on and drown the world.

Xar.

Haplo struggled, briefly. It was hard—hard to leave. Especially now that he was finally beginning to understand . . .

Beginning. Xar was talking to him, cajoling him. Something about the Seventh Gate. A child's poem. End is the beginning.

A muffled whimper came from beneath the stone bed, was louder than Xar's voice. Haplo found just strength enough to move his hand. He felt a wet lick. He smiled, fondled the dog's silky ears.

"Our last journey together, boy," he said. "But no sausages . . ."

The pain was back. Bad. Very bad.

A hand took hold of his. A hand gnarled and old, strong and supportive.

"Easy, my son," said Xar, holding fast. "Rest easy. Give up the struggle. Let go . . ."

The pain was agony.

"Let go . . ."

Closing his eyes, Haplo sighed his last breath and sank beneath the waves.

CHAPTER ◆ 9

THE NECROPOLIS

THE LABYRINTH

◆

Xar clasped his hand around Haplo's wrist. The lord kept his hand on the wrist even when he could no longer feel life pulsing through it. Xar sat silently, staring into the darkness, seeing nothing at first. And then, as time passed and the flesh in his fingers grew cool, Xar saw himself.

An old man, alone with his dead.

An old man, sitting in a dungeon cell far below the surface of a world that was its own tomb. An old man, head bowed, stoop-shouldered, grieving over his loss. Haplo. Dearer to him than any son he'd fathered. But more than Haplo.

Closing his eyes against the bitter darkness, Xar saw another darkness, the terrible darkness that had fallen over the Final Gate. He saw the faces of his people, lifted to him in hope. He saw that hope change to disbelief, then to fear in some, anger in others, before his ship swept him into Death's Gate.

He could remember a time, countless times, when he'd emerged from the Labyrinth, weary, wounded, but triumphant. His people, stern and taciturn, had not said much, but their very silence was eloquent. In their eyes he saw respect, love, admiration . . .

Xar looked into Haplo's eyes—wide open and staring—and the lord saw only emptiness.

Xar let fall Haplo's wrist. The lord gazed in dull despair around the dark cell.

"How have I come to this?" he asked himself. "How, from where I began, did I end up here?"

And he thought he heard, in the darkness, sibilant, hissing laughter.

Furious, Xar bounded to his feet. "Who is there?" he called.

No reply, but the sounds ceased.

His moment of self-doubt was over, however. That hissing laughter had caused the emptiness to fill with rage.

"My people are disappointed in me now," Xar muttered to himself. He turned back, slowly and purposefully, to the corpse. "But when I rejoin them in victory, coming to them through the Seventh Gate, bringing to them a single world to conquer, to rule—then they will revere me as never before!"

"The Seventh Gate," Xar whispered, as he gently, tenderly, composed the body's limbs, folding the flaccid arms across the chest, stretching out the legs. Last, he shut the staring, empty eyes. "The Seventh Gate, my son. When you were a living man, you wanted to take me there. Now you will have the chance. And I will be grateful, my son. Do this for me, and I will grant you rest."

The flesh was cool beneath his fingers now. The heart-rune—with its dreadful, gaping wound—was beneath his hand. All he had to do was close the sigil, mend it, then work the magic of the necromancy on Haplo's corpse, on all the rest of the runes tattooed upon the body.

Xar rested his fingers on the heart-rune, the words of mending on his lips. Abruptly, he drew his hand back. His fingertips were stained with blood. His hand, which had always held firm in battle against his foes, began to tremble.

Again a sound, outside the cell. Not a hissing sound, but a shuffling. Xar turned, staring hard into the darkness. "I know you are there. I hear you. Are you spying on me? What do you want?"

In response, a figure advanced on the cell. It was one of the lazar, one of the frightful living dead of Abarrach. Xar eyed the shambling corpse suspiciously, thinking it might be Kleitus. Former Dynast of Abarrach, now a lazar, murdered by his own people, the Sartan Kleitus would have been quite happy to return the favor by murdering Xar. The lazar had tried and failed, but was ever on the lookout for another opportunity.

This lazar was not Kleitus, however. Xar breathed an involuntary sigh. He was not afraid of Kleitus, but the Lord of the Nexus had other, more important matters to consider now. He did not presume to waste his magical talents fighting a dead man.

"Who are you? What do you want here?" Xar demanded testily. He thought he recognized the lazar, but could not be certain. One dead Sartan looked a great deal like another to the Patryn.

"My name is Jonathon," said the lazar.

". . . Jonathon . . ." came the echo that was the trapped soul, forever trying to free itself from the body.

"I come, not to you, but to him."

". . . to him . . ."

The lazar's strange eyes, which were sometimes the blank eyes of the dead and sometimes the pain-filled eyes of one living in torment, fixed on Haplo.

"The dead call to us," the lazar continued. "We hear their voices . . ."

". . . voices . . ." whispered the echo sadly.

"Well, this is one call you needn't bother to answer," Xar said sharply. "You may depart. I have need of this corpse myself."

"Perhaps you could use my assistance," the lazar offered.

". . . assistance . . ."

Xar started to rebuff the lazar, bid it be gone. Then he remembered that the last time he'd tried to use the necromancy on Samah's corpse, the spell had failed. Giving life to Haplo was far too important to Xar to take a chance. The lord glanced distrustfully at the lazar, doubting its motives.

All he saw was a being in torment, like every other lazar on Abarrach. The ghouls had only one ambition, so far as Xar knew, and that was to turn other beings into horrid copies of themselves.

"Very well," Xar said, his back to the lazar. "You may stay. But do not interfere unless you see me doing something wrong."

And that would not happen. The Lord of the Nexus was confident. This time, his spell would succeed.

The lord went resolutely back to work. Swiftly now, ignoring the blood on his hands, he closed the heart-rune on Haplo's body. Then, mindful of the spell, he began to trace over the other sigla, muttering the runes as he worked.

The lazar stood silent, unmoving, outside the cell door. Soon, concentrating solely on his spell-casting, Xar forgot all about the undead. He moved slowly, patiently, taking his time. Hours passed.

And suddenly, an eerie blue glow began to spread over the dead body. The glow started at the heart-rune, then spread slowly, one sigil catching fire from another. Xar's spell was causing each individual sigil to burn with a mockery of life.

The lord drew in a shivering breath. He was shaking with eagerness, elation. The spell was working! Working! Soon the body would rise to its feet, soon it would lead him to the Seventh Gate.

He lost all feeling, all pity, all grief. The man he'd loved as a son was dead. The corpse was no longer known to Xar. It was an it. A means to an end. A tool. A key to unlock the door of Xar's ambition. When the last sigil flared to life, Xar was so excited that, for a moment, he actually struggled to recall the corpse's name— an essential in the concluding moments of the spell.

"Haplo," said the lazar softly.

". . . Haplo . . ." sighed the echo.

The name seemed whispered by the darkness. Xar never noticed who spoke it, nor did he notice the scrabbling, scuffling sound that came from behind the stone bier on which the corpse lay.

"Haplo!" Xar said. "Of course. I must be wearier than I thought. When this is done, I shall rest. I will need all my strength to work the magic of the Seventh Gate."

The Lord of the Nexus paused, going over everything one last time in his mind. All was perfect. He had not made a single error, as was evidenced by the shimmering blue of the runes on the dead body.

Xar raised his hands. "You will serve me in death, Haplo, as you served me in life. Stand. Walk. Return to the land of the living."

The corpse did not move.

Xar frowned, studied the runes intently. There was no change. None whatsoever. The sigla continued to glow; the corpse continued to lie on the bier.

Xar repeated his command, a hint of sternness in his voice. It seemed impossible that Haplo should, even now, continue to defy him.

"You will serve me!" Xar repeated.

No response. No change. Except that perhaps the blue glow was starting to fade.

Xar hurriedly repeated the most critical of the rune-structures and the blue glow strengthened.

But still the corpse did not move.

Frustrated, the Lord of the Nexus turned to the lazar, waiting patiently outside the cell.

"Well, what is wrong?" Xar demanded. "No, don't go into long explanations," he added irritably, when the lazar started to speak. "Just . . . whatever it is, fix it!" He waved his hand at the corpse.

"I cannot, Lord," said the lazar.

". . . cannot . . ." came the echo.

"What? Why?" Xar was aghast, then furious. "What trick is this? I'll cast you into oblivion—"

"No trick, Lord Xar," said Jonathon. "This corpse cannot be raised. It has no soul."

Xar glared at the lazar, wanting to doubt, yet something in the back of his mind was nudging him painfully toward the truth.

No soul.

"The dog!" Xar gasped, outrage and frustration combining to nearly choke him.

The sound he'd heard, from behind the bier. Xar dashed behind it, arrived just in time to see the tip of a plumy tail disappear around the front.

The dog sped for the cell door, which had been left standing wide open. Rounding the corner, the animal skidded on the damp stone floor, went down on its hind legs. Xar called on his magic to halt it, but the necromancy had left him weak. The dog, with a wild scramble, managed to get its legs underneath it and sped off through the corridor of cells.

Xar reached the cell door, planning to vent his anger on the lazar. He had at last recalled where he'd seen this particular dead Sartan before. This "Jonathon" had been present at the death of Samah. Xar's spell had also failed to resurrect that corpse. Was this lazar deliberately thwarting him? Why? And how?

But Xar's questions went unanswered. The lazar was gone.

The dungeons of Necropolis are a maze of intersecting and bisecting corridors, burrowing far beneath the surface of the stone world. Xar stood in the doorway of Haplo's cell and stared down first one corridor, then another, as far as he could see by the fitful, sputtering torchlight.

No sign, no sound of anything living—or dead.

Xar turned back, glared at the body on the stone bier. The runes glowed faintly, the spell preserving the flesh. He had only to catch that fool dog . . .

"The creature won't go far," Xar reasoned, when he was at last calm enough to reason. "It will stay in the dungeons, near its master's body. I will set an army of Patryns to the task of searching for it.

"As for the lazar, I will put out search teams for it, too. Kleitus said something about this Jonathon," Xar mused. "Something about a prophecy. 'Life to the dead . . . for him the gate will open . . .' All nonsense. A prophecy implies a higher power, a higher *ruling* power, and I am the ruler of this world and any other I care to take over."

Xar started to leave, to order his Patryns to their various tasks. Pausing, he glanced back a final time at Haplo's corpse.

Ruling power . . .

"Of course I am," Xar repeated and left.

CHAPTER ◆ 10

THE NECROPOLIS

ABARRACH

◆

THE DOG WAS CONFUSED. IT COULD HEAR ITS MASTER'S VOICE CLEARLY, BUT ITS master was not around. Haplo lay in a cell far from the dog's current hiding place. The dog knew something was terribly wrong with Haplo, but every time the animal attempted to go back to help, a sharp and peremptory voice—Haplo's voice, sounding very near, almost as if Haplo were right beside it—ordered the dog to lie still, stay put.

But Haplo wasn't here. Was he?

People—other people—were passing back and forth outside the dark cell where the dog crouched hidden in a corner. These people were searching for the dog, whistling, calling, cajoling. The dog wasn't particularly in the mood for people, but it did have the thought that perhaps they could help its master. They were, after all, the same kind of people. And, formerly, some of them had even been friends.

Not now, apparently.

The unhappy animal whimpered a little, to indicate that it *was* unhappy and lonely and forlorn. Haplo's voice ordered the dog sharply to keep quiet. And with no conciliatory pat on the head to mitigate the severity of the command. A pat that would indicate "I know you don't understand, but you must obey."

The dog's only comfort—a bleak one—was that it sensed from its master's tone that Haplo was also unhappy, confused, and frightened. He himself didn't seem to quite know what was going on. And if the master was frightened . . .

Nose on its paws, the dog lay shivering in the darkness, its body pressed against the damp stone floor of a cell, and wondered what to do.

Xar sat in his library, the Sartan book of necromancy on a table nearby, but unopened, unread. Why bother? He knew it by rote, could have recited it in his sleep.

The lord picked up one of the rectangular rune-bones lying on his desk. Idly, lost in thought, he tapped the rune-bone rhythmically against the kairn-grass desktop, tapping the bone on one corner, sliding the bone through his fingers, tapping it on the next corner of the rectangle, sliding it down, and so on. Tap, slide. Tap, slide. Tap, slide. He had been sitting thus for so long that he'd entered into a trancelike state. His body—except for the hand with the rune-bone—felt numb, heavy, unable to move, as if he were asleep. Yet he was aware of being awake.

Xar was confounded, completely, totally confounded. He had never before come up against such an insurmountable obstacle. He had no idea what to do, where to turn, how to act. At first he'd been raging, furious. Anger gave way to frustration. Now he was . . . bemused.

The dog might be anywhere. A legion of tytans could hide in that rat's nest of a tunnel system and no one stumble across them, let alone one insignificant animal. And suppose I do find the dog? Xar wondered, tapping the rune-bone, sliding it through his fingers. What do I do then? Kill it? Would that force Haplo's soul back to his body? Or would I kill the soul? Cause Haplo to die as Samah died—of no use to me.

And how to find the Seventh Gate without him? I *must* find the Seventh Gate! Swiftly. My people are fighting, dying in the Labyrinth. I promised them . . . I promised them I would return . . .

Tap, slide. Tap, slide. Tap, slide.

Xar closed his eyes. A man of action, who had fought and overcome every enemy he had ever faced, he was now relegated to sitting at a desk, doing nothing. Because there was absolutely nothing he could do. He slid the problem through his mind, as he slid the rune-bone through his fingers. Examined it from every angle.

Nothing. Tap, slide. Nothing. Tap, slide. Nothing.

How, from where he began, had he arrived here?

Failure . . . he would fail . . .

"My Lord!"

Xar jerked to full consciousness. The rune-bone flew from his fingers, clattered onto the desk.

"Yes, what is it?" he said harshly. Hastily, he flipped open the book, pretended to be reading.

A Patryn entered the library, stood in respectful silence, waiting for Xar to complete the task at hand.

The lord permitted himself another moment to completely restore his wandering mental faculties; then he glanced up.

"What news? Have you found the dog?"

"No, Lord. I have been sent to report to you that Death's Gate in Abarrach has been opened."

"Someone's entered," Xar said, his interest caught. A premonition of what he was about to hear surged through him. He was fully awake, fully functional now. "Marit!"

"Yes, Lord!" The Patryn regarded him with admiration.

"Did she come alone? Who is with her?"

"She arrived by ship—one of yours, My Lord. From the Nexus. I recognized the runes. Two men are with her. One of them is a mensch."

Xar was not interested in mensch.

The Patryn continued, "The other is a Sartan."

"Ah!" Xar had a good idea who. "A tall, balding, clumsy-looking Sartan?"

"Yes, Lord."

Xar rubbed his hands together. He could see the plan now, see it leap out of the darkness with extraordinary clarity, as an object is suddenly and brilliantly illuminated during a lightning storm.

"What did you do?" Xar regarded the Patryn with narrowed eyes. "Did you accost them?"

"No, Lord. I left immediately to report to you. The others are keeping watch on the three. When I left, they were still on the ship, conferring together. What are your orders, Lord? Do we bring them to you?"

Xar considered his plan a moment longer. He picked up the rune-bone, slid it through his fingers swiftly.

Tap. Tap. Tap. Tap. All angles covered. Perfect.

"This is what you will do . . ."

CHAPTER ◆ 11

SAFE HARBOR

ABARRACH

◆

THE PATRYN SHIP, DESIGNED AND BUILT BY LORD XAR FOR HIS JOURNEYS through Death's Gate, hovered over the Fire Sea—a river of molten lava that winds through Abarrach. The ship's runes protected it from the searing heat, which would have set an ordinary wooden ship ablaze. Alfred had brought the ship down near a dock running out into the Fire Sea, a dock belonging to an abandoned town known as Safe Harbor.

He stood near the porthole, gazing out on the churning river of flame, and recalled with vivid and terrifying clarity the last time he'd been in this dread world.

He could see it all so clearly. He and Haplo had barely reached their ship alive, fleeing the murderous lazar, led by the former Dynast, Kleitus. The lazar had only one goal—to destroy all the living and, when they were dead, grant them a terrible form of tormented, eternal life. Safely on board ship, Alfred watched in shock as the young Sartan nobleman, Jonathon, gave himself—a willing victim—into the bloodstained hands of his own murdered wife.

What had Jonathon seen, in the so-called Chamber of the Damned, that led him to commit that tragic act?

Or had he truly seen anything? Alfred wondered sadly. Perhaps Jonathon had gone mad, driven insane by his grief, the horror.

Alfred knew, he understood . . .

◆

. . . The ship moves beneath my feet, nearly throwing me off balance. I look back at Haplo. The Patryn has his hands on the steering stone. The sigla glow a bright, intense blue. Sails shiver, ropes tighten. The dragon ship spreads its wings, prepares to fly. On the pier, the dead begin to clamor and clash their weapons together. The lazar lift their horrible visages, move as a group toward the ship.

Apart from them, at the far end of the dock, Jonathon rises to his feet. He is a lazar; he has become one of the dead who is not dead, one of the living who is not living. He begins walking toward the ship.

"Stay! Stop!" I cry to Haplo. I press my face against the glass, trying to see more clearly. "Can't we wait a minute longer?"

Haplo shrugs. "You can go back if you want to, Sartan. You've served your purpose. I don't need you any longer. Go on, get out!"

The ship begins to move. Haplo's magical energies flow through it . . .

I should go. Jonathon had faith enough. He was willing to die for what he believed. I should be able to do the same.

I start toward the ladder. Outside the ship, I can hear the chill voices of the dead, shouting in fury, enraged to see their prey escaping. I can hear Kleitus and the other lazar raise their voices in a chant. They are attempting to break down our ship's fragile protective rune-structure.

The ship lurches, begins to sink.

A spell comes, unbidden, to my mind. I can enhance Haplo's failing energy.

The lazar that was Jonathon stands apart from the other lazar. The eyes of his soul—not quite torn from the body—gaze up at the ship, gaze through the runes, through the wood, through the glass, through flesh and bone into my heart . . .

◆

"Sartan! Alfred!"

Alfred turned fearfully, fell back against the bulkheads. "I'm not! I can't! . . ." He blinked. "Oh, it's you."

"Of course it's me. Why did you bring us to this forsaken place?" Marit demanded. "Necropolis is over there, on the other side. How are we going to get across the Fire Sea?"

Alfred looked helpless. "You said that Xar would have Death's Gate watched—"

"Yes, but if you'd done what I told you to do and flown the ship straight to Necropolis, we could be safely hidden in the tunnels by now."

"It's just that I— Well, that I . . ." Alfred lifted his head, glanced around. "It sounds foolish, I know, but . . . but . . . I was hoping to meet someone here."

"Meet someone!" Marit repeated grimly. "The only people we're likely to meet are my lord's guards."

"Yes, I suppose you're right." Alfred looked out at the empty dock and sighed. "What should we do now?" he asked meekly. "Fly the ship to Necropolis?"

"No, it's too late for that. We've been seen. They're probably already coming for us. We'll have to bluff our way out of this."

"Marit," Alfred said hesitantly, "if you are so certain of your lord, why are you afraid to meet him?"

"I wouldn't be, if I were by myself. But I'm not. I'm traveling with a mensch and a Sartan. Come on," she said abruptly, turning away. "We better disembark. I need to strengthen the runes protecting the ship."

The ship, similar in build and design to the dragon ships of Arianus, floated only a few feet above the dock. Marit jumped easily from the foredeck, landed lightly on her feet. Alfred, after a few false starts, launched himself overboard, caught his foot in one of the ropes, and ended by dangling upside down above the molten lava. Marit, her face grim, managed to free him, get him standing more or less upright on the dock.

Hugh the Hand had been staring in awe and disbelief at the new and terrifying world into which they'd flown. He leapt off the ship, landed on the dock. But almost immediately he stumbled to his knees. His hand clutched his throat. He began to choke, gasp for air.

"Thus did the mensch on this world die, so many long years ago," came a voice.

Alfred turned fearfully.

A figure emerged from the sulfurous haze that hung over the Fire Sea.

"One of the lazar," Marit said in disgust. Her hand closed over the hilt of her sword. "Begone!" she shouted.

"No, wait!" Alfred cried, staring hard at the shambling corpse. "I know . . . Jonathon!"

"I am here, Alfred. I've been here, all this time."

". . . all this time . . ."

Hugh the Hand lifted his head, gazed in disbelief at the terrifying apparition, at its waxen visage, the death-marks upon its throat, the eyes that were sometimes empty and dead, sometimes bright with life. Hugh tried to speak, but each breath he drew carried poisonous fumes into his lungs. He coughed until he gagged.

"He can't survive here," Alfred said, hovering over Hugh anxiously. "Not without magic to protect him."

"We'd best get him back on board the ship, then," Marit said, with a distrustful glance at the lazar, which stood silently watching them. "The runes will maintain an atmosphere he can breathe."

Hugh the Hand shook his head. Reaching out his hand, he caught hold of Alfred. "You promised . . . you could help me!" He managed to gasp. "I'm . . . going with . . . you!"

"I never promised!" Alfred protested, stooping over the choking man. "I never did!"

"Whether he did or he didn't, Hugh, you better get back on board. You—"

At that moment, Hugh pitched forward onto the dock, writhing in agony, his hands clutching at his throat.

"I'll take him," Alfred offered.

"You better hurry," Marit said, eyeing the mensch. "He's about finished."

Alfred began to sing the runes, performed a graceful and solemn dance around Hugh. Sigla sparkled in the brimstone air, twinkling around the Hand like a thousand fireflies. He disappeared.

"He's back on board," Alfred said, ceasing his dance. He glanced at the ship nervously. "But what if he tries to leave again—"

"I'll fix that." Marit drew a sigil in the air. It burst into flame, soared upward, hit a sigil burned into the ship's outer hull. The fire flared, spread from rune to rune more swiftly than the eyes could follow. "There. He cannot leave. And nothing can get inside."

"Poor man. He is like me, isn't he?" Jonathon asked.

". . . like me . . ." came the sad echo.

"No!" Alfred spoke sharply, so sharply that Marit stared at him in amazement. "No, he is *not* . . . like you!"

"I do not mean a lazar. His death was noble. He died sacrificing himself for one he loved. And he was brought back, not by hatred, but out of love and compassion. Still," Jonathon added softly, "he is like me."

Alfred's face was red, mottled with white. He stared down at his shoes. "I . . . I never meant this to happen."

"None of this was *meant* to happen," Jonathon replied. "The Sartan did not mean to lose control of their new creation. The mensch were not meant to die. We were not meant to practice necromancy. But all this did happen, and now we must take the responsibility. *You* must take it. Hugh is right. You can save him. Inside the Seventh Gate."

". . . Seventh Gate . . ."

"The one place I dare not go," Alfred murmured.

"True. Lord Xar searches for it. So does Kleitus."

Alfred gazed across the Fire Sea at the city of Necropolis, a towering structure of black rock, its walls reflecting the red glow of the lava river.

"I won't go back," said Alfred. "I'm not certain I could find the way."

"It would find you," said Jonathon.

". . . find you . . ."

Alfred paled. "I'm here to look for my friend. Haplo. You remember him? Have you seen him? Is he safe? Could you take us to him?" In his anxiety, he stretched out his hand to the lazar.

Jonathon backed up, away from the warm flesh reaching toward it. Its voice was stern. "My help is not for the living. It is for the living to help each other."

"But if you could just tell us? . . ."

Jonathon had turned around and was walking, with the undead's halting gait, down the dock, toward the abandoned town.

"Let the thing go," Marit said. "We've got other problems."

Turning, Alfred saw Patryn runes light the air. The next moment, three Patryns stepped out of the fiery circle of magic and stood on the dock in front of them.

Marit wasn't surprised. She'd been expecting this.

"Play along with me," she said softly, beneath her breath. "No matter what I do or say."

Alfred gulped, nodded.

Taking hold of his arm, Marit gave the Sartan a rough tug that nearly jerked him off his feet. She advanced to meet the Patryns, dragging the stumbling Alfred along with her.

"I must see Lord Xar," Marit called. She thrust Alfred forward. "I've brought a prisoner."

Fortunately, Alfred generally always managed to appear as wretched as if he'd just been taken captive by someone. He didn't need to act to look forlorn and desperately unhappy. He only had to stand on the dock, his head bowed, his expression guilty, his feet shuffling.

Does he trust me? Marit wondered. Or does he think I've betrayed him? Not that it matters what he thinks. This is our only hope.

She had decided on this plan of action before they had even left the Labyrinth. Knowing that the Patryns would be watching Death's Gate, Marit guessed that she and Alfred would be accosted. If they tried to flee or fight, they would be captured and imprisoned, possibly killed. But if she were transporting a Sartan prisoner to Lord Xar . . .

Marit brushed back the hair on her forehead. She had washed away the blood. The sigil of joining between herself and Xar was broken by a slashing weal. But his mark on her was still plainly visible.

"I must speak to Xar immediately. As you see," Marit added proudly, "I bear our lord's authority."

"You are wounded," said the Patryn, studying the mark.

"A terrible battle is being fought in the Labyrinth," Marit returned. "An evil force is attempting to seal shut the Final Gate."

"The Sartan?" asked the Patryn, with a baleful glance at Alfred.

"No," Marit replied. "Not the Sartan. That is why I must see Lord Xar. The situation is dire. Unless help arrives, I fear . . ." She drew a deep breath. "I fear we are lost."

The Patryn was troubled. The bond between Patryns as a race is strong; he knew Marit wasn't lying. He was alarmed, shocked by the news.

Perhaps this man has a wife, children, left behind in the Nexus. Perhaps the woman with him has a husband, parents, still caught in the Labyrinth.

"If the Final Gate shuts," Marit continued, "our people will be trapped inside that terrible place forever. Hasn't our lord told you any of this?" she asked, almost wistfully.

"No, he has not," said the woman.

"But I am certain Lord Xar had good reason," the man added coldly. He paused, thinking, then said, "I will take you to Lord Xar."

The other guard started to argue. "But our orders—"

"I know my orders!" the man said.

"Then you know that we are supposed—"

The guards drew off to one side of the dock, began to talk in undertones, an edge of tension audible in the conversation.

Marit sighed. All was going as she had hoped. She remained standing where she was, arms crossed over her chest, in seeming unconcern. But her heart was heavy. Xar hadn't told his people about the struggle in the Labyrinth. Perhaps he is trying to spare them pain, she argued. But something whispered back: perhaps he feared they might rebel against him.

As Haplo had rebelled . . .

Marit put her hand to her forehead, rubbed the sigil, which burned and itched. What was she doing? Wasting time. She needed to talk to Alfred. The guards were still debating, keeping only casual watch on their prisoners.

They know we're not going anywhere, Marit said to herself bitterly. Moving slowly, so as not to draw attention to herself, she sidled closer to the Sartan.

"Alfred!" she whispered out of the side of her mouth.

He jumped, startled.

"Oh! What—"

"Shut up and listen!" she hissed. "When we arrive in Necropolis, I want you to cast a spell on these three."

Alfred's eyes bulged. He went nearly as white as a lazar and began shaking his head emphatically. "No! I couldn't! I wouldn't know—"

Marit was keeping an eye on her fellow Patryns, who seemed to be near reaching some consensus. "Your people once fought mine!" she said coldly. " I'm not asking you to kill anyone! Surely there's some type of spell you can use that will incapacitate these guards long enough for us to—"

She was forced to break off, move away. The Patryns had ended their discussion and were returning.

"We will take you to Lord Xar," said the guard.

"About time!" Marit returned irritably.

Fortunately, her irritation could be mistaken as eagerness to see her lord, not eagerness to shake Alfred until his teeth rattled.

He was silently pleading with her, begging her not to force this on him. He looked truly pathetic, pitiful.

And suddenly Marit realized why. He had never, in his entire life, cast a magical spell in anger on a fellow being, Patryn or mensch. He had gone to great lengths to avoid it, in fact—fainting, leaving himself defenseless, accepting the possibility that he might be killed rather than use his immense power to kill others.

The three guards, working together, began to redraw the sigla in the air. Concentrating on their magic, they were not paying close attention to their prisoners. Marit took firm hold of Alfred's arm, as she might well have done if he were really her prisoner.

Digging her nails through the velvet fabric of his coat, she whispered urgently, "This is for Haplo. It's our only chance."

Alfred made a whimpering sound. She could feel him trembling in her grasp.

Marit only dug her nails in more deeply.

The Patryn leader motioned to them. The other two Patryns came to lead them forward. The sigil burned in the air, a flaring circle of flame.

Alfred pulled back. "No, don't make me!" he said to Marit.

One of the Patryn guards laughed grimly. "He knows what lies ahead of him."

"Yes, he does," said Marit, staring hard at Alfred, granting him no reprieve, no hope of reprieve.

Taking firm hold of him, she pulled him into the fiery ring of magic.

CHAPTER ◆ 12

NECROPOLIS

ABARRACH

◆

I'M NOT ASKING YOU TO KILL! THE REALIZATION STRUCK ALFRED. INCAPACITATE. Of course. That's what she'd said. Incapacitate.

What had he been thinking? A shudder, starting inside the marrow of his bones, shook Alfred's body. All he'd been able to think of was killing.

And he'd actually considered it!

It's this world, he decided, horrified at himself. This world of death where nothing is permitted to die. That and the battle in the Labyrinth. And his anxiety, his soul-wrenching anxiety over Haplo. Alfred was so close to finding his friend, and these—his enemies—were blocking his way. Fear, anger . . .

"Make all the excuses you want," Alfred accused himself. "But the truth of the matter is this—for one single instant, I was looking forward to it! When Marit told me to cast a spell, I saw the bodies of those Patryns lying at my feet and I was glad they were dead!"

He sighed. " 'You created us,' the dragon-snakes said. And now I see how . . ."

Marit's elbow dug into his ribs. Alfred came back to himself with a start that must have been perceptible, for the Patryns were looking at him oddly.

"I—I recognize this place," he said for the sake of saying something.

And he did, much to his regret. They had walked through the

Patryns' magical tunnel, created by the possibility that they were here and not there. Now they stood in Necropolis.

A city of tunnels and corridors, burrowing far beneath the world's stone surface, Necropolis had been a desolate, depressing place when Alfred last stood on its winding streets. But then, at least, it had been filled with people—his people, remnants of a race of demigods who had discovered, too late, that they weren't.

Now the streets were empty, empty and blood-spattered. For it was here in these streets, in these houses, in the palace itself, where the dead Sartan had taken out their fury on the living. The dead roamed the hallways now. The terrifying lazar watched him from the shadows with their ever-shifting eyes—hating, despairing, vengeful.

The Patryns guided their prisoners down the empty, echoing streets, heading for the palace. One of the lazar joined them, trailed after, its shuffling footfalls scraping behind, its cold voice, with its eerie double, telling of what it would like to do to them.

Alfred shivered all over, and even the steel-nerved Patryns appeared shaken. Their faces tightened; the tattoos on their arms flared in defensive response. Marit had gone extremely pale; her jaw was clenched. She did not look at the thing, but walked forward, grimly resolute.

She's thinking of Haplo, Alfred realized, and he himself was sick with horror. What if Haplo . . . what if he is now one of them? . . .

Alfred broke out in a chill sweat; his stomach wrenched. He felt faint—truly faint, sick and dizzy.

He came to a halt, forced to lean against a wall to support himself.

The Patryns stopped, turned. "What's the matter with him?"

"He's a Sartan," Marit answered, her tone scornful. "He's weak. What do you expect? I'll deal with him."

She turned toward him and Alfred saw—in her eyes—eagerness, expectation.

Blessed Sartan! She thinks this is an act! That I'm shamming, preparing to . . . to cast the spell!

No! Alfred wanted to cry. No, you've got it all wrong. Not now . . . I wasn't thinking . . . I can't think . . .

But he knew he had to go through with it. The Patryns weren't suspicious at the moment, but in about another half a second—as he stood staring and stammering—they would be.

What can I do? he wondered frantically. He had never fought a Patryn, never fought someone with magic that worked the same— only opposite—as his own. To make matters worse, the Patryns' magical defenses were already raised, protecting them from the lazar. Possibilities whirled through Alfred's mind, dazzling, confusing, terrifying.

I'll make the cavern roof collapse.

(No, that would kill us all!)

I'll bring a fire dragon up through the floor.

(No, same outcome!)

A flower garden will suddenly appear out of nowhere.

(What good will that do?!)

The lazar will attack.

(Someone might get hurt . . .)

The floor will open and swallow me up . . .

(Yes! That's it!)

"Hang on!" Alfred grabbed hold of Marit.

He began to do a dance, hopping from one foot to the other, faster and faster.

Marit clung to him. Alfred's dance grew more frantic, his feet pounding on the rock floor.

The Patryns, who had at first assumed Alfred had gone mad, suddenly became suspicious. They made a lunge for him.

The magic sparked, the possibility occurred. The floor beneath Alfred's feet crumbled. A hole gaped in the rock. He jumped into it, pulled Marit in with him. The two tumbled down through rock and choking dust, plunging into darkness.

The fall was a short one. As Alfred knew from his last visit, Necropolis was a warren of tunnels stacked up one on top of the other. He had assumed (or at least desperately hoped) that another corridor would be running under the one in which they were standing. It didn't occur to him until *after* he'd cast the spell that there were also immense pools of lava beneath the city . . .

Fortunately, they landed in a dark tunnel. Above them, light poured through a hole in the ceiling. The Patryn guards had surrounded the hole, were peering down at them, talking together in urgent tones.

"Close it!" Marit cried, shaking Alfred. "They're going to come after us!"

Imagining how he might have dropped them into a pool of lava, Alfred had momentarily gone blank. Now, realizing their danger, he belatedly summoned the possibility that the hole had never existed.

The hole disappeared. Darkness—thick and heavy—closed over them. It was soon lit by the glimmer of the sigla tattooed on Marit's body.

"Are . . . are you all right?" Alfred quavered.

Instead of answering, Marit shoved him. "Run!"

"Which way?" he gasped.

"It doesn't matter!" She pointed up at the ceiling. "They can use the magic too, remember?"

The glow of Marit's runes increased, giving them light enough to see by. They ran down the corridor, not knowing where they were going, not caring, hoping only to shake off pursuit.

At length, they came to a halt, paused to listen.

"I think we lost them," Alfred ventured a guess.

"By losing ourselves. You know, though, I don't believe they even tried to pursue us." Marit frowned. "That's strange."

"Maybe they went to report to Lord Xar."

"Possibly." She looked up and down the dark tunnel. "We have to figure out where we are. *I* don't have any idea. Do you?"

"No," Alfred said, shaking his head. "But I know how to find out."

He knelt down, touched the bottom of the corridor, sang softly beneath his breath. A sigil glimmered to life beneath his fingers. Its glow spread to another sigil, and another, until a line of runes burned with a soft, soothing light along the bottom of the wall.

Marit breathed a sigh. "The Sartan runes. I forgot they were here. Where will they lead us?"

"Wherever we want to go," Alfred said simply.

"To Haplo," she said.

Alfred heard the hope in her voice. He had no hope himself. He dreaded what they would find.

"Where would Xar have taken Haplo? Not . . . not to the lord's own chambers?"

"To the dungeons," Marit said. "It was where he took Samah and . . . and the others he . . ." Her voice trailed off. She turned away. "We better hurry. It won't take them long to figure out where we've gone. *Then* they'll come after us."

"Why didn't they come after us before?" Alfred asked.

Marit didn't answer. She didn't need to. Alfred knew well enough anyway.

Because Xar already knows where we're going!

They were walking into a trap. They had been—all along, Alfred realized unhappily. The Patryn guards had not only let him and Marit escape, they had actually provided the opportunity.

Their magic could have taken us directly to Xar. Planted us on his very doorstep, as it were, Alfred thought. But no. The Patryns take us into Necropolis, into empty streets. They let us go and don't even bother to pursue us.

And just when all seemed most dark, Alfred was startled to notice a tiny bit of hope flickering to life inside him.

If Haplo was dead, and Lord Xar had used the necromancy on him, then the lord would already be in the Seventh Gate. He wouldn't need us.

Something's gone wrong . . . or right.

The sigla flared on the wall, burning with the speed of a brushfire. In some places, where cracks on the wall had broken the sigla, the runes remained dark. The Sartan living on Abarrach had forgotten how to restore their magic. But the breaks never completely stopped the flow. The magical light would leap over a broken sigil, catch the next one, and so on. All he had to do was keep the image of the dungeons on his mind and the sigla would guide them to them.

To what? Alfred wondered fearfully.

He formed a resolve, there and then. If I am wrong and Xar has turned Haplo into one of the wretched undead, I will end such a terrible existence for him. I will grant him peace. No matter what anyone says or does to try to stop me.

The sigla led them steadily downward. Alfred had been in the dungeons before, knew they were going in the right direction. So did Marit. She led the way, walking rapidly, eagerly. Both kept watch, but saw nothing. Not even the dead roamed these corridors.

They walked for so long, seeing nothing except the Sartan runes on the wall and the glimmer of the Patryn runes on Marit's body, that Alfred fell into a sort of waking horrific dream.

When Marit stopped suddenly, Alfred—walking trancelike—ran right into her.

She shoved him back against the wall with a hissing shush.

"I see light ahead," she said in a low voice. "Torchlight. And now I know where we are. Ahead of us are the cells. Haplo's probably being held in one of them."

"It seems very quiet down here," Alfred whispered. "*Very* quiet."

Ignoring him, Marit started down the corridor, heading for the torchlight.

It did not take Alfred long to find the right cell. The sigla on the walls no longer guided him; in the dungeons, most of the Sartan runes had been either broken or deliberately obliterated. But he moved toward the right place unerringly, as if invisible runes, brought into being by his heart, flared before his eyes.

Alfred looked into the cell first, for which he was grateful. Haplo lay on a stone bier. His eyes were closed, his hands folded over his chest. He did not move, did not draw breath.

Marit was following behind, keeping watch. Alfred had a moment to deal with his own emotions before Marit, seeing the Sartan come to a halt, guessed instantly what he had found.

He tried to catch hold of her, but she broke free, ran past him. Hastily, Alfred removed the cell bars with a spoken word of magic or Marit would have torn right through them.

She stood a moment over the stone bier, then—with a sob—she sank onto her knees. Lifting Haplo's cold and lifeless hand, she started to chafe it, as if she could warm it. The runes tattooed on his body glimmered faintly, but there was no life in the chill flesh.

"Marit," Alfred began awkwardly, softly. "There's nothing you can do."

Burning tears stung his eyes, tears of grief and bitter sorrow, yet tears of relief as well. Haplo was dead, yes. But he was *dead!* No terrible magical life burned inside him, like a candle inside a skull. His body lay composed on the bier. His eyes were closed, his face smooth, free of pain.

"He's at peace now," Alfred murmured.

He entered the cell slowly, came to stand beside his enemy, his friend.

Marit had replaced the flaccid hand on Haplo's chest, over the heart-rune. Now she sat hunched on the floor, grieving alone in fierce, aching silence.

Alfred knew he should say something, pay tribute, homage. But words were inadequate. What did you say to a man who had looked inside you and seen—not what you were—but what you could be? What did you say to a man who had wrenched that other, better person hiding inside of you outside? What did you say to a man who had taught you how to live, when you would much rather have died?

Haplo had done all this. And now Haplo was dead. He gave his life for me, for the mensch, for his people. Each of us drew on his strength and perhaps, unknowingly, each of us ended up draining a little of his life away.

"My dear friend," Alfred whispered, his voice choked. He bent down, rested his hand on Haplo's, over the heart-rune. "I promise you. I will continue the fight. I will do what I can, take up where you left off. You rest. Don't worry about it anymore. Farewell, my friend. Fare—"

At that moment, Alfred was interrupted by a *whuff.*

CHAPTER ◆ 13

NECROPOLIS

ABARRACH

◆

"No, boy! stay!"

Haplo's voice was insistent, peremptory. His command was final, the law. Yet . . .

The dog squirmed, whimpered. Here were trusted friends. Here were people who could make things right. And, above all else, here were people who were desperately unhappy. Here were people who needed a dog.

The dog half rose.

"Dog, no!" Haplo's voice, sharp, warning. "Don't! It's a trap . . ."

Well, there, you see? A trap! Here were trusted friends, walking into a trap. And, obviously, the master was only thinking of his faithful dog's safety. Which, so far as the dog could determine, left the decision up to it.

With a glad and excited *whuff,* the dog leapt from its hiding place and bounded joyfully down the corridor.

"What was that?" Alfred glanced fearfully around. "I heard something . . ."

He looked out into the corridor and saw a dog. Alfred sat down on the floor, very hard and very unexpectedly.

"Oh, my!" he repeated over and over. "Oh, my!"

The animal bounded into the cell, jumped into Alfred's lap, and licked his face.

Alfred flung his arms around the dog's neck and wept.

Objecting to being slobbered on, the dog wriggled free of Alfred's embrace and pattered over to Marit. Very gently, the dog lifted a paw, placed it on her arm.

She touched the offered paw, then buried her face in the dog's neck and began to sob. The dog whined in sympathy, looked pleadingly at Alfred.

"Don't cry, my dear! He's alive!" Alfred wiped away his own tears. Kneeling down beside Marit, he put his hands on her shoulders, forced her to lift her face, to look at him. "The dog. Haplo's not dead, not yet. Don't you see?"

Marit stared at the Sartan as if he'd gone mad.

"I don't know how!" Alfred was babbling. "I can't understand it myself. Probably the necromancy spell. Or perhaps Jonathon had something to do with it. Or maybe all together. Or none at all. Anyhow, my dear, because the dog is alive, Haplo is *alive!*"

"I don't . . ." Marit was bewildered.

"Let me see if I can explain."

Completely forgetting where he was, Alfred settled himself on the floor, prepared to launch into explanations. The dog had other plans, however. Catching hold of the toe of Alfred's over-large shoe in its mouth, the dog sank in its teeth and began to tug.

"When Haplo was a young man . . . Good dog," Alfred interrupted himself, attempted to free his shoe from the dog's mouth. "A young man in the Labyrinth, he—Haplo . . . Nice doggie. Let go. I . . . Oh, dear."

The dog had released the shoe, was now tugging at Alfred's coat sleeve.

"The dog wants us to leave," said Marit.

She stood up, somewhat unsteadily. The dog, giving up on Alfred, switched its attention to her. Pressing its large body against her legs, it tried to herd her toward the cell door.

"I'm not going anywhere," she said, getting a firm grip on the loose skin around the dog's neck and hanging on. "I'm not leaving Haplo until I understand what's happened."

"I'm trying to tell you," Alfred said plaintively. "Only I keep getting interrupted. It all has to do with Haplo's 'good' impulses— pity, compassion, mercy, love. Haplo was raised to believe that such feelings were weaknesses."

The dog muttered in its throat, nearly knocked Marit down trying again to shove her toward the cell door.

"Stop it, dog!" she ordered and turned back to Alfred. "Go on."

Alfred sighed. "Haplo found it increasingly difficult to reconcile his true feelings with what he believed he *should* be feeling. Did you know he searched for you? After you left him? He realized he loved you, but he couldn't admit it—either to himself or to you."

Marit's gaze went to the body on the stone bier. Unable to speak, she shook her head.

"When Haplo believed he had lost you, he grew increasingly unhappy and confused," Alfred went on. "His confusion angered him. He concentrated all his energy on beating the Labyrinth, on escaping it. And then his goal was in sight—the Final Gate. When he reached it, he knew he had won, but winning didn't please him, as he had assumed it would. Rather, it terrified him. After he passed through that Gate, what would life hold for him? Nothing.

"When Haplo was attacked at the Gate, he fought desperately. His instinct for survival is strong. But when he was severely wounded by the chaodyn, he saw his chance. He could find death at the hands of the enemy. This death would be an honorable one. No one would say otherwise, and it would free him from the terrible feelings of guilt, self-doubt, and regret.

"Part of Haplo was determined to die, but another part—the best part of him—refused to give up. At that point, wounded and weak in body and spirit, angry with himself, Haplo solved his problem. He did so unconsciously. He created the dog."

The animal in question had, by this time, given up on attempting to drag everyone out of the cell. Flopping down on its belly, it rested its head on the floor between its paws and regarded Alfred with a resigned, doleful expression. Whatever happened now was not its fault.

"He created the dog?" Marit was incredulous. "Then—it's not real."

"Oh, it's real." Alfred smiled, rather sadly. "As real as the souls of the elves, fluttering in their garden. As real as the phantasms, trapped by the lazar."

"And now?" Marit stared doubtfully at the animal. "What is it now?"

Alfred shrugged, helpless. "I'm not sure. Haplo's body appears to be in some sort of suspended state, like the stasis sleep of my people . . ."

The dog jumped up suddenly. Tense, hackles raised, it glared out into the dark corridor.

"There's someone there," Alfred said, stumbling to his feet.

Marit didn't move. Her eyes shifted from Haplo to the dog.

"Perhaps you're right. The runes on his skin *are* glowing." She looked at Alfred. "There must be a way to bring him back. Perhaps if you used the necromancy—"

Alfred blanched, backed away. "No! Please don't ask me!"

"What do you mean, *no*? No, it can't be done? Or no, you won't do it?" Marit demanded.

"It can't . . ." Alfred began lamely.

"Yes, it can!" someone said, speaking from the corridor.

". . . it can . . ." came a dismal echo.

The dog barked a sharp warning.

The lazar that had once been the Dynast, ruler of Abarrach, shambled into the cell.

Marit drew her sword. "Kleitus." Her tone was cool, though her voice shook slightly. "What do you want here?"

The lazar paid no attention to her, or to the dog, or to the body on the stone bier.

"The Seventh Gate!" Kleitus said, the dead eyes horribly alive.

". . . Gate . . ." sighed the echo.

"I . . . I don't know what you mean," Alfred said faintly. He had gone extremely pale. Sweat beaded on his bald head.

"Yes, you do!" Kleitus returned. "You are a Sartan! Enter the Seventh Gate and you will find the way to release your friend."

The blood-mottled hand of the lazar pointed at Haplo. "You will bring him back to life."

"Is that true?" Marit asked, turning to Alfred.

All around him, the cell walls were starting to shrink and shrivel, to writhe and crawl. The darkness began to grow huge, swell and expand. It seemed about to jump on him, swallow him . . .

"Don't faint, damn it!" said a voice.

A familiar voice. Haplo's voice!

Alfred's eyes flared open. The darkness retreated. He looked for the source of the voice, found the dog's liquid eyes fixed intently on his face.

Alfred blinked, gulped. "Blessed Sartan!"

"Don't listen to the lazar. It's a trap," Haplo's voice continued, and it was coming from inside Alfred, from inside his head. Or perhaps from that elusive part of him that was his own soul.

"It's a trap," Alfred repeated aloud, without being truly conscious of what he was saying.

"Don't go to the Seventh Gate. Don't let the lazar talk you into it. Or anyone else, for that matter. Don't go."

"I won't go." Alfred had the confused impression of sounding very much like the lazar's echo. He added to Marit, "I'm sorry . . ."

"Don't apologize!" Haplo ordered irritably. "And don't let Kleitus fool you. The lazar knows where the Seventh Gate is. He died in that room."

"But he can't get back inside!" Alfred said in sudden understanding. "The warding runes prevent him!"

"And he's *not* worried about me," Haplo added dryly. "He's thinking of himself. Maybe hoping you'll bring *him* back!"

"I won't be the one to let you in," Alfred said.

"A mistake, Sartan!" The lazar snarled.

". . . mistake, Sartan . . ."

"I am on your side! We are brothers." Kleitus advanced several shuffling steps into the cell. "If you bring me back, I will be strong, powerful. Far stronger than Xar! He knows this and he fears me. Come! Swiftly! This is your only chance to escape him!"

"I won't!" Alfred shuddered.

The lazar moved toward him. Alfred fell back until he hit the wall and could go no farther. He pressed both hands against the stone, as if he would seep into it. "I won't . . ."

"You've got to get out of here!" Haplo urged. "You and Marit! You're in danger! If Xar finds you here . . ."

"What about you?" Alfred asked.

Marit was looking at him strangely, suspiciously. "What about me?"

"No, no!" Alfred was losing control. "I . . . I was talking to Haplo."

Her eyes widened. "Haplo?"

"Can't you hear him?" Alfred asked and realized, in the instant of asking, that she could not. She and Haplo had been close, but they had not exchanged souls, as had Haplo and Alfred, that one time, crossing through Death's Gate.

Alfred wavered.

"Never mind me! Just leave, damn it!" Haplo urged. "Use your magic!"

Alfred swallowed. Licking dry lips with a dry tongue, trying ineffectually to moisten a parched throat, he began to sing the runes in a cracked, almost inaudible voice.

Kleitus understood the forgotten rune-language enough to realize what Alfred was doing. Reaching out its wasted hand, the lazar caught hold of Marit.

She tried to break free, tried to stab the lazar with her sword. But the dead know no physical limitations. With inhuman strength, Kleitus wrested the sword from Marit's grasp. The lazar wrapped its bloodstained hand around her throat.

The sigla on Marit's skin flared, her magic acting to defend her. Another living being would have been paralyzed by the shock, but the corpse of the Dynast absorbed the punishment without apparent harm. The long blue nails of the skeletal hand dug into Marit's flesh.

She flinched in pain, choked back a cry. Blood trickled down her skin.

"Sing one more rune," Kleitus warned Alfred, "and I will turn her into the undead."

Alfred's tongue clicked against the roof of his mouth, froze there. Before he could cast the spell, Marit would be dead.

"Take me to the Seventh Gate!" Kleitus demanded. He stabbed his fingers deeper into Marit's throat.

She cried out. Her hands tore frantically at the corpse's.

The dog whined and whimpered.

Marit began to gulp, gasp for breath. Kleitus was slowly strangling her.

"Do something!" Haplo ordered furiously.

"What?" Alfred cried.

"*This* is what you do, Sartan."

Lord Xar entered the cell. He lifted his hand, formed a sigil in the air, and sent it flashing toward Kleitus.

CHAPTER ♦ 14

NECROPOLIS

ABARRACH

♦

THE SIGIL STRUCK THE LAZAR IN THE CHEST, EXPLODED. KLEITUS CRIED OUT IN rage; the corpse felt no pain. It fell to the floor, the dead limbs jerking and twitching spasmodically.

But Kleitus fought against the magic. The corpse seemed about to win, was struggling to regain its feet.

Xar spoke sharply. The single rune expanded. Its arms became tentacles, surrounding, subduing the writhing corpse.

At length, the lazar shuddered, then lay still.

Lord Xar regarded it suspiciously, thinking it was shamming. He had not killed it. He couldn't kill something that was already dead. But he had rendered it harmless, for the moment. The sigil, burning feebly, flickered and died out. The spell ended. The lazar did not move.

Satisfied, Xar turned to Alfred.

"Well met, Serpent Mage," said the Lord of the Nexus. "At last."

The Sartan's eyes were bulging out of his balding head. His jaw worked; no sound came out. Xar thought he had never seen such a pitiful, wretched-looking specimen. But he wasn't fooled by outward appearances. This Sartan was powerful, extraordinarily powerful. The weak and foolish act of his was just that—an act.

"Although I must say that I am disappointed in you, Alfred," Xar continued. No harm in letting the Sartan think he was succeeding in his foolery. Xar prodded the unmoving lazar with his toe. "You could have done this yourself, or so I presume."

The lord bent over Marit. "You are not hurt badly, are you, Daughter?"

Weak and shaken, Marit shrank back from him, but there was nowhere for her to go. She had come up against the stone bier.

Xar took hold of her. She cringed, but he was gentle. He helped her to her feet. She swayed, unsteady, and he supported her.

"The wounds burn where he touched you. Yes, I know, Daughter. I, too, have felt the lazar's foul touch. Some type of poison, I would guess. But I can give you ease."

He placed his hand on her forehead. Brushing aside her hair, his fingers lightly, delicately retraced the sigil mark that had been there, the mark he had slashed in the Labyrinth. At his touch, the rune closed, healed completely.

Marit did not notice. She was burning with fever, dizzy and disoriented. Xar alleviated her pain somewhat, but not entirely.

"Soon you will feel better. Sit here"—Xar guided Marit to the edge of Haplo's stone bier—"and rest. I have certain matters to discuss with the Sartan."

"My Lord!" Marit grasped hold of Xar's hand, clung to him. "My Lord! The Labyrinth! Our people are fighting for their lives."

Xar's face hardened. "I am aware of this, Daughter. I plan to return. They will be able to hold out until—"

"Lord! You don't understand! The dragon-snakes have set fire to the Nexus. The city is in flames! Our people . . . dying . . ."

Xar was aghast. He could not believe what he was hearing. It wasn't possible. "The Nexus, burning?"

He thought at first she was lying. But they were now joined again and he saw the truth in her mind. He saw the Nexus, beautiful, white-spired city; *his* city. Never mind the fact that his enemy had built it. He had first set foot in it. He had first claimed it. He had won it with blood and unceasing toil. He had brought his people to it. His people had made that city their home.

Now, in Marit's eyes, he saw the Nexus red with flame, black with smoke and death.

"All I worked for . . . gone . . . ," he murmured. His grip on her loosened.

"Lord, if you went back . . ." Marit held fast to his hand. "If you returned to them, the people would have hope. Go to them, Lord. They need you!"

Xar hesitated. Remembered. . . .

. . . He did not walk through the Final Gate. He crawled, dragged himself between its rune-covered stone supports on his belly. He left a trail of blood behind him, a trail that marked his path through the Labyrinth itself. Some of the blood was his; more of it belonged to his enemies.

Pulling himself across the border, he collapsed onto the soft grass. He rolled over onto his back, stared up into a twilight sky, a sky of blush reds and hazy purples, banded with gold and orange. He should heal himself, sleep. And he would, in time. But for a moment, he wanted to feel everything, including the pain. This was his moment of triumph, and when he remembered it, he wanted to remember the pain with it.

The pain, the suffering. The hatred.

When he knew he must soon heal himself or die, he raised up on one elbow and looked around for shelter.

And he saw, for the first time, the city his enemies had named the Nexus.

It was beautiful—white stone shimmering with the colors of perpetual sunset. Xar saw the beauty, but he also saw something more.

He saw people; his people, living and working in peace and safety. No longer afraid of the wolfen, the snog, the dragon.

He had survived the Labyrinth. He had beaten it. He had escaped. He was the first. The very first. And he would not be alone. He would go back. Tomorrow, when he was completely healed and rested, he would go back through the Gate and would bring out someone else.

The next day, he would return again. And the day after that.

He would go back into that dread prison and he would lead his people to freedom. He would bring them to this city, this sanctuary.

Tears blinded him. Tears wrung from him by pain and weariness and—for the first time in his dark life—hope.

Later, much later, Xar would look at that city with clear, cold eyes and he would see armies.

But not then. Then he saw, through his tears, children playing . . .

And now the twilight skies were black with smoke. The bodies of the children lay charred and twisted in the streets.

Xar's hand stole to his heart-rune, tattooed long, long ago on his chest. His name, then . . . What had been his name? The name of the man who had dragged himself through the Final Gate? Xar couldn't remember. He had obliterated it, written it over with runes of strength and power.

Just as he had written over his vision.

If only he could think of his name . . .

"I will return to the Nexus." Xar spoke into the awe-tinged silence that emanated from him. A silence that had, for a moment, bound them all together in hope. Bound even his enemy to him. "I will return . . . through the Seventh Gate."

Xar's gaze fixed on the Sartan. Alfred, he called himself. Not *his* real name either. "And you will take me there."

The dog barked loudly, almost a command. But it might have spared itself the trouble.

"No," Alfred said, his voice mild, sad. "I won't."

Xar looked at Haplo, at the body lying on the cold stone bier. "He still lives. You are right about that. But he might as well be dead. What do you intend to do about it?"

Alfred's face was exceedingly pale. He licked dry lips. "Nothing," he said, swallowing. "There is nothing I can do."

"Isn't there?" Lord Xar asked, pleasantly. "The necromancy spell I cast preserves his flesh. His essence—or soul, as you call it—is trapped inside the dog. Inside the body of a dumb animal."

"Some might say we are all trapped that way," Alfred said, but he spoke in a low voice and no one, except the dog, heard him.

"You can change all that," Xar was saying. "You can bring Haplo back to life."

The Sartan shuddered. "No, I can't."

"A Sartan—lying!" Xar smiled. "I wouldn't have said it was possible."

"I'm *not* lying," Alfred returned, drawing himself up. "You cast the necromancy spell using Patryn magic. I can't undo it or change it—"

"Ah, but you could," Xar interrupted. "Inside the Seventh Gate."

Alfred raised his hands as if to ward off an attack, though no one had made a move toward him. He backed into a corner, staring around the prison cell, perhaps seeing it—for the first time—as a prison. "You can't ask that of me!"

"But we do, don't we, Daughter?" Xar said, turning to Marit.

She was shivering, feverish. Reaching out her shaking hand, she touched Haplo's chill flesh.

"Alfred . . ."

"No!" Alfred shrank back against the wall. "Don't ask me! Xar doesn't care about Haplo, Marit. Your lord plans to destroy the world!"

"I plan to undo what you Sartan did!" Xar snarled, losing patience. "To return the four worlds to one—"

"Which *you* would rule! Only you wouldn't. Any more than Samah was able to rule the worlds he created. What he did was wrong. But he has answered for his crimes. Over time, the wrong has been made right. The mensch have built new lives on these worlds. If you commit this act, millions of innocents will die—"

"The survivors will be better off," Xar returned. "Isn't that what Samah said?"

"And what of your people, caught inside the Labyrinth?" Alfred demanded.

"They will be free! I will free them!"

"You will doom them. They may escape the Labyrinth. But they will never escape the new prison you will build for them. A prison of fear. I know," he added sadly, softly. "I have lived in one like it almost all my life."

Xar was silent. He was not pondering Alfred's words; he had ceased paying attention to the sniveling Sartan. Xar was trying to figure out how to coerce the wretch into doing his will. The lord recognized Alfred's power, probably more than Alfred did himself. Xar had no doubt he could win a battle, should one take place between the two of them. But he would not come out unscathed and the Sartan would likely be dead. Considering Xar's luck with necromancy so far, such an outcome was not advisable.

There was one possibility . . .

"I think you had better move to a safe place, Daughter." Xar took firm hold of Marit, drew her away from the stone bier on which lay Haplo's body.

The Lord of the Nexus traced a series of runes on the base of the bier, spoke the command.

The stone burst into flame.

"What . . . what are you doing?" Marit cried.

"I could not succeed in raising Haplo's body," Xar said off-handedly. "The Sartan will not use his power to restore him. The corpse is, therefore, of no use to me. This will be Haplo's funeral pyre."

"You can't!" Marit hurled herself at Xar. She clutched at his robes, pleading. "You can't, Lord! Please! This . . . this will destroy him!"

The sigla spread slowly around the bottom of the stone bier, forming a fiery circle. Flames licked upward, devouring the magic, since they had no other fuel.

Until they reached the body.

Marit sank to her knees, too weak and ill from the effects of the poison to stand. "Lord, please!"

Xar reached down, stroked back her hair. "You plead with the wrong person, Daughter. The Sartan has it in his power to save Haplo. Beg him!"

The flames were growing stronger, rising higher. The heat was increasing.

"I—" Alfred opened his mouth.

"Don't!" Haplo commanded.

The dog regarded Alfred sternly, growled warningly.

"But"—Alfred stared at the flames—"if your body is burned—"

"Let it! If Xar opens the Seventh Gate, then what? You said yourself what would happen."

Alfred gulped, gasped for air. "I can't stand here and watch—"

"Then faint, damn it!" Haplo said irritably. "This would be the one time in your life when passing out might be of some use!"

"I won't," Alfred said, recovering himself. He even managed to smile bleakly. "I am afraid I must put you in *my* prison for a while, my friend."

The Sartan began to dance, moving solemnly to music he hummed beneath his breath.

Xar watched with suspicion, wondering what the Serpent Mage was up to. Surely not an offensive spell. That would be too dangerous in the small cell.

"Dog, go to Marit!" Alfred murmured, doing a graceful slide-step around the animal. "Now!"

The animal ran to Marit's side, stood protectively near her. At the same instant, two crystal coffins sprang into being. One covered Haplo's body. The other surrounded Lord Xar.

Inside Haplo's coffin, the flames dwindled, died.

Inside the other coffin, Xar fought to free himself, fumed in impotent rage.

Alfred took hold of Marit, helped her escape the cell. They ran into the dark corridor. The dog dashed along behind.

"Out!" Alfred gasped for the benefit of the magic. "We want out!"

Blue sigla flashed along the base of the wall. Supporting Marit, Alfred followed the sigla's lead, stumbling blindly through the rune-lit darkness, with no idea where he was or which way he was going. But it seemed to Alfred that they were going down, descending deeper into Abarrach . . .

And then the terrifying thought came to him that the runes

might be guiding him right to the Seventh Gate! After all, the runes would take him to wherever it was he wanted to go and the Seventh Gate had certainly been on his mind.

"Well, put the thought *out* of your mind!" Haplo ordered. "Think about Death's Gate! Concentrate on that!"

"Yes," Alfred panted. "Death's Gate . . ."

The sigla suddenly flashed, went out, leaving them in fearful, mind-numbing darkness.

CHAPTER ◆ 15

NECROPOLIS

ABARRACH

◆

ENTOMBED IN SARTAN MAGIC, XAR QUELLED HIS ANGER, RELIED ON PATIENCE and calm to free himself. His brain, like a sharp knife, slid into each chink in the Sartan runes, searching for a weakness. He found it, and worked at it patiently, breaking down the sigil, chipping away at the magic. One crack, and the rest of the hastily designed structure shattered.

Xar gave Alfred credit; the Serpent Mage was good. Never before had any magic completely stopped and confounded the Lord of the Nexus. Had the situation not been so critical, so dire, Xar would have enjoyed the mental exercise.

He stood in the prison cell, alone except for Kleitus, and that heap of bones and rotting flesh scarcely counted. The lazar continued under the constraints of Xar's spell and did not move. Xar ignored it. He walked over to stand beside Haplo's body, encased in the Sartan's magical coffin.

The funeral fire had been snuffed out. Xar could always start it again. He could break the magic that protected Haplo as the lord had broken that which had imprisoned him.

But he did not.

He gazed down at the body and smiled.

"They won't abandon you, my son. No matter how much you try to persuade them otherwise. Because of you, Alfred will lead me to the Seventh Gate!"

Xar touched the sigil on his own forehead, the rune-mark he had drawn, destroyed, then redrawn on Marit's forehead. Once again, they were joined. Once again, he could share her thoughts, hear her words. Except that this time, provided he was careful, she wouldn't be conscious of his presence.

Xar left the dungeons, began his pursuit.

No sigla lit their path. Alfred guessed this was a result of the confusion in his own mind—he couldn't decide where he wanted to go. And then he considered that it might be safer to travel without guidance. If he didn't know where he was going, no one else would, either. Or such was his rather confused logic.

He spoke a sigil, caused it to burn softly in the air in front of him, giving them light enough to walk by. They stumbled on, as fast as they could, until Marit could go no farther.

She was very ill. He could feel the poison's heat on her skin. Her body shook with chills; pain gripped her, twisted her. She'd fought gamely to keep up, but the last few hundred paces or so, he'd been forced to almost carry her. Now her body was dead weight. His arms were trembling and limp with fatigue. He let go of her. She sagged to the floor.

Alfred knelt down beside her. The dog whined, nosed her limp hand.

"Give me time . . . to heal myself." She gasped for breath.

"I can help you." Alfred hovered over her, peering at her in the darkness. The sigla on her skin barely glimmered.

"No. Keep watch," she ordered. "Your magic won't stop Xar . . . for long."

She hunched into a ball, bringing her knees to her chin, resting her head on her knees. Wrapping her arms around her body, she closed her eyes, closed the circle of her being. The sigla on her arms glowed more warmly. Her chills and shivering ceased. She huddled in the darkness, enveloped in warmth.

Alfred watched anxiously. Generally a healing sleep was required to make Patryns perfectly well. He wondered if she had fallen asleep, wondered what he would do if she did. He was very tempted to let her rest. He'd seen no sign that Xar was following them.

Timidly, he reached out his hand to smooth back the damp hair from her forehead. And he saw, suddenly, with a pang of fear, that the sigil Xar had marked on her forehead, the sigil joining the two together, was once more whole. Swiftly, Alfred snatched his hand away.

"What?" Startled at his chill touch, Marit lifted her head. "What is it? What's wrong?"

"N-nothing," Alfred stammered. "I . . . thought you might want to sleep . . ."

"Sleep? Are you crazy?"

Refusing his help, Marit rose slowly to her feet.

She was no longer feverish, but the marks on her throat were still plainly visible—black slashes, cutting through the rune-light. She gingerly touched the wounds, winced, as if they burned. "Where are we going?"

"Out of here!" Haplo ordered peremptorily. "Off of Abarrach. Go back through Death's Gate."

Alfred looked at the dog, didn't know quite how to respond.

Marit saw his glance, understood. She shook her head.

"I won't leave Haplo."

"My dear, there's nothing we can do for him . . ."

Alfred's lie trailed into silence. There was something *he* could do. Kleitus had spoken the truth. Alfred had, by this time, given a lot of thought to the Seventh Gate. He had gone over all that he'd heard about it from Orlah, who had described to him how Samah and the Council used the magic of the Seventh Gate to sunder the world. Alfred had also delved deep in his own memory, recalling passages he'd read in the books of the Sartan. From his research, he guessed that, once inside, he could use the Gate's powerful magic to work wonders beyond belief. He could restore Haplo to life. He could grant Hugh the Hand peace in death. He could, perhaps, even come to the aid of those fighting for their lives in the Labyrinth.

But the Seventh Gate was the one place in the four worlds where Alfred dared not go. Not with Xar watching, waiting for him to do that very thing.

The dog pattered nervously back and forth, up and down the corridor.

"Get *yourself* out of here, Sartan!" Haplo told Alfred, reading his thoughts as usual. "You're the one Xar wants."

"But I can't leave you," Alfred protested.

"You're not." Marit gave him a puzzled look. "No one ever said you were."

"All right, then." Haplo was talking at the same moment. "*Don't* leave me. Take the damn dog with you! So long as the dog is safe, Xar can't do anything to me."

Alfred, listening to two voices speaking simultaneously, opened and shut his mouth in hopeless confusion. "The dog . . ." he murmured, attempting to grasp one solid point in the strange conversation.

"You and Marit take the dog to a world where it will be safe," Haplo repeated, patiently, insistently. "Where Xar can't possibly find it. Pryan, maybe . . ."

The suggestion sounded good, made sense—take the dog and themselves out of harm's way. But something about it wasn't quite right. Alfred knew that if he could only take the time to stop and think about the matter long and hard, he'd discover what was wrong with it. But between fear, confusion, and amazement at being able to communicate with Haplo at all, Alfred was completely befuddled.

Marit leaned against the wall, her eyes closed. Her magic was too much weakened by her injury to sustain her, apparently. She was once more shivering, in obvious pain. The dog crouched at her feet, gazed up at her forlornly.

"If she doesn't heal herself—or if you don't heal her, Sartan—she's going to die!" Haplo said urgently.

"Yes, you're right."

Alfred made up his mind. He put his arm around Marit, who stiffened at his touch but then went limp against him.

A very bad sign.

"Who are you talking to?" she murmured.

"Never mind," Alfred said quietly. "Come along . . ."

Marit's eyes opened wide. For an instant, strength suffused her body, hope eased her suffering. "Haplo! You're talking to Haplo! How is that possible?"

"We shared consciousness once. In Death's Gate. Our minds exchanged bodies . . . At least"—Alfred sighed—"that's the only explanation I can think of."

Marit was silent long moments; then she said in a low voice, "We could go to the Seventh Gate now. While my lord is still imprisoned by your magic."

Alfred hesitated. And, as the thought came into his mind, the sigla on the wall suddenly flared to life, lit up a corridor previously dark. So dark, they had never, before now, suspected its existence.

"That's it," Marit said, awed. "That's the way . . ."

Alfred gulped, excited, tempted . . . afraid.

But then, when in his life *hadn't* he been afraid?

"Don't go!" Haplo warned. "I don't like this. Xar must have unraveled your spell by now."

Alfred blenched. "Do you know where he is? Can you see him?"

"What I see, I see through the dog's eyes. So long as the mutt's with you, I'm with you, for all the good that's likely to do any of us. Forget the Seventh Gate. Get off of Abarrach while you still have a chance."

"Alfred, please!" Marit begged. She pushed away from him, tried to stand on her own. "Look, I'm well enough—"

The dog barked sharply, leapt to its feet.

Alfred's heart lurched.

"I don't . . . Haplo's right. Xar is searching for us. We've got to leave Abarrach! We'll take the dog with us," Alfred said to Marit, who was glaring at him, the glow of the runes bright in her feverish eyes. "We'll go someplace where we can rest and you can heal yourself. Then we'll come back. I promise—"

Marit shoved him out of her way, prepared to go around him, over him, through him, if necessary. "If you won't take me to the Seventh Gate, I'll find—"

Her words were cut off. A spasm shook her body. She clutched at her throat, fighting to breathe. Doubling over, she fell to her hands and knees.

"Marit!" Alfred gathered her into his arms. "You have to save yourself before you can save Haplo."

"Very well," she whispered, half choked. "But . . . we're coming back for him."

"I promise," Alfred said, no doubt at all remaining in him. "We'll go to the ship."

The sigla lighting the way to the Seventh Gate flickered and died.

Alfred began to sing the runes, softly, sonorously. Sparkling, shimmering runes enveloped him, Marit, and the dog. He continued to sing the runes, the runes that would stretch forth into the possibility that they were safely on board the ship . . .

And within a heartbeat, Alfred and Marit and the dog were standing on the deck.

And there, waiting for them, was Lord Xar.

CHAPTER ◆ 16

SAFE HARBOR

ABARRACH

◆

Alfred blinked, stared. Marit clutched at him, nearly falling.

Xar ignored them both. He reached out his hand to grab the dog, which was standing stiff-legged, teeth bared, growling.

"Dragon!" said Haplo.

Dragon!

Alfred grasped at the possibility, at the spell. He sprang high into the air, his body twisting and dancing with the magic. And suddenly Alfred was no longer on the ship but flying high above it. Xar was not a threatening figure standing next to the Sartan, but a small insignificant one far below, staring up at him.

Marit clung groggily to Alfred's back. She had been hanging on to his coat when the spell transformed him and apparently the magic had taken her with him. But the dog was still down on the deck, dashing back and forth, gazing up at Alfred and barking.

"Give up, Sartan!" Xar called. "You're trapped. You cannot leave Abarrach."

"You can leave, Alfred!" Haplo said to him. "You are stronger than he is! Attack him! Take back the ship!"

"But I might hurt the dog . . ." Alfred wavered.

Xar now had hold of the animal, hanging on to it by the scruff of its neck. "You might well be able to take back your ship from me, Sartan. But what will you do then? Leave without your friend? The dog cannot pass through Death's Gate."

The dog cannot pass through Death's Gate.

"Is that true, Haplo?" Alfred demanded. He answered his own question, realizing that Haplo wouldn't. "It is, isn't it. I knew something about that suggestion of yours wasn't right. The dog can't go through Death's Gate! Not without you!"

Haplo did not respond.

The dragon circled, unhappy, irresolute. Down below, the dog, caught in Xar's grasp, watched them and whined.

"You won't leave your friend here alone to die, Alfred," Xar shouted. "You can't. Love breaks the heart, doesn't it, Sartan . . ."

The dragon wavered. Its wings dipped. Alfred prepared to surrender.

"No!" Haplo shouted.

The dog twisted in Xar's grasp, snapped viciously at him. Its slashing teeth tore through the sleeve of the lord's black robes. Xar let loose, backed up a step from the slavering animal.

The dog leapt from the deck, landed on the dock. It raced off, running as fast as it could run, heading for the abandoned town of Safe Harbor.

The dragon swooped down, flew protectively above the dog until it had disappeared into the shadows of the crumbling buildings. Creeping into an empty house, the dog waited, panting, to see if it was pursued.

It wasn't.

The Lord of the Nexus could have stopped the dog. He could have killed it with a single spoken sigil. But he let the animal go. He had accomplished his purpose. Alfred would never leave Abarrach now. And, sooner or later, he would lead Xar to the Seventh Gate.

Love breaks the heart.

Smiling, pleased with himself, Xar left the ship, returned to his library to consider what to do next. As he went, he rubbed the sigil on his forehead.

Barely conscious, clinging to the dragon's back, Marit moaned.

♦

The dragon circled above the abandoned town of Safe Harbor, waiting to see what Xar would do. Alfred was prepared for anything except the lord's sudden departure.

When Xar disappeared, Alfred waited and watched, thinking it might be a trick. Or perhaps the lord had gone to fetch reinforcements.

Nothing happened. No one came.

"Alfred," Marit said weakly. "You better land. I . . . don't think I can hang on much longer."

"Take her to Salfag Caverns," Haplo suggested. "They're up ahead, not far. The dog knows the way."

The dog emerged from hiding, dashed out into the middle of the empty street. Gazing up at Alfred, the animal barked once, then trotted off down the road.

The dragon flew after the dog, veering sharply over Safe Harbor, followed a road up the coastline of the Fire Sea until the road itself disappeared. The dog began to pick its way among gigantic boulders, jutting out from the shoreline. Recognizing the place as near the entrance to Salfag Caverns, the dragon spiraled downward, seeking a suitable landing site.

As he did so, as he flew closer to the ground, Alfred thought he detected movement—a shadow detaching itself from a jumble of rocks and dead trees and hurrying away, losing itself in more shadows. He stared hard at the site, could see nothing. Finding a clear spot among a jumble of boulders, the dragon settled to the ground.

Marit slid from the dragon's back, slumped down among the rocks, and did not move. Alfred changed back to his usual form, bent over her anxiously.

Her healing powers had kept her from dying, but not much beyond. The poison still coursed through her veins. She was burning with fever and struggled to draw every breath. She seemed to be in pain. She lifted her hand to her forehead, pressed on it.

Alfred brushed back her hair. He saw the sigil—Xar's sigil—glowing with an eerie light. Alfred understood, sighed deeply.

"No wonder Xar let us go," he said. "Wherever we go, she'll lead him right to us."

"You've got to heal her," Haplo said. "But not here. Inside the cavern. She'll need to sleep."

"Yes, of course."

Alfred gently lifted Marit in his arms. The dog, knowing Alfred, regarded this maneuver dubiously. The animal obviously expected that at any moment it would have to save both of them from tumbling headlong into the Fire Sea.

Alfred began to hum to himself, singing the runes as he might have sung a lullaby to a child. Marit relaxed in his arms, ceased to cry out. She drew a deep and peaceful breath. Her head lolled on his shoulder. Smiling to himself, Alfred carried her easily, without slipping once, to the entrance to Salfag Caverns. He started to enter.

The dog refused to follow. It sniffed the air. Its legs went stiff, its hackles rose. It growled warningly.

"Something's in there," Haplo said. "Hiding in the shadows. To your right."

Alfred blinked, unable to see in the dark after the lurid light of the Fire Sea. "It . . . It's not the lazar . . ." His voice quavered nervously.

"No," said Haplo.

The dog crept closer, growling softly.

"This person's alive. I think . . ." Haplo paused. "Do you remember Balthazar? That Sartan necromancer we left behind when we fled Abarrach?"

"Balthazar!" Alfred couldn't believe it. "But he must be dead. All the Sartan with him. The lazar must have destroyed them."

"Apparently not. My guess is we've stumbled onto where Balthazar and his people have been hiding. Remember, this is where we came across them the first time."

"Balthazar!" Alfred repeated in disbelief. He peered into the shadows, attempted to see. "Please, I need help," he called, speaking Sartan. "I was here once before. Do you remember me? My name is—"

"Alfred," said a dry, rasping voice from the shadows. A Sartan clad in ragged, threadbare black robes stepped out from the shadows. "Yes, I remember you."

The dog stood protectively in front of Alfred, barked a warning that said *Keep your distance.*

"Don't be afraid. I won't harm you. I haven't the strength to harm anyone," Balthazar added, a bitter tinge to his voice.

The Sartan had been slightly built to begin with; suffering and deprivation had left him thin and wasted. His beard and hair, once shining black—unusual among Sartan—were now prematurely streaked with gray. Though movement obviously fatigued him, he managed to carry himself with dignity and pride. But the tattered black robes that marked a necromancer hung from bony shoulders, as if they covered a skeleton.

"Balthazar," said Alfred in shocked recognition. "It *is* you. I . . . wasn't certain."

The pity in his voice was all too apparent. Balthazar's black eyes flashed in anger. He drew himself up, clasped his emaciated arms across his shrunken chest.

"Yes, Balthazar! Whose people you left to die on the docks of Safe Harbor!"

The dog, having recognized Balthazar, had been about to make advances in friendly fashion. The animal growled, backed up to stand near its charges.

"You know why we left you behind. I could not permit you to take necromancy into the other worlds," Alfred said quietly. "Especially after I'd seen the harm done to this one."

Balthazar sighed. His anger had been more reflexive than real, a flickering spark, all that was left of a fire that had long since died. His arms, clasped across his chest, slid apart, dropped wearily to his sides.

"I understand. I didn't then, of course. And I can't help my anger. You have no idea"—the black eyes were shadowed, filled with anguish and pain—"what we have suffered. But what you say is true. We brought this evil upon ourselves by our own rash actions. It is up to us to deal with it. What is wrong with the woman?"

Balthazar eyed Marit closely. "She must belong to the same

race of people as that friend of yours—what was his name? Haplo.
I recognize the rune-markings on the skin."

"She was attacked by one of the lazar," Alfred explained, gazing down at Marit. She was no longer in pain. She was unconscious.

Balthazar's expression grew dark, grim. "Some of our people
have met the same fate. There is nothing that can be done for her, I
fear."

"On the contrary." Alfred flushed. "I can heal her. But she
needs to be someplace quiet, where she can sleep undisturbed for
many hours."

Balthazar gazed at Alfred with unblinking eyes. "I forgot," the
necromancer said at last. "I forgot you possessed skills that we
have lost . . . or no longer have the strength to practice. Bring her
inside. She will be safe here . . . as safe as anywhere in this
doomed world."

The necromancer led the way deeper into the cave. As they
went, they passed by another Sartan, a young woman. Balthazar
nodded to her, made her a sign. She cast one curious glance at
Alfred and his companions, then left, heading outside. Within a
few moments, two other Sartan appeared.

"If you want, they will take the woman on ahead to our living
area, make her comfortable," Balthazar suggested.

Alfred hesitated. He wasn't entirely certain he trusted these
people . . . his people.

"I will only keep you a few moments," Balthazar said. "But I
would like to talk with you."

The black eyes penetrated, probed. Alfred had the uneasy feeling that they were seeing much more than he wanted them to see.
And it was obvious the necromancer wasn't going to permit Alfred
to do anything for Marit until Balthazar's curiosity—or whatever it
was—was satisfied.

Reluctantly, Alfred relinquished Marit to the care of the Sartan.
They treated her with tenderness and bore her carefully back to the
interior of the cavern. He couldn't help noting, however, that
the two Sartan who had taken charge of Marit were almost as
weak as the injured Patryn.

"You were warned of our coming," Alfred said, thinking back to the person he'd seen moving among the rocks.

"We keep watch for the lazar," Balthazar answered. "Please, let us sit a moment. Walking fatigues me." He sank down, almost collapsing, upon a boulder.

"You're not using the dead . . . for scouts," Alfred said slowly, remembering the last time he'd been on this world. "Or to fight for you?"

Balthazar cast him a sharp, shrewd glance. "No, we are not." His gaze shifted to the shadows that had deepened around them as they moved farther into the cave. "We do not practice the necromancy anymore."

"I am glad," Alfred said emotionally. "So very glad. Your decision was the right one. The power of necromancy has already done great harm to our people."

"The ability to bring the dead back to life is a strong temptation, arising as it does out of what we call love and compassion." Balthazar sighed. "Unfortunately, it is really only the selfish desire to hold on to something we should let go. Shortsighted and arrogant, we imagine that this mortal state is the apex, the best we can achieve. We have learned that such is not the case."

Alfred regarded him with astonishment. "You have learned? How?"

"My prince, my cherished Edmund, had the courage to show us. We honor his memory. The souls of our dead are free to depart now, their bodies laid to rest with respect.

"Unfortunately," he added, the bitterness returning, "burying our dead is a task that has become all too common . . ."

Lowering his head into his hand, he sought vainly to hide his tears. The dog pattered forward, willing to forgive the earlier misunderstanding. It placed its paw on the necromancer's knee, gazed up at him with sympathetic eyes.

"We fled inland to escape the lazar. But they caught up with us. We fought them, a losing battle, as we well knew. Then one of their number—a young nobleman known as Jonathon—stepped forward. He freed Prince Edmund, sent his spirit to rest, and proved to us that what we had feared all these centuries was not true. The soul does not fall into oblivion, but lives on. We had been wrong to chain that soul to its prison of flesh. Jonathon held off Kleitus and the other lazar, gave us time to escape to safety.

"We hid in the outback for as long as we could. But our food supplies were scarce, our magic weakening daily. Finally, driven by hunger, we came back to this abandoned town, scavenged what meagre supplies remained, and moved into this cave. Now our food is almost completely gone and we have no hope of obtaining more. What little we have left goes to feed the very young, the sick . . ."

Balthazar paused, shut his eyes. He seemed about to faint. Alfred put his arm around him, supported him until he was able to sit by himself.

"Thank you," Balthazar said, with a wan smile. "I am better now. These dizzy spells are a weakness with me."

"A weakness brought on by lack of sustenance. My guess is that you have been depriving yourself of food so that your people could eat. But you are their leader. What will happen to them if you fall ill?"

"The same thing that will happen to them whether I live or die," Balthazar said grimly. "We have no hope. No means of escape. We wait only for death." His voice softened. "And after seeing what peace my prince found, I must confess that I am looking forward to it."

"Come, come," Alfred said hastily, alarmed by such talk. "We're wasting time. If you have any food left at all, I can use my magic to provide more."

Balthazar smiled wanly. "That would be a great help. And undoubtedly you have large stores of food on your ship."

"Well, yes, of course, I—" Alfred stopped. His tongue stuck to the roof of his mouth.

"Now you've done it," Haplo muttered.

"So that ship we saw *is* yours!" Balthazar's eyes burned with a fevered glow. He stretched forth a skeletal hand, clutched at Alfred's faded velvet lapel. "At last we can escape! Leave this world of death!"

"I—I—I—" Alfred stammered. "That is . . . you see . . ."

Alfred could see—could see exactly where all this had been leading. He rose, trembling, to his feet.

"We will discuss this later. I need to be with my friend. To heal her. Then I will do what I can to help your people."

Balthazar also stood up. He leaned near Alfred. "We will escape!" he said softly. "No one will stop us this time."

Alfred gulped, backed up a pace. He said nothing. Balthazar said nothing. The two walked on, moving deeper into the cavern. The necromancer walked slowly and weakly, but he politely refused any type of aid. Alfred, miserable and unhappy, could not control his wandering feet. If it hadn't been for the dog, he would have tumbled down any number of crevices, fallen over any number of rocks.

A mensch saying came to Alfred's mind.

"Out of the frying pan. Into the fire."

CHAPTER ◆ 17

SALFAG CAVERNS

ABARRACH

◆

Bᴀʟᴛʜᴀᴢᴀʀ ʀᴇᴍᴀɪɴᴇᴅ sɪʟᴇɴᴛ ᴅᴜʀɪɴɢ ᴛʜᴇɪʀ ᴡᴀʟᴋ, ꜰᴏʀ ᴡʜɪᴄʜ ᴀʟꜰʀᴇᴅ ᴡᴀs extremely grateful. Having endeavored to extricate himself from one problem, he had—as usual—become embroiled in another. Now he had to find a way out of both. Try as he might, he could see no solution to either.

They walked on, the dog pattering watchfully behind. And then they came to the portion of the cavern in which the Sartan lived.

Alfred peered through the darkness. His worries about Haplo and Marit, his suspicions of Balthazar, were submerged beneath a wave of pity and shock. Fifty or so Sartan men, women, and a few —far too few—children were sheltered in this dismal cavern. The sight of them, their wretched plight, was heart-wrenching. Starvation had taken its terrible toll, but worse than physical deprivation, terror and fear and despair had left their souls as emaciated as their bodies.

Balthazar had done what he could to keep up their spirits, but he was near the end himself. Many of the Sartan had given up. They lay on the hard, cold floor of the cavern, doing nothing but staring into the darkness, as if beseeching it to come down and wrap around them. Alfred knew such hopelessness well, knew where it could lead, for he himself had once walked that dread

road. If it had not been for the coming of Haplo—and Haplo's dog
—Alfred might have followed the road to its bitter conclusion.

"This is what we live on," Balthazar said, gesturing to a large
sack. "Kairn-grass seed, meant to be used for planting, salvaged
from Safe Harbor. We grind the seeds, mix them with water to
make gruel. And this is the last sack. When it is gone . . ."

The necromancer shrugged.

What magical powers the Sartan had left were being used to
simply stay alive, to breathe the poisonous air of Abarrach.

"Don't worry," said Alfred. "I will aid you. But first, I must
heal Marit."

"Certainly," Balthazar said.

Marit lay on a pile of ragged blankets. Several Sartan women
were tending her, doing what they could to make her comfortable.
She'd been warmly covered, given water. (Alfred couldn't help
wondering at the apparent abundance of fresh water; the last time
he'd been on Abarrach, water had been extremely scarce. He
would have to remember to ask.)

Thanks to these ministrations, Marit had regained consciousness. She was quick to catch sight of Alfred. Weakly raising her
hand, she reached out to him. He started to kneel beside her. Marit
grabbed hold of him, nearly pulled him off-balance.

"What . . . where are we?" she asked through teeth clenched
against the chills that shook her. "Who are these?"

"Sartan," said Alfred, soothing her, trying to coax her to lie
back down. "You are safe here. I'm going to heal you, then you
need sleep."

An expression of defiance hardened Marit's face. Alfred was
reminded of the time—another time—in Abarrach, when he'd
healed Haplo, against his will.

"I can take care of myself," Marit began, but her words were
choked off. She couldn't catch her breath.

Alfred took hold of her hands, her right in his left, her left in his
right, completing, sharing the circle of their beings.

She attempted feebly to snatch her hand away, but Alfred was
stronger now than she was. He held on to her tightly and began to
sing the runes.

His warmth and strength flowed into Marit. Her pain and suffering and loneliness entered his. The circle wrapped around them, bound them together, and for just a brief instant, Haplo was included within it.

Alfred had a strange, eerie image of the three of them, floating on a wave of light and air and time, talking to each other.

"You have to leave Abarrach, Alfred," Haplo said. "You and Marit. Go someplace safe, where Xar can't find you."

"But we can't take the dog, can we?" Alfred argued. "Xar is right. The dog cannot pass through Death's Gate. Not without you."

"We won't go," Marit said. "We won't leave you."

She seemed surrounded by light, was beautiful in Alfred's eyes. She leaned near Haplo, reached out her hand to him, but he couldn't touch her. She couldn't touch him. The wave carried them, supported them, but it also separated them.

"I lost you once, Haplo. I left you because I didn't have the courage to love you. I have the courage now. I love you and I won't lose you again. If the situation were reversed," Marit continued, not letting him speak, "and I were the one lying back there on that stone bier, would you leave me? Then how can you think I am less strong than you are?"

Haplo's voice faltered. "I don't ask you to be less strong than I am. I ask you to be stronger. You must find the strength to leave me, Marit. Remember our people, fighting for their lives in the Labyrinth. Remember what will happen to them and to everyone in the four worlds if our lord succeeds in closing the Seventh Gate."

"I can't leave you," Marit said.

Her love poured out from her. Haplo's love flowed from him, and Alfred was the fine silk cloth through which both passed. The tragedy of their separation grieved him deeply. If he could have given them ease by tearing himself apart, he would have done so. As it was, he could only be a poor sort of go-between.

What made it worse was that he knew Haplo was speaking to him, too—to Alfred as well as Marit. Alfred, too, must find the strength to leave someone he had come to love.

"But in the meantime, what do I do about Balthazar?" Alfred asked.

Before Haplo could answer, the light began to fade, the warmth receded. The wave ebbed, leaving Alfred stranded and alone in darkness. He sighed deeply, shudderingly, not wanting to let go, not wanting to return. And, as he did so, he heard his name.

"Alfred." Marit was half sitting up, propped on her elbow. The fever had left her eyes, although the lids were now heavy with the longing for sleep. "Alfred," she repeated urgently, struggling to remain awake.

"Yes, my dear, I am here," he replied, close to tears. "You should be lying down."

She sank back onto the blankets, permitted him to fuss over her, because she was too distracted to stop him. When he started to leave, she caught hold of his hand.

"Ask the Sartan . . . about the Seventh Gate," she whispered. "What he knows about it."

"Do you really think that's wise?" Alfred demurred.

Now that he had seen Balthazar again, he was reminded of the power of the necromancer. And though weakened from anxiety and lack of food, Balthazar would regain his strength quickly enough if he thought he'd found a way out for him and his people.

"I'm not certain I want Balthazar to find the Seventh Gate, any more than Lord Xar. Perhaps I shouldn't bring it up."

"Just ask what he knows," Marit pleaded. "What harm can there be in that?"

Alfred was reluctant. "I doubt if Balthazar knows anything . . ."

Marit held fast to his hand, squeezed it painfully. "Ask him. Please!"

"Ask me what?"

Balthazar had been standing at a distance, watching the healing process with intense interest. Now, hearing his name, he glided forward. "What is it you want to know?"

"Go ahead," said Haplo's voice suddenly, startling Alfred. "Ask him. See what he says."

Alfred sighed, gulped. "We were wondering, Balthazar, have you ever heard of . . . of something called the Seventh Gate?"

"Certainly," Balthazar answered calmly, but with a stabbing glance of his black eyes that slid through Alfred like a sharp blade. "All on Abarrach have heard of the Seventh Gate. Every child learns the litany."

"What . . . what litany would that be?" Alfred asked faintly.

" 'The Earth was destroyed,' " Balthazar began, repeating the words in a high, thin voice. " 'Four worlds were created out of the ruin. Worlds for ourselves and the mensch: Air, Fire, Stone, Water. Four Gates connect each world to the other: Arianus to Pryan to Abarrach to Chelestra. A house of correction was built for our enemies: the Labyrinth. The Labyrinth is connected to the other worlds through the Fifth Gate: the Nexus. The Sixth Gate is the center, permits entry: the Vortex. And all was accomplished through the Seventh Gate. The end was the beginning.' "

"So *that* was how you knew about Death's Gate, about the other worlds," Alfred said, recalling the first time he'd met Balthazar, how the necromancer had seen through the lies Haplo had used to conceal his true identity. "And you say this is taught to children?"

"It *was*," Balthazar said, with rueful emphasis on the word. "When we had leisure to teach our children other things besides how to die."

"How did your people come to be in this condition?" Marit asked, fighting drowsiness, fighting sleep. "What happened to this world?"

"Greed is what happened," Balthazar replied. "Greed and desperation. When the magic that kept this world alive started to fail, our people began to die. We turned to necromancy, to hold on to those dear to us, at first. Then, eventually, we used that black art to increase our numbers, to add soldiers to our armies, servants to our houses. But things grew worse instead of better for us."

"Abarrach was always intended to be dependent on the other three worlds for its survival," Alfred explained. "Conduits, known on this world as colossi, were meant to channel energy flowing from the citadels of Pryan into Abarrach. The energy would provide light and heat, enable the people to live near the surface, where the air is breathable. The plan did not work out. When the Kicksey-winsey failed, the light of Pryan's citadels failed as well, and Abarrach was left in the darkness."

He stopped. His didactic lecture had worked. Marit's eyes were closed, her breathing deep and even. Alfred smiled slightly, carefully tucked the blankets around her to keep her warm. Then he stole silently away. Balthazar, after a glance at Marit, followed Alfred.

"Why do you ask about the Seventh Gate?"

Another one of the stabbing glances penetrated Alfred, who was immediately rendered incoherent.

"I . . . I . . . curious . . . heard . . . somewhere . . . something . . ."

Balthazar frowned. "What are you trying to find out, Brother? The location? Believe me, if I had any idea where the Seventh Gate was, I would have used it myself, to help my people escape this terrible place."

"Yes, of course."

"What else do you want to know about it, then?"

"Nothing, really. Just . . . just curious. Let's go see what we can do about feeding your people."

Truly concerned for his people's welfare, the necromancer said nothing more. But it was apparent to Alfred that, as he had feared, his sudden interest in the Seventh Gate had aroused Balthazar's interest as well. And the necromancer was a great deal like Haplo's dog. Once he had something in his teeth, he would not easily let go.

Alfred began replicating sacks of the kairn-grass seed,[1] providing enough so that the Sartan could turn it into flour, bake it into

---

[1] Sartan and Patryn magic can replicate already existing food supplies. This can be done quite easily, merely by advancing the possibility that one sack of grain is twenty sacks of grain. Certain powerful magic-users are able to alter

hardbread—far more substantial and nourishing than the gruel. As he worked, he glanced surreptitiously around the cavern. No dead Sartan served the living, as had been the case the last time Alfred had visited these people. No soldier-corpses guarded the entrance, no cadaver-king tried to rule. Wherever the dead lay, they lay at rest—as Balthazar had said.

Alfred looked at the children huddled around him, begging for a handful of seed that, on Arianus, he would have thrown to the birds.

His eyes filled with tears, and that reminded him of a question. He turned to Balthazar, who kept near him, watching each spell Alfred cast, almost as hungry for the magic as he was for the food.

The necromancer had, at Alfred's insistence, eaten a small amount and was looking somewhat stronger—although the renewal of hope probably accounted more for the change than the unappetizing kairn-grass paste he had consumed.

"You seem to have plenty of water," Alfred remarked. "That's different from when I was here last."

Balthazar nodded. "You recall that one of the colossi stands not far from here. We had assumed it was dead, its power gone out. But, quite suddenly, not too long ago, its magic returned to life."

Alfred brightened. "Indeed? Do you have any idea why?"

"There has been no change on *this* world. I can only assume that there have been changes on others."

"Why, yes! You're right!" Alfred was all eager enthusiasm. "The Kicksey-winsey . . . and the citadels on Pryan . . . they're working now! . . . Why, this means—"

"—nothing to us," Balthazar finished coolly. "Change comes too late. Suppose the heat from the conduits has returned, suppose it is causing the ice that rimes this world to begin to melt. We once

---

the possibilities to produce food out of objects not normally edible, such as changing stone into bread. Or they might change one food substance into another—turn a fish into a beefsteak. Alfred could undoubtedly perform such magic, but it would require a tremendous expenditure of will and energy.

again find water. But it will be many, many lifetimes before this world of the dead can be inhabited by the living. And by then the living will be no more. The dead alone will rule Abarrach."

"You are determined to leave," Alfred said, troubled.

"Or die trying," Balthazar said grimly. "Can you envisage a future for us, for our children, here, on Abarrach?"

Alfred couldn't answer. He handed over more food. Balthazar took it and left, doling it out to his people.

"I can't blame them for wanting to leave," Alfred said quietly. "I want to leave very badly myself at this moment. But I know perfectly well what will happen when these Sartan arrive on the other worlds. It will only be a matter of time before they begin to try to take over, disrupting the lives of the mensch."

"They're a sad-looking lot," Haplo said.

Alfred, not realizing he'd spoken aloud, jumped to hear Haplo's voice. Or maybe he hadn't spoken aloud. Haplo had always been able to read his thoughts.

"You're right," Haplo went on. "These Sartan are weak now, but once they are able to quit using their magic for survival, their magic will strengthen. They'll discover its power."

"And then there are your people." Alfred glanced at the sleeping Marit. The dog lay protectively at her side, growling warningly at anyone who ventured near her. "If they escape from the Labyrinth and enter the worlds, who can say what will happen? Patryns have sucked in hatred with their mothers' milk, and who can blame them?"

Alfred began to tremble. He dropped the food, pressed his hands to his burning eyes. "I see it all happening again! The rivalries, the wars, the deadly confrontations. The innocent victims caught up in it, dying for something they don't understand . . . All . . . all ending in disaster!"

The last burst from Alfred in a hollow cry. Looking up, he encountered the necromancer's glittering black-eyed gaze. Balthazar had returned. Alfred had the sudden, uncanny impression that the necromancer had followed every twist and turn of his thoughts. Balthazar had seen what Alfred had seen, shared the vision that had led to his horrified cry.

"I *will* leave Abarrach," Balthazar said to Alfred, softly. "You cannot stop me."

Alfred, shaken and disturbed, was forced to quit using his magic. He didn't feel strong enough to turn ice to water on a hot summer's day.

"It was a mistake to come here," he muttered.

"But if we hadn't, they would have all died," Haplo observed.

"Perhaps it would have been best." Alfred stared at his hands —large, with large-boned wrists; slender, tapering fingers; graceful, elegant . . . and capable of causing so much harm. He could use them for good, too, but at the moment he was not disposed to see that. "It would be best for the mensch if we all died."

"If their 'gods' left them, you mean?"

" 'Gods'!" Alfred repeated, with contempt. " 'Enslavers' is nearer the mark. I would rid the universe of us and our corrupt 'power'!"

"You know, my friend"—Haplo sounded thoughtful—"there may be something in what you say . . ."

"There may be?" Alfred was startled. He'd been babbling, flailing about mentally, not expecting to hit anything. "What exactly *did* I say?"

"Don't worry about it. Go make yourself useful."

"Do you have any suggestions?" Alfred asked meekly.

"You might want to find out what Balthazar's scouts are reporting to him," Haplo suggested dryly. "Or hadn't you noticed that they'd returned?"

Alfred hadn't noticed, as a matter of fact. His head jerked up, his body twitched. The Sartan he'd seen posted near the cavern's entrance—the one Balthazar had sent on some sort of errand—was back. Balthazar brought the young woman food. She was eating ravenously, but between mouthfuls, she was talking to him, their discussion low-voiced and intense.

Alfred started to stand up, slipped on a smattering of kairn-grass seeds, and sat back down again.

"Stay here," Haplo said. He gave the dog a silent command.

The animal rose to its feet. Padding silently over to Balthazar, the dog flopped down at his feet.

"He sent her to inspect the ship. He's going to try to seize it," Haplo reported, hearing through the dog's ears.

"But they can't, can they?" Alfred protested. "Marit surrounded it with Patryn runes . . ."

"Under ordinary circumstances, no," Haplo said. "But apparently someone else on Abarrach has had the same idea. Someone else is also trying to steal the ship."

Alfred was astonished. "Surely not Xar . . ."

"No, my lord has no need for that ship. But someone else on this world does."

Suddenly, Alfred knew the answer.

"Kleitus!"

CHAPTER ◆ 18

SALFAG CAVERNS

ABARRACH

◆

"I WISH WE WERE STRONGER!" BALTHAZAR WAS SAYING, AS ALFRED HESITANTLY approached the necromancer and the guard. The dog, tail wagging, pattered over to greet Alfred.

"Our numbers greater! But . . . it will have to suffice." The necromancer glanced around. "How many of us are physically capable . . ."

"Um . . . what's going on?" Alfred remembered just in time to pretend that he didn't know.

"The lazar, Kleitus, is attempting to steal your ship," Balthazar reported, with a calm that astonished Alfred. "Of course, the fiend must be stopped."

So that you can take it yourself, Alfred added, but he added it silently. "The . . . um . . . that is . . . Patryn rune-magic guards the ship. I don't think it can be broken . . ."

Balthazar smiled, thin-lipped, grim. "As you recall, I once saw a demonstration of 'Patryn' magic. The rune-structures are visible, they glow with light when they are activated. Isn't that true?"

Alfred, wary, nodded.

"Half the sigla on your ship are now dark," Balthazar reported. "Kleitus is unraveling it."

"That's impossible!" Alfred protested in disbelief. "How could the lazar have learned such a skill—"

"From Xar," Haplo said. "Kleitus has been watching my lord

and the rest of my people. The lazar has discovered the secret of the rune-magic.''

''The lazar are capable of learning,'' Balthazar was saying at the same time, ''because of the soul's proximity to the body. And they have long wanted to leave Abarrach. They can find no living flesh here on which to feed. I do not need to tell you what terrible tragedies will befall in the other worlds if the lazar succeed in entering Death's Gate.''

He was right. He had no need to tell Alfred, who could envision such horror all too clearly. Kleitus had to be stopped, but— once the lazar was stopped, *if* it was—who was going to stop Balthazar?

Alfred sank down on a rock ledge, stared unseeing into the darkness. ''Will it never end? Will we go on forever perpetuating the misery and the sorrow?''

The dog flopped down, whined a little in sympathy. Balthazar stood near, black eyes probing, prodding. Alfred flinched, as if the sharp gaze had drawn blood. He had the distinct feeling he knew what Balthazar was going to say next.

Balthazar placed his gaunt, wasted hand on Alfred's shoulder.

Leaning over him, the necromancer spoke in low tones. ''Once I might have been able to cast such spells as are required. But not now. You, on the other hand . . .''

Alfred blenched, shrank away from the man's touch. ''I . . . couldn't! I wouldn't know how . . .''

''I do,'' Balthazar said smoothly. ''I have been thinking long on the matter, as you might guess. The lazar are dangerous because— unlike the ordinary dead—the living soul remains attached to the dead. If that attachment were to be severed, the soul wrenched from the body, I believe the lazar would be destroyed.''

''You 'believe'?'' Alfred retorted. ''You don't know for certain.''

''As I said, I have not been strong enough to conduct such an experiment myself.''

''I couldn't,'' Alfred said flatly. ''I couldn't possibly.''

''Yet he's right,'' said Haplo. ''Kleitus must be stopped. Balthazar's too weak to do it.''

Alfred groaned again. What do I do about Balthazar? he asked silently, conscious of the necromancer hovering at his elbow. How do I stop *him*?

"Worry about one thing at a time," Haplo returned.

Alfred shook his head dismally.

"Look at these Sartan," Haplo told him. "They can barely walk. The ship is a Patryn ship, covered with Patryn runes—inside and out. Even if Kleitus destroys all the runes, new ones will have to be crafted to enable the ship to fly. Balthazar won't be leaving anytime soon. Plus I don't think Lord Xar will be too pleased with the idea of letting these Sartan escape him."

Alfred did not find this cheering. "But that will mean more fighting, more killing . . ."

"One problem at a time, Sartan," Haplo said, with an inexplicable calm. "One problem at a time. Can you work this magic the necromancer proposes?"

"Yes," said Alfred softly, subdued. He sighed. "Yes, I believe I can."

"You can work the magic?" The voice was Balthazar's. "Is that what you are talking about?"

"Yes," Alfred said, flushing.

Balthazar's black eyes narrowed. "With what—or with whom —do you commune, Brother?"

The dog, not liking the man's tone, raised its head and growled.

Alfred smiled, reached out to pat it. "Myself," he said quietly.

Balthazar insisted on taking all of his people with them.

"We will seize control of the ship, begin to work on it immediately," he told Alfred. "The strongest among us will stand guard for any attack. Barring interruptions, we should be able to leave Abarrach in a relatively short time."

There will be interruptions, Alfred said silently. Lord Xar will not let you go. And I cannot go. I can't leave Haplo behind. Yet I can't stay. Xar is hunting me, to lead him to the Seventh Gate. What do I do? What do I do?

"What you must," Haplo answered calmly, quietly.

And it was then Alfred realized Haplo had a plan.

Alfred's heart quivered with hope. "You have an idea . . ."

"I beg your pardon?" Balthazar turned to him. "What were you saying?"

"Shut up, Alfred!" Haplo ordered. "Don't say a word. It's nothing firm yet. And circumstances may not work out. But, just in case, be ready. Now, go wake up Marit."

Alfred started to protest, felt the heat of Haplo's irritation wash over him—an uncomfortable and uncanny experience.

"She'll be weak, but you're going to need help and she's the only one who can provide it."

Alfred nodded, did as he was told. The Sartan were gathering together their few belongings, preparing to move out. Word had spread among them rapidly: a ship, escape, hope. They spoke in awed tones of fleeing this dread land, of finding new lives in beautiful new worlds. It was all Alfred could do to keep from shrieking in frustration.

He knelt down beside Marit. She slept so peacefully, so deeply, it seemed criminal to wake her. Looking at her, untroubled as she was by dreams or memories, he was suddenly and shockingly reminded of another—Hugh the Hand—free of the burdens and pain of life, finding a haven and a sanctuary in death . . . until wrenched back . . .

Alfred's throat constricted. He choked, attempted to clear his throat—and at the strange sound, Marit woke up.

"What? What is it? What's wrong?"

Patryns are accustomed to waking instantly, mindful always—even in slumber—of the danger that surrounds them in the Labyrinth. Marit sat up, her hand fumbling for her weapon, almost before Alfred could comprehend that she was awake and moving.

"It's . . . it's all right." He hastened to reassure her.

She blinked, brushed back her hair. Alfred saw, again, the sigil on her forehead. His heart sank. He'd forgotten. Xar would know . . . every move . . . Perhaps he should tell her.

"Don't say a word," Haplo counseled him swiftly. "Yes, Xar knows, through her, what is happening. But that may work to our advantage. Don't let *him* know *you* know."

"What is it?" Marit demanded. "Why are you staring at me?"

"You . . . look . . . much better," Alfred managed.

"Thanks to you," she said, smiling, relaxing. When she did, he saw that she was still ill, still weak. She glanced around, was immediately aware of the sudden activity.

"What's going on?"

"Kleitus is attempting to steal the ship," Alfred explained.

"My ship!" Marit stood up swiftly; too swiftly. She almost fell.

"I'm going to try to stop him," Alfred said, rising awkwardly himself.

"And who's going to stop them?" Marit demanded, with an impatient, sweeping gesture that encompassed all the Sartan in the cave. "They're packing up! Moving out! In my ship!"

Alfred didn't know what to say; Haplo gave him no help. Alfred blinked at her like a baffled owl and stammered something unintelligible.

Marit strapped her sword around her waist. "I understand," she said to him, calm, grim. "I forgot. They're your people. Of course you'll be glad to help them escape."

"Keep quiet . . ." Haplo cautioned.

Alfred clamped his lips shut tightly, to avoid temptation. If he opened his mouth at all, even to breathe, he was afraid the words would come spewing out. Not that he could actually tell Marit anything constructive. He didn't know what Haplo was plotting.

Alfred had the strange impression of Haplo's mind racing down a track, like the flashrafts of the Kicksey-winsey, the great iron carriages that scuttled along on iron rails, powered by the lightning of the 'lectric zingers. Alfred was being carried along with it and he feared he was going to be in for an unnerving jolt whenever Haplo arrived at the end of the line. Meanwhile, the Sartan had no choice but to bumble on and hope that somehow, somewhere, he managed to do his part right.

Balthazar's people had joined together to form a tiny army that looked more dead than the dead they were going out to face. Their thin, wan faces hardened by determination, they moved slowly, but with resolve. Alfred admired them. He could have wept for them.

Yet, looking at them, he saw the beginning of evil, not an end to it.

The Sartan left Salfag Caverns, traveling along the broken road that led to the town of Safe Harbor. With characteristic logic, Balthazar had seen to it that the younger Sartan, who served to guard their people, had been given food enough to keep up their strength. These Sartan were in relatively good condition, though their numbers were few. They moved out in front, acting as advance guards and scouts.

But for the most part, it was a ragged, shabby, and pitifully weak group of people who trudged along the shore of the burning sea, intending to make a stand against the dead, which could not be harmed, which could not die.

Alfred and Marit accompanied them. Alfred's mind was in such turmoil over the spell he would have to cast—a spell he had never ever even considered casting—that he paid no attention to where he was going or how he got there. He lurched into boulders, fell over the feet of his companions, if they were available; tumbled over his own feet if not.

The dog was kept busy hauling Alfred out of one potential disaster after another and, within a short time, even that faithful animal begin to evince signs of irritation with the man. A snap and a snarl warned Alfred away from a bubbling mud pit, when before a gentle nudge would have taken him clear.

Marit marched silently, her hand on her sword hilt. She, too, was plotting something, but obviously had no intention of sharing her strategy. Alfred had become—once again—one of the enemy.

The thought made him miserable, but he couldn't blame her. He didn't dare trust her either; not with Xar's mark on her.

Evil beginning again . . . without end. Without end.

At Balthazar's command, the Sartan left the road before they came near the town, moving into the dark shadows created by the lurid light glowing from the Fire Sea. The Sartan herded the children and those too weak to keep going into abandoned buildings.

The younger Sartan went with their leader to view—from hidden vantage points—the dock and the Patryn ship.

Kleitus was alone; none of the other lazar were working with him, which Alfred found inexplicable at first. Then it occurred to him that these lazar probably didn't trust each other. Kleitus would jealously guard the secrets he had learned from Xar. Crouched in the shadows, the Sartan watched the lazar slowly, patiently, unravel the complex Patryn rune-structure.

"It is well we came when we did," Balthazar whispered, before moving off to issue commands to his people.

Alfred was too harried and flurried to reply. Marit also had no comment. She was staring, amazed and aghast, at her ship. Almost two-thirds of the runes protecting the ship were destroyed, their magical power broken. Perhaps she hadn't believed the Sartan. Now she knew they were telling the truth.

"Do you suppose Xar put Kleitus up to this?" Alfred was, in truth, asking Haplo, but Marit apparently thought he was talking to her.

Her eyes flashed. "My lord would never have permitted the lazar to learn the rune-magic! Besides, what purpose would this serve?"

Alfred flushed, stung by her anger. "You must admit, this is a convenient way to rid himself of the lazar . . . and keep us trapped here on Abarrach."

Marit shook her head, refusing to consider the idea. She lifted her hand to her forehead, to rub the sigil put there by Xar. Catching Alfred watching her, she snatched her hand away, wrapped her fingers tightly about her sword hilt.

"What do you plan to do?" she asked coldly. "Are you going to change into the dragon?"

"No." Alfred spoke reluctantly, not wanting to think about what he was going to do, what he was going to *have* to do. "It will take all my energy to perform the spell to free this tormented soul." His sad-eyed gaze was on the lazar. "I couldn't do that and be the dragon, too."

He added softly, first checking to make certain Balthazar was nowhere near, "Marit, I'm not going to let the Sartan have the ship."

She regarded him silently, thoughtfully, taking his measure. Finally she nodded, once, abruptly.

"How are you going to stop them?"

"Marit . . ." Alfred licked dry lips. "What if I were to destroy the ship?"

She was thoughtful, did not protest.

"We'd be trapped in Abarrach. There would be no other way out for us," he said to her, wanting to make certain she understood.

"Yes, there is," Marit replied. "The Seventh Gate."

CHAPTER ◆ 19

SAFE HARBOR

ABARRACH

◆

"MY LORD!" A PATRYN ENTERED XAR'S LIBRARY. "A GROUP OF WHAT APPEAR TO be Sartan have arrived in Safe Harbor. The scouts believe they are going to attempt to seize the ship."

Xar knew, of course, what was transpiring. He had been with Marit mentally, following events through her ears and eyes, although she had no idea she was being used for such a purpose. He made no mention of this fact, however, but looked up with interest at the Patryn making the report.

"Indeed. Sartan—native to Abarrach. I heard rumor of this before our arrival, but the lazar led me to believe all the Sartan were dead."

"They might as well be, Lord. They are a ragged, wretched-looking lot. Half starved."

"How many of them?"

"Perhaps fifty or so, My Lord. Including children."

"Children . . ." Xar was nonplussed. Marit had made no mention of children. He hadn't figured them into his calculations.

Still, he reminded himself coldly, they are *Sartan* children.

"What is Kleitus doing?"

"Attempting to destroy the rune-magic protecting the ship, My Lord. He appears to be oblivious to all else."

Xar made an impatient gesture. "Of course he is. He, too, is half starved—for fresh blood."

"What are your orders, My Lord?"

What indeed? Xar had been pondering this ever since he had known, from Marit's whispered conversation with Alfred, what was being planned. Alfred was going to attempt to wrench the soul from the lazar's body. Xar had a great deal of respect for the Serpent Mage—more respect for Alfred than Alfred had for himself. He might very well be capable of ending the lazar's tormented existence.

Xar didn't care a rune-bone what happened to the lazar. If they all turned to dust, if they fled Abarrach—it was all the same to him. He would be happy to be rid of them. But once Kleitus was destroyed, Alfred would be free to take over the ship. True, he had told Marit he intended to destroy it. But Xar didn't trust the Sartan.

The Lord of the Nexus made his decision. He rose to his feet.

"I will come," he said. "Send all our people to the Anvil. Have my ship there, ready to sail. We must be prepared to move . . . and move swiftly."

Out beyond the New Provinces, directly across from Safe Harbor, stood a promontory of jagged rock known—for its black color and distinctive shape—as the Anvil. The Anvil guarded the mouth of a bay created eons ago when a tremor had caused part of the rock peak to crack and break off. It had slid into the sea, creating an opening in the cliff that permitted the magma to flow into a low-lying section of land.

This created a bay, which was named Firepool. The lava, fed continually by the Fire Sea and surrounded by sheer rock walls on all sides, formed a slow-moving, sluggish maelstrom.

Around and around flowed the viscous magma, carrying chunks of black rock on its glowing surface. A person standing on the Anvil could pick out a particular rock and watch it being carried inexorably to its doom. Watch it enter the Firepool, watch it revolve around the outer surface, watch it drift nearer and nearer the Firepool's heart, watch it vanish, dragged down into the sucking maw of the fiery maelstrom.

Xar often came to the Anvil, often stood and stared into the mesmerizing swirl of fiery lava. When he was in a fatalistic mood, he compared the Firepool to life. No matter what a man did, how much he struggled and fought to avoid his fate, the end was always the same.

But Xar was not indulging in such morbid thoughts this day. He looked down on the maelstrom and saw—not rocks, but one of the iron, steam- and magic-driven ships built by the Sartan to sail the Fire Sea. The iron ship floated in the bay, hidden from the eyes of the dead and the living.

Perched on the Anvil, Xar gazed across the Fire Sea at the abandoned town of Safe Harbor, at the dock, at Marit's ship and the lazar Kleitus. Xar had no fear of being observed. He was too far away, a black-robed figure against black rocks. The iron ship was out of sight behind the promontory. Besides, he doubted that anyone over there—lazar or Sartan—would bother to look for him. They had more urgent matters at hand.

All Patryns remaining on Abarrach, with the sole exception of Haplo, lying in the dungeons below Necropolis, were on board the ship. They awaited the signal of their lord to sail out of the bay, surge across the Fire Sea. They were prepared to intercept Alfred should he attempt to leave Abarrach.

The Patryns were also—and this Xar considered an incredible thing, but one he was driven to by necessity—prepared to save Alfred should anything go wrong.

Xar used the rune-magic to enhance his vision. He had a clear view of the docks of Safe Harbor, of Kleitus working to unravel Marit's spells. Xar could even see, through a porthole in the ship, what appeared to be a mensch—the human assassin, Hugh the Hand—moving from one side of the ship to the other, nervously watching the lazar at work.

The mensch—another walking corpse, Xar thought, somewhat bitterly. It irritated him that Alfred had been able to work the necromancy by giving life back to the mensch, whereas Xar had been able to do nothing with necromancy except provide a dog a soul.

Xar could see, but he could not hear, for which he was grateful. He had no need to hear what was going on, and the echo of

Kleitus's soul, trapped in the dead body, had been getting on his nerves lately. It was bad enough watching the corpse shuffling and shambling about the dock, the imprisoned phantasm struggling constantly to break free. The chained soul undulating around the body gave the lazar a fuzzy look, as if Xar were watching it through a flawed crystal. He found himself constantly blinking, trying to bring the watery image into focus.

And then came a figure, stepping out onto the docks, a figure that was sharp and clear, if somewhat stoop-shouldered and faltering. Two figures walked beside it—one clad in the black robes of a necromancer, the other one a woman, a Patryn.

Xar's eyes narrowed. He smiled.

"Make ready," he said to the Patryn standing beside him, who gave a signal to the ship, waiting below.

"I think it will be much better if I go on ahead alone," Alfred said to a disapproving Balthazar and a skeptical Marit. "If Kleitus sees an army approaching, he will feel threatened and immediately attack. But if he just sees me—"

"—he'll laugh?" Balthazar suggested.

"Perhaps," Alfred replied gravely. "At least he might not pay me much heed. And that will give me time to cast the spell."

"How long will this take?" Marit demanded, dubious, her gaze on the lazar, her hand on the hilt of her sword.

Alfred flushed, embarrassed.

"You don't know."

Alfred shook his head.

Balthazar looked back at his people, huddled in the shadows of the buildings, the weak who could walk supporting those weaker who couldn't. Children—faces pinched, eyes huge and staring—clung to their parents or, in those cases where the parents were dead, to those who now held their responsibility. After all, what help could his people give?

The necromancer sighed. "Very well," he said grudgingly. "Do this your way. We will come to your aid if need be."

"At least let me go with you, Alfred," Marit urged.

He again shook his head, cast a swift, oblique glance at Baltha-zar.

Marit saw the look, understood, made no further argument. She was to watch the necromancer, prevent him from trying to seize control of the ship, which he might do while Alfred was busy with the lazar.

"*We* will wait for you here," Marit said, giving the word emphasis to indicate she understood.

Alfred nodded, rather dismally. Now that he had achieved his aim, he was extremely sorry he'd done so. What if his spell failed? Kleitus would attempt to murder him, make him one of the lazar. Alfred looked at the corpse, scarred with the marks of its own violent death. He looked at the hapless phantasm, struggling to escape, and at the waxen hands, longing to end life—his life. He remembered Kleitus's attack on Marit, the poison . . . Even now, she was not free of it. Her cheeks had an unnatural flush; her eyes were too bright. The slashes on her throat were inflamed, painful.

Alfred went hot and then extremely cold. The words to the spell slipped out of his mind, fluttering like the butterfly souls of the elves of Arianus, flapping off in a thousand different directions.

"You think too damn much," came Haplo's voice. "Just go out there and do what you have to do!"

Do what you have to do. Yes, Alfred told himself. I will do what I have to do.

Taking a deep breath, he stepped out of the shadows and headed for the docks.

The dog, knowing Alfred and foreseeing a hundred obstacles in his path, trotted along watchfully at his side.

The runes surrounding the ship were now more than three-quarters dark. From her vantage point in the shadows of a ruined building, Marit could see Hugh the Hand, moving about restlessly on board, keeping watch on the ghastly being walking about the ship. She wondered suddenly how the Cursed Blade would react to Kleitus. He was Sartan, or had been. Most likely, the blade would fight for the lazar. She hoped Hugh had sense enough *not* to intervene, wished she had thought to warn Alfred of this additional danger.

Too late, though. Her duty was here. She cast a sidelong glance at Balthazar. His gaze slid across hers like a fencer's sword, testing, seeking out his opponent's weakness.

Marit caught herself just before she laughed aloud. Weakness! Both of us so damn weak neither one could likely melt butter. What a fight that would be. What an inglorious battle. Yet we would fight. Until both dropped down dead.

Tears filled her eyes. Angry, she blinked them away.

She was beginning, at last, to understand Alfred.

Kleitus was systematically unraveling the magic. The blood-mottled, waxen hand made plucking motions in the air, as if he were ripping apart a woven rug. The glimmering rune-structure surrounding the ship was fading, flickering, dying. Kleitus was watching Alfred. Or rather, the trapped phantasm was watching Alfred. The shambling corpse of the Dynast paid the approaching Sartan scant attention, preferring to concentrate instead on the destruction of the ship's protective magic.

Alfred crept closer, the dog pressed against his leg, offering both its support and—if the truth be known—urging the reluctant Sartan along.

Alfred was terribly, horribly frightened, more frightened of this than he'd ever been of anything, even the red dragon in the Labyrinth. He looked at Kleitus and he saw himself. Saw—with awful fascination—the blood on the decomposing hands, saw the hunger for blood in the dead, living eyes. A hunger that might well become his own. He saw, in the brief flicker of the imprisoned phantasm, peering out of the moldering body, the suffering, the torment of a trapped soul. He saw . . .

Suffering.

Alfred stopped walking so suddenly that the dog pattered on ahead a few steps before realizing it was alone. Turning, the animal fixed Alfred with a stern look, suspecting he was about to cut and run.

This is a person suffering. This is a being in torment.

I've been thinking about this all wrong. I'm not going to kill this man. I'm going to give him rest, ease.

Keep thinking that, Alfred told himself, resuming his advance, somewhat stronger now. Keep thinking about that. Don't think about the fact that, in order to cast this spell, you must grasp the lazar's dead hands . . .

Kleitus ceased his work, turned to face Alfred. The phantasm flicked in and out of the eyes.

"Come to share immortal life?" the lazar asked.

". . . life . . ." moaned the phantasm.

"I . . . don't want immortality," Alfred managed to gasp from a throat closing with fear.

Somewhere on board the ship, Hugh the Hand watched and listened. Perhaps he was exultant. *Now* you understand!

Now I understand . . .

The lazar's bluish lips drew back in a smiling grimace.

The dog growled low in its chest.

"Stay behind," Alfred said softly, with a brief touch on the animal's head. "You can't do anything for me now."

The dog eyed him dubiously, then—hearing another word of command—fell back meekly, to watch and to wait.

"You are responsible!" Kleitus accused. The dead eyes were cold and empty, the living eyes filled with hatred . . . and pleading. "You brought this on us!"

". . . us . . ." hissed the echo.

"You brought it on yourselves," Alfred said sadly. He had to take hold of the dead hand. He stared at it, and his own flesh crawled. He saw again the long nails digging savagely into Marit's flesh. He felt them closing over his own throat.

Alfred tried to drive himself to do what he had to do . . . and then he had no choice.

Kleitus sprang at him. The hands of the lazar grappled for Alfred's neck, seeking to choke the life from him.

Acting on instinct, in self-defense, Alfred grabbed hold of the lazar's wrists. But instead of trying to break Kleitus's hold, Alfred clasped the lazar's hands even tighter, closed his eyes to blot out the horror of the murdered corpse's twisted, anguished face so near his own.

Alfred began to extend the circle of his being. He let his own soul flow into that of Kleitus. He sought to draw the tormented soul into his own.

"No!" the lazar said softly, "Yours will be mine!"

To his horror and astonishment, Alfred was suddenly aware of brutal hands reaching inside him. Kleitus had grasped hold of Alfred's soul and was attempting to wrench it from his body.

Alfred shrank back in panic, released his hold on Kleitus to defend himself. The battle was an unequal one, Alfred realized in despair. He could not win, because he had too much to lose. Kleitus had nothing, feared nothing.

Alfred heard shouts behind him. He was vaguely aware of the dog leaping and snarling, of Marit attempting to drive Kleitus away from his victim, of Balthazar frantically summoning weak magic.

But they could not save Alfred. The fight had been joined on an immortal plane. These others were like insects buzzing far, far away. Kleitus's dead hands were tearing apart Alfred's being as surely as they were ripping apart his flesh.

Alfred struggled, fought, and knew he was losing.

And then a powerful explosion of rune-magic dazzled his eyes. The starlit blast burst between him and his enemy. Kleitus reeled back, dead mouth open and screaming. The lazar's hands released Alfred's soul and he fell amid a shower of glittering runes, landing heavily on the dock.

Lying on his back, Alfred looked up, with fast-beating heart, to see a white-robed Sartan, standing above him.

"Samah . . ." Alfred murmured, his failing senses catching only the vague outline of the man's features.

"I am not Samah. I am Samah's son, Ramu," the Sartan corrected, his voice cold and flaring as the starbursts of his magic. "You are Alfred Montbank. What horror was that thing?"

Alfred, dazzled, dazed, clutched his soul to him and struggled to sit up. Fearful, he gazed around, bleary-eyed. Kleitus was nowhere to be seen. The lazar had vanished.

Destroyed? Alfred didn't think it likely.

Driven off, escaped. To wait. Bide its time. There would be other ships. Death's Gate would always be open . . .

Alfred shuddered. Marit knelt beside him, put her arm around him. The dog—which entertained bad memories of Ramu—stood over them both protectively.

Other white-robed Sartan were proceeding down the dock. Above them floated an enormous vessel, its blue protective Sartan runes flaring brightly in Abarrach's sullen, red-tinged darkness.

"Who is this Sartan? What does he want?" Marit demanded, suspicious.

Ramu's gaze was on her, on the sigla that flared defensively on her skin.

"I see we come in good time. The warning we received was well founded."

Alfred looked up, dazed. "What warning? Why *have* you come? Why did you leave Chelestra?"

Ramu was cold, grim. "We were warned that the Patryns had broken out of their prison, that they had launched an assault on the Final Gate. We are sailing to the Labyrinth. We intend to return the prisoners to their cells, keep them trapped there. We will close the Final Gate. We will make certain—once and for all—that our enemy never again escapes."

CHAPTER ◆ 20

SAFE HARBOR

ABARRACH

◆

Aᴄʀᴏꜱꜱ ᴛʜᴇ ꜰɪʀᴇ ꜱᴇᴀ, Xᴀʀ, ʟᴏʀᴅ ᴏꜰ ᴛʜᴇ ɴᴇxᴜꜱ, ꜱᴀᴡ ʜɪꜱ ᴄᴀʀᴇꜰᴜʟʟʏ ᴄᴏɴᴄᴇɪᴠᴇᴅ plans sucked down into chaos, like chunks of broken rock caught in the maelstrom.

The Sartan ship had appeared out of nowhere, materializing above the Fire Sea in a shimmering blaze of blue sigla. An enormous construction, long and sleek, with a swanlike shape, it hovered over the magma river as if loath to touch it. Those people aboard it dropped ladders of magic from the sides, rune-constructs that carried them down to the docks below.

Xar heard Ramu's words through Marit's ears, heard them as clearly as if he had been standing beside her. *We will close the Final Gate. We will make certain—once and for all—that our enemy never again escapes.*

The Sartan ship was visible to the Patryns waiting on board their own iron dragon ship, floating above the molten lava in the bay below. A group of them were now scaling the rocks, hastening to join their lord.

Xar remained standing, silent, unmoving.

Several Patryns, arriving on the promontory, prepared for action, came up against the high, chill wall of Xar's silence. He paid no attention to them, to their arrival. They glanced at each other, uncertain. Eventually, one of them—the eldest—moved forward.

"Sartan, My Lord!" he ventured.

Xar did not reply aloud. He nodded grimly, thought, We are outnumbered almost four to one.

"We will fight, Lord," said the Patryn eagerly. "Give us the word . . ."

Fight! Battle! Revenge at last on the ancient enemy. The anticipation, the desire clenched Xar's stomach, burned the breath from his lungs, nearly burst his heart. It was like being young again and waiting to meet a lover.

The fire was doused swiftly by the icy waters of logic.

"Ramu is lying," Xar said to himself. "This talk of going to the Labyrinth is a ruse, a diversion. He's hoping we'll abandon Abarrach. He wants this world for his own. He came here to find the Seventh Gate."

"My Lord!" cried the Patryn, peering across the Fire Sea. "They have captured Marit! They're taking her prisoner!"

"What is your command, Lord?" His people clamored for, yearned for blood.

Outnumbered four to one. Yet my people are strong. If I was with them . . .

"No." Xar spoke harshly. "Keep watch on the Sartan. See what they do, where they go. They claim they are bound for the Labyrinth."

"The Labyrinth, Lord!" His people must have heard rumors of the fighting there.

"They plan to finish us for good this time," one said.

"Over my dead body," said another.

Over many, many dead bodies, Xar thought. "I don't trust them," he said aloud. "I don't believe they really plan to go to the Labyrinth. However, it is well to be prepared. Don't interfere with them here. Make ready to sail. If they actually enter Death's Gate, follow them."

"Do we take all our people, Lord?"

Xar pondered a moment. "Yes," he said at last. If Ramu *was* sending his forces into the Labyrinth, the Patryns would need all the manpower they could muster. "Yes, take everyone. I put you in charge, Sadet. In my absence."

"But, My Lord—" The Patryn started to protest, to question.

Xar's flashing glare halted the words on the man's lips. "Yes, My Lord."

Xar waited to see his orders being carried out. The Patryns left the Anvil, slid down the rocks back to their iron ship below. Once they were gone and he was alone, the Lord of the Nexus began tracing a circle of fiery runes in the air. When the circle was complete, he stepped through it and vanished.

The Patryns left behind saw the sigla flare on top of the Anvil. They watched until the rune-circle had flickered and died. Then, slowly, cautiously, they eased their iron dragon ship out of the bay, moved into position to keep watch on their enemy, made ready to sail into Death's Gate.

"Fool Sartan, you have this all wrong!"

Surrounded by a shell of protective blue and red light, her own runes acting to defend her, Marit faced Ramu defiantly. In her hand she held her sigla-covered sword. "Ask one of your own, if you don't believe me. Ask Alfred. He has been in the Labyrinth! He has seen what is happening!"

"She is telling the truth," Alfred said earnestly. "The serpents —those you know as dragon-snakes—are the ones attempting to shut the Final Gate. The Patryns are defending themselves against this terrible evil. I know! I've been there!"

"Yes, you've been there." Ramu sneered. "And that is why I do not believe you. As my father said, you are more Patryn than Sartan."

"You can see the truth in my words—"[1]

Ramu rounded on him. "I see Patryns massing around the Final Gate. I see the city we built for them in flames. I see hordes of evil creatures, coming to their aid, *including* the dragon-snakes . . . Do you deny any of this?"

---

[1] The Sartan language is capable of causing images to form in the minds of those hearing the words. Alfred is projecting what he has seen to Ramu, who receives a clear picture of it as a result. The way he interprets that picture, however, is up to him.

"Yes," Alfred said, trying desperately to keep everyone calm, to keep the situation from deteriorating. "You see, Ramu, but you are *not* seeing!"

Marit could have told Alfred he was wasting his time.

Ramu could have told him he was wasting his time.

Alfred included them both in a despairing, pleading glance.

Marit ignored him.

Ramu turned away in disgust. "Some of you—disarm her." He gestured to Marit. "Take her prisoner, bring her on board her own ship. We will use that ship to transport our Abarrach brethren."

The Sartan moved to surround Marit. She paid no heed to them. Her gaze was fixed, intent on Ramu.

"Several of you come with me," he continued. "We will finish breaking down the rune-structure."

The odds were impossibly against Marit. She was weak from the effects of the poison, not completely healed. Yet she had determined to fight Ramu, to overwhelm and destroy him. Her fury at the sight of this sleek, complacent Sartan, talking so coolly of sentencing her people to further torment, when they were now fighting for their very lives, drove her to madness.

She would kill him, though killing him would cost her own life, for the other Sartan would be swift to retaliate.

That doesn't matter now anyway, she said to herself. I have lost Haplo. We will never find the Seventh Gate. I will never see him alive again. But I will see to it that his final wishes are carried out, that our people are safe. I will see to it that this Sartan does not make it to the Labyrinth.

The spell Marit was going to cast was powerful, deadly, and would take Ramu completely by surprise.

The fool had turned his back on her.

Having never before fought a Patryn, Ramu knew them only by repute, could have never conceived that Marit would be willing to sacrifice her own life to end his.

But Alfred knew, knew even before Haplo's voice warned him of what Marit was planning.

"I'll stop her," Haplo told him. "You deal with Ramu."

Still shaking from his terrible encounter with the lazar, Alfred prepared to work his magic. He peered dazedly into the possibilities—and discovered them so jumbled up and confused that he couldn't sort one from the other. Panic took hold of him. Marit was going to die. She was already speaking the runes; he could see her lips moving, though no sound came out. Ramu was walking off—but he would never, could never walk far enough. The dog was gathering itself together for a great leap . . .

And that gave Alfred an idea. He gathered *himself* together for a great leap.

The dog jumped at Marit.

Alfred jumped—arms and legs flailing wildly—straight at Ramu.

The dog hurled itself onto Marit's protective rune-shell. Sigla crackled and flared. The animal yelped in pain and fell, lifeless, to the wooden dock.

Marit cried out in dismay. The spell, her concentration, her will were shattered. She sank down beside the animal, gathered its limp head into her arms and bowed over it.

Alfred jumped on Ramu's back, knocked him flat.

For an instant, all was confusion.

The Councillor landed face first with a bone-breaking thud. The air left his lungs and, for a terrifying moment, he couldn't breathe. Flares burst in his vision; a heavy weight crushed him down, prevented him from drawing a breath.

And then the weight was suddenly removed. Hands helped him stand. Ramu rounded on his assailant, more furious than he'd ever been in his life.

Alfred jabbered incoherently, trying vainly to explain.

Ramu wasn't interested. "Traitor! Imprison him along with his Patryn friend!"

"No, Councillor," cried several Sartan. "The brother saved your life."

Ramu stared at them wordlessly, not believing, not wanting to believe.

They pointed to Marit.

She sat on the dock, the dog cradled in her arms. The sigla glimmered only faintly on her skin.

"She was going to attack you," one of the Sartan explained. "The brother threw himself on top of you, shielded you with his own body. If she had cast her spell, she would have killed him, Councillor, not you."

Ramu stared hard, intently at Alfred, who had suddenly ceased talking. He didn't look guilty or innocent, only extremely foolish and considerably confused. Ramu suspected the Sartan of some devious ulterior motive, though what that might be he couldn't begin to conceive. All would be made plain, no doubt.

The Patryn runes surrounding the Patryn ship were almost all destroyed. His people had worked swiftly and well. Ramu gave the orders to have both Marit and Alfred taken on board. The Patryn female, as one might have expected, seemed determined to resist, though she was so weak she could barely walk. She refused to leave the dog.

It was Alfred who finally convinced her to come.

He put his arm around her, whispered something to her—probably another plot. She suffered herself to be taken aboard, though she continued to look behind her at the dog.

Ramu thought the animal was dead, discovered his mistake when he walked up to it.

Snapping jaws missed his ankles by inches.

"Dog! Here, dog!" A scandalized Alfred whistled for the beast.

Ramu would have liked to have pitched it into the Fire Sea, but he would look ridiculous—venting his spleen on a dumb animal. He coldly ignored it, went on with his business.

The dog rose groggily to its feet, shook itself, and staggered—listing slightly to one side—after the Sartan and Marit.

Ramu left the docks, entered the main street of the abandoned town. He had arranged a meeting with the leader of the Abarrach Sartan, found the man—a necromancer, by report. Ramu was shocked at the sight of the man, who was pale, wasted, and weak. Recalling what he knew of the Sartan who lived on Abarrach (knowledge gained from Alfred), Ramu regarded this brother with pity and curiosity.

"My name is Balthazar," said the Sartan in the black robes. He smiled faintly. "Welcome to Abarrach, World of Stone, Brother."

Ramu didn't like that smile, didn't like the man's dark and piercing gaze. The black eyes jabbed—knifelike—through Ramu's head.

"Your greeting seems less than cordial, Brother," Ramu observed.

"Forgive me, Brother." Balthazar bowed stiffly. "We have been waiting over a thousand years to give it."

Ramu frowned.

Balthazar fixed his brother with the dagger-gaze. "We've been *dying* to see you."

Ramu's frown deepened. Angry words came to his lips, but at that moment, Balthazar shifted his gaze to his people, huddled, ragged, starving, and then to Ramu's people, well fed, well dressed, in excellent health. Ramu swallowed his anger, actually felt moved enough to be gracious.

"I am sorry for your plight, Brother. Truly sorry. We heard of it some time back from the one who calls himself Alfred. We would have come to your aid, but circumstances . . ."

Ramu's voice trailed off. Sartan cannot lie to each other and what he had been going to say was a lie. Samah had come to Abarrach, but not to help his desperate brethren. He had come to learn the necromancy.

Ramu had the grace to feel and look ashamed.

"We have had our troubles, too, though, I admit, not as dire as yours. If we had known . . . but I could not believe that false Sartan."

Ramu's grim gaze turned in the direction of Alfred, who was assisting a faltering Marit to board her own ship. Balthazar followed Ramu's glance, looked back at the Councillor.

"The one of whom you speak so disparagingly has been the only one of our people to help us," Balthazar returned. "Even though he was shocked and appalled—rightly so—by what we had done to ourselves, to this world, he did what he could to save lives."

"He had his reasons, you may be sure," Ramu said, sneering.

"Yes, I believe he did," Balthazar replied. "Pity, mercy, compassion. And why have *you* come to us now?" he asked coolly, catching Ramu by surprise.

The Councillor was not accustomed to being confronted in this insolent manner, nor did he like this Sartan. The words he spoke were Sartan words, but—as Alfred had discovered when he had first visited Abarrach—they conjured up images of death and suffering, images that Ramu found quite distasteful. He was forced, however, into admitting the truth. He hadn't come to give aid, but to beg for it.

Briefly, he explained what was happening in the Labyrinth, how the Patryns were attempting to break out of their prison, how they would—undoubtedly—seek to rule the four worlds.

"Whereas we alone should be allowed to rule," Balthazar said. "As we have ruled here. Look around you. See what a magnificent job we've done."

Ramu was outraged, but he took care not to let his anger show. He sensed in this black-robed Sartan a latent power, a power perhaps as great as Ramu's own. Looking ahead into the future, a future where the Sartan *would* rule the four worlds, the Councillor saw a potential rival. One who knew the necromancy. It would never do to reveal weakness.

"Take your people on board our ships," Ramu said. "We will give them aid and succor. I presume you want to leave this world?" he added, with his own measure of sarcasm.

Balthazar paled; the dark eyes narrowed. "Yes," he said quietly, "we want to leave. We are grateful to you, Brother, for making this possible. Grateful for any aid you can give us."

"And, in turn, I will be grateful for any aid you can give me," Ramu replied.

He guessed they understood each other, though what the necromancer might be thinking was as murky as the poisonous air in this hellish cavern.

Ramu bowed and left. He saw no point in continuing the conversation. Time was running out; every moment that passed was a moment the Patryns were nearer to breaking free.

Once Balthazar was healed and fed and rested, once he was

inside the Nexus and came face to face with the savage Patryns, he would understand. He would fight. Of that, Ramu was confident. Balthazar would use every means at his disposal to win the battle. Including the necromancy. And he'd be happy to teach it to others. Ramu would see to that.

He returned to the docks to make preparations for the Sartan of Abarrach to be transported onto the former Patryn ship. Boarding, he made a quick inspection, began working out his strategy.

The journey to the Nexus, through Death's Gate, would ordinarily be a quick one. But now he'd have to allow time for these Abarrach Sartan to heal, if they were going to make an effective fighting force.

Considering this, trying to figure how long the healing would take, Ramu came across Alfred. The Sartan leaned dolefully against the ship's rail. The dog crouched, tense and nervous, at his side. The Patryn female sat huddled dejectedly on the deck. Sartan stood guard at her side.

Ramu frowned. The Patryn female was taking all this much too calmly. She'd surrendered too easily. So had Alfred. They must be plotting something . . .

A strong arm grabbed Ramu from behind, encircled his throat. A sharp object prodded him in the ribs.

"I don't know who you are, you bastard, or why you're here," grated a harsh voice—a mensch voice—in Ramu's ear. "I don't much care. But if you so much as twitch I'll drive this knife into your heart. Let Marit and Alfred go."

CHAPTER ◆ 21

SAFE HARBOR

ABARRACH

◆

ALFRED HAD BEEN LEANING OVER THE SHIP'S RAIL, STARING AT NOTHING, WON-dering despairingly what to do. On the one hand, it seemed vitally important that he travel to the Labyrinth with Ramu.

I have to continue to try to make the Councillor understand the true situation. Make him understand that the serpents are the true enemy, that the Patryns and Sartan *must* join forces against this evil or it will end up devouring us.

"Not only ourselves," Alfred said to himself, "but the mensch. We brought them to these worlds, they're our responsibility."

Yes, in this his duty was clear, although just how he was going to convince Ramu of the danger was rather foggy in Alfred's mind at this moment.

But, on the other hand, there was Haplo.

"I can't leave you," Alfred argued, and waited in some trepida-tion for Haplo to argue back. But his friend's voice had been strangely silent lately, ever since he had ordered the dog to stop Marit. This silence was ominous, made Alfred uneasy. He won-dered if it was Haplo's way of forcing them to leave him. Haplo would sacrifice himself in a minute if he thought that by doing so he could help his people . . .

All this was what Alfred had been thinking when Marit sprang to her feet with a startled cry.

"Alfred!" She clutched at his arm, nearly sent him backward over the rail. "Alfred! Look!"

"Blessed Sartan!" Alfred whispered in shock.

He had forgotten about Hugh the Hand, had forgotten that the assassin was on board the ship. And now Hugh had hold of Ramu, had the Cursed Blade pointed at the Sartan's throat.

Alfred understood all too clearly what must have happened.

Hidden in the cabin, Hugh had witnessed the arrival of the Sartan. He had watched them take Marit and Alfred captive. His one thought—as their friend and companion and self-appointed bodyguard—would be to secure their freedom. His only weapon—the Sartan blade.

But he could not realize that these were the very Sartan who had forged that blade.

"Don't any of you move," Hugh the Hand warned, his gaze taking in all on board the ship. He clenched Ramu tighter, nearly bending the man over backward. The Hand exhibited enough of the knife to the horrified watchers to let them know he was in earnest. "Or your leader will find six inches of steel in his neck. Alfred, Marit, come over and stand by me."

Alfred didn't move. He couldn't.

How will the magical blade react? he wondered frantically. Its first loyalty was to its wielder, Hugh the Hand. The knife might well stab Ramu—especially if he attempted to use magic against it —before it knew its mistake.

And if Ramu died, there would be an end to all hope of bringing the Patryns and Sartan together.

As it was, the other Sartan were staring at the two in amazement, not quite realizing what was going on. Ramu himself appeared stunned. Probably never in his life had such an outrage been perpetrated against him. He didn't know how to react. But he was quick-thinking. He soon would . . .

"Councillor!" Alfred cried desperately. "The weapon that man holds is a magic one. *Don't* use magic against it! That will only make things worse!"

"Well done!" Marit said to him softly. "Keep him busy."

Alfred was horrified. She'd completely misread his intentions. "No, Marit. I didn't mean that . . . Marit, don't . . ."

She wasn't listening. Her sword lay on the deck, guarded by Sartan. Sartan who were staring in stunned disbelief at their leader. Marit grabbed her sword easily, ran across the deck toward Hugh. Alfred tried to stop her, but he wasn't watching where he was going and fell headlong over the dog. The animal, yelping painfully, bristled and barked at everyone on general principle.

The Sartan, confused, looked to Ramu for orders.

"Please! Stay calm. Don't anybody do anything!" Alfred was pleading, but no one heard him over the dog's frantic barks, and it would probably have made no difference if they had.

At that moment, Ramu cast a paralyzing jolt of electricity through Hugh's body.

Hugh collapsed, writhing in agony. But the jolt did more than fell the assassin. The shock galvanized the Cursed Blade. It recognized the magic—Sartan magic—recognized the fact that Hugh, the one who wielded the blade, was in peril. The blade sensed Marit, approaching at a run, as the enemy.

The Cursed Blade reacted. As it had been trained to do, it summoned the strongest force available in the vicinity to fight its foe.

Kleitus the lazar appeared on the deck of the ship. Within the space of a heartbeat, the dead of Abarrach were crawling up and over the ship's rails.

"Control the magic!" Alfred cried. "Ramu—you have to regain control of the magic!"

The blade had merely summoned the dead to its aid; it had no control over them. Control was not the blade's purpose. Having fulfilled its creator's intent, it changed back to its original form, fell to the deck beside a groaning Hugh the Hand.

Kleitus lunged for Marit, his wasted hands grasping for her throat. Marit struck him with her sword—a blow that sliced open one of the bony arms. No blood flowed; the dead flesh hung in tatters. Kleitus never felt the wound.

Marit could strike the lazar as often as she liked, without the least effect. Its nails scraped across her skin, and she gasped in pain. She was weakening rapidly. She could not last long against the formidable lazar.

The dog jumped at Kleitus. A savage kick sent the animal rolling. Now there was no one to help Marit, even if they could have. The Sartan on board ship were battling for their own lives.

Summoned by the blade, the dead smelled the warm blood of the living, a smell they craved and hated. Ramu watched, helpless and appalled, as the lazar attacked his people.

Alfred bumbled his way through the melee, disrupting magic, tripping up the shambling corpses, leaving confusion and chaos in his wake. But he managed to reach Ramu.

"These dead . . . are ours!" Ramu whispered, awed. "This horror . . . our people . . ."

Alfred ignored him. "The blade! Where's the blade?"

He had seen it fall near Hugh the Hand. He knelt by the assassin's side, searched frantically for the knife. He couldn't find it. The blade was gone. Tramping feet had kicked it aside, perhaps.

Marit was nearly finished. The sigla on her skin no longer glowed. She had dropped the useless sword, was fighting Kleitus with her bare hands. The lazar was slowly choking the life out of her.

"Here!" Hugh the Hand rolled over, shoved something at Alfred. It was the knife. He'd been lying on it, his body hiding it.

Alfred hesitated, but only an instant. If this was what it took to save Marit . . . He picked up the blade, felt it squirm in his hand. He was about to launch an attack at Kleitus when a black-robed form stopped him.

"Our creation," said Balthazar grimly. "Our responsibility."

The necromancer advanced on Kleitus. Intent on its kill, the lazar was unaware of Balthazar's approach.

The necromancer reached out, took hold of one of Kleitus's arms, and began to speak the words of a spell.

Balthazar had hold of Kleitus's soul.

Feeling the dread touch, realizing his doom, Kleitus released Marit. With a fearful shriek, the lazar turned on Balthazar, attempted to destroy the necromancer's soul.

The battle was a strange and terrifying one, for it appeared to those watching that the two were locked in an embrace, an embrace which might have been—but for the hideous contortion of the faces—a loving one.

Balthazar was nearly as pale as a corpse himself, but he held firm. A slight gasp escaped him. Kleitus's dead eyes widened. The phantasm flitted in and out of the lazar's body, a prisoner longing for freedom yet fearful of venturing into the unknown.

Balthazar forced Kleitus to his knees. The lazar's screams and curses were frightful to hear, echoed mournfully by the man's own soul.

And then Balthazar's grim expression relaxed. His hands, which had been exerting deadly force, eased their grip, though they held the lazar firmly.

"Let go," he said. "The torment is ended."

Kleitus made a final, desperate effort, but the necromancer's spell had strengthened the phantasm, weakened the decaying body. The phantasm wrenched itself free. The body crumpled, collapsed onto the deck. The phantasm hovered over it, regretfully; then it drifted off, as if blown away by the breath of a whispered prayer.

Alfred's shaking hand closed tightly over the blade's hilt. "Stop!" He gave the magical command to the blade in a quivering voice.

The battle ended abruptly. The lazar, either frightened by the loss of their leader or commanded by the magic of the blade, broke off the attack. The dead disappeared.

Balthazar, weak almost to the point of falling, turned slowly.

"Still want to learn necromancy?" Balthazar asked Ramu with a strained and bitter smile.

Ramu looked down at the ghastly remains of the Sartan who had once been the Dynast of Abarrach. The Councillor made no reply.

Balthazar shrugged. He knelt down beside Marit, began to do what he could to aid her.

Alfred started to go to Marit, discovered Ramu blocking his way.

Before Alfred quite knew what was happening, Ramu had

taken hold of the Cursed Blade, wrenched it from Alfred's grasp. The Councillor examined the knife curiously at first, and then with dawning recognition.

"Yes," he said quietly. "I remember weapons like this."

"Heinous weapons," Alfred said in a low voice. "Designed to help the mensch kill. And be killed in their turn. For us—their protectors, their defenders. Their gods."

Ramu flushed in swift anger. But he could not deny the truth of the words, or deny the ugly thing he held in his hand. The blade quivered with life. Ramu grimaced; his hand flinched. He seemed loath to touch it, but he could not very well relinquish it.

"Let me have it," said Alfred.

Ramu thrust it into the belt of his robes.

"No, Brother. As Balthazar said, it is our responsibility. You may leave it in my care. Safely," he added, his gaze meeting Alfred's.

"Let him have it," said Hugh the Hand. "I'll be glad to be rid of the damn thing."

"Councillor," Alfred begged, "you've seen what terrible forces our power can unleash. You've seen the evil we've brought on ourselves and others. Don't perpetuate it . . ."

Ramu snorted. "What happened here the Patryn brought on herself. She and her kind will continue to cause disruption unless they are finally halted. We sail for the Labyrinth, as planned. You had best prepare for departure."

He walked off.

Alfred sighed. Well, at least when they reached the Labyrinth he would see to it that . . .

At any rate he would . . .

Or then he might . . .

Confused, miserable, he tried once again to go to Marit.

This time, the dog blocked his way.

Alfred attempted to circle around the animal.

The dog thwarted him, dodging to its left when Alfred went to his right, jumped to its right when Alfred veered to his left. Becoming hopelessly entangled in his own feet, Alfred halted. He regarded the animal with perplexity.

"What are you doing? Why are you keeping me away from Marit?"

The dog barked loudly.

Alfred attempted to shoo it aside.

The dog would not be shooed and, in fact, took offense at the suggestion. It growled and bared its teeth at him.

Startled, Alfred stumbled several steps backward.

The dog, pleased, trotted forward.

"But . . . Marit! She needs me," Alfred said and made a clumsy attempt to outflank the dog.

Quick off the mark, as if it were herding sheep, the dog swerved in. Nipping at Alfred's ankles, the animal continued to drive him backward across the deck.

Balthazar raised his head; the black eyes pierced Alfred.

"She will be well cared for, I promise you, Brother. Go do what you must without fear for her. As to the people of the Labyrinth, I have heard what you said. I will make my own judgments, based on the hard lessons I have learned. Farewell, Alfred." Balthazar added, with a smile, "Or whatever your name might be."

"But I'm not going anywhere—" Alfred protested.

The dog leapt, hit Alfred squarely in the chest, and knocked him over the ship's rail, into the Fire Sea.

CHAPTER ◆ 22

FIRE SEA

ABARRACH

◆

SNAPPING JAWS CAUGHT HOLD OF THE COLLAR OF ALFRED'S FRAYED VELVET coat. A gigantic dragon—its scales the red-orange of the flaming sea in which it lived—caught the Sartan in midair and carried him, curled up like a frightened spider, to her back, where she deposited him gently. The dog's teeth sank into the rear of his breeches, took firm hold of him, steadied him.

Alfred required several moments to recover himself, to realize that he was *not* being immolated in the Fire Sea. He was, instead, seated on the back of a fire dragon next to Hugh the Hand and the lazar Jonathon.

"What?" Alfred gasped feebly, and could only continue to repeat the word in a confused manner. "What? What?"

No one answered him. Jonathon was speaking to the fire dragon. Hugh the Hand, a cloth over his nose and mouth, was doing his best to try to stay alive.

"You might help him," Haplo advised.

Alfred emitted a final faint "What?" Then, compassion causing him to forget about himself, he began to sing a song in his reedy, thin voice, his hands fluttering, weaving the magic around Hugh the Hand. The mensch coughed, retched, drew in a deep breath—and looked startled.

"Who said that?" Hugh the Hand eyed Alfred; then, his eyes

widening, he stared at the dog. "I heard Haplo's voice! That animal has learned to talk!"

Alfred gargled. "How can he hear you? I don't understand . . . Of course," he added on reflection, "I'm not certain how *I* can hear you."

"The mensch is as much in my realm as I am in his," Haplo said. "He hears my voice. So does Jonathon. I asked Jonathon to bring the fire dragon here, to snatch you off that ship, if necessary."

"But . . . why?"

"Do you remember what we talked about, back in Salfag Caverns? How the Sartan would go out into the four worlds and then the Patryns after them and the fighting would start all over again?"

"Yes," Alfred said quietly, sadly.

"That gave me an idea, made me realize what we had to do to stop Xar's threat, to help both our peoples, and the mensch. I was trying to think of the best way to go about it, when suddenly Ramu arrived and took the matter out of my hands. He settled everything far better than I could have. And so I—"

"But . . . Ramu's going to the Labyrinth!" Alfred cried. "To fight your people!"

"Precisely." Haplo was grim. "That's just where I want him."

"It is?" Alfred was beyond amazement, well into bewilderment.

"It is. I explained my plan to Jonathon. He agreed to accompany us, so long as we brought Hugh the Hand with us."

"Us." Alfred gulped.

"I'm sorry, old friend." Haplo's voice softened. "I didn't want you involved. But Jonathon insisted. He's right. I need you."

"For what?" Alfred was about to ask, wondered unhappily if he truly wanted to know.

The fire dragon skimmed across the lava sea, heading for the shoreline, for Necropolis. Marit's ship, now bright with Sartan runes, was preparing to depart, as was the Sartan ship from Chelestra. Alfred glanced up as their dragon sailed beneath the prow and caught a glimpse of Ramu, glaring at them. The Councillor was grim, stony-faced. He turned coldly away. Probably considered Alfred's abrupt departure good riddance. One person, watching from the rail, did not turn away. Balthazar raised his hand in farewell.

"I will take care of Marit," he called out. "Have no fear for her."

Alfred waved disconsolately back. He recalled the necromancer's words, spoken just before the dog tumbled Alfred over the side.

Go do what you must . . .

Which was? . . .

"Would someone mind telling me what's happening?" Alfred asked meekly. "Where are you taking me?"

"To the Seventh Gate," Haplo replied.

Alfred lost his grip on the dragon's mane, nearly fell overboard. This time it was Hugh the Hand who caught hold of him. "But . . . Lord Xar . . ."

"A risk we have to take," Haplo replied.

Alfred shook his head.

"Listen, my friend." Haplo spoke earnestly. "This is the chance you've wanted. Look—look at the ships sailing away, sailing for Death's Gate."

Alfred lifted his gaze. The two ships, both flaring with Sartan runes, soared up into the smoke-tinged air of Abarrach. The sigla glowed brilliant blue against the black shadows of the vast cavern's ceiling. Both ships, under Ramu's guidance, were headed for Death's Gate. And beyond that, the Nexus, the Labyrinth, the four worlds.

"And there!" Jonathon lifted his wasted, waxen hand, pointed. "There, look what follows."

". . . follows . . ." mourned the echo.

Another ship, this one forged in the shape of an iron dragon, covered with Patryn runes, soared up from a hidden bay. It was taking the same course as the Sartan ship, its sigla burning red with the heat and the magical power that propelled it.

"Patryns!" Alfred said, staring in disbelief. "Where are they going?"

"They are chasing Ramu. He will lead them to the Labyrinth, where they will join the battle."

"Perhaps Xar is with them?" Alfred was hopeful.

"Perhaps . . ." Haplo wasn't.

Alfred heaved a deep sigh. "But this accomplishes nothing . . . except more bloodshed . . ."

"Think about it, my friend. The Sartan and the Patryns—now gathered together in one place. All of them in the Labyrinth. And with them—the serpents."

Alfred raised his head, blinked.

"Blessed Sartan," he murmured. He was beginning to see, beginning to understand.

"The worlds: Arianus, Pryan, Chelestra, Abarrach—free of them. Free of us. The elves and humans and dwarves left to live and die, love and hate all on their own. No interference from demigods or the evil we create."

"That's all very well now," Alfred pointed out, hope slipping again. "But the Sartan won't stay in the Labyrinth. Neither will your people. No matter who wins . . . or loses."

"That's why we have to find the Seventh Gate," Haplo said. "We find it . . . and we destroy it."

Alfred was amazed. Then appalled. The enormity of the task confounded him. It was too unreal even to be frightening.

Bitter, mortal enemies, with a legacy of hatred passed down through generations, locked up in a prison of their own creation with an immortal enemy: a product of their hatred. Sartan, Patryn, serpents—battling through eternity with no way to escape.

Or was there no way? Alfred looked over at the dog, reached out his hand to give it a timid pat. He and Haplo had once been mortal, bitter enemies. Alfred thought about Marit and Balthazar, two enemies drawn together by shared suffering, sorrow.

A handful of seeds, fallen onto burned, charred ground, had taken root, found nourishment in love, pity, compassion. If these seeds could blossom and grow strong, why not others?

The dread city of Necropolis was very close now, the fire dragon sailing toward it rapidly. Alfred couldn't believe this was happening to him and wondered rather wistfully if he weren't really on that Sartan ship, perhaps suffering from a blow to the head.

But the mane of the fire dragon, with its glistening bright red scales, pricked his flesh uncomfortably. The heat from the Fire Sea radiated around him. Beside him, the dog shivered in terror (it had never grown accustomed to riding dragon-back) and Hugh the Hand stared around at this strange new world in awe. Near him sat Jonathon—like Hugh, dead, not dead. One brought back by love, the other by hate.

Perhaps there was hope, after all. Or perhaps . . .

"Destroying the Seventh Gate might well destroy everything," he observed in a low voice, after giving the matter some thought.

Haplo was silent a moment, then said, "And what will happen when Ramu and the Sartan arrive in the Labyrinth, along with my people and Lord Xar? The wars they wage will be meat and drink to the evil of the dragon-snakes, who will grow fat and sleek and urge them on. Perhaps my people will flee through Death's Gate. Your people will chase after them. The battles will escalate, expand out into the four worlds. The mensch will be sucked in, as they were the last time. We will arm them, give them weapons like the Cursed Blade.

"You see the dilemma we face, my friend," Haplo added, after a pause to allow Alfred a good long look. "You understand?"

Alfred shuddered. He covered his face with his hands. "What will happen to the worlds if we do shut Death's Gate?" He lifted his head. His face was pale, his voice quivering. "They need each other. The citadels need the energy from the Kicksey-winsey. Such energy could stabilize the sun in Chelestra. And because of the citadels, the conduits on Abarrach are starting to carry water . . ."

"If the mensch have to, they can manage on their own," Haplo said. "What would be better for them, my friend? To allow them to control their own destiny? Or to be pawns in ours?"

Alfred sat hunched in silent thought. He glanced back, one last time, at the ships. The Sartan vessels gleamed faintly, bright specks against the darkness. The Patryn ship tracked them, magic burning.

"You are right, Haplo," Alfred said, with a deep sigh. He stared after the ships. "You let Marit go with them."

"I had to," Haplo said quietly. "She is marked by Lord Xar's sigil, bound to him. He would know our plans through her. Besides, there's another reason."

Alfred drew in a shivering breath.

"In destroying the Seventh Gate, we may well destroy ourselves," Haplo said calmly. "I am sorry to bring this fate upon you, my friend, but, as I said, I need you. I couldn't do this without you."

Alfred's eyes dimmed with tears. For long minutes, he couldn't speak for the lump in his throat. If Haplo had been there, Alfred would have reached out, clasped his friend's hand. Haplo wasn't. His body lay, still and lifeless, back in the chill dungeon cell. It was difficult to touch a spirit, but Alfred did his best. He reached out his hand anyway. The dog, with a glad bark, jumped down to be comforted. The animal would be relieved to get off the dragon.

Alfred smoothed the silky fur.

"This is the greatest compliment you could have paid me, Haplo. You are right. We must take this chance."

Alfred continued to pet the dog's head; his hand began to tremble slightly. He spoke his doubts aloud. "But have you considered, my friend, the doom we might bring on our people? By closing Death's Gate, we seal off their only escape route. They could be trapped forever inside the Labyrinth, forever battling the serpents, forever battling each other."

"I've thought about that," Haplo answered. "The choice would be theirs, wouldn't it? To keep fighting . . . or to try to find peace. And remember, the good dragons are in the Labyrinth now, too. The Wave could correct itself."

"Or drown us all," Alfred said.

CHAPTER ◆ 23

NECROPOLIS

ABARRACH

◆

The fire dragon carried them as near the city of Necropolis as she could, swimming into the very bay in which the Patryns had been hiding their ship. The dragon kept close to shore, avoiding the massive whirlpool rotating slowly in the center of the bay. Alfred glanced once at the whirlpool, at the molten rock sluggishly spiraling downward, at the steam and smoke lazily coiling up from the gaping maw in the center. He hastily averted his gaze.

"I always knew there was something strange about that dog," remarked Hugh the Hand.

Alfred smiled tremulously; then the smile faded. There was one other problem he had to resolve. One for which he had to take responsibility.

"Sir Hugh," Alfred began hesitantly, "did you understand . . . any of what you heard?"

Hugh the Hand eyed him shrewdly, shrugged. "Doesn't seem to me it much matters whether I understand or not, does it?"

"No," Alfred answered in some confusion. "I guess it doesn't." He cleared his throat. "We're . . . um . . . going to a place known as the Seventh Gate. Here, I think . . . I believe . . . I may be wrong, but—"

"That's where I'll die?" Hugh asked bluntly.

Alfred gulped, licked dry lips. His face burned, and not from the heat of the Fire Sea. "If that is truly what you want . . ."

"I do," Hugh the Hand said firmly. "I'm not supposed to be here. I'm a ghost. Things happen and I can't feel them anymore."

"I don't understand." Alfred was puzzled. "It wasn't that way at the beginning. When I"—he swallowed, but he *had* to take responsibility—"when I first brought you back."

"Perhaps I can explain," Jonathon offered. "When Hugh came back to the realm of the living, he left that of the dead far behind. He clung to life, to the people in his life. Thus he remained closely bound to the living. But one by one, he has severed those ties. He has come to realize that he has nothing more to give them. They have nothing to give him. He had everything. And now he can only mourn its loss."

". . . loss . . ." sighed the echo.

"But there was a woman who loved him," Alfred said in a low voice. "She loves him still."

"Her love is only a very small fraction of the love he found. Mortal love is our introduction to the immortal."

Alfred was chagrined, aggrieved.

"Don't be too hard on yourself, Brother," Jonathon said. The phantasm entered the body, gleamed in the dead eyes. "You used the necromancy out of compassion, not for gain or hatred or vengeance. Those among the living who have encountered this man have learned from him—some to their despair and fear. But he has given others hope."

Alfred sighed, nodded. He still didn't understand, not completely, but he thought he might perhaps forgive himself.

"Good luck in your endeavors," said the dragon, when she deposited them on the jagged-toothed shore surrounding the Firepool. "And if you are responsible for ridding the world of those who have ravaged it, you have my gratitude."

They meant well, Alfred said to himself. That seemed the saddest indictment of all.

Samah meant well. The Sartan all meant well. Undoubtedly Ramu meant well. Maybe even, in his own way, Xar meant well.

They simply lacked imagination.

Though the dragon had taken them as near as she could, the journey from the bay to Necropolis was still a long one, particularly on foot. Particularly on Alfred's feet. He had no sooner stumbled onto shore when he nearly fell into a bubbling pool of boiling-hot mud. Hugh the Hand dragged him back from the edge.

"Use your magic," Haplo suggested wryly, "or you'll never make it to the Chamber of the Damned alive."

Alfred considered this suggestion, hesitated. "I can't take us inside the Chamber itself."

"Why not? All you have to do is visualize it in your mind. You've been there before." Haplo sounded irritated.

"Yes, but the warding runes would prevent us from entering. They would block my magic. Besides"—Alfred sighed—"I can't see it all that clearly. I believe I must have blotted it out of my memory. It was a horrifying experience."

"In some ways," Haplo said, thoughtful. "Not in others."

"Yes, you are right about that."

Though neither would admit it at the time, their experience in the Chamber of the Damned had brought the two enemies closer together, had proved to them that they were not as different as each had believed.

"I remember one part," Alfred said softly. "I remember the part where we entered the minds and bodies of those who lived—and died—in that Chamber centuries ago . . ."

. . . A sense of regret and sadness filled Alfred. And though painful to him, the feelings of sorrow and unhappiness were better —far better—than not feeling anything, the emptiness he'd experienced before joining this brotherhood. Then he had been a husk, a shell containing nothing. The dead—dreadful creations of those who were beginning to dabble in necromancy—had more life than he. Alfred sighed deeply, lifted his head. A glance around the table revealed feelings similar to his softening the faces of the men and women gathered together in this sacred chamber.

His sadness, his regret wasn't bitter. Bitterness comes to those who have brought tragedy on themselves through their own mis-

deeds. But unless they changed, Alfred foresaw a time for his people when bitter sorrow must encompass them all. The madness
must be halted. He sighed again. Just moments before, he had been
radiant with joy; peace had spread like a balm over the boiling
magma sea of his doubts and fears. But that heady sense of exalta-
tion could not last in this world. He must return to face its problems and perils and, thus, the sadness, the regret.

A hand reached out, clasped his. The hand's grip was firm, the
skin smooth and unwrinkled, a contrast to Alfred's aged, parch-
ment-paper skin, his weakened grasp.

"Hope, Brother," said the young man quietly. "We must have
hope."

Alfred turned to look at the young man seated beside him. The
Sartan's face was handsome, strong, resolute—fine steel emerging
from a forging fire. No doubts marred its shining surface; its blade
was honed to a sharp, cutting edge. The young man looked familiar to Alfred. He could almost put a name to him, but not quite.

Now he could. The man had been Haplo.

Alfred smiled. "I remember the feeling of elation, of knowing
that I wasn't alone in the universe, that a higher power was watching over me, caring for me and about me. I remember that, for the
first time in my life, I wasn't afraid."

He paused, shook his head. "But that's all I do remember."

"Very well," Haplo said, resigned. "You can't take us to the
Chamber. Where *can* you take us? How close can we come?"

"Your dungeon cell?" Alfred suggested in a low, subdued
voice.

Haplo was silent. Then, "If that's the best you can do, do it," he
muttered.

Alfred invoked the possibility that they were there and not here
and, quite suddenly, they were there.

"Ancestors protect me," Hugh the Hand murmured.

They stood in the cell. A sigil, formed by Alfred, glowed with a soft white radiance above Haplo's body. The Patryn lay cold and seemingly lifeless on the stone bed.

"He's dead!" Hugh cast a dark and suspicious glance at the dog. "Then whose voice am I hearing?"

Alfred was about to launch into an explanation—all about the dog and Haplo's soul—when the dog sank its teeth into Alfred's velvet breeches and began tugging him toward the cell door.

A thought occurred to Alfred. "Haplo. What . . . what will happen to you?"

"It doesn't matter," Haplo said shortly. "Get moving. We don't have much time. If Xar should find us—"

Alfred gasped. "But you said Lord Xar went to the Labyrinth!"

"I said *maybe*," Haplo retorted grimly. "Stop wasting time."

Alfred wavered. "The dog can't enter Death's Gate. Maybe it can't enter the Seventh Gate, either. Not without you. Jonathon, do you know? What will happen?"

The lazar shrugged. "Haplo is not dead. He lives, though only barely. My care is for those who have passed beyond."

". . . beyond . . ."

"You don't have any choice, Alfred," Haplo said impatiently. "Get on with it!"

The dog growled.

Alfred sighed. He had a choice. There was always a choice. And he always seemed to make the wrong one. He peered down the hallway that traveled into impenetrable night. The white sigil he had lit above Haplo's body faded; its light died. They stood blind in the darkness.

Alfred thought back a long, long time, to when he had first met Haplo on Arianus. He remembered the night he'd cast the magical sleep on Haplo, had lifted the bandages that hid his hands, had discovered the sigla tattooed on the flesh. Alfred recalled his despair, his stark terror, his bewilderment.

The ancient enemy has returned! What do I do?

And in the end, he'd done very little, it seemed. Nothing calamitous or catastrophic. He had followed the precepts of his heart, had acted for what he believed to be the best. *Was* there a higher power guiding his way?

Alfred looked down at the dog, crowding against his leg. At that moment, he thought he understood.

He began to sing the runes softly, in a nasal tone that echoed eerily in the tunnel.

Blue sigla flared to life on the base of the wall at his feet. The darkness was banished.

"What's that?" Hugh the Hand had been standing near the wall. At the flare of magic, he jumped away from it.

"The runes," said Alfred. "They will lead us to what is known on this world as the Chamber of the Damned."

"Sounds appropriate," Hugh the Hand said dryly.

The last time Alfred had made this journey, he'd been running in fear for his life. He thought he'd forgotten the way, but now that the runes were flickering—lighting the darkness—he began to recognize his surroundings.

The corridor sloped downward, as if it were leading them to the very core of the world. Obviously ancient, but in good repair, the tunnel—unlike most of the catacombs in this unstable world—was smooth and wide. It had been intended to accommodate vast numbers of people. Alfred had thought this odd the last time he'd walked this path. But then, he hadn't known where the corridor led.

Now he knew and now he understood. The Seventh Gate. The place from which the Sartan had worked the magic that had sundered a world.

"Do you have any idea how the magic worked?" Haplo asked. He spoke in a hushed, subdued voice, though only inner ears could hear him.

"Orlah told me," Alfred replied, pausing occasionally in his explanation to softly chant the runes. "After they made the decision to sunder the world, Samah and the Council members brought together all the Sartan population and those of the mensch they deemed worthy. They transported these fortunate few to a place which was probably similar to the time well we saw used in Abri—a well in which there exists the possibility that no possibilities exist. Here the people would be safe until the Sartan could transport them to the new worlds.

"The most talented of the Sartan came together with Samah inside a chamber he termed the Seventh Gate. Aware that the casting of such powerful magic, which would break apart one world and forge new ones, would drain the strongest magic-user, Samah and the Council endowed the chamber itself with a great deal of their power. It would operate rather like one of the Kicksey-winsey machines Limbeck calls a 'gen'rator.'

"The Seventh Gate stored up the magical power left there in reserve. The Sartan called on it when their own magic waned and diminished. The danger was, of course, that once the power was transferred to the Seventh Gate, the magic would always remain inside. Only by destroying the Seventh Gate could Samah destroy the magic. He should have done so, of course, but he was afraid."

"Of what?" Haplo demanded.

Alfred hesitated. "Upon first entering the Seventh Gate, after they had endowed it with power, the Council members encountered something they hadn't expected."

"A power greater than their own."

"Yes. I'm not sure how or why; Orlah couldn't tell me much. The experience was an awful one for the Sartan. Rather like what we experienced when we entered. But whereas ours was comforting and uplifting, theirs was terrible. Samah was made aware of the enormity of his actions, of the horrendous consequences of what he planned. He was given to know that he had—in essence—overstepped his bounds. But he was also made aware that he had the free will to continue, if he chose.

"Appalled by what they had seen and heard, the Council members began to doubt themselves. This led to violent arguments. But their fear of their enemy—the Patryns—was great. The memory of the experience in the Chamber faded. The Patryn threat was very real. Led by Samah, the Council voted to proceed with the Sundering. Those Sartan who opposed them were cast, along with the Patryns, into the Labyrinth."

Alfred shook his head. "Fear—our downfall. Even after he had successfully sundered a world and built four new ones, after he had locked his enemies into prison, Samah was still afraid. He feared what he had discovered inside the Seventh Gate, but he also feared he might have need of the Seventh Gate again and so, instead of destroying it, he sent it away."

"I was with Samah when he died," Jonathon said. "He told Lord Xar he did not know where the Seventh Gate was."

"Probably not," Alfred conceded. "But Samah could have found it easily enough. He had my description to go on—I told him all about the Chamber of the Damned."

"My people found it," Jonathon said. "We recognized its power, but we had forgotten how to use it."

". . . use it . . ." repeated the echo.

"Something for which we should be grateful. Can you imagine what would have happened had Kleitus discovered how to use the true power of the Seventh Gate?" Alfred shuddered.

"What I find interesting is that through all the magical upheaval and turmoil, those we derisively refer to as 'the mensch' prevailed. The humans and elves and dwarves have had their problems, but they have—by and large—managed to thrive and prosper. What you call the Wave has kept them afloat."

"Let's hope they continue," Haplo said. "This next Wave—should it crash down on top of them—might be the end."

They continued traversing the corridors, traveling always downward. Alfred sang the runes softly, beneath his breath. The sigla on the wall burned brightly, led them on.

The tunnel narrowed. They were forced to walk in single file, Alfred leading the way, followed by Jonathon. The dog and Hugh the Hand brought up the rear.

Either the air was thinner down here—something Alfred didn't remember from last time—or his nervousness was robbing him of breath. The rune-song seemed to cling to his raw throat; he had difficulty forcing it out. He was afraid and at the same time excited, quivering, filled with a nervous anticipation.

Not that the sigla seemed to need his song now anyway. They flashed into light almost joyfully, moving far more rapidly than he and the others could keep up. Alfred eventually ceased singing, saved his breath for what was coming.

Perhaps you're worrying about nothing. It could all be so easy, so simple, he told himself. A touch of magic and the Seventh Gate is destroyed, Death's Gate is shut forever . . .

The dog barked, suddenly, loudly.

The unexpected sound, echoing in the tunnel, nearly caused Alfred's heart to stop. As it was, it gave a great lurch, ending up in his throat, momentarily blocking his windpipe.

"What?" Alfred choked, coughed.

"Hsst! Quiet! Stop a moment," ordered Hugh the Hand.

All of them halted. The blue of the sigla reflected in their eyes— the living and the dead.

"The dog heard something. And so did I," Hugh the Hand continued grimly. "Someone's following along behind us."

Alfred's heart slid from his throat right out of his body.

Lord Xar.

"Go on," said Haplo. "We've come too far to stop now. Go on."

"No need," said Alfred faintly, almost without a voice.

The sigla left the base of the wall, traveled upward to form an arch of glowing blue light. Blue light that changed to glaring, ominous red at his approach.

"We are here. The Seventh Gate."

CHAPTER ◆ 24

THE SEVENTH

GATE

◆

THE RUNES OUTLINED AN ARCHED ENTRYWAY, WHICH LED—ALFRED REMEM-bered—to a wide and airy tunnel. And Alfred remembered sud-denly, too, the feeling of peace and tranquillity that had enveloped him when he had stepped into that tunnel. He longed for that sensation again, longed for it as a grown man sometimes longs to rest his head on a comforting breast; to feel gentle arms around him; to hear a voice, softly singing, lulling him to sleep with songs of his childhood.

Alfred stood before the archway, watching the sigla flicker and glimmer. To anyone else looking at the runes inscribed on the wall, the sigla would have appeared similar to those running along the base of the wall. Harmless runes, meant to serve as guides. But Alfred could read the subtle differences: a dot placed over a line instead of beneath; a cross instead of a star; a square drawn around a circle. Such differences changed these runes of guiding into runes of warding—the strongest a Sartan could forge. Anyone approach-ing this arch—

"What the devil are you waiting for?" Hugh the Hand de-manded. He glared at Alfred dubiously. "You're not feeling faint, are you?"

"No, Sir Hugh, but— Wait! Don't!"

Hugh the Hand brushed past Alfred, headed straight for the arch.

The blue runes changed color, flaring from blue to red. The Hand, somewhat startled, halted, eyed the runes suspiciously.

Nothing happened. Alfred kept silent. The mensch probably wouldn't have believed him anyway. He was the type who had to find out for himself.

Hugh took a step forward. The sigla smoldered, burst into flame. The archway was surrounded by an arc of fire.

The dog cringed away.

"Damn!" Hugh the Hand muttered, impressed. He backed off precipitously.

The moment he stepped away from the arch, the fire died. The sigla once again gleamed a sullen red, did not change back to blue. The heat of the flames lingered in the hallway.

"We are not meant to pass," said Alfred quietly.

"I gathered that," Hugh the Hand growled, rubbing his arms where the flames had singed the thick, dark hair. "How in the name of the ancestors do we get inside?"

"I can break the runes," Alfred said, but he made no move to do so.

"Dithering?" said Haplo.

"No," Alfred replied, defensive. "It's just . . ." He glanced back down the corridor, down the way they'd come.

The blue runes on the wall's base had faded by now, but at his look, his thought, they began to glow again. They would lead back to the cell, to Haplo.

Alfred looked down at the dog. "I have to know what will happen to you."

"It doesn't matter."

"But—"

"Damn it, I don't know what will happen!" Haplo returned, losing patience. "But I do know what will happen if we fail here. And so do you."

Alfred said nothing more. He began to dance.

His movements were graceful, slow, solemn. He accompanied himself with a song, his hands weaving the sigla to the melody, his feet marking out the same intricate pattern on the stone floor. The dance, the magic entered him, like intoxicating bubbles in his blood. His body, which oftentimes felt so awkward and clumsy, as if it belonged to someone else and was only on loan to him, was sloughed off, shed like a snake's skin. The magic was his flesh, his bone, his blood. He was light and air and water. He was happy, content, and unafraid.

The red light of the warding runes flared once, brightly, then faded and died altogether.

Darkness floated down into the corridor. Darkness extinguished Alfred.

The bubbles burst and grew flat, stale. The magic seeped out of him. His old heavy body hung before him, like a massive coat on a hook. He had to struggle into it again, feel its weight drag on his shoulders, try to walk around again in the flesh, which was too cumbersome, which didn't fit.

Alfred's feet shuffled to a halt. He sighed once, then said quietly, "We can pass now. The runes will light again once we are through the arch. Perhaps that will stop Lord Xar."

Haplo grunted, didn't even bother to respond.

Alfred led the way. Hugh the Hand followed, keeping a wary eye on the runes, obviously expecting them to burst into flame at any moment. The dog, looking bored, trotted along at Hugh's heels. Jonathon entered last, the lazar's shuffling steps leaving a path in the dust. Alfred glanced down, was intrigued and somewhat disquieted to see his own footprints, left in the dust from the last time they had passed through the arch. He knew them by their erratic pattern, that wandered aimlessly all over the place.

And Haplo's footprints—walking in a straight line, with fixed purpose and determination. On leaving that room, his walk had been less certain. His path altered drastically, the course of his life forever changed.

And Jonathon. He had been a living man, the last time they'd come here. Now his corpse—neither living nor dead—walked through the dust, obscuring the path he'd left in life. But the dog's tracks from that last time were not visible. Even now, it left no trace of its passing. Alfred stared, marveling that he'd never noticed this before.

Or maybe I saw tracks, he thought, smiling wistfully, because I wanted to see them.

He reached down, patted the animal's smooth head. The dog looked up at him with its liquid, bright eyes. Its mouth opened, parted in what might have been a grin.

"I *am* real," it seemed to say. "In fact, maybe I'm the only reality."

Alfred turned. His feet no longer stumbled. He walked upright and steadily toward the Seventh Gate, known to those who once lived on Abarrach as the Chamber of the Damned.

As it had the last time, the tunnel led them straight to a blank wall made of solid black rock. Two sets of runes marked it. The first set were simple locking sigla, undoubtedly inscribed by Samah himself. The other sigla had been added by those early Sartan living on Abarrach. While attempting to contact their brethren on other worlds, they had accidentally stumbled across the Seventh Gate. Inside, they found peace, self-knowledge, fulfillment —granted to them by a higher power, a power beyond their comprehension and understanding. And so they had marked this chamber sacred, holy.

In this chamber, they had died.

In this chamber, Kleitus had died.

Alfred, recalling that terrible experience, shuddered. His hand had been touching the runes on the wall. Now it dropped, trembling, to his side. He could see with horrible clarity the skeletons lying on the floor. Mass murder. Mass suicide.

Any who bring violence into this chamber will find it visited upon themselves.

So it was written on the walls. Alfred had wondered at the time how and why. Now he thought he understood. Fear—it came down always to fear. Who knew for certain what Samah had feared or why,[1] but he had been afraid, even in this chamber

---

[1] See Appendix I, "Being a Concise History of the Seventh Gate . . ."

which the Council had endowed with its most powerful magic. It had been meant to destroy the Council's enemies. It had ended up destroying its creators.

A chill hand touched Alfred's. He jumped, startled, and found Jonathon standing at his side.

"Do not be afraid of what is within."

". . . within . . ." came the sad echo.

"The dead are now, at long last, at rest. No trace remains of their tragic end. I have seen to that myself."

". . . myself . . ."

"You have entered here?" Alfred asked, amazed.

"Many times." And it seemed the lazar smiled, the phantasm lighting the dead, dark eyes. "I enter, I leave. This chamber has been—as much as any place can be—my home. Here I can find ease from the torment of my existence. Here I am given patience to endure, to wait, until the end."

"The end?" Alfred didn't quite like the sound of that.

The lazar said nothing; the phantasm slid out of the corpse, fluttered restlessly near the body.

Alfred drew in a shivering breath; what confidence he'd felt was rapidly oozing out of him.

"What happens if we fail?"

Repeating Haplo's words, Alfred placed his hands on the walls, began to chant the runes. The rock dissolved beneath his fingers. The sigla, glowing blue, framed a doorway that led, not into darkness, as it had the last time they had entered the Chamber, but into light.

The Seventh Gate was a room with seven marble walls, covered by a domed ceiling. A globe suspended from the ceiling cast a soft, white glow. As Jonathon had promised, the dead whose bodies had littered the floor were gone. But the words of warning remained inscribed on the walls: *Any who bring violence into this chamber will find it visited upon themselves.*

Alfred stepped over the threshold. He felt again that same enveloping, loving warmth he'd experienced the first time he'd walked into this chamber. The feeling of comfort and calm spread like a balm over his troubled soul. He drew near the oblong table, carved of pure white wood—wood that had come from the ancient, sundered world—and regarded it with reverence and sadness.

Jonathon moved over to stand beside the table. If Alfred had been paying attention, he would have noticed a change come over the lazar when it entered this room. The phantasm remained outside the body, no longer writhing, struggling to escape. Its vague, shapeless form coalesced into a shimmering image of the duke as he had been when Alfred first knew him: young, vibrant, joyful. The corpse was, it seemed, the soul's shadow.

Alfred didn't notice, however. He stared at the runes carved on the table, stared at them as if hypnotized, unable to look away. He drew nearer, nearer.

Hugh the Hand stood in the doorway, gazing into the chamber with awe, perhaps reluctant—now that the moment was at hand— to cross the threshold.

The dog nudged Hugh, urged him forward, reassuringly wagging its tail.

Hugh's grim face relaxed. He smiled. "Well, if you say so," he said to the animal and walked inside. Glancing around, taking in everything, he walked over to the white table and, placing his hands on it, began idly to trace the runes with his fingers.

The dog pattered inside the room . . . and vanished.

The door to the Seventh Gate slid shut.

Alfred didn't notice Hugh. Alfred didn't see the dog disappear. He didn't hear the door close. He was standing at the table. Stretching out his hands, he placed his fingers gently, reverently on the white wood . . .

"We are come today, Brethren," said Samah from his place at the head of the table, "to sunder the world."

CHAPTER ◆ 25

THE SEVENTH

GATE

◆

THE CHAMBER KNOWN AS THE SEVENTH GATE WAS CROWDED WITH SARTAN. THE Council of Seven sat around the table; all others stood. Alfred was shoved against a wall near the back, near one of the seven doors. The doors themselves and a series of seven squares on the floor in front of each were left clear.

The faces so near his were strained, pale, haggard. It was, Alfred thought, like seeing himself in a mirror. He must look exactly the same, for he felt exactly the same. Only Samah—seen occasionally when there was a shift in the numbers of people who surrounded him—appeared master of himself and the situation. Stern and implacable, he was the dire force holding them all together.

If his will falters, the rest of us will crumble like moldy cheese.

Alfred shifted from one foot to the other, trying to ease the discomfort of standing for such an interminably long period. He was not normally claustrophobic, but the tension, the fear, the crowded conditions were creating the impression that the walls were about to close in on him. It was hard to breathe. The room suddenly seemed a vacuum.

He pressed back against the wall, wishing it would give way behind him. He had wonderful, wild visions of the marble blocks collapsing, the fresh air flowing inside, the vast expanse of blue sky opening above him. He would flee this place, flee Samah and the Council guards, escape back *into* the world, instead of away from it.

"Brethren." Samah rose to his feet. The entire Council was now standing. "It is time. Prepare yourselves to cast the magic."

Alfred could see Orlah now. She was pale, but composed. He knew her reluctance, knew how vehemently she had fought this decision. She could. She was Samah's wife. He would never cast her into the prison along with their enemies, not as he had done some of the others.

The Sartan stood with heads bowed, hands folded, eyes closed. They had begun sinking into the relaxed, meditative state required to summon such vast magical power as Samah and the Council were demanding.

Alfred endeavored to do the same, but his thoughts refused to focus, went dashing about desperately, running hither and yon with no escape, like mice trapped in a box with a cat.

"You seem unable to concentrate, Brother," said a low, calm voice, very near Alfred.

Startled, Alfred looked for the voice's source, saw a man leaning on the wall beside him. The man was young, but beyond that it was difficult to tell much about him. His head was covered by the cowl of his robe and his hands were swathed in bandages.

Bandages. Alfred stared at the white linen wrappings covering the man's hands, wrists, and forearms, and was filled with a vague sense of dread.

The young man turned to him and smiled—a quiet smile.

"The Sartan will come to regret this day, Brother." His voice changed, grew bitter. "Not that their regret will ease the suffering of the innocent victims. But at least, before the end, the Sartan will come to understand the enormity of what they have done. If that is of any comfort to you."

"We will understand," Alfred said, hesitantly, "but will understanding help us? Will the future be better for it?"

"That remains to be seen, Brother," said Haplo.

It *is* Haplo! And I am Alfred, not some nameless, faceless Sartan who once, long, long ago, stood trembling in this very chamber. And yet, at the same time, I am that unhappy Sartan. I am here and I was there.

"I should have been more courageous," Alfred whispered. Sweat trickled down his balding head, soaked the collar of his robes. "I should have spoken up, tried to stop this madness. But I'm such a coward. I saw what happened to the others. I . . . couldn't face it. Though now, perhaps, I think it would have been better . . . At least I could live with myself, though I wouldn't live long. Now I must carry this burden with me the rest of my life."

"It isn't your fault," said Haplo. "For the last time, quit apologizing."

"Yes, it is . . ." Alfred said. "Yes, it is. For each of us who have turned a blind eye to prejudice, hatred, intolerance . . . it is our fault . . ."

"Reach out, Brethren," Samah was saying. "Reach out with your minds to the farthest point of your power and then reach beyond that. Envision the possibility that this world is not one, but has been reduced to its elemental parts: earth, air, fire, and water."

A single sigil began to shine blue in the centers of four doors. Alfred recognized the symbols—one for each of the four elements. These, then, were the doors which would lead to the new worlds. He began to shiver.

"Our enemies, the Patryns, have been confined to prison. They are now contained, immobilized," Samah continued. "We could have easily destroyed them, but we do not seek their destruction. We seek their redemption, their rehabilitation. Their prison house —no, let us term it a correction center—is ready to be sealed shut."

A sigil on the fifth door burst into flame, burned an angry, fiery red. The Labyrinth. Redemption. Haplo laughed harshly.

"You must stop this, Samah!" Alfred wanted to shout frantically. "The Labyrinth is not a prison but a torture chamber. It hears the hatred and the fear that lie hidden behind your words. The Labyrinth will use that hatred to murder and destroy."

But Alfred didn't speak aloud. He was too afraid.

"We created a haven for the Patryns." Samah smiled, tight-lipped, grim. "Once they have learned their hard lesson, the Labyrinth will free them. We will build for them a city, teach them how to live like civilized people."

"Yes," Alfred said to himself, "the Patryns will continue to study the 'lesson.' The lesson of hate you taught them. They will emerge from the Labyrinth stronger in their fury than ever. Except for some. Some like Haplo, who learned that true strength lies in love."

The sixth door began to glimmer with twilight colors, soft, shimmering. The Nexus.

"And last," said Samah, with a gesture toward the door that stood behind him, a door that—as he moved his hand—slowly began to open, "we create the path that will take us to these worlds. We create Death's Gate. As this world dies, newer, better worlds will be born from it. And now the time has come."

Samah turned slowly, faced the door, which now stood wide open. Alfred tried to catch a glimpse of what it revealed. Standing on his toes, he peered over the heads of the restive crowd.

Blue sky, white clouds, green trees, rolling oceans . . . The old world . . .

"Take it apart, my brethren," Samah commanded. "Take the world apart."

Alfred couldn't cast the magic. He couldn't. He saw the faces of the "regrettable but necessary civilian casualties." He saw their disbelief, their fear, their panic. Thousands and thousands, running to their own ends, for there was no refuge, no sanctuary.

He was weeping, blubbering. He couldn't help it, he couldn't stop himself.

Haplo rested a bandaged hand on his shoulder. "Pull yourself together. This won't help. Samah is watching you."

Fearfully Alfred raised his head. His eyes met Samah's and he saw the fear and anger in the man.

And then Samah wasn't Samah any longer.

He was Xar.

CHAPTER ◆ 26

THE SEVENTH

GATE

◆

"ALFRED!"

The voice called to him across a vast distance, through time and space. It was faint, yet compelling. Urging him to leave, withdraw, return . . .

"Alfred!"

A hand on his shoulder, shaking him. Alfred looked down at the hand, saw it was bandaged. He was frightened, tried to get away, but he couldn't. The hand gripped him tightly.

"No, please, let me alone!" Alfred whimpered. "I'm in my tomb. I'm safe. It's peaceful and quiet. No one can hurt me here. Let me go!"

The hand didn't let him go. It kept fast hold of him and drew him on, its strong grip no longer frightening, but welcome and comforting, supportive and reassuring. It was drawing him back, back into the world of the living.

And then, before he was quite there yet, the hand pulled away. The bandages fell off. He saw that the hand was covered with blood. Pity filled his heart. The hand was outstretched, reaching for him.

"Alfred, I need you."

And there, at his feet, was the dog, gazing up at him with liquid eyes.

"I need you."

Alfred reached out, caught hold of the hand . . .

The hand squeezed his painfully, jerked him backward, dragged him completely off his feet. He tumbled to the floor.

"And stay away from that damn table, will you?" Haplo ordered, standing over him, glaring down at him. "We almost lost you for good that time." He eyed Alfred grimly, but with a touch of concern in the quiet smile. "Are you all right?"

Crouched on his hands and knees on the dusty marble, Alfred had no answer. He could only gaze in wordless astonishment at Haplo—Haplo, standing right there in front of him, Haplo whole, alive!

"You look," said Haplo, suddenly grinning, "exactly like the dog."

"My friend . . ." Alfred sat back on his heels. His eyes filled with tears. "My friend . . ."

"Now don't start blubbering," Haplo warned. "And get up, damn it. We don't have much time. Lord Xar—"

"He's here!" Alfred said fearfully, clambering to his feet. He stumbled around to face the head of the table.

Alfred blinked. Not Samah. Certainly not Xar. Jonathon stood at the table's head. Beside him, grim and tense, was Hugh the Hand.

"Why . . . I saw Xar . . ." Another thought occurred to Alfred. "You!" He staggered back around to face Haplo. "You. Are *you* real?"

"Flesh and blood," said Haplo.

His hand—sigla-covered, strong and warm—took hold of Alfred, steadied the Sartan, who was extremely pale and wobbly.

Timidly, Alfred extended a bony finger, poked cautiously at Haplo. "You *seem* real," he said, still dubious. He glanced around. "The dog?"

"The mutt's run off," said Haplo. He smiled. "Probably smelled sausages."

"Not run off," said Alfred tremulously. "Part of you. At last. But how did it all happen?"

"This chamber," Jonathon answered. "Cursed . . . and blessed. In Haplo's case, the rune-magic kept his body alive. The magic in this chamber, inside the Seventh Gate, has enabled the soul to rejoin the body."

"When Prince Edmund came in here," Alfred said, remembering, "his soul was freed from his body."

"He was dead," Jonathon replied. "And raised through the necromancy. His soul was in thrall. That is the difference."

"Ah," said Alfred, "I think I'm beginning to understand—"

"I'm very glad for you," Haplo interrupted. "How many years do you think it might take you to completely understand? As I said, we don't have much time. We have to establish contact with the higher power—"

"I know how! I was there, during the Sundering! Samah was here and the Council members were all gathered around the table. And you were here . . . Never mind," Alfred concluded meekly, catching Haplo's impatient glance. "I'll tell you that later, too.

"Those four doors"—Alfred pointed—"the ones that are slightly ajar, each lead to the four worlds. The door over there leads to the Labyrinth. That door—the one that is shut—must go to the Vortex, which, if you'll remember, collapsed, and that door"—the pointing finger shook slightly—"*that* door, the one that's wide open, leads to Death's Gate."

Haplo grunted. "I told you to stay away from that damn table. *That* door doesn't lead anywhere except out into the hall. In case you've forgotten, my friend, that was the door we went through last time we were in here. Although, as I recall, you shut it when we left. Or rather, it almost shut you."

"But that was in Abarrach," Alfred argued. He looked around helplessly, the knowledge suddenly terrifying. "We're not in the Chamber of the Damned. We're not on Abarrach. We are inside the Seventh Gate."

Haplo frowned, skeptical.

"You're here," Alfred said. "How did you get here?"

Haplo shrugged again. "I woke up, half frozen, in a prison cell. I was alone. No one was around. I walked out into the corridor and saw the blue runes shining on the wall. I followed them. Then I heard your voice, chanting. The warding runes let me pass. I came down here, found the door open. I walked inside. You were sitting at that damn table, whimpering and apologizing . . . as usual."

Perplexed, Alfred looked at Jonathon. "*Are* we on Abarrach still? I don't understand."

"Because you went *to* the Seventh Gate, you found the Seventh Gate. You are now in the Seventh Gate."

". . . Seventh Gate . . ." said the echo and it had a joyous sound.

"That door"—Jonathon glanced in the direction of the door with the sigil marking it as Death's Gate—"has stood open all these centuries. To close Death's Gate, that is the door you must shut."

The enormity of the task overwhelmed Alfred. It had taken the Council of Seven, and hundreds of other powerful Sartan, to create and open that door. To shut it—only him.

"Then how did I get here?" Haplo demanded, obviously still not believing. "I didn't use any magic—"

"Not magic," Jonathon replied. "Knowledge. Self-knowledge. That is the key to the Seventh Gate. If my people, who found this place long ago, had truly known themselves, they could have discovered its power. They came close. But not close enough. They could not let go."

". . . let go . . ."

"I need proof. Open a door," said Haplo. "Not that one!" He purposefully avoided going near the door that already stood ajar. "Open another door, one that's closed. Let's see what's out there."

"Which door?" Alfred asked, gulping.

Haplo was silent a moment, then said, "The one that you claim leads to the Labyrinth."

Alfred slowly nodded. He thought back to the Chamber as he had seen it just before the Sundering. He saw again the door with the fiery red sigil.

He located the correct door. Edging his way around the table— careful not to touch the runes on the white wood—he came to stand before the door.

He reached out his hand, gently touched the sigil etched into the marble. He began to sing, very softly; then his song grew stronger. He traced over the sigil with his fingers and the sigil flared to life, glowed red.

The song caught in Alfred's throat. He coughed, swallowed, tried to continue singing, though now the song was cracked and off-key. He pushed on the door.

The door swung silently open.

And they were inside the Labyrinth.

CHAPTER 27

THE LABYRINTH

✦

Traveling through death's gate, the two sartan ships arrived in the Nexus. The ships landed near what had once been Lord Xar's house, now a mass of charred wood. On landing, the Sartan stared out the portholes, shocked into stunned silence at the sight of the destruction.

"You see the magnitude of the hatred these Patryns bear us," Ramu could be heard saying. "They wreak destruction upon the city and land we made for them, although it means they will be the ones who suffer. There is no reasoning with such savagery. These people will never be fit to live among civilized men."

Marit could have told him the truth—that it was the serpents who had destroyed the Nexus—but she knew he would never believe her and she refused to let him provoke her into a meaningless argument. She maintained a haughty, dignified silence, kept her face averted so that they would not see her tears.

Ordering the majority of the Sartan to remain safely on board ship, where the runes could protect them, Ramu sent out scouting parties.

While the scouts were abroad, the Sartan of Chelestra came to tend to the needs of their Abarrach brethren. They were gentle, patient, and kind, giving of their own strength unstintingly. Several Sartan, passing by Marit, even paused to ask if they could do anything to aid her. She refused their help, of course, but—astonished and touched by the offers—she managed to be gracious about it.

The only Sartan she came close to trusting (and not all that close, either) was Balthazar. She couldn't quite explain why. Perhaps it was because he and his people also knew what it was to watch their children die. Or perhaps it was because he had taken the time to talk to her on their journey through Death's Gate, to ask *her* what was happening in the Labyrinth.

Marit waited impatiently for the return of the Sartan scouts, who went immediately to Ramu. Marit would have given several gates to have heard their report. She could do nothing but wait, however.

At last Ramu left his cabin. He motioned—grudgingly, Marit thought—to Balthazar. The Councillor obviously didn't like sharing his position of authority, but he had little choice. The Abarrach Sartan had made it clear during the journey that they would follow no leader but their own.

"I don't like what I am hearing," Ramu said in a low voice. "The scouts' reports are conflicting. They tell me—"

Marit could not hear what the scouts reported, but she could guess. The scouts would see whatever it was the serpents wanted the scouts to see.

Balthazar listened, then halted Ramu with a polite gesture. The necromancer looked over to Marit, motioned to her to join them.

Ramu frowned. "Do you think that wise? She is a prisoner. I do not like giving away our plans to the enemy."

"As you say, she is a prisoner and would find it difficult—if not impossible—to escape. I would like to hear what she has to say."

"If you are interested in lies, then, by all means, Brother, let us hear her," Ramu said bitingly.

Marit came up, stood silently between the two.

"Please continue, Councillor," said Balthazar.

Ramu remained silent for a moment, displeased and angry, forced to rethink what and how much he was going to reveal. "I was going to say that I plan to go to the Final Gate. I want to see for myself what is transpiring."

"Excellent idea," Balthazar agreed. "I will accompany you."

Ramu did not appear pleased. "I would think, Brother, that you would prefer to remain on board. You are still very weak."

Balthazar shrugged this off. "I am the representative of my people. Their ruler, if you will. You cannot, by Sartan law, refuse my request, Councillor."

Ramu bowed. "I was thinking only of your health."

"Of course you were," Balthazar said smiling, smooth. "And I will take Marit along to act as my adviser."

Caught completely by surprise, she stared at him in astonishment.

"Absolutely not." Ramu refused to consider the matter. "She is far too dangerous. She will stay here, under guard."

"Be sensible, Councillor," Balthazar returned coolly. "This woman has lived both in the Nexus and in the Labyrinth itself. She is familiar with the surroundings, with the inhabitants. *She* knows what is transpiring—something that, in my mind, your scouts do not."

Ramu flushed in outrage. He was not accustomed to having his authority challenged. The other Council members, overhearing, looked uncomfortable, exchanged uneasy glances.

Balthazar remained polite, politic. Ramu had no choice but to acquiesce. He needed the help of the Abarrach Sartan and this was neither the time nor the place for the Councillor to challenge Balthazar's authority.

"Very well," Ramu said unpleasantly. "She may accompany *you*, but she is to be kept under strict watch. If anything happens—"

"I take full responsibility for her upon myself," Balthazar said humbly.

Ramu, with a dark glance at Marit, turned on his heel and left.

Outright confrontation had been avoided. But every Sartan who witnessed the clash of these two strong wills knew that war had been declared. Two suns do not travel in the same orbit, as the saying goes.

"I want to thank you, Balthazar," Marit began awkwardly.

"Do not thank me," he said coldly, cutting her words off. Placing his thin, wasted hand on her arm, he drew her over to one of the portholes. "Look out here a moment. I want you to explain something to me."

The bony fingers dug into Marit's arm with such force that the sigla beneath them began to glow, defending her. She didn't like his touch, started to pull away. His grip tightened.

"Watch for your chance," he said softly, urgently, before she could speak. "When it comes, take it. I will do what I can for you."

Escape! Marit knew instantly what he had meant. But why? She held back, suspicious.

He glanced over his shoulder. A few Sartan were watching them, but they were his people, whom he could trust. The other Sartan had either left with Ramu or were occupied with helping their brethren.

Balthazar turned back to Marit, spoke in a low voice. "Ramu does not know this, but I sent out my own scouts. They report that vast armies of terrible creatures—red dragons, wolves who walk like men, gigantic insects—are massed around the Final Gate. You might be interested to know that Ramu's scouts captured one of your people, interrogated him, forced him to talk."

"A Patryn?" Marit was bewildered. "But there are no Patryns left in the Nexus. I told you—the serpents drove all my people back through the Final Gate."

"There was something odd about this Patryn," Balthazar went on, studying her intently. "He had very strange eyes."

"Let me guess. The eyes glowed red. That wasn't one of my people! It was one of the serpents. They can take any form—"

"Yes. From what little you said, I gathered this might be something like that. The Patryn admitted that his people are in league with the serpents, fighting to open the Final Gate."

"That part is true!" Marit cried, feeling helpless. "We have to! If the Final Gate closes, my people will be trapped inside forever . . ."

Fear and despair choked her. For a moment she could not go on. Desperately, she fought to maintain control, speak calmly. "But we are *not* in league with the serpents. We know them for what they are. We would remain locked inside the Labyrinth forever before we would side with them! How can that fool Ramu believe such a thing!"

"He believes what he wants to believe, Marit. What serves his purpose. Or perhaps he is blind to their evil." The necromancer smiled, thin-lipped, rueful. "We are not. We have looked inside that dark mirror. We recognize the reflection."

Balthazar sighed; his face had gone exceedingly pale. He was, as Ramu had pointed out, still weak. But he refused Marit's suggestion that he return to his quarters, lie down.

"You need to get word to your people, Marit. Tell them we are here. We must ally together to fight these creatures, or all of us will be destroyed. If only there was some one of your people who could talk to Ramu, convince him—"

"But there is!" Marit gasped, clutched at Balthazar. "Headman Vasu! He is part Sartan himself! I will try to reach him. I can use my magic to go to him. But Ramu will see what I'm doing and try to stop me."

"How long do you need?"

"Long enough to draw the runes. A count of thirty heartbeats, no more."

Balthazar smiled. "Wait and watch."

Marit stood huddled beside a wall surrounding the burned-out shells of what had once been the beautiful buildings of the Nexus. The city that had shone like the first star of the evening, gleaming bright against the twilit sky, was a mass of blackened stone. Its windows were dark and empty as the eyes of its dead. Smoke from still smoldering beams of wood clouded the sky, brought a dirty and ugly night—lit by patches of orange—to the land.

Two Sartan were supposed to be keeping watch on her, but they only glanced at her occasionally, more interested in what was transpiring beyond the Gate than in one subdued and seemingly harmless Patryn prisoner.

What she saw beyond the Gate weakened Marit far more than any Sartan magic.

"The reports were correct," Ramu was saying grimly. "Armies of darkness massing for an assault against the Final Gate. We have arrived here just in time, it seems."

"You fool!" Marit told him bitterly. "Those armies are massing for an assault against *us*."

"Don't believe her, Sartan," hissed a sibilant voice from behind the walls. "It is a trick. She lies. Their armies will break through the Final Gate and, from there, advance into the four worlds."

A huge, snakelike head reared up from behind the wall, loomed over them, swaying slowly back and forth. Its eyes glinted red; its tongue flicked in and out of toothless jaws. Its skin was old and wrinkled and hung loose on its sinuous body. It stank of death and corruption and burned-out ruins.

Balthazar recoiled in horror. "What ghastly creature is this?"

"Don't you know?" The red eyes glinted in what might have been laughter. "You created us . . ."

The two Sartan guards were pale and shaking. This was Marit's chance to flee, but the serpent's terrible gaze was on her, or so it seemed, and she could not move or think or do anything except watch in dread fascination.

Only Ramu was proof against its dire spell. "And so you are here, in league with your friends, the Patryns. One of their own people told me as much."

The snake's head sank. Its eyes were hooded, the red glint fading. "You wrong us, Councillor. We are here to help you. As you surmised, the Patryns are attempting to break out of their prison. They have summoned hordes of dragons to fight at their behest. Even now, their armies approach the Final Gate."

The head slid over the wall, followed by part of the enormous, foul-smelling body. Ramu could not help himself. He fell back before it, but only a step or two. Then he held his ground.

"Your kind are with them."

The snake's head oscillated. "We serve our creators. Give the command, and we will destroy the Patryns and seal shut the Final Gate forever!"

The serpent rested its head on the ground in front of Ramu. Its red eyes closed in servile submission.

"And when they have destroyed us, they will turn against you, Ramu!" Marit warned. "You will find yourself inside the Labyrinth! Or worse!"

The serpent ignored her. And so did Ramu.

"Why should we trust you? You attacked us on Chelestra—"

The giant reptile lifted its head. Its red eyes flared in hurt indignation. "It was the wicked mensch who attacked you, Councillor. Not us. There is proof. When your city was flooded with the magic-nullifying seawater, when you were bereft of your power, weak and helpless, did we harm you? We could have."

The red eyes glinted for an instant; then—again—the hooded lids shadowed them. "But we did not. Your esteemed father—honor to his memory—opened Death's Gate for us. We were only too happy to flee our mensch persecutors. And a good thing we did. Otherwise, you would now face this threat from your most terrible enemies alone."

"You do face it alone, Ramu. In the end, we will all face it alone," Marit said softly.

"This from one who helped murder your father!" the serpent hissed. "She listened to his screams and she laughed!"

Ramu went deathly pale. He turned to look at Marit.

"I didn't laugh," she said through trembling lips. She remembered Samah's screams. Burning tears stung her eyelids. "I didn't laugh."

Ramu's fist clenched.

"Kill her . . ." whispered the dragon-snake. "Kill her now . . . Take your just revenge."

Ramu reached into his robes, drew forth the Sartan knife, the Cursed Blade. He stared at it, looked back at her.

Marit came forward, apparently eager, ready to fight.

Balthazar stepped in between the two.

"Are you mad, Ramu? Look what this foul snake has driven you to do! Don't trust it! I know it. I recognize it! I've seen it before."

Ramu seemed ready to shove Balthazar aside. "Get out of my way. Or by my father's memory, I will kill you, too!"

The serpent watched, grew fatter, sleeker.

The two Sartan guards looked on in horror, not certain what to do.

The Cursed Blade in Ramu's hand was wriggling, starting to come to life. Marit drew a magical circle of blue and red sigla. Its fire shone brightly. Speaking the name "Vasu," she stepped through the rune-circle and was gone.

Ramu thrust the Cursed Blade back into its sheath. Cold with anger, he turned on the necromancer.

"You helped her escape. An act of treason! When this is ended, you will be brought up on charges before the Council!"

"Don't be a fool, Ramu!" Balthazar returned. "Marit was right. Look at that foul serpent! Don't you know it? Haven't you seen it before? Take a good look—inside yourself!"

Ramu regarded Balthazar grimly, then turned back to face the serpent. The creature was bloated, surfeited. The red eyes smiled and winked.

"I will ally myself with you. Attack the Patryns," Ramu ordered. "Kill them. Kill them all."

"Yes, Master!" The serpent bowed low.

CHAPTER 28

THE SEVENTH

GATE

◆

"YOU SEE WHAT IS HAPPENING?" SAID HAPLO.

Alfred shook his head. "It is hopeless. We will never learn. Our people will destroy each other . . ." His shoulders slumped in despair.

Haplo rested a hand on his arm. "It may not be that bad, my friend. If your people and mine can find a way to meet in peace, they will see the evil of the serpents. The dragon-snakes can't keep playing one side off the other if both sides stand together. We have people like Marit and Balthazar and Vasu . . . They are our hope. But the Gate must be closed!"

"Yes." Alfred lifted his head, a tinge of color in his gray cheeks. He stared at the door, the door marked Death's Gate. "Yes, you're right. The Gate must be shut and sealed. At least we can contain the evil, keep it from spreading."

"Can you do it?"

Alfred flushed. "Yes, I believe I can. The spell is not all that difficult. It involves, you see, the possibility that—"

"No need to explain," Haplo interrupted. "No time."

"Oh, um, yes." Alfred blinked. Approaching the door, he eyed it wistfully, sadly. "If only this had never come to be. I'm not sure, you know, what will happen when the Gate is shut." He waved his hand. "To this chamber, I mean. There exists the possibility that . . . that it could be destroyed."

"And us with it," Haplo said quietly.

Alfred nodded.

"Then I guess that's a risk we'll have to take."

Alfred looked back into the door leading to the Labyrinth. The serpents twined about the ruins of the Nexus, their huge bodies roiling over the blackened stones and broken, charred beams. Red eyes glinted. He could hear their laughter.

"Yes," Alfred said softly, exhaling an indrawn breath. "And now—"

"Wait a minute!" Hugh the Hand was standing near the door through which they'd entered. "I've got a question. This involves me as well," he added harshly.

"Of course, Sir Hugh," Alfred said, flustered, apologizing. "Please forgive . . . I'm sorry . . . I wasn't thinking—"

Hugh the Hand made an impatient gesture, cut off Alfred's rambling.

"Once you shut the Gate, what will happen to the four mensch worlds?"

"I've been considering that," Alfred pondered. "From my earlier studies, I think it highly possible that the conduits which connect each world to the other will continue working, even though the Gate is shut. Thus the Kicksey-winsey on Arianus will still send energy to the citadels on Pryan, which will beam energy to the conduits on Abarrach, which will in turn send—"

"So all the worlds would continue to function."

"I'm not certain, of course, but the probability is such that—"

"But no one could travel between them."

"No. Of that, I am certain," Alfred said gravely. "Once Death's Gate is shut, the only way to go from world to world would be to fly through space. Which is—given the mensch's present state of magical development—the only way they could have traveled from one world to another anyway. So far as we know, the child Bane was the only mensch ever to enter Death's Gate, and he did so only—"

A sharp nudge from an elbow caught Alfred in the ribs.

"I want to talk to you for a moment." Haplo motioned Alfred over to stand near the table.

"Certainly," Alfred replied, "just after I finish explaining to Hugh—"

"Now," Haplo said. "Don't you find that an odd question?" he asked beneath his breath.

"Why, no," Alfred said, defending a brilliant pupil. "In fact, I thought it quite a good one. If you remember, you and I discussed this on Arianus."

"Exactly," said Haplo beneath his breath, looking at Hugh the Hand through narrowed eyes. "*We* discussed it. What's it to an assassin from Arianus whether or not the mensch on Pryan can go visit their cousins on Chelestra? Why should he care?"

"I don't understand." Alfred was puzzled.

Haplo was silent, eyeing Hugh the Hand. He had shoved open one of the doors, was peering through it. Haplo saw, in the distance, the floating continent of Drevlin. Once shrouded in storm clouds, Drevlin now basked in sunshine. Light glinted and flashed off the gold and silver and brass parts of the fabulous Kicksey-winsey.

"I'm not sure I understand, either," Haplo said at last. "But I think you'd better cut short the academics, get on with your magic."

"Very well," Alfred replied, troubled. "But I'll have to go back in time."

"Back? Back where?"

"Back to the Sundering." Alfred looked down at the white table, shivered. "I don't want to, but it's the only way. I must know how Samah cast the spell."

"Do it, then," Haplo said. "But don't forget to return. And don't get yourself sundered in the process."

Alfred smiled wanly. "No," he said, blushing. "No, I'll be careful . . ."

Slowly, reluctantly, fingers trembling, he placed his hands on the white table . . .

◆

. . . Chaos swirled around him. Alfred stood, terrified, in the center of a storm of magic. Howling winds buffeted him, slammed him back against the wall, breaking his bones. Crashing waves washed over him. He was drowning, suffocating. Lightning flared, crackled, blinded; thunder rumbled in his head. Flames roared, burned, consumed his flesh. He was sobbing in fear and in pain; he was dying.

"A single drop, though it falls into an ocean, will yet cause a ripple. I need all of you! Don't give up. The magic!" Samah was shouting to be heard over the tumult. "Use the magic or none of us will survive!"

The magic drifted toward Alfred like a bit of flotsam on a storm-tossed sea. He saw hands reaching out for it, saw some grasp it, saw others miss and disappear. He made a desperate grab.

His fingers closed over something solid. The noise and terror subsided for an instant, and he saw the world—whole, beautiful, shining blue-green in the blackness of space. He must break the world, or the power of the chaotic magic would break him.

"I'm sorry!" he wept and repeated the words over and over. "I'm sorry. I'm sorry . . ."

A single drop . . .

The world exploded.

Alfred reached desperately for the possibility that it could be re-formed, and he felt hundreds of other Sartan minds surge toward the same goal. Yet he still wept, even as he created, and his tears flowed into a sea of gently swelling waves . . .

Alfred lifted his head. Jonathon sat opposite him, on the other side of the table. The lazar said nothing, the eyes sometimes alive, sometimes dead. But Alfred knew that the eyes had seen.

"So many died!" Alfred cried, shuddering. He couldn't breathe; spasmodic sobs choked him. "So many!"

"Alfred!" Haplo shook him. "Let go! Leave it!"

Alfred sat hunched over, his head in his hands, shoulders heaving.

"Alfred . . ." Haplo urged quietly. "Time . . ."

"Yes," Alfred said, drawing in a shivering breath. "Yes, I'm all right. And . . . I know how. I know how to shut Death's Gate."

He looked up at Haplo. "It will be for the best. I have no more doubts. Sundering the world was a great evil. But attempting to 'fix' one evil by means of another—by collapsing the worlds back into one—would be even more devastating. And Lord Xar might not succeed. There is a chance the magic could fail utterly. The worlds might break apart, never to be re-formed. Those living on the worlds would all die. Xar could be left with nothing but motes of dust, droplets of water, wisps of smoke, and blood . . ."

Haplo smiled his quiet smile.

"I know something else, too." Alfred rose, tall and dignified, elegant and graceful, to his feet. "I can cast the spell myself. I don't need your help, my friend. You can go back." He gestured toward the door marked Labyrinth. "They need you there. Your people. Mine."

Haplo looked in that direction, looked back at a land he had once despised, a land that now held everything dear to him. He shook his head.

Alfred, prepared for this, launched into his argument. "You are needed there. I will do what has to be done. It's best this way. I'm not afraid. Well, not much," he amended. "The point is, there's nothing for you to do here. I don't need you. And they do."

Haplo said nothing, continued to shake his head.

"Marit loves you!" Alfred prodded at the weak point in Haplo's armor. "You love her. Go back to her. My friend," he continued earnestly, "for me to know that you two are together . . . well . . . it would make what I have to do so much easier . . ."

Haplo was still shaking his head.

Alfred looked pained. "You don't trust me. I don't blame you. I know that in the past I've let you down, but, truly, I'm strong now. I am—"

"I know you are," Haplo said. "I trust you. I want you to trust me."

Alfred stared, blinked.

"Listen to me. In order to cast the spell, you'll have to leave this chamber, enter Death's Gate. Right?"

"Yes, but—"

"Then I'm staying here." Haplo was firm.

"Why? I don't—"

"To stand guard," Haplo said.

Alfred's hopes, which had been bright, were suddenly dimmed; a dark cloud passed over his sun. "Lord Xar. I forgot. But surely if he was going to try to stop us, he would have done so by now—"

"Just get on with the spell," Haplo said sharply.

Alfred regarded him anxiously, sadly. "You know something. Something you're not telling me. Something's wrong. You're in danger. Perhaps I shouldn't leave . . ."

"You and I don't matter. Think of them," Haplo said quietly.

"Let go," said Jonathon. "And take hold."

". . . let go . . . take hold . . ." The phantasm's voice was strong; stronger, almost, than that of the body.

"Cast the spell," said Hugh the Hand. "Set me free."

A single drop, though it falls into an ocean, will yet cause a ripple.

"I will," said Alfred suddenly, lifting his head. "I can."

Turning to Haplo, Alfred reached out his hand.

"Farewell, my friend," he said. "Thank you. For bringing me back to life."

Haplo took Alfred's hand, then embraced the embarrassed and startled Sartan.

"Thank you," Haplo said, his voice gruff, "for giving me life. Farewell, my friend."

Alfred was extremely red. He patted Haplo's back awkwardly, then turned away, wiping his eyes and nose with his coat sleeve.

"You know," said Alfred, voice muffled, his face averted, "I . . . I miss the dog."

"You know," said Haplo, grinning, "so do I."

With a last fond look, Alfred turned and walked over to the door marked with the sigil meaning "death."

He didn't stumble once.

CHAPTER ◆ 29

THE SEVENTH

GATE

◆

Haplo stood near death's gate, watched as Alfred entered. The Patryn was aware of a presence near him. Hugh the Hand had come up to stand at his side, join him in his vigil. Haplo did not turn around, did not take his gaze from the doorway.

Alfred placed his hand on the sigil, spoke the rune.

The door swung open. Alfred, without a look behind, entered and disappeared.

Hugh the Hand began walking toward the door.

"I wouldn't go any farther," Haplo advised mildly.

The assassin halted, glanced back. "I only want to see what's going on."

"If you take another step, My Lord," Haplo said, and his voice was respectful, "I will be forced to stop you."

" 'My Lord?' " Hugh the Hand appeared puzzled.

Haplo moved to stand between the Hand and the door.

"Do no violence," Jonathon warned quietly.

". . . no violence . . ."

Hugh the Hand stared at the Patryn intently; then he shrugged and spoke several words—words in the Patryn language. Words a mensch could not possibly know.

A shower of sparkling runes swirled around the assassin. The light was dazzling; Haplo was forced to squint against it. When he could see, Hugh the Hand was gone. Lord Xar stood in his place.

"The question about the four worlds," Xar said. "That's what gave me away."

"Yes, My Lord." Haplo smiled, shook his head. "It wasn't the type of question a mensch would ask. Hugh the Hand didn't much care about his one world, let alone three others. Where is he, by the way?"

Xar shrugged; his gaze was now concentrated on Death's Gate. "In the Fire Sea. In the Labyrinth. Who knows? The last I saw of him, he was on board the Sartan ship. While you were fooling with that bumbling Sartan, I was able to assume Hugh's form, take his place on the back of the fire dragon. That thing knew the truth." Xar's gaze flicked to Jonathon.

The lazar remained seated at the table, seemingly uncaring, oblivious.

"But what do the living mean to those walking corpses? You were a fool to trust it. It has betrayed you."

"Do no violence," Jonathon repeated softly.

". . . no violence . . ."

Xar snorted. The glittering eyes flicked back to Haplo. "So you truly intend—you and this Sartan master you serve—to shut Death's Gate."

"I do," said Haplo.

The lord's eyes narrowed. "You doom your own people! You doom the woman you love. You doom your child! Yes, she is alive. But she won't remain alive if you permit the Sartan to shut the Gate."

Haplo said nothing, tried to maintain his outward composure. Xar was swift to read the clenched jaw muscle, the faint pallor, the swift and doubtful glance toward the door that led to the Labyrinth.

"Go to her, my son," Xar said gently. "Go to Marit, find your child. I found her. I know where she is. She is not far, not far at all. Take her and her mother to the Nexus. You will be safe there. When my work here is complete"—the lord made an all-encompassing gesture with his hands—"I will return in triumph to join you. Together, we will defeat our enemies, lock the Sartan in the prison they designed for us! And we will be free!"

Again, Haplo said nothing. But he did not move, did not step aside. He remained, blocking the door.

Xar looked past Haplo, inside Death's Gate. He could not see Alfred, but he could see the swirl of chaos, guessed that Alfred must be having a difficult time of it. So long as chaos prevailed, Xar had nothing to worry about. He had time. He glanced at the runes glowing on the walls. He could read their warning. The Lord of the Nexus turned back to Haplo, who was blocking his way.

"Alfred has tricked you, my son," Xar warned. "He is using you. He will turn on you in the end. Mark my words. He will cast *you* back into prison!"

Haplo did not move.

Xar was beginning to grow angry. He marched forward until he stood directly in front of Haplo. "Your loyalty belongs to me, my son. I gave you life."

Haplo remained silent. His left hand moved to his chest, to the scars over the heart-rune.

Xar reached out, gripped that hand, nails digging into the flesh. "Yes, I let you die! It was my right to take your life, if I needed it. You pledged as much to me there"—the gnarled finger pointed back to the Labyrinth—"in front of the Final Gate."

"Yes, Lord. It was your right."

"I could have killed you, my son. I could have. I did not. Love breaks the heart." Xar sighed. "There is a weakness in me. I admit it—"

"Not a weakness, Lord. Our strength," said Haplo. "That is why we have survived."

"Hatred!" Xar was displeased, his voice cold. "That is why we have survived! And now vengeance is within our grasp! Not only vengeance, but a chance to put the great wrong right! The four worlds will become one again—under our rule!"

"Thousands, millions will die," said Haplo.

"Mensch!" Xar was scornful; then—glancing back at Haplo's face—the lord realized he'd said the wrong thing.

But he was distracted. Keeping one eye on Death's Gate, Xar could see the mad whirl of chaos slowing. He had not overestimated Alfred's power. The Serpent Mage might actually be able to pull this off.

Xar was running out of time. "Forgive my callous attitude, my son. I spoke hastily, without thought. You know that I will do what I can to save as many of the mensch as possible. We will need them to help us rebuild. Tell me the names of those mensch you particularly want protected and I will arrange for them to be transported to the Nexus. You yourself can watch over them. You will be the guarantor of their safety—something you cannot do if Death's Gate is shut. I will not be able to rescue them then. Go to Death's Gate. Take this opportunity. I will send you back to Marit, to your child—"

Haplo did not hesitate. "No, My Lord."

Xar was furious, frustrated. He saw that the chaos inside Death's Gate was ending. A door, at the far end of a long corridor, stood open. Alfred was reaching out his hand to shut it . . .

The Lord of the Nexus had no choice.

"You have thwarted my wishes for the last time, my son!" Xar stretched forth *his* hand, began to chant the runes.

Jonathon's voice rose. "Do no violence!"

The phantasm repeated the warning, but its voice could no longer be heard.

CHAPTER ◆ 30

DEATH'S GATE

◆

ALFRED HAD FORGOTTEN THE TERROR OF JOURNEYING THROUGH DEATH'S GATE, which compresses and combines, sorts out and divides all possibilities at precisely the same moment in time.

Thus he found himself entering an immense, cavernous corridor that was a small aperture growing smaller all the time. The walls and floors and ceiling rushed away from him, expanding ever outward, as the corridor collapsed in on him, crushing him with emptiness.

"I have to ignore this, or I'll go mad!" he realized frantically. "I have to focus on something . . . on the Gate. On shutting the Gate. Where . . . where is it?"

He looked and instantly the possibility that he had found the Gate caused it to appear, even as the possibility that he would never find it made it vanish. He refused to admit the second possibility, held on fast to the first, and he saw—at the far end of the corridor, in front of him, to his rear, moving rapidly toward him, continually receding, growing ever more distant the closer he came —a door.

It was marked with a sigil, the same sigil as the door he'd entered. In between the two doors was the corridor known as Death's Gate. Shut both doors, and he would shut off that corridor forever.

But in order to shut that far door, he had to walk down the corridor.

Chaos danced and shifted around him, the possibilities happening simultaneously, no two at the same time. He was shivering with cold because he was too hot. He had eaten so much he was starving to death. His voice was too loud; he couldn't hear it. He moved extremely fast and never left the place where he was floating, standing, hopping, running, on his head, on his feet, sideways.

"Control," Alfred said to himself desperately. "Control the chaos."

He focused, concentrated, grappled with the possibilities, and finally the corridor was a corridor and it remained a corridor and the ceiling was up and the floor was down and all things were where they should be. The door was at the end of the corridor. It was open. He had only to shut it.

Alfred started forward.

The door moved backward.

He stopped. It kept going.

It stopped. He kept going. Away from it.

"Let go," Jonathon's voice echoed. "And take hold."

"Of course!" Alfred cried. "That is my mistake! That was Samah's mistake. That has always been our mistake, all through the centuries! We seek to control the uncontrollable. Let go . . . let go."

But letting go was not an easy thing to do. It meant giving himself up completely to the chaos.

Alfred tried. He opened his hands. The corridor began to shift; the walls closed in, flew outward. Alfred clenched his fists tight over nothing and held on for dear life.

"I don't think I'm doing this right," he said miserably. "Perhaps I wasn't meant to let go completely. Surely it won't hurt if I hold on to just a tiny piece . . ."

A joyful *whuff* sounded at the far end of the corridor. Alfred whirled about, standing stock-still, and saw a dog—mouth open in a wide grin, tongue lolling—bounding down the corridor, heading straight for him.

"No!" Alfred shouted, raising his hands to ward off the animal.

"No! There's a good boy. Don't come any closer! Nice dog! Good dog! No!"

The dog leapt, struck Alfred squarely in the chest. The Sartan tumbled head over feet backward. Pieces of the magic flew everywhere. He was falling up, soaring down . . .

And there was the door, right in front of him.

Alfred slammed to a halt. And he remained halted.

Thankfully, he mopped his sweating head with his shirt sleeve. It was all so easy, really.

In front of him—an ordinary wooden door with a silver handle. Not very prepossessing, almost a disappointment. Alfred looked through the door, saw the four worlds, saw the Nexus, the Labyrinth, the shattered Vortex.

The Labyrinth. Patryns and Sartan stood drawn up in battle formation on either side of a charred and blackened wall. High above the armies flew the good dragons of Pryan, but few could see them through the smoke and darkness. Everyone could see the Labyrinth's creatures, terrible monsters that lurked in the forests, waiting to fall on the victor. If there could ever be a victor in this hopeless battle.

Other than the serpents.

Bloated, fat with the hatred and the fear, the serpents slithered along on either side of the wall, aiding both armies, whispering, urging, exhorting, lying, fanning the flames of war.

Horrified, sickened, Alfred reached out to slam shut the door.

One of the serpents caught sight of sudden movement, reared its head. It looked up, through the chaos, and saw Alfred.

Death's Gate stood wide open, visible to anyone who knew where to find it.

The snake's red eyes flared in alarm. It saw the danger: forever trapped in the Labyrinth. The way to the lush mensch worlds closed off.

Shrieking a warning, the serpent uncoiled its huge body. Red eyes caught Alfred in their lurid gaze. The serpent screeched hideous threats, conjured up terrifying images of pain-racked torment. Toothless maw gaping wide, the dragon-snake surged toward the open door, moving with the speed and force of a cyclone.

Alfred's hand closed over the silver handle. Shutting out the serpent's hideous voice, the Sartan fought to pull the door shut.

And then, from far, far behind him, he heard a distant voice— Lord Xar's voice.

"You have thwarted my wishes for the last time, my son!"

And Jonathon's voice, "Do no violence!"

Haplo's voice, a cry of pain and anguish . . . and a shouted warning to Alfred.

Too late.

A sigil, red and flaming, shot down the corridor. It burst, like a lightning blast, on Alfred's chest.

Blinded, consumed by fire, he lost his grip on the door handle.

The door swung wide open.

The serpent roared inside.

CHAPTER ◆ 31

THE SEVENTH

GATE

◆

THE SERPENT BURST THROUGH THE DOOR AND INTO DEATH'S GATE AT THE PRE-
cise moment that Xar's sigil struck Alfred.

Chaos broke free of Alfred's fragile grasp and began to feed off
the serpent, which, in turn, fed off chaos. The serpent cast one
glance at the Sartan, saw him horribly injured, probably dying.
Satisfied that Alfred posed no threat, the serpent slithered through
the corridor, heading for the chamber.

Alfred could not stop it. Xar's deadly magic seared his skin like
molten iron. Falling to his knees, Alfred clutched his chest in agony. Sartan of ancient times would have known how to defend
themselves. Alfred had never fought a Patryn. He had never been
trained in warfare. The burning pain robbed him of his senses; he
couldn't think. He only wanted to die and end the torment. But
then he heard Haplo's hoarse shout.

Fear for his friend penetrated the blazing wall of agony. Hardly
knowing what he was doing, acting out of instinct, Alfred began to
do what Ramu would have known to do immediately. Alfred
started to unravel Xar's lethal magic.

The moment he broke the first rune-structure, the pain eased.
Breaking down the rest of the sigla was simple after that, similar to
ripping out a seam once the first thread has been pulled. But
though he was no longer dying, he had let the magical attack go on
too long. It had hurt him, wounded him.

Weakened, Alfred cast a despairing glance at the door leading from Death's Gate into the Labyrinth. He could never shut it now. Chaos buffeted it like a hurricane wind.

He turned, looked down the corridor, trying to see what was happening in the Chamber. But the other door was far, far away from him and so small; he might have been trying to enter a child's dollhouse. The hall leading back to the door undulated and swayed, the floor now the wall, the wall now the ceiling, the ceiling now the floor.

"Violence," Alfred said to himself in despair. "Violence has entered the Sacred Chamber."

What was happening in there? Was Haplo alive or dead?

Alfred tried to stand, but chaos ripped the floor out from under his feet. He tumbled down, landed heavily, gasping for breath. He was too weak to fight, in too much pain, too distracted by his own fear. His clothes hung from him in charred rags. He was afraid to look at the flesh beneath, afraid of what he would see. Gripping hold of the remnants of his faded velvet jacket, he drew the cloth over the wound, hid it from sight.

His hands came away covered with blood.

But he had to do something. He couldn't just sit here. If Haplo was alive, he was fighting his enemies alone . . .

Alfred was about to make another effort to stand when movement caught his attention. He looked out of Death's Gate into the Labyrinth. Hundreds of serpents were surging for the open door.

Haplo lay sprawled on the floor in front of the doorway leading to Death's Gate. He was either unconscious or dead; Xar didn't know which and he didn't care. The lord had also dealt with the so-called Serpent Mage. Another glance showed him Alfred bleeding, weak, crawling about aimlessly on his hands and knees. So much for the powerful Sartan.

Certain he was now safe from interference, Xar immediately turned his attention to the doors leading to the four mensch worlds, began to chant the spell that would collapse all the worlds into one. He paid no attention to the lazar, which was ranting on about bringing violence into the Sacred Chamber.

Xar knew the spell. The Lord of the Nexus, in the guise of Hugh the Hand, had been sitting at the white table. He had shared Alfred's visions of the Sundering. Alfred had, in fact, seen him—a lapse on Xar's part. Fortunately, the Sartan had been so unnerved by the entire experience that he had not known what he'd seen. At that point, Alfred could have made Xar's task far more difficult. As it was now, the Lord of the Nexus had only to reach into the possibilities.

It had taken hundreds of Sartan to work the magic that had broken the world apart. Xar was not daunted by the task, however. It would be far easier to collapse the world, especially since he could call on the power imbued in the Seventh Gate.

Lord Xar had a clear view of each of the four worlds. He began to draw the runes swiftly in the air, sigla of destruction, of reversal and upheaval.

Ferocious storm clouds massed on Arianus.

The four bright suns on Pryan went dark.

The seawaters of Chelestra bubbled and boiled.

Tremors shook the unstable world of Abarrach.

"Your power is immense, Lord of the Nexus," hissed a voice behind Xar. "All honor to you."

Xar turned. A serpent in man's form—resembling one of Xar's own people—stood in the center of the Chamber. The serpent looked exactly like a Patryn in all respects, except that the sigla tattooed on its skin were meaningless scrawls.

Xar was wary. He knew enough about the serpents now not to trust them. He also knew they were powerful in magic. This one might very well disrupt his spell, although it had not done so yet.

"Who are you?" Xar demanded. "What do you want?"

"You know me, Lord," said the serpent. "I am Sang-drax."

"Sang-drax is dead," Xar said crisply. "The serpent died in the Labyrinth."

"Yet here I stand, very much alive. I told your minion"—a red-eyed glance at the fallen Haplo—"and I tell you, Lord of the

Nexus, that we cannot die. We have always been. We will always be."

Xar snorted. "What are you doing here, then? The last I saw, you and your kind were in the Labyrinth, killing my people!"

The serpent was shocked, saddened. "Alas that you refused to take time to let us explain, Lord of the Nexus. Those we attacked in the Labyrinth are not your people, not true Patryns. No, they are an evil mixture—Patryn blood mingled with Sartan. Such a weak strain should not be perpetuated, don't you agree? After all," Sang-drax added, eyes glittering red through hooded lids, "you were there. You could have stopped us."

Xar waved this aside as unimportant. "I heard something of this from Haplo. I do not like the idea, but *I* will deal with these half-breeds when I return to the Labyrinth. I ask you again, why are you here? What do you want?"

"To serve you, My Lord," said the serpent, bowing.

"Then keep watch on Death's Gate," Xar ordered. "I don't want that fool Sartan interfering."

"As you command, My Lord."

Xar kept watch on the serpent from the corner of his eye. Sang-drax moved obediently to take up his post. The lord no longer trusted the serpents, and he understood that he would eventually have to prove to them, once and for all, who was master. But, for now, the serpent was probably telling the truth. It was here to serve, its interests coinciding with his own. He turned back to his magic, which had already started to wane, gave it his full and complete attention.

The moment Xar's back was turned, Sang-drax examined Haplo's body. The Patryn appeared to be dead. The sigla on his skin did not glow in the serpent's presence. Sang-drax, glancing back at Xar, surreptitiously kicked the fallen Patryn with a toe of his boot.

Haplo didn't move.

Engulfed by his magic, Xar didn't notice.

Sang-drax reached into the folds of his clothing, drew forth a dagger, wrought in the shape of a striking snake.

◆

Playing dead had saved Haplo's life more than once in the Labyrinth. The trick was to control the magic, his body's natural defense; prevent the sigla from reacting. The drawback was that this did, in fact, leave him defenseless. But Haplo knew that this Sang-drax the Second or the Second Millionth or whatever the serpent termed itself was not interested in him. The serpent was playing for far larger stakes. It was playing for control of the universe.

Forcing himself to relax, Haplo let his body go limp, absorbed the kick from the serpent without flinching. Fear and revulsion surged through him, his body aching to fight, to defend and protect against the evil that was nearly overwhelming his senses. Haplo grit his teeth. He risked a glance, peering through half-closed eyelids.

He saw Sang-drax and he saw the dagger—a hideous, sinuously curved blade the same gray color as, in its other form, the dragon-snake's scaled body. Sang-drax had no further interest in Haplo. The serpent's red-eyed gaze was fixed on Xar.

Haplo risked surveying the Chamber. Jonathon continued to sit at the white table. The lazar had made no move, seemed unconcerned, uncaring, dead. Haplo glanced back at the door leading to Death's Gate. He couldn't see Alfred through the swirling madness of the chaos, had no idea if the Sartan was dead or alive.

"If he's alive, he's probably fighting his own battle," Haplo reasoned. "Sang-drax undoubtedly brought reinforcements."

As if in response, he heard Alfred give a low cry of horror and despair. He wouldn't be coming to Haplo's aid. And there was nothing Haplo could do to help the Sartan.

Haplo had problems of his own.

Against a ghastly backdrop of storms and fire, of darkness and churning seas, Lord Xar was drawing the intricate pattern of runes that would, when complete, cause the elements of the four worlds to shift and alter, to break apart and collapse. Intent on his spell-casting, Xar did not dare allow his concentration to shift for even a minuscule fraction of a second. So difficult, so immense was the spell, he was forced to pour every portion of his being into it. His own defenses were lowered; the sigla on his wrinkled skin barely glowed.

The magic was a blazing inferno in front of the Lord of the Nexus. His back was unprotected.

Sang-drax raised the dagger. The serpent's red eyes focused on the base of the lord's skull, the place where the protective runes ended.

Silently, the serpent glided toward its victim. But in order to reach Xar, Sang-drax would have to go around Haplo.

If my lord dies, the spell he is casting will be disrupted. The worlds will be safe. I should let Xar die.

As he let me die.

I should do nothing. Let my lord die . . .

I must . . .

"My Lord!" Haplo shouted as he sprang to his feet. "Behind you!"

CHAPTER 32

THE SEVENTH

GATE

◆

ALFRED STARED IN HORROR THROUGH DEATH'S GATE. OTHER SERPENTS HAD LEFT the battle in the Labyrinth, were speeding toward the open door. One, in the vanguard, was almost there.

"Haplo!" Alfred started to call for help and at that moment heard Haplo's warning shout to Lord Xar.

Glancing back over his shoulder, down the chaotic corridor, Alfred could see the Patryn springing to attack the serpent.

Alfred choked back his own cry. He turned helplessly to the open doorway, to the serpent—red eyes gleaming—lunging for it. If that serpent succeeded in entering, it would join its fellow, and Haplo would be fighting two of them. His chances against one were slim; against two the odds would be insurmountable, particularly if Xar turned against him, as seemed very likely.

"I have to stop this one myself!" Alfred said, groping around within himself for the courage, for the other Alfred, for the Alfred whose name was truly Coren—The Chosen.

And suddenly the possibility was enacted that Alfred was back inside the mausoleum of Arianus.

He couldn't believe it. He stared around, confused, yet immeasurably relieved, thankful, as if he'd wakened in his bed to find that the preceding had all been nothing but a terrible nightmare.

The tomb was peaceful, silent. He was secure, safe. The coffins of his friends, sleeping in tranquillity, surrounded him. And as he gazed around in thankful bewilderment, wondering what all this meant, Alfred saw the door of his own coffin open.

He had only to crawl inside, lie down, close his eyes.

Gratefully, he took a step toward it . . . and fell over the dog.

He tumbled to the cold marble floor of the mausoleum, entangled in a confused flurry of paws and plumy tail. The animal yelped in pain. Alfred had landed squarely on top of it.

Crawling out from underneath the spread-eagled Sartan, the animal shook itself indignantly, regarded him with reproachful eyes.

"I'm sorry . . ." Alfred stammered.

His apology echoed through the chamber like the voice of a phantasm. The dog barked irritably.

"You're right," Alfred said, flushing, smiling faintly. "There I go—apologizing. I won't let it happen again."

The door to the coffin slammed shut.

He was back in Death's Gate, inside the corridor, and the serpent was in the doorway.

Alfred let go . . . and seized hold.

A green-scaled and golden-winged dragon, its burnished crest shining like a sun, shattered the corridor of chaos, burst out of Death's Gate, and attacked the serpent.

The dragon's powerful back claws slammed into the serpent's body, slid through the gray-scaled skin, dug deep into flesh.

The serpent, impaled on the dragon's claws, writhed and twisted in an attempt to free itself, but the movement only drove the claws deeper into its body. In terrible pain, the serpent fought back, its toothless, powerful jaws attempting to close around the dragon's slender neck, crack and break it.

The dragon's fangs closed over the snake's snapping jaws, sank into the head, between the red, hate-filled eyes. Blood spurted, raining down on the Labyrinth. The serpent shrieked in its death throes, and its cries reached its fellows.

They began to close ranks around the dragon, preparing to rush in for the kill.

Alfred loosed his claws from the dead serpent, let it fall to the ground. He longed to return to the Chamber, to come to Haplo's aid, but Alfred dared not leave the door unguarded.

The green and golden dragon flew before Death's Gate, awaited the onslaught.

Haplo's cry jolted Xar from his magic. He had no need to look around to know what was happening. The serpent had betrayed him. Xar had barely time enough to reestablish his body's own magical defenses when he was hit from behind. A flash of pain seared the back of his head.

Xar stumbled, turned to defend himself.

Haplo was struggling with Sang-drax, both of them grappling for a bloodstained dagger.

"Lord Xar! This traitor tried to kill you!" Sang-drax snarled, striking viciously at Haplo.

Haplo said nothing, his breath coming in sharp, painful gasps. The sigla on his skin flared blue. There was blood on his hands.

Xar reached to touch the wound, drew back fingers wet with blood.

"Indeed," he said and watched the battle between Haplo and the serpent with a strange detachment. The pain was a distraction, but he didn't have time to heal himself. The rune-construct he had created blazed with a bright light in front of the four doors—the doors that led to the four worlds. But, here and there, the light was starting to fade. Bereft of the lord's power, the magic he had cast was starting to unravel.

Xar irritably wiped away the blood that was starting to ooze down his neck and into his robes. The blood might have been someone else's for all the thought he gave it.

Sang-drax struck Haplo again and again—savage, vicious blows that cracked open the rune-magic, began to bruise and batter flesh and bone. Haplo's face was smeared with blood. He was half-blind, stunned, could do little to halt the brutal attack. Blow after blow drove Haplo to his knees. A vicious kick in the face sent him reeling backward. He fell, lay unconscious. On the floor near him was the snake-shaped dagger.

Sang-drax turned to face Xar.

The Lord of the Nexus tensed. The serpent stood between Xar and the magical rune-construct.

Sang-drax pointed at the fallen Haplo.

"This treacherous servant of yours tried to murder you, Lord of the Nexus! Fortunately, I was able to stop him. Say the word and I will end his life."

Haplo rolled over, lay face first on the blood-spattered floor.

"You needn't waste your time," Xar said, drawing closer to Haplo, to the serpent, to the magic. "I will deal with him. Stand aside."

The serpent's red eyes gleamed with a bright, suspicious light. Swiftly, Sang-drax hooded his emotion, lowering the eyelids.

"I am only too pleased to obey you, Lord. First"—the serpent swooped down—"allow me to retrieve the traitor's dagger. He might be shamming again."

Sang-drax's hand closed over empty air.

Xar—quite by inadvertence—had placed his foot on the blood-covered blade. He knelt beside Haplo, all the while keeping an eye on Sang-drax. The lord grasped hold—not gently—of Haplo's chin, turned his face to the light. A savage cut had split open Haplo's forehead, practically to the bone.

The lord traced, swiftly, obliquely, a healing sigil over the wound, closing it, stopping the bleeding. Then, after a moment's hesitation, Xar traced another sigil on Haplo's forehead, a copy of the one over Xar's own heart. He traced it in blood; it wouldn't last. It had no power . . . no magical power.

At his lord's touch, Haplo groaned; his eyes flickered open. Xar increased the pressure, digging his gnarled fingers deep into Haplo's flesh.

Haplo looked up, blinked. He was having difficulty focusing, and when he could see, he seemed puzzled. Then he sighed and smiled. Reaching out his hand, he clasped Xar's wrist.

"My Lord," Haplo murmured. "I'm here . . . I've reached it. The Final Gate."

"What is he talking about, Lord?" Sang-drax demanded nervously. "What is he telling you? Lies, My Lord. Lies."

"He's not saying anything important," Xar replied. "He imagines he is back in the Labyrinth."

Haplo shuddered. His voice hardened, grew strong. "I beat it, Lord. I defeated it."

"You did, my son," Xar said. "You won a great victory."

Haplo smiled. He clung to Xar's hand a moment longer, then let go. "Thank you for your help, My Lord, but I do not need you now. I can walk through the Gate on my own."

"So you can, my son," said Xar softly. "So you can."

Sang-drax spoke a sigil—a Sartan sigil—and drew a Patryn sigil in the air at the same time. The two runes flared, flashed, and flew toward the construct Xar had created.

But the Lord of the Nexus had been watching, waiting for the serpent to make just such a move. He reacted swiftly, cast his own rune. The constructs met, burst, exploded in a shower of sparks, and canceled each other out.

Xar rose to his feet. He held the snake dagger in his hand.

"I know the real traitor," he said, watching Sang-drax, who watched the lord through narrowed, glittering red eyes. "I know who has tried to bring my people to ruin."

"You want to see the person who has brought destruction to his people?" Sang-drax sneered, mocking. "Look in a mirror, Lord of the Nexus!"

"Yes," said Xar quietly, "I look in a mirror."

Sang-drax shed the Patryn body, took on serpent form, growing, expanding until the great, slime-covered bulk filled the Chamber of the Damned.

"Thank you, Lord of the Nexus, for casting the spell to tear down the worlds," said the serpent, its head rearing upward. "It was, I admit, a plan we had not considered. But it will work out well for us. We will feed off the turmoil and chaos for eons to come. And your people, trapped forever in the Labyrinth. I regret you will not live to see it, Lord Xar, but you are far too dangerous—"

The serpent's toothless maw opened. Xar looked at his doom. Then he turned away.

He gave his attention to the magic, to the wondrous rune-construct he had created. The magic he had spent his life creating—a dream forged out of hatred.

He knew the snake was attacking, lethal jaws opening wide to devour him.

With a steady hand, he drew the sigil in the air. Its fire glowed blue, then red, then hot white, blazing, blinding. Xar spoke the command, his voice firm, clear, loud.

The sigil struck the magical rune-construct, burst on it like an exploding star, tore the heart out of the spell.

Snapping jaws closed over the Lord of the Nexus.

CHAPTER ◆ 33

THE SEVENTH

GATE

◆

THE SERPENTS FLEW TOWARD DEATH'S GATE. THE OPENING WAS CLEARLY VISIBLE now, a black patch in the gray, smoke-filled sky above the Labyrinth. Below, the Final Gate remained open, but the Sartan were massing their forces along it; the Patryns were doing the same on the opposite side.

Alfred tried to contain his despair, but he could not hope to hold the Gate against the enormous power of the enemy. Frightful sounds from the Chamber behind him unnerved him, distracted his attention when he needed to concentrate on his magic. Frantically, he searched through the possibilities, trying to find one that would come to his aid, but it seemed he was seeking to do the impossible.

Whatever spell he cast, the serpents had the ability to rip it asunder. He had never realized before how truly powerful the creatures were—either that or they were gaining strength and power from the war below. Sick at heart, the green and golden dragon kept guard before Death's Gate and waited for the end.

A shape loomed into view, swooping at him from the side.

Bracing himself, Alfred swerved to fight.

He faced an old man seated on a dragon's back. The old man was dressed in mouse-colored robes, his white hair flew out wildly behind.

"Red Leader to Red One!" the old man howled. "Come in, Red One!"

The serpents were spreading out, sending some to deal with Alfred. The rest were massing to enter Death's Gate.

"Break off the attack, Red One," the old man shouted and waved a hand. "Go rescue the princess! My squadron'll take over!"

Behind the old man, legions of dragons of Pryan flew out of the smoke of the burning Nexus.

"How do you like my ship?" The old man patted the dragon's neck. "Made the Kessel run in six parsecs!"

The dragon dropped suddenly from the skies, diving for one of the serpents. The old man gave Alfred a salute before he disappeared from view. The other Pryan dragons followed, soaring into the battle against their enemies.

Alfred no longer had to deal with his enemies alone. He could return to the Chamber of the Damned. He flew inside Death's Gate. Once there, he altered his form, was again the tall and gangling, balding, velvet-coated Sartan. He stood for a moment watching the fight.

Confronted by a courageous, determined foe, most of the serpents were fleeing.

"Good-bye, Zifnab," Alfred said quietly.

Sighing, he turned back to face the chaos reverberating throughout the hall behind him.

And, as he did so, he heard a faint cry.

"The name's . . . Luke . . ."

Inside the Chamber of the Damned, the serpent crushed Xar in its toothless mouth, then flung the broken and bloodied body into the softly glowing walls of the Chamber of the Damned.

The lord's body hit with a bone-crushing thud, slid down the wall, leaving a smear of blood on the white marble. Xar lay in a crumpled heap at the bottom. The serpent shrieked in triumph.

"My Lord!" Haplo was on his feet, dizzy and weak, but no longer disoriented.

"There is nothing you can do," said the serpent. "The Lord of the Nexus is dead."

The serpent's red eyes turned on Haplo.

Through the four doors behind him, Haplo could see the four worlds. The storms on Arianus were beginning to abate. The seas of Chelestra were once more calm. Pryan's suns shone with blinding brilliance. Abarrach's crust shuddered and was still. The crumpled body of his lord lay in a pool of blood.

Seated at the white table, Jonathon intoned, "Do no violence."

"It's a little late for that," Haplo said grimly.

The serpent loomed over him, its huge head weaving hypnotically back and forth, red eyes staring down at him.

Haplo's only weapon was the snake-shaped dagger. He was surprised to feel how well it fit his hand, the hilt seeming to adapt itself to his touch. But the short blade would be less than an insect bite on the thick and magical skin of the serpent.

Haplo gripped the weapon, eyed the monster, waited for the attack. The sigla on his skin flared brightly.

The serpent began to shift form, dwindling in size until, within the span of an eyeblink, an elf lord stood in the Chamber.

Giving Haplo an ingratiating smile, Sang-drax began to sidle closer.

"Far enough," said Haplo, raising the knife.

Sang-drax halted. Slender, delicate hands raised, palms facing outward, in a gesture of surrender and conciliation. He looked hurt, disappointed.

"Is this how you thank me, Haplo?" Sang-drax made a graceful gesture toward Xar. "But for my intervention, he would have taken your life."

Haplo cast Xar's body a glance, quickly brought his attention back to Sang-drax, who—in the intervening time—had once again attempted to draw near the Patryn.

"You killed my liege lord," said Haplo quietly.

Sang-drax laughed in disbelief. "Liege lord! I killed the lord who ordered Bane to have you assassinated. The lord who seduced the woman you love, then convinced her to murder you. The lord who was going to chain you to a life of torment among the undead! That's your liege lord for you."

"If my lord required my death as payment for my life, then that was his right," Haplo returned, holding the dagger high and steady. "You are wasting my time. Whatever it is you mean to do to me, get on with it."

He wondered where Alfred was, could only assume the Sartan was dead.

Sang-drax was perplexed. "My dear Haplo, I have no weapons. I am not a threat to you. No, I want to serve you. My people want to serve you. Once I bowed down to you and called you 'Master.' I do so again."

The serpent in elf form made a low and servile bow, red eyes lowered, hooded. Crouching like a toad, he made another attempt to creep up on Haplo, halted at the flash of the snake-shaped blade.

"The Sartan have arrived in the Nexus," Sang-drax continued, voice sibilant. "Do you know that, Haplo? Ramu plans to seal shut the Final Gate. I can stop them. My people and I can destroy them. You have only to say the word, and your enemy's blood will be sweet wine for you to savor. We ask one small favor in return."

"And that is—?" Haplo asked.

Sang-drax looked toward the four doors; the red eyes glinted eagerly, hungrily. "Cast the spell, the one your lord was weaving. You can do it, Haplo. You are as powerful as Xar. And I will be glad to offer my poor help—"

Haplo smiled grimly, shook his head.

"Surely you don't refuse?" Sang-drax was pained, sadly astonished.

Haplo didn't answer. Instead, he began walking backward, toward the first door—Arianus.

Sang-drax watched, red eyes narrowing. "What are you doing, Haplo, my friend?"

"Shutting the door, Sang-drax, my friend," Haplo returned. "Shutting *all* the doors."

"A mistake, Haplo." The serpent hissed softly. "A terrible mistake."

Haplo looked down onto Arianus, world of air. The storm clouds were being blown apart; Solarus was shining. He could see the continent of Drevlin, the metal parts of the great Kicksey-winsey flashing in the intermittent sunlight. He could picture Limbeck the dwarf, peering nearsightedly through his thick lenses, giving a speech to which no one was listening, except Jarre. And perhaps, someday, a host of small Limbecks who would change a world with their "whys."

Haplo smiled, said good-bye, and slammed shut the door.

Sang-drax hissed again in displeasure.

Haplo didn't look at the serpent; he could tell by the fact that the light was growing dark in the Chamber that the creature was once more altering its shape.

The next door, Pryan, world of fire. Blinding sunlight, a contrast to the growing shadows gathering around him. Tiny silver stars were glittering jewels set in a green velvet jungle. The citadels, come to life, beamed their light and energy out into the universe. Paithan and Rega, Aleatha and Roland and the dwarf Drugar—mankind, elfkind, dwarfkind—loving, fighting, living, dying. According to Xar, they had learned the secret of the tytans. They were operating the citadels. Haplo would never know their fate. But he was confident that—resilient, strong in their many weaknesses, with an indomitable spirit—the mensch would thrive when the gods who had brought them to this world were gone and forgotten.

Haplo said good-bye and slammed shut the door.

"You have doomed yourself, Patryn," warned a sibilant voice. "You will meet the same end as your lord."

Haplo didn't look. He could hear the serpent's huge body scraping against the stone floor, could smell the foul odor of death and decay, could almost feel the slime on his skin.

He took a quick look at Abarrach, a dead world, populated by the dead. Jonathon had wanted to free them, free himself. That would not happen, apparently.

I have failed them, too, Haplo said to himself.

"I'm sorry," he said as he closed the door, and he smiled rue-fully. He sounded very much like Alfred.

He reached the fourth door, Chelestra, world of water. On this world he had, at last, come to know himself. He heard the serpent hiss behind him, but steadfastly ignored the sound. The dwarf maid Grundle had probably married her Hartmut by now. The wedding would have been quite a party: the elves, dwarves, and humans gathering together to celebrate. Haplo wondered how Grundle had done in the ax-throwing contest.

He whispered good-bye and good luck to her and to her hus-band, and shut the door softly, with a momentary pang of regret. Then he turned to face Sang-drax.

The snake-shaped dagger in Haplo's hand changed to a sword, made of fine steel, gleaming, heavy. His magic had not altered it. The serpent must have.

The gigantic gray body towered over him, its very presence crushing. The serpent could have struck him from behind at any time, but it didn't want him to die without a struggle, without a fight, without pain and fear . . .

Haplo raised the sword, braced himself for the attack.

"Don't, Haplo! Put the weapon down!"

Alfred tumbled out of Death's Gate. He would have gone sprawling on the floor, but he saved himself by grabbing hold of the white table. Clinging to it, he gasped, *"Don't* fight!"

"Yes, Haplo," the serpent mocked, "put the sword down! Your dying will be so much faster that way."

There was blood on Haplo's shirt. The wound over his heart had broken open, was bleeding again. Oddly, the dagger wound he'd taken on his forehead didn't pain him at all.

"Use nothing." Alfred sucked in a gulping breath, struggling to remain calm. "Refuse to fight. It's the fight the creature wants!" The Sartan pointed to the body of Lord Xar. " 'Those who bring violence in this place will find it turned against them.' "

Haplo hesitated. All his life, he had fought to survive. Now he was being asked to cast away his weapon, refuse to fight, meekly await torture, torment, death . . . Worse, endure the knowledge that his enemy would live to destroy others.

"You're asking too much, Alfred," he said harshly. "Next, I suppose you'll want me to faint!"

Alfred stretched forth his hands. "Haplo, I beg—"

The serpent's huge tail slashed around, struck the Sartan a blow across his back that doubled him over the white table.

Sang-drax reared up. The serpent's head hung poised over Alfred. The red eyes focused on Haplo. "The next blow will break his spine. And the one after that will crush his body. Fight, Haplo, or the Sartan dies."

Alfred managed to lift his head. His nose was broken, his lip split. Blood smeared his face. "Don't listen, Haplo! If you fight, you are doomed!"

The serpent waited, smug, knowing it had won.

Burning with anger and the strong need to kill this loathsome being, Haplo cast a bitter, frustrated glance at Alfred. "Do you expect me to stand here and die?"

"Trust me, Haplo!" Alfred pleaded. "It's all I've ever asked of you! Trust me!"

"Trust a Sartan!" Sang-drax laughed horribly. "Trust your mortal enemy! Trust those who sent you to the Labyrinth, who are responsible for the deaths of how many thousands of your people? Your parents, Haplo. Do you remember how they died? Your mother's screams. She screamed a long, long time, didn't she, before they finally left her to die of her wounds. And you saw it. You saw what they did to her. This man—responsible. And he begs you to trust him . . ."

Haplo closed his eyes. His head had begun to hurt; he felt blood sticky on his hands. He was that child again, cowering in the bushes, stunned and dazed from the blow inflicted by his father. The blow had been intended to knock him out, to keep him silent and safe while his parents drew their attackers away from their child. But his parents had not been able to run far. Haplo had regained consciousness.

His own wail of fear and terror was choked off by his horror. And hate. Hate for those who had done this, who were responsible . . .

Haplo gripped the sword tightly, waited for the blood-red tinge to fade from his eyes so that he could see his prey . . . and nearly dropped the weapon when he felt the quick swipe of a wet tongue.

There came a reassuring whine, a paw on his knee.

Haplo reached down his hand, stroked the silky ears. The dog's head pressed against his knee. He felt the hard bone, the warmth, the soft fur. And yet he wasn't surprised to find, when he opened his eyes, that no dog stood beside him.

Haplo threw down his sword.

Sang-drax laughed in derision. The serpent reared up. It would smash the helpless Patryn, crush him. But in its eager rage, the serpent miscalculated. It grew too big, soared upward too far. The gigantic head crashed through the marble ceiling of the Chamber of the Damned.

The runes traced on the ceiling crackled and flared; arcs of blue and red flame surged through the serpent's body. Sang-drax shrieked in agony, writhed and twisted, attempting to escape the jolting flashes. But the serpent couldn't pull itself out from the wreckage of the ceiling. It was trapped. It flailed wildly, furiously to free itself. Cracks in the ceiling started to expand, splitting the walls.

The Chamber of the Damned—the Seventh Gate—was crumbling. And there was only one way out—Death's Gate.

Haplo took a step. The serpent's tail thrashed out. Even in its agony, it was intent on killing him.

Haplo twisted to one side, but could not avoid the blow. It caught him on his left shoulder, already aching from the reopening of the wound over the heart-rune. He gasped with the pain, fought the blackness of unconsciousness stealing over him.

Slowly, he raised himself to his feet. His hand had, inexplicably, closed over the hilt of his sword.

"Fight me!" the serpent urged. "Fight me . . ."

Haplo lifted the sword, sent it crashing down upon the white stone table. The blade broke in two. Haplo raised the hilt for the serpent to see, then tossed it away.

The serpent tried desperately to free itself, but the magic of the Seventh Gate held it enthralled. Arcs of blue flame danced over the slime-covered body. It lashed out once again.

Haplo made a dive for Alfred, who lay bleeding and dazed on top of the white table. The serpent's tail smacked into the table, cracked it. But the serpent was in its death throes. Blind, in terrible pain, it could no longer see its prey. In a last desperate attempt to free itself, the serpent lunged against the forces of magic that bound it in place. The ceiling began to break apart under the strain. A large chunk of marble fell down, missing Alfred by only inches. Another block landed on the serpent's now feebly twitching tail. A wooden beam crashed down, smashing the white table into two complete and separate halves.

Stumbling through the raining debris, choking on the dust, Haplo managed to reach Alfred. He grabbed hold of the first part of the Sartan that came to hand—the back of Alfred's velvet coat—and pulled him up on his feet.

Alfred flopped and staggered, limp as a maltreated doll.

Haplo peered through the dust and ruin. "Jonathon!" he shouted.

He thought he could see the lazar, still sitting calmly at one half of the broken table, oblivious to the destruction that was soon going to encompass it.

"Jonathon!" Haplo called.

No answer. And then he couldn't see the lazar at all. An enormous slab of marble smashed down between them.

Alfred slumped to the floor.

Haplo hooked his hand firmly in the Sartan's coat collar, began dragging him through the tumult. The runes tattooed on the Patryn's skin burned red and blue, protecting him from the falling debris. He expanded the aura of his magic to include Alfred. A glowing shell of runes encompassed them. Blocks of stone hit and bounced off. But each time something struck the shell, a sigil weakened. Soon one would give. And the unraveling would begin.

Haplo counted fifteen, maybe twenty steps to reach Death's Gate.

He didn't say to himself *to reach the safety of Death's Gate*, because for all he knew, once inside, they faced worse odds. But death was a possibility there, here a certainty. Already, he could see one sigil in the shell start to go dark . . .

He hauled Alfred across the floor, heading for the doorway, when suddenly the floor that had been in front of him wasn't anymore.

A gaping hole opened into endless nothing. Chunks of marble and splintered white wood slid into the crack and disappeared. Death's Gate glimmered on the other side.

The crack wasn't wide. Haplo could have jumped across it easily. But he couldn't jump across it and carry Alfred with him. He dragged Alfred to his feet. The Sartan's knees turned inward; his body sagged.

"Damn it!" Haplo shook the Sartan, hauled him to his feet again.

Alfred was conscious, but he was staring around him with the befuddled expression of one whose wits are wandering.

"So what else is new," Haplo muttered. "Alfred!" He smacked the Sartan across the face.

Alfred gasped, gargled. His eyes focused. He stared around him in horror. "What—"

Haplo didn't let him finish. He didn't dare give Alfred time to think about what he was going to have to do.

"When I say 'jump,' you jump."

Haplo spun Alfred around, positioned the muddled Sartan on the very edge of the gaping crack in the floor. "Jump!"

Not fully cognizant of what was happening, numb with terror and astonishment, Alfred did as he was told. He gave a convulsive leap, legs jerking like a galvanized spider, and flung himself across the crack.

His toes hooked the opposite edge. He landed flat on his stomach, the breath knocked from his body. Haplo cast a swift glance down into the abysmal darkness beneath him; then he jumped.

Landing easily on the other side, Haplo caught hold of Alfred. Together, the two stumbled out of the Chamber of the Damned and into the opening of Death's Gate.

Haplo, looking back, saw the Seventh Gate collapse in on itself.

And with the sickening sensation of sliding down a chute, Haplo felt himself falling into the chaos.

CHAPTER 34

THE SEVENTH

GATE

◆

"WHAT THE DEVIL'S HAPPENING?" HAPLO CRIED, SCRABBLING TO HANG ON. HIS hands could find no purchase on the slick, listing floor. "What's going on?"

Alfred, too, was slowly sliding downward. The corridor that was Death's Gate had become a cyclone, whirling and spiraling, a vortex whose heart was the Chamber of the Damned—the Seventh Gate.

"Merciful Sartan!" Alfred gasped in shock. "The Seventh Gate is collapsing and taking the rest of creation with it!"

They were sliding right back into the Chamber of the Damned; Death's Gate was sliding back into the Chamber, and after that, everything else. Frantically, the Sartan tried to stop his fall, but there was nothing to hang on to; the floor was too slick.

"What do we do?" Haplo shouted.

"I can think of only one thing! And it might be the right thing and it might be the wrong. You see—"

"Just do it!" Haplo bellowed. He was very near the door.

"We've got . . . to shut Death's Gate!"

They were falling into the ruined Chamber with a rapidity that made Alfred sick to watch. He had the horrible impression that he was sliding into the serpent's gaping maw. He could swear that he saw two red eyes, burning with hunger . . .

"The spell, damn it!" Haplo yelled, trying vainly to halt his fall.

This is the moment in my life I've been dreading! Alfred thought. The one I've tried all my life to avoid. Everything depends on me.

He shut his eyes, tried to concentrate, reached forth into the possibilities. He was close, so very close. He began singing the runes in a trembling voice. His hand touched the door. He pushed on it . . .

Pushed hard, harder . . .

The door wouldn't budge.

Fearfully, Alfred opened his eyes. Whatever he had done had at least slowed their descent. But Death's Gate remained open; the universe was still tumbling down into it.

"Haplo! I need your help!" Alfred quavered.

"Are you mad? Patryn magic and Sartan magic can't work together!"

"How do we know?" Alfred returned desperately. "Just because it's never been done, at least that we're aware of. Who knows but that somewhere, sometime in the past—"

"All right! All right! Shutting Death's Gate. That's it? That's what we've got to do?"

"Concentrate on that!" Alfred cried. Their rate of descent was increasing once again.

Haplo spoke the runes. Alfred sang them. Sigla flared in the middle of the slanting corridor. The rune-structures were similar, but the differences were clearly obvious—appallingly obvious. The two magicks hung far apart, glowing with a weak and sullen flame that would soon flicker and die. Alfred stared at them, despaired.

"Well, we tried . . ."

Haplo swore in frustration. "It won't end like this! Try harder. Sing, damn you! Sing!"

Alfred sucked in a deep breath, began to sing.

To his astonishment, Haplo joined him. The Patryn's baritone slid in under, lifted, and supported Alfred's high-pitched tenor.

A warmth flooded through Alfred. His voice grew stronger; he sang louder and with more assurance. Uncertain of the melody, Haplo scrambled around the notes, hitting them as near he could, depending on volume rather than accuracy.

The sigla began to burn brighter. The runes moved closer together, and soon it was apparent to Alfred that the differences in the structures were designed to complement each other, just as the incisions on a latchkey adapt to the wards of a lock.

A flare of radiance, brighter than the white-glowing heart of Pryan's four suns, seared Alfred's eyeballs. He shut his eyes, but the light burned through them, dazzling, explosive, bursting inside his head.

He heard a muffled thud, as of, somewhere in the distance, a door slammed shut.

And then everything was dark. He was floating, not in a sickening spiral, but gently, as if his body were made of thistledown and he were riding on a rolling wave.

"I think it worked," he said to himself.

And the thought came to him that he could die now, without apology.

CHAPTER ◆ 35

THE LABYRINTH

◆

Haplo was hurt and exhausted. He'd spent the day running from his foes, turning and fighting when they had him cornered. Now, at last, he'd eluded them. But he was weak, wandering, needing desperately to stop and heal himself. But he dared not. He was alone in the Labyrinth. To lie down and sleep was to lie down and die.

Alone. It was what his name meant, after all. Haplo. Single. Alone.

And then a voice said softly, "You are not alone."

Haplo lifted his dimming eyes. "Marit?" He was disbelieving. She was illusion, the result of his pain, of his terrible longing and despair.

Strong arms, warm and supporting, reached around his shoulders, bore him up when he would have fallen. He leaned thankfully against her. Gently, she eased him to the ground, pillowed his hurting body on a bed of leaves. He looked up at her. She knelt beside him.

"I've been searching for you," he said.

"You've found me," she answered.

Smiling, she placed her hand over his torn heart-rune. Her touch eased his pain. He could see her clearly now.

"It will never heal completely, I'm afraid," she said.

He reached up his hand, brushed back her hair. The sigil on her skin, Xar's sigil, was starting to fade. But it, too, would never heal.

She flinched at his touch, but she continued to smile. Taking hold of his hand, she pressed her lips against the palm.

Full consciousness brought awareness, the danger . . .

"We can't stay here," he said, sitting up.

She stopped him, hands against his shoulders. "We're safe. At least for the moment. Let go, Haplo. Let go of the fear and the hatred. It is all ended now."

She was partly wrong. It had only just begun.

He lay back down in the leaves, drew her to lie beside him.

"I won't let go of you," he said.

She laid her head on his chest, over the heart-rune, the name-rune.

A single sigil, torn in two.

Stronger for the break.

CHAPTER ◆ 36

THE LABYRINTH

◆

"WHAT'S THE MATTER WITH HIM?" ASKED A WOMAN. SHE SOUNDED FAMILIAR, but Alfred couldn't place the voice. "Is he hurt?"

"No," a man answered. "He's likely just fainted."

I have not! Alfred wanted to return indignantly. I'm dead! I—

He heard himself make a noise, a croak.

"There, what did I tell you? He's coming round."

Alfred cautiously opened his eyes. He looked up into the branches of a tree. He was lying on soft grass. A woman knelt beside him.

"Marit?" he said, staring at her in wonder. "Haplo?"

His friend stood near.

Marit smiled down at Alfred, placed her hand gently on his forehead. "How do you feel?"

"I'm . . . I'm not sure." Alfred gingerly examined his various body parts, was surprised not to experience any pain. But then, of course, he wouldn't, would he? "Are you dead, too?"

"You're not dead," said Haplo grimly. "Not yet, at any rate."

"Not yet . . ."

"You're in the Labyrinth, my friend. And likely to be here for a good long time."

"Then it worked!" Alfred breathed. He sat up. Tears filled his eyes. "Our magic worked! Death's Gate is—"

"Closed," said Haplo and he smiled his quiet smile. "The Seventh Gate destroyed. The magic dumped us here, apparently. And, like I said, we're going to be here a while."

Alfred sat up. "Is there fighting?"

Haplo's face darkened. "About to begin, according to Vasu. He's been trying to open negotiations with Ramu, but the Councillor refuses to even talk. Claims it's only a trap."

"The wolfen and the chaodyn are massing for an assault," Marit added. "There've already been skirmishes along the edges of the forest. If the Sartan would join together with us, but—" She shrugged, shook her head. "We thought maybe you could talk to Ramu."

Alfred staggered to his feet. He still couldn't quite believe that he wasn't dead. He gave himself a surreptitious pinch, winced in pain. Perhaps he *was* alive . . .

"I don't think I'd be of much help," he said ruefully. "Ramu thinks I'm every bit as bad as any Patryn who ever lived. Or maybe worse. And if he ever found out I combined my magic with yours . . ."

"And that they worked," Haplo added, grinning.

Alfred nodded, smiled back. He knew he should be downhearted over this, but couldn't help himself. Joy seemed to be bubbling up in his heart. He glanced around his surroundings, caught his breath.

Two bodies lay on a bower of leaves in the center of a glade. One was clad in black robes, gnarled hands rested across the chest. The other was the body of a mensch, a human.

"Hugh the Hand!" Alfred didn't know whether to be glad or to weep. "Is he . . . is he . . ."

"He is dead," said Marit gently. "He gave his life fighting to defend my people. We found him alongside the bodies of several chaodyn. He was as you see him now. At rest, at peace. When I found him dead"—her voice broke, and Haplo moved near, put his arm around her—"I knew that something awful had happened in Death's Gate. And I knew I should be afraid, but I wasn't."

Alfred could only nod, unable to speak. Next to Hugh lay Xar, Lord of the Nexus.

Haplo followed his gaze, guessed what he was thinking. "We found him here, like this."

With subdued heart and a mixture of conflicting emotions, Alfred approached the dead.

Xar's face, in death, looked far older than it had in life. Lines and wrinkles that had been drawn to a taut fierceness by the lord's hatred and his indomitable will sagged now, revealing hidden pain and suffering, deep and abiding sorrow. He stared up at the sky with dark, unseeing eyes, stared up at the sky of the prison house he had escaped, only to find himself back again.

Alfred knelt down beside the body. Reaching out a gentle hand, he closed the staring eyes.

"He understood . . . at the end," came a voice, very near them. "Do not grieve for him."

Jonathon stood behind them.

And it *was* Jonathon! It wasn't the dreadful lazar, the walking corpse, covered with its own blood, the marks of its painful death visible upon it. It was Jonathon, the young man, as they had known him . . .

"Alive!" Alfred cried.

Jonathon shook his head. "I am no longer one of the tormented undead. But neither have I returned to life. Nor would I. As the prophecy foretold, the Gate has opened. I will soon go back to the worlds and lead forth those souls trapped within them. I remained only to free these two."

He gestured to Lord Xar and to Hugh the Hand.

"They have both passed beyond. And this will be the last time I walk among the living. Farewell."

Jonathon began to walk away. And, as he did so, his corporeal body started to fade, until he became as dust, glittering faintly in a shaft of bright sunlight.

"Wait!" Alfred cried desperately, running after, stumbling over rocks in his effort to catch up with the ephemeral being. "Wait! You must tell me what has happened. I don't understand!"

Jonathon did not pause.

"Please!" Alfred begged. "I feel strangely at peace. The same way I felt the first time I was in the Chamber of the Damned. Does . . . does this mean I can contact the higher power?"

There came no answer. Jonathon had disappeared.

"You rang?"

The pointed end of a disreputable-looking hat appeared from around the bole of a tree. The rest of the hat followed along, bringing with it an old wizard in mouse-colored robes.

"Zifnab," Haplo muttered. "Surely not—"

"Don't call me Shirley!" the old man snapped. Entering the glade, he stared around in vague confusion. "My name's . . . well . . . it's . . . Oh, the hell with it! Call me Shirley if you want. Rather a pleasant name. Grows on you. Now, what was the question?"

Alfred was staring at Zifnab in sudden, dawning comprehension. "You! You're the higher power. You are God!"

Zifnab stroked his beard, attempted to look modest. "Well, now that you mention it—"

"No, sir. Absolutely not." An enormous dragon emerged from the forest.

"Why not?" Zifnab appeared nettled, drew himself up indignantly. "I was a god once, you know."

"Was that before or after you joined Her Majesty's Secret Service, sir?" responded the dragon in a sepulchral tone.

"You needn't be insulting." Zifnab sniffed. He sidled close to Alfred, kept his voice low. "I was so too a god. They find out in the last chapter. He's just jealous, you know . . ."

"I beg your pardon, sir?" said the dragon. "I couldn't quite hear that."

"Zealous," Zifnab amended hastily. "Said you were zealous."

"You are not a god, sir," repeated the dragon. "You must come to understand that."

"Sounds like my therapist," Zifnab said, but he didn't say it very loudly. Heaving a sigh, he twiddled his hat in his hand. "Oh, have it your way. Around here, I'm pretty much the same as all the

rest of you. But I don't mind saying I'm extremely miffed about it."
He cast a baleful glare at the dragon.

"But," Alfred argued, "then where is the higher power? I know
there is one. Samah encountered it. The Abarrach Sartan who entered the Chamber ages ago discovered it."

"The Sartan on Chelestra did the same," Haplo added.

"So they did," said Zifnab. "So have you."

"Oh!" Alfred's face was alight, aglow. Then, slowly, his glow
faded. "But I didn't *see* anything."

"Of course not," said Zifnab. "You looked in the wrong place.
You've always looked in the wrong place."

"In a mirror," Haplo murmured, remembering his lord's last
words.

"Ah, ha!" Zifnab shouted. "That's the ticket!" The old man
reached out a skinny hand, jabbed Alfred on the breast. "Look in a
mirror."

"D-dear me, no!" Alfred blushed, stammered. "I don't! I can't!
I'm not the higher power!"

"But you are." Zifnab smiled, waved his arms. "And so is
Haplo. And so am I. So is—let's see, on Arianus, we have four
thousand six hundred and thirty-seven inhabitants of the Mid
Realms alone. Their names, in alphabetical order, are Aaltje, Aal-
truide, Aaron . . ."

"We get your point, sir," said the dragon sternly.

The old man was ticking them off on his fingers. "Aastami,
Abbie . . ."

"But we can't *all* be gods," Alfred protested, confused.

"Don't know why not." Zifnab huffed. "Might be a damn good
thing. Make us think twice. But if you don't like that notion, think
of yourself as a teardrop in an ocean."

"The Wave," said Haplo.

"All of us, drops in the ocean, forming the Wave. Usually we
keep the Wave in balance—water lapping gently on the shoreline,
hula girls swaying in the sand," said Zifnab dreamily. "But sometimes we throw the Wave out of kilter. Tsunami. Tidal distur-
bances. Hula girls washed out to sea. But the Wave will always act

to correct itself. Unfortunately"—he sighed—"that sometimes sends water foaming up in the opposite direction."

"I still don't understand, I'm afraid," Alfred said sadly.

"You will, old chap." Zifnab smote him on the back. "You're destined to write a book on the subject. Nobody will read it, of course, but—hey—that's the publishing game for you. It's the creative process that counts. Consider Emily Dickinson. Wrote for years in an attic. Nobody ever read—"

"Excuse me, sir," the dragon mercifully interrupted. "But we don't have time to discuss Miss Dickinson. There is the matter of the impending battle."

"What? Ah, yes." Zifnab tugged on his beard. "I can't quite see how we're going to get out of this one. Ramu is a thickheaded, hardhearted, stubborn old—"

"If I may say so, sir," said the dragon, "it was *you* who gave him the wrong information—"

"Got him here, didn't I!" Zifnab cried triumphantly. "You think he would have come otherwise? Not on your Great-Aunt Minnie! He'd still be hanging around Chelestra, causing no end of trouble. Now, here, he's—"

"Causing no end of trouble," concluded the dragon gloomily.

"Well, actually, that's not precisely true anymore."

Headman Vasu, accompanied by Balthazar, entered the glade.

"We bring good news. For the time being, there will be no battle. At least not among ourselves. Ramu has been forced to resign his post as Councillor. I have taken over. Our people"— Balthazar glanced at Headman Vasu, who smiled—"are now forming an alliance. Working together, we should be able to drive back the armies of evil."

"That is truly good news, sir. My kind will welcome it. You both realize," the dragon added gravely, "that this battle will not be the end. The evil present in the Labyrinth will remain here forever, although its effect will be lessened by the advent of trust and reconciliation between your two peoples." The dragon glanced at Alfred. "The Wave correcting itself, sir."

"Yes, I see," said Alfred thoughtfully.

"And here remain our cousins, the serpents. They can never be defeated, I'm afraid. But they can be contained, and, I am thankful to say, most of them are now trapped in the Labyrinth. Very few live among the mensch on the four worlds."

"What will happen to the mensch, now that Death's Gate is closed?" Alfred asked wistfully. "Will all they have accomplished be wasted? Will they be completely shut off from each other?"

"The Gate is closed, but the conduits remain open. The great Kicksey-winsey continues working. Its energy beams through the conduits to the citadels. The citadels amplify that energy and send it to Chelestra and Abarrach. Chelestra's sun is starting to stabilize, which means that the seamoons will awaken. Life there will flourish."

"And Abarrach?"

"Ah, we are not certain about Abarrach. The dead have left it, of course. The citadels will warm the conduits, which will melt its icy shell. Regions now gripped by cold will be habitable once more."

"But who will come to repopulate it?" Alfred asked sadly. "Death's Gate is closed. The mensch could not have traveled through it anyway."

"No," said the dragon, "but one mensch currently living on Pryan—an elf named Paithan Quindiniar—is working on experiments begun by his father. Experiments having to do with rocketry. The mensch might reach Abarrach sooner than you think."

"As for us, life for our peoples will not be easy," said Vasu. "But if we work together, we can hold back the evil and bring a measure of peace and stability—even to the Labyrinth."

"We will rebuild the Nexus," said Balthazar. "Tear down the wall and the Final Gate. Perhaps, someday, our two peoples will be able to live there together in harmony."

"I am truly grateful. Truly thankful." Alfred wiped his eyes with the frayed lace of his collar.

"So am I," said Haplo. He put his arm around Marit, held her close. "All we need to do now is to find our daughter—"

"We'll find her," said Marit. "Together."

"But," said Alfred, with a sudden thought, "what in the name

of the Labyrinth happened to Ramu? What caused him to relinquish command?"

"A peculiar incident," said Balthazar gravely. "He was
wounded, I'm afraid. In rather a tender spot. And, what's truly
odd, he can't seem to heal himself."

"What wounded him? A dragon-snake?"

"No." Balthazar glanced shrewdly at Haplo, almost smiled. "It
seems poor Ramu was bitten by a dog."

EPILOGUE

◆

THE STRANGE STORM THAT HAD SWEPT OVER ARIANUS ABATED AS QUICKLY AS IT had come up. There had never been a storm to equal it, not even on the continent of Drevlin, which was—or had been—subjected to severe storms on a nearly hourly basis. Some of the terrified inhabitants of the floating continents feared that the world was coming to an end, though the more rational among them—this included Limbeck Bolttightner—knew better.

"It is an environmental flux," he said to Jarre, or rather what he assumed to be Jarre, but which was, in fact, a broom. He had broken his glasses during the storm. Jarre, used to this, moved the broom and took its place, without the nearsighted Limbeck knowing the difference. "An environmental flux, no doubt caused by the increased activity of the Kicksey-winsey, which has created a heating up of the atmosphere. I will call it Winsey-warming."

Which he did, and made a speech about it that very night, to which no one listened, due to the fact that they were mopping up the water.

The ferocious storm winds threatened to cause considerable damage to the cities of the Mid Realms, particularly elven cities, which are large and densely populated. But at the height of the storm's fury, human mysteriarchs—high-ranking wizards of the Seventh House—arrived and, with their magical ability to exert control over the natural elements, did much to protect the elves.

Damage was kept to a minimum and injuries were minor. Most important, this unasked-for and unlooked-for aid did much to ease tensions between former bitter enemies.

The only building to suffer extensive damage in the storm was the Cathedral of the Albedo, the repository for the souls of the dead.

The Kenkari elves had formed the Cathedral of crystal, stone, and magic. Its crystal-paned dome protected an exotic garden of rare and beautiful plants, some purportedly dating back to pre-Sundering times—plants brought from a world whose very existence was now mostly forgotten. Inside this garden, the souls of elves of royal blood fluttered among the leaves and the fragrant roses.

Each elf, before he or she died, bequeathed the soul to the Kenkari, leaving it in the care of keeper elves, who were known as geir or weesham. The geir brought the soul, imprisoned in an ornate box, to the Cathedral, where the Kenkari set it loose among the other souls held in the garden. It was believed, among the elves, that these souls of the dead granted the gift of strength and wisdom gained in life to the living.

The ancient custom had been started by the holy elf-woman Krenka-Anris, the souls of her own dead sons having returned to save their mother from a dragon.

The Kenkari elves lived in the Cathedral, tending to the souls, accepting and releasing new souls into the garden. At least, that was what had been done in the past. When it became clear to the Kenkari that the elven emperor Agah'ran was having young elves murdered in order to obtain their souls to aid his corrupt rule, the Kenkari closed the Cathedral, forbade the acceptance of any more souls.

Agah'ran was overthrown by his son, Prince Rees'ahn, and the human rulers Stephen and Anne of Volkaran. The emperor fled and disappeared. The elves and humans formed an alliance. The peace was an uneasy one, its overseers working hard to keep it, constantly forced to put out fires, quell riots, rein in headstrong followers. So far, it was working.

But the Kenkari had no idea what to do. Their last instructions, given to them by the Keeper of the Soul, revealed to him by Krenka-Anris, was to keep the Cathedral closed. And so they did. Every day, the three Keepers—Soul, Book, and Door—approached the altar and asked for guidance.

They were told to wait.

And then came the storm.

The wind began rising unexpectedly around midday. Frightful-looking dark clouds formed in the skies above and below the Mid Realms, completely obscured Solarus. Day turned to night in an instant. All commerce ceased in the city. People ran out into the streets, staring nervously at the sky. Ships plying the air between isles sought safe haven as fast as they could, putting down in any harbor close by, which meant that elves were landing in human ports, humans seeking refuge in elven towns.

The winds continued to rise. The brittle hargast trees shattered and cracked. Flimsy buildings were flattened as if smashed by a giant fist. The strong fortresses of the humans shook and shuddered. It was said that even the Kir death monks, who pay little attention to what is transpiring in the world of the living, actually emerged from their monasteries, looked up at the sky, nodded gloomily to themselves in anticipation of the end.

In the Cathedral, the Keepers of the Soul, the Book, and the Door all gathered together before the altar of Krenka-Anris to pray.

Now the rain began, slanting from the dark clouds like spears thrown by a fearsome army. Hailstones large as the head of a soldier's mace pelted the Cathedral's glass dome.

"Krenka-Anris," prayed Soul, "hear our—"

A cracking sound—loud and violent, like the blast of a pyrotechnic display—split the air. Door gasped. Book flinched. The Keeper of the Soul, shaken, halted in mid-prayer.

"The souls in the garden are highly agitated," said the Keeper.

Though the souls themselves were not visible to the eye, the leaves of the trees trembled and quivered. Petals were shaken from the flowers.

Another crack, sharp, ominous.

"Thunder?" ventured the Keeper of the Door, forgetting—in his fear—that he was not to speak unless spoken to.

The Keeper of the Soul rose to his feet and looked through the crystal window into the garden. With an incoherent cry, he staggered backward, grasping at the altar for support. The other two hastened to his side.

"What is it?" Book asked, her voice nearly failing her.

"The ceiling!" Soul gasped, pointing. "It is starting to break!"

They could all see the crack now, a jagged line, slanting like lightning, cutting through the crystal dome. As they watched, the crack grew longer, wider. A piece of glass broke loose, fell into the garden with a crash.

"Krenka-Anris, save us!" Book whispered.

"I do not think we are the ones she is saving," said the Keeper of the Soul. He was suddenly extremely calm. "Come. We must leave, seek shelter in the rooms underground. Quickly, now." He left the altar, headed for the door. Book and Door hastened behind, practically tripping on his heels.

Behind them, they could hear the shattering of more falling glass, the splintering of the great trees sheltered beneath the dome.

The Keeper of the Soul rang the bell that called the Kenkari together for prayer—except that this time he called them together for action.

"The great dome is being split asunder," he told his shocked followers. "There is nothing to be done to save it. This is the will of Krenka-Anris. We have been told to seek shelter. The matter is out of our hands. We have done what we could to help. Now we must pray."

"What did we do to help?" the Keeper of the Door whispered to the Keeper of the Book as they hastened after Soul down the stairs leading to the underground chambers.

The Keeper of the Soul, overhearing, looked around with a smile. "We helped a lost man find a dog."

The storm grew more and more fierce. All knew now that Arianus was doomed.

And then the tempest ended with the same suddenness with which it had begun. The dark clouds vanished, as if sucked through a gigantic open doorway. Solarus returned, dazzling the dazed elves with its bright light.

The Kenkari emerged from below ground to find the Cathedral completely and utterly destroyed. The crystal dome was shattered. The trees and flowers inside were cut to ribbons by shards of glass, buried beneath hailstones.

"The souls?" asked the Keeper of the Door, awed, stunned.

"Gone," said the Keeper of the Book sadly.

"Free," said the Keeper of the Soul.

APPENDIX ◆ I

Being a Concise History of
the Seventh Gate, the Sundering, and the Tragic Downfall
of the Sartan in the New Worlds

compiled by Alfred Montbank

◆

Author's Note: I wish to gratefully acknowledge the assistance of those Sartan who were witnesses to the events I have endeavored to record in this monograph. Their help and candor have been invaluable.

DROPS OF WATER

"We each have within ourselves the ability to shape our own destinies. That much we understand. But, more important, each of us has an equal ability to shape the destiny of the universe. Ah, that you find more difficult to believe. But I tell you it is so. You do not have to be the leader of the Council of Seven. You do not have to be elven king or human monarch or the head of a dwarven clan to have a significant impact on the world around you.

"In the vastness of the ocean, is any drop of water greater than another?

" 'No,' you answer, 'and neither has a single drop the ability to cause a tidal wave.'

" 'But,' I argue, 'if a single drop falls into the ocean, it creates ripples. And these ripples spread. And perhaps—who knows—these ripples may grow and swell and eventually break foaming upon the shore.

"Like a drop in the vast ocean, each of us causes ripples as we move through our lives. The effects of whatever we do—insignifi-

cant as it may seem—spread out beyond us. We may never know
what far-reaching impact even the simplest action might have on
our fellow mortals. Thus we need to be conscious, all of the time,
of our place in the ocean, of our place in the world, of our place
among our fellow creatures.

"For if enough of us join forces, we can swell the tide of events
—for good or for evil."

The above is a portion of a speech made to the Council of Seven
in the days just prior to the Sundering, shortly after the creation of
the Seventh Gate. The speaker was an elder Sartan of great wisdom. His true Sartan name may not be given here, since he is still
alive and I do not have his permission to reveal it. (His permission
cannot be obtained, because he has tragically lost all memory of
what he was.) We know him now as Zifnab.

In the remainder of the speech, the elder Sartan—who was formerly Councillor before Samah—goes on to argue passionately
against the proposal to sunder the world. Many of the Council
members who heard him that day remember being deeply moved
by his speech, and more than a few were starting to waver in their
decision.

The Head of the Council, Samah—having listened with cold
politeness—spoke afterward. Samah portrayed in vivid detail the
rising power of the Patryns, how they had taken over mensch
kingdoms, how they were raising armies with the intent to conquer and overthrow the Sartan.

The Council members recall being elevated by the elder
Sartan's image of the world and terribly frightened by Samah's.
Needless to say, fear won out over what Samah termed "worthy
but impractical idealism." The Council voted to proceed with the
Sundering, the capture and incarceration of their enemies.

THE CREATION
OF THE SEVENTH GATE

Were the Patryns actually plotting to conquer the world?

We have no way of knowing for certain, since—unlike the Sartan—no Patryns remain alive from that period in time. Knowing the nature of sentient beings, I think it quite probable that Samah had his counterpart on the Patryn side. We have some indication of this in the later portion of the elder Sartan's speech, in which he refers to a now forgotten Patryn leader by name and urges the Council to consider negotiating with this person, rather than fighting.

Perhaps negotiation would have been impossible. Perhaps war between the two powerful forces was inevitable. Perhaps just as much or more destruction and suffering would have come from such a war as from the Sundering. Those are questions to which we will never know the answers.

Having made its decision, the Council was faced with a monumental task, the working of magicks the likes of which had never been seen before in the universe.

First, the Council created a headquarters, an actual structure with a physical presence in the world. This is the room I knew later as the Chamber of the Damned. Samah referred to this room as the Seventh Gate, after the plan proposed by himself for the re-creation of the world, a plan which would in later days be reduced to a meaningless litany.

The Earth was destroyed.

Four worlds were created out of the ruin. Worlds for ourselves and the mensch: Air, Fire, Stone, Water.

Four Gates connect each world to the other: Arianus to Pryan to Abarrach to Chelestra.

A house of correction was built for our enemies: the Labyrinth.

The Labyrinth is connected to the other worlds through the Fifth Gate: the Nexus.

The Sixth Gate is the center, permits entry: the Vortex.

And all was accomplished through the Seventh Gate.

The end was the beginning.

◆

Once the Seventh Gate had physical existence, the Sartan gave it existence on a magical plane, making it a "well" similar to that constructed by the Patryns on Abri—a hole in the fabric of magic wherein the possibility exists that no possibilities exist.

When this magical slate had been wiped clean, so to speak, the Sartan were able to go in and imbue this chamber with the specific rune-magic necessary to bring about (1) the defeat and imprisonment of their enemies, (2) the salvation of those mensch considered worthy of saving, (3) the destruction of the world, (4) the building of four new worlds. A monstrous undertaking. But the Sartan were strong in magic and desperate in their fear. Creating the Seventh Gate took them many years of work, during which they lived in constant terror that the Patryns would discover them before they were ready to act.

Finally, however, the Seventh Gate was completed, its magic ready. The Sartan entered and discovered, to their astonishment and terror and chagrin, that they were not alone. A possibility existed that they had never before considered—they were *not* the masters of the universe. A power existed that was far greater than themselves.

BITTER WATER

How was this power manifested? How did the Sartan discover it? I could not find a single Sartan willing to discuss the experience, which each described as soul-shattering. Based on my own experience the first time I entered the Chamber of the Damned, I must conclude that the perceptions of the higher power are varied and highly personal. In my own case, I felt, for the first time in my life, loved and accepted, at peace with myself. But I gather that, for other Sartan, the revelations were not so pleasant.

(Certainly, it was—as Haplo has suggested—this very same force that drove the Sartan on Pryan out of their protected fortress-citadels and into the jungles, which they had created, but for which they refused to accept responsibility. I will return to this event later in the text.)

Unfortunately, the knowledge that a power existed in the universe greater than his own did not deter Samah from his plans. Rather, it fed his fear. What if the Patryns discovered this power? Could they somehow tap into it? Perhaps they already had! Samah and the Council members and the majority of the Sartan gave in to their fear. The drops of bitter water swelled to form a wave of terrible force and power, which crashed down on the world.

Those Sartan like Zifnab who protested against the Council's decision, who refused to join it, were considered traitors. In order to keep such treachery from contaminating and weakening the magic of the Seventh Gate, these traitor Sartan were rounded up and sent into the Labyrinth along with the Patryns.

THE DOWNFALL
OF THE PATRYNS

One might think that the capture and incarceration of the Patryns would have proved extremely difficult, provoking magical battles of the most tremendous magnitude. That the Sartan were afraid of this very outcome is witnessed by the fact that they created magical weapons such as the Cursed Blade and armed and trained the mensch to fight for the Sartan "cause."

But, in the end, according to the Sartan with whom I spoke, the capture of the Patryns was relatively simple, made so by the very nature of the Patryns themselves.

Unlike the gregarious Sartan, the Patryns tended to be loners, living for the most part by themselves or in small family groups. They were a selfish, haughty, proud people, having little compassion even for each other, no compassion for anyone else. Such were their jealousies and rivalries that they found it impossible to unite, even against a common foe. (This was one reason they preferred to live among the mensch, whom they could intimidate and control.) Thus, the Patryns were picked off one by one, easy prey for the united forces of the Sartan.

THE BEGINNING
OF THE END

The elder Sartan whom we now know as Zifnab refused to leave the world. When the Sartan guards (of whom Ramu was one) came to arrest him, the old Sartan could not be found. He had been tipped off, forewarned. (Was it Orlah who warned him? She never said, but I often wonder.) The Sartan searched for him. To give them credit, they did not want any of their number to face the horror of what they knew was coming. But he eluded them. He remained in the world and witnessed the Sundering.

The sight drove him mad, and he would undoubtedly have perished, but he made his way—somehow—to the Vortex and from there entered the Labyrinth. How he managed this is not known, for Zifnab himself has no memory of it. The dragons of Pryan—the manifestation of the higher power in its form for good —might have had something to do with his rescue, but, if so, they refuse to discuss it.

The remaining Sartan removed those mensch deemed worthy to repopulate the new worlds, took them to a safe place (the Vortex). The Sartan then shut themselves up in the Seventh Gate and worked the magic. (I will not go into that here. You will find a description of what I saw and experienced when I was magically transported back to that time in Haplo's more extensive notes on the subject, compiled under the title *The Seventh Gate*.)

THE END
OF THE BEGINNING

Once the Sundering was complete and the new worlds were created, the Sartan—those who had survived the horrific forces they had themselves unleashed—were sent out to begin new lives in new worlds. They took the mensch with them, intending to shepherd them like flocks of sheep.

Samah and the Council members chose Chelestra as their base of operation. At this point, Samah should have destroyed the Seventh Gate. (I believe that he had actually been directed by the Council to do so and that, in leaving the Gate intact, he directly disobeyed Council commands. I have no proof of this, however. The Council members to whom I spoke were all very evasive on the subject. They are still intent on honoring Samah's memory. Ah, well, he was not an evil man, merely a frightened one.)

I think it likely that Samah intended to destroy the Seventh Gate, but that circumstances combined to convince him that he should leave it open. He almost immediately ran into trouble in his new world. Events strange and unforeseen were happening—events over which the Sartan had no control.

THE SERPENTS

The seawater of Chelestra turned out to have a devastating effect on Sartan magic, rendering it useless, themselves powerless. The Sartan were baffled. They had certainly not created such a magic-nullifying ocean. Who had? And how and why?

But this was not the worst.

The tremendous magical eruption had upset the delicate balance of creation—what the dwarves on Chelestra would later come to refer to as "the Wave." Think of the Wave as the sea on a calm day, the waves flowing in to shore, one after the other, falling and rising, falling and rising. Now, imagine a tidal wave—a wave out of control, rising and rising and rising. The wave would naturally seek to correct itself and, in this instance, it did so. The evil that had always existed in the world prior to the Sundering had now gained the power to take on physical shape and form. Evil was manifested in the serpents or dragon-snakes.

The serpents followed Samah to Chelestra, hoping, undoubtedly, to learn more about the new world in which they suddenly found themselves. They knew of the existence of Death's Gate, but not how it worked. They could enter it only if the Sartan opened it for them. Perhaps they were also searching for the Seventh Gate, although that is conjecture. At any rate, their appearance was another bitter shock for the Sartan, who couldn't imagine how such loathsome creatures came into existence. Alas, it was the Sartan themselves who brought them into being.

They told Samah, "You created us," and, in a sense, he did. We all did. We all do, through fear and hatred and intolerance.

But I digress.

THE GOOD DRAGONS
OF PRYAN

Fortunately for the mensch and the Sartan—although they couldn't know it at the time—the Wave continued to try to correct itself. The evil of the dragon-snakes was balanced by good manifesting itself in the form of the dragons of Pryan. If Death's Gate had remained open, as was intended, the evil and the good would have balanced each other out—the Wave would have succeeded in correcting itself.

But, again, fear ruled Samah's life. Afraid of the dragon-snakes, and now afraid of the mensch—whose slight magical powers were not affected by the seawater—Samah sent out calls to other Sartan on other worlds, asking them to come to his aid, to fight and subdue these new foes.

His calls were never answered, or at least that is what Samah told his people. According to Orlah, Samah's wife, the calls *were* answered. The Sartan on the other worlds told Samah that they were powerless to come to his aid because they themselves were in serious trouble. Samah lied to spare his people—some of whom had relatives and friends in these other worlds—the terrible truth. The grand design was beginning to shatter.

SHUTTING DEATH'S GATE

According to Orlah, at this point in time, Samah was baffled, angry. He had lost control of events and he had no idea how or why. The plan should have worked. It had all been so logical, rational. He laid blame on the mensch. He laid blame on weak Sartan. But that did not solve his immediate problem.

If the serpents attacked the Chalice—the Sartan's home base— the Sartan had no way to defend themselves. All the serpents had to do was toss a bucket of magic-nullifying water on the Sartan and they were finished. The mensch were quarreling among themselves, blaming the Sartan for the appearance of the serpents. Worse, the mensch had seen the Sartan humbled, chastened, routed by the serpents. Samah sent the mensch away from the Chalice, sent them out into the sea to find their own way in the world.

Some might consider this an appalling act. After all, Samah might well have been sending the mensch into the toothless maws of the serpents. But according to Orlah, Samah guessed—rightly— that the serpents were not interested in the mensch. Their main goal was to enter Death's Gate, and to do that they had to rely on the Sartan.

Fearing that the evil serpents would spread from Chelestra into the other three worlds, Samah felt he had no recourse but to shut Death's Gate. He should have destroyed the Seventh Gate at this time, but he thought that perhaps its powerful magic might once again be needed. He cast the Seventh Gate into oblivion.

Once this was accomplished, Samah and his people sent themselves into a stasis sleep, planning to wake up in a hundred years. By that time, Samah reasoned, matters would have stabilized on the other worlds. The Kicksey-winsey would be up and running, the citadels in operation. When he awoke, life would be better.

Such was not the case.

THE SERPENTS FROZEN

Again I find an example of the Wave correcting itself.

Due to the fact that Sartan magic had no effect on the ocean of Chelestra, its sun remained unstable. The sun was supposed to be locked into position in the center of the water world, warming the inside of the globe, leaving the outer portion a shell of ice. But the sun could not be constrained and so it wandered, drifting slowly through the water, warming parts of that world, while the rest remained locked in ice.

When the Sartan first moved onto Chelestra, the sun warmed their portion of that world—a part known as the Chalice. (For a more complete description, refer to the volume Haplo called—over my objections—*Serpent Mage*.) But as time passed and the Sartan slept on, the sun began to drift away.

The evil serpents saw their doom too late. Unable to flee through Death's Gate and unwilling to leave the Sartan in case they woke up, the serpents waited too long to escape. When the sun wandered off, the serpents did not follow it and so were frozen in the ice-bound ocean.

The Wave was almost back to normal. The good serpents on Pryan, so as not to disturb the balance, went underground, doing what they could to avoid contact with the mensch and the Sartan.

THE WAVE ROLLS ON

Arianus

Time passed while the Sartan slumbered. Samah's glorious vision of four worlds interconnected, working together, failed to materialize. The Sartan population dwindled. The numbers of mensch—who were now thriving on the new worlds (with the exception of Abarrach)—increased. Their populations grew too large for the few remaining Sartan to control. The Sartan retreated, hoping to fall back and regroup, waiting all the while for contact with their brethren on the other worlds—contact that would never come.

On Arianus, the great Kicksey-winsey went to work, but it lacked direction. The mensch had no idea what it was supposed to do. The Sartan left directions for the operation of the Kicksey-winsey with the Kenkari elves—a race the Sartan considered most trustworthy.

But the elves on Arianus were divided among themselves in a bitter power struggle. And all the elves feared and detested the humans, who in turn had no use for the elves. The Kenkari, reading the book on the Kicksey-winsey, realized that the machine would bring the lands of the elves and the humans together, that the dwarves would have control over the machine. This the elves deemed intolerable. The Kenkari hid the book in the libraries of the Cathedral of the Albedo, where it lay forgotten for many centuries.

After turning over the book, the Sartan on Arianus went into hiding in tunnels they had built underground. They sent their young people into stasis sleep, hoping again that when they woke up, things would have improved. Unfortunately, most of the young Sartan on Arianus died in that sleep. (I think it is likely that these mysterious deaths were due to the practice of necromancy on Abarrach, for so it is written that when one life is restored untimely another dies untimely. This is speculation, however. Hopefully, my theory will never be proved!)

Pryan

The Sartan on Pryan lived in the citadels with the mensch whom they had brought to this world. The Sartan ran the star chambers, which were designed to work with the Kicksey-winsey to beam energy to the other worlds. The Sartan were endeavoring to make the star chambers work, and were also trying to control the mensch, whose numbers were rapidly increasing.

Cooped up in the citadels, the mensch races began to fight among themselves. The Sartan, considering the mensch as annoying as quarrelsome children, treated them as such. Instead of working with the mensch to negotiate their problems, the Sartan created "nursemaids." Thus were born the tytans—fearsome giants who were meant to operate the star chambers (should they ever start functioning!) and serve as nannies to the mensch. Acting out of fear and blind prejudice, the Sartan made matters worse instead of better. The tytans proved too powerful a creation; they turned on their creators.

How or why the Sartan on Pryan came into contact with the higher power is open to conjecture. On his visit to Pryan, Haplo entered one of the citadels and there discovered a room that he describes as an almost exact replica of the Seventh Gate. I can only assume that the Sartan on Pryan constructed what might be called a miniature Seventh Gate, perhaps in the hope of reestablishing communication with their brethren on other worlds or even in a desperate attempt to reopen Death's Gate.

The Sartan on Pryan claimed that they were forced by this

higher power to leave the citadels. I think it more likely that they found it easier to flee their problems than to seek solutions. They laid the blame conveniently on the higher power, rather than on where it belonged—on themselves.

Abarrach

As for the Sartan on Abarrach, their situation was the most desperate of all. The mensch they had brought to Abarrach had almost all died due to the poisonous atmosphere. The Sartan were faced with the knowledge that unless help came soon, they were doomed as well. It was a group of Sartan on Abarrach who, seeking to regain contact with their lost brethren, stumbled onto the Seventh Gate.

The Sartan knew they had found a tremendous source of power, but—having lost much of their ability to perform Sartan magic—they had no idea what it was they had discovered. These Sartan came closest of all who had gone before to understanding the higher power. But their own evil—brought about by greed for power, exacerbated by the heinous practice of necromancy—proved their downfall. Violence entered the sacred chamber and all within were destroyed.

Appalled, terrified, the Sartan who survived inscribed runes of warding on what was now called the Chamber of the Damned. No one dared enter it, and eventually, all knowledge of the location of the Seventh Gate was lost.

The Labyrinth

The Labyrinth had become a prison house of horrors. According to Orlah, Samah had intended that the Sartan serve as wardens of this prison, monitoring it as well as their prisoners' progress toward rehabilitation. When the Sartan lost control of their own lives, they could not hope to control the Labyrinth. The dark magic of the Labyrinth fed off the Sartan's hatred and fear. It turned deadly. And from the Labyrinth, born of hatred, came Lord Xar.

XAR, LORD OF
THE NEXUS

The history of Xar's early life is unknown, but certainly it must have been similar to the countless histories of those Patryns who were born in that dreadful prison. Xar is different in that he was the first Patryn[1] to escape the Labyrinth, to fight his way out through the Final Gate. He was the first Patryn to see the Nexus.

To give Xar credit, he worked unselfishly, often in dire peril of his own life, to save his fellow Patryns from the Labyrinth. It is no wonder that, to this day, the lord's memory is still honored among them.

Xar's ambition was his downfall. He was not content to lead his people, but on discovering that four worlds existed, sought to rule them as well. He learned how to open Death's Gate—not completely, only a crack. But this was enough. He was able to enter, and this brought about catastrophic change. Xar's rise to power caused the Wave to shift out of balance.

Death's Gate opened. The first Patryn, Haplo, left the Nexus, entered Arianus. At the same time, Chelestra's sun floated back around to the Chalice. The warmth caused the ice to melt, freeing the serpents. The knowledge that their cousins were awake caused the good dragons of Pryan to come out of hiding. These events, occurring simultaneously, might be taken as coincidence. I prefer to see in them the Wave attempting, once again, to restore the balance.

---

[1] I make the distinction—first Patryn—because the Sartan known as Zifnab apparently managed to escape the Labyrinth and enter the Nexus. He claims to have written a large portion of the manuscripts and books which Xar found in the Nexus. These works are mostly lost to us now, having been destroyed in the fire set by the serpents—one reason that Haplo and I are working to replace them.

No one (including Zifnab himself!) is quite certain how he managed to leave the Nexus. During his more lucid moments, he claims that the good dragons of Pryan traveled to the Nexus and found him there. Impressed with his abilities as a great and powerful wizard, they turned to him for leadership and guidance.

The dragons of Pryan tell quite a different story, one which I refrain from repeating, since it might unnecessarily hurt the old man's feelings.

What happened after that I will not describe here. Suffice it to say that by a curious series of incidents, I met Haplo and his remarkable dog.

Those interested in reading more about the exciting adventures of Haplo and the humbler adventures of myself can find them in what has come to be known as the *Death Gate Cycle*.

In closing, I will add, for those who might be interested, that the Wave continues to ebb and flow. The Patryns and the Sartan now live together in an uneasy peace. The Sartan have split into two factions: one led by Balthazar, which desires alliance with the Patryns; the other led by Ramu, who—though still somewhat bothered by his unfortunate injury—refuses to trust the Patryns at all.

Headman Vasu is leader of the Patryns. He and Haplo and Marit have formed bands of what are known as Rescuers, brave men and women—both Patryn and Sartan—who risk their lives venturing deep into the Labyrinth to try to aid those still trapped in the prison. I am proud to say that I am myself a Rescuer.

The evil serpents are diminished in power, but are present still and will be forever, I suppose. They are kept in check by the dragons of Pryan, however, and by the concerted efforts of the Rescuers.

We have no knowledge of what is transpiring in the worlds of the mensch, but I hope all is well with them. I like to think of them traveling between worlds in fantastical ships, propelled by hope and curiosity.

Haplo and Marit set out on a search for their daughter—and returned with numerous daughters, all orphans whom they rescued from the Labyrinth. Haplo states proudly that any one of them could be his child, and Marit always agrees. They have several sons now as well. They all call me "Grandfather Alfred" and tease me unmercifully about my big feet.

Haplo has a dog now. A real one.

The mad old Sartan Zifnab wanders the Labyrinth happily, watched over by his dragon. He hardly ever remembers the bad times, and we take care not to remind him.

He has decided, now, that he *is* God.

And who are we to argue with him?

APPENDIX ✦ II

Concerning the Theory
and Practice of Chaos, Order,
and the Power of Magic

✦

Author's Note: I have elsewhere noted the history of the Seventh Gate and the Sundering (see Appendix I) and the chronology of events that brings us to our present era. It occurred to me, however, that there may be students of the magical arts who might have wondered what went wrong with the Sundering and why the Sartan vision of the Sundered Realms did not work as they had hoped. To this end I now write.

In reviewing the histories I note there is but one recorded instance of Sartan and Patryn magical structures being used together—that being when Haplo and I fought our final fight. While reflecting on the various treatises of magic that have attempted to illuminate this chronicle—as well as the now seemingly incredible events in which we have played a part—I was moved to pen these observations.

Is there a greater power than rune magic? Most certainly. Is this a benevolent mind in the realm of spirit that exists beyond our physical world, or the combined essence of our joint spirits? Are these musings the window to where we have come from and how we arrived at our present state? Are they the key to our future hope? I cannot say. It is left to our children and their children to answer such questions fully. As for me, I am at peace with what I believe.

—Alfred Montbank

DEFINITION IN MAGIC

The quest for magical power has, throughout the ages, been a quest for definition. This is inherent in both Sartan and Patryn rune magic. Both forms look into the Omniwave in search of a possibility that the rune wizard wishes to bring into existence. Once the possibility is found, the wizard then uses rune structures to weave the possibility found in the Wave into the reality of existence. These basic principles form the foundation of all magic. These principles have been thoroughly studied for uncounted ages.[1] Yet the question of definition—being able to fully define the possibility that the rune magician has in mind—has never been resolved completely.

Patryn magic came closer to understanding in this regard than did that of the Sartan. While Sartan magic talked about looking, "concentrating on the Wave of possibilities," the Patryns spoke in terms of an object's "true name." Patryn magic saw itself as a search for the true name of a possibility and the calling of that true name into reality. Naming an object *completely* was the ultimate objective of Patryn magic.[2] While Sartan magic viewed this process in more nebulous terms, it is essentially this process of defining *completely* the probability required that was the essence of all magic.

THE GRAIN OF MAGIC

The flaw in all our epochs of magical theory and practice came down to a single word: *completely*. The Patryns were first to understand the limits of their own rune structures through the insights of Sendric Klausten.[3] Rune magic is constructed of runes within

---

[1] *Dragon Wing,* vol. 1 of *The Death Gate Cycle,* Appendix titled "Magic in the Sundered Realms: Excerpt from a Sartan's Musings," for a detailed explanation of the Wave and the basic principles of rune magic.

[2] *Elven Star,* vol. 2 of *The Death Gate Cycle,* Appendix titled "Patryn Runes and the Variability of Magic." See text under heading Patryn Rune Magic: Theory and Practice.

[3] *Ibid.* See text under heading Grain of Magic and Variability.

runes. Before Klausten it was believed that this succession could be infinite—rather like cutting an apple in half, then cutting the half in half, then cutting the half of the half in half, and so on an infinite number of times. Klausten, however, realized that there came a point in writing the definition where the presence of the rune itself affected the definition—and beyond which magic rune structures could not go.

The Sartan of Abarrach also discovered this limitation during their research into Necromancy.[4] The limits of the runes they defined as the "Runestate Boundary" in necromantic writings. Other advanced research writings in Patryn magic talk about the "Barrier of Uncertainty," beyond which runes are too coarse in structure to pass. Both of these terms speak to the same limits written of by the Patryn Klausten: the inability to define any magic beyond the grain of the runes themselves.

BEYOND THE BOUNDARY: FINE AND COARSE STRUCTURES

Both magicks attempted to come to grips with this Runestate Boundary or Barrier of Uncertainty, and how to pass beyond it in different ways and for different reasons.

Patryn Magic and the Barrier of Uncertainty

Sage Rethis[5] established the laws of Patryn rune magic. While Patryn magic certainly existed before Rethis, his attempts at defining the magic itself became the touchstone for Patryn magical thought for many ages and included the writings of Klausten in their defi-

---

[4] *Fire Sea*, vol. 3 of *The Death Gate Cycle*, Appendix titled "Necromancy." See text under heading Material as Coarse Existence Structure.

[5] *Elven Star*, vol. 2 of *The Death Gate Cycle*, Appendix titled "Patryn Runes and the Variability of Magic."

nition. His thoughts shaped Patryn approaches to the barrier from that moment on. His basic laws are:

First Law of Rethis: An object's name has balance. For a Patryn rune to work—or that of a Sartan, for that matter—the rune structure must be balanced. A pillar whose base is not square with its sides will not stand upright. Nor will that pillar stand if one side is heavier than the other. So it is with rune structures.

The problem came when the "true name" of the object—the name that was fully balanced—extended past the Barrier of Uncertainty, where the rune structure could no longer fully define it. No matter how carefully the rune was constructed, it remained unbalanced because the true name required a balance that had a finer grain of definition than the runes could provide.

Rethis reasoned that if this alone were true, all advanced and intricate magic would be unbalanced and, therefore, could not work. This he knew from experience was just not true. His research at this point was taken as somewhat ridiculous by some fellow Patryns and as bordering on heretical by others: Why did Patryn magic work at all? His research turned in astonishing results and led him to his second and third laws.

Second Law of Rethis: An unbalanced name tends to balance itself. This has also been called the Equilibrium Factor. He found that the Wave of probabilities from which all magic was born was not a static state entity but rather a dynamic force that obeyed laws of its own beyond the Barrier of Uncertainty. The Wave itself—from beyond this barrier—acted to correct for any small imbalances and imperfections of the rune structure itself.

Third Law of Rethis: No rune has infinite balance. In the end, I believe, Rethis gave the equivalent of a shrug in his third law. Essentially he was saying, since no rune has infinite balance and since the Wave will correct for any small imperfections anyway—well, why worry? Make your magicks, trust that the Wave will correct for any small flaws in its balance, and get on with getting out of the Labyrinth.

It was this Third Law of Rethis that attracted the attention and the praise of Patryn researchers and popular thought. From that time on, Patryns explored ways of influencing the Wave in their approaches to the barrier in order to bring the exact probability they wanted into existence.

Forgotten in the thunderous clamor over the third law was the astounding implications of the second law, that the Wave itself may have something to say about the fate of all creation.

Sartan Necromancy and the Runestate Boundary

In their attempts at Necromancy, the Abarrach Sartan had more success in penetrating their Runestate Boundary than the Patryns had with their Barrier of Uncertainty—although both proved to be the same thing.

The first major insights came from an aging Sartan mage named Delsart Sparanga,[6] who discovered the Delsart Near State, or Delsart Similitude. Delsart said that the "spiritual state of all things is a much finer reflection of the physical state. All things that exist in the physical are also expressed in this spiritual state. Delsart taught that no thing exists in what he terms the coarse physical state except that it also have existence in the spiritual state."[7] This spiritual reflection of all things was thought to exist beyond the Runestate Boundary; thus all things existed in a coarse physical state (accessible by runes) and a spiritual state (beyond runes).[8]

The mensch have had many gods in all their wonderful and varied lands. They have always believed in the spirit state. We— the Sartan and the Patryns—thought such whisperings to be fool-

---

[6] *Fire Sea*, vol. 3 of *The Death Gate Cycle*, Appendix titled "Necromancy." See text under heading The Delsart Solution.

[7] *Ibid.*

[8] *Ibid.* See text under Cycle 290: Coarse and Fine Existence.

ish and childlike imaginings. How could we have known that in our ignorance of such things we would cause such misery on an unprecedented scale.

THE NATURE OF CHAOS

Both Sartan and Patryn had considered the working of the universe to be something like a Geg machine: If you turned the wheelie then the lifter-arm would raise. The universe was absolutely predictable. No matter how often you turned the wheelie, that lifter-arm would raise just the same.

All of this was fine in the coarse state—that crude physical world that we had increasingly come to recognize as the domain of the runes. However, the runes' power shattered entirely at the Runestate Boundary. Beyond that lay a realm of Chaos where entropic forces were at work. It was truly an "Uncertainty Barrier" in that nothing that happened beyond it could be predicted with any surety.

However, this image of complete chaos was incongruent with Delsart's teachings of the Near State as a finer reflection of the physical state, as well as with the Second Law of Rethis. If complete chaos reigned beyond the barrier, why then did the spiritual effects of Necromancy work? Further, why did the Omniwave, which by definition existed on both sides of the barrier, act dynamically toward a stable, ordered state when chaos and entropy were the accepted rule beyond the barrier?

The problems of spiritual essence were not confined to the realms of rune magic alone but were also reflected in the lesser magicks of the mensch as well. The Kenkari elf practice of trapping the souls of their ancestors[9] for the enhancement of their own crude magicks touched on this spiritual world beyond. They, too, had no context in which to put their discoveries and, like both the Sartan and the Patryns, covered their ignorance with cobbled-together theory that either masked or excused the truth.

---

[9] *The Hand of Chaos*, vol. 5 of *The Death Gate Cycle*. See also *Dragon Wing*, vol. 1 of *The Death Gate Cycle*.

DEATH'S GATE

The Sundering, in the light of the knowledge we have gained since that time, was an arrogant folly of unparalleled proportions. In structuring the complex runes to sunder creation into the realms, we had supposed that the magic would be perfect in all its detail. Yet the magic was coarse even in its finest detail when it came to the Uncertainty Barrier. Its magic had no choice but to extend itself beyond that boundary and into the spiritual realms. In doing so, the Wave corrected as best it could to such a catastrophic inclusion.

Part of that correction, I believe, involved the rune structures that gave name to "Death's Gate." Imperfect as it was and heavily intrusive into the realms of the finer spiritual structures, the calling of Death's Gate into reality was more apt than the original designers had supposed.

Death may well be a gate: a spiritual gate through which our finer selves pass on to other realms and other realities. Indeed, I am left to ponder if we truly exist more in that spirit state than in this physical one. Who is to say which is real and which is ephemeral?

When the Sundering opened Death's Gate in the physical, coarse reality, I believe it closed the spiritual gate beyond the Uncertainty Barrier. Our actions not only brought suffering and horror in the physical realms but damned the souls of our countless dead as well, cutting us off from whatever higher existence we would have beyond this physical realm as well as from other spirits that may already exist in that finer place.

Yet we were not entirely cut off, for the Wave continued to correct itself. We may have upset the boat, but the waves of our foolishness subside and the pond again becomes placid and at peace.

THE ORDER BEYOND

Who or what observes the Wave in the realms beyond? Are there gods of the spirit with powers higher than our own? Were the mensch far wiser in this than we with all our power?

I believe now that there is an existence beyond the physical whose purpose we can only now guess at. It is in that realm of the spirit that the greatest power of all is found, somewhere in the correcting Wave. If there is something or someone out there beyond this life, I know I shall find it when the time is come. We have closed the physical gate; the spirit gate is now open once again.

Only in closing the gate on our prison are we now truly free.

Closing the Seventh Gate

Alfred, Haplo, Dog

by Janet Pack

Alfred

Alfred

Haplo, Dog

"Woof"

"Woof"   "Woof"

"Woof"

Haplo

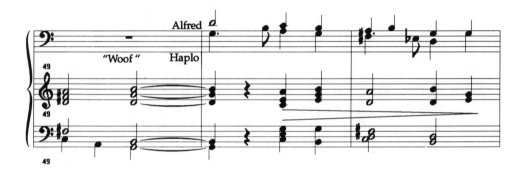

Alfred

"Woof" Haplo

"Woof"

"Woof"

"Woof" "Woof"

"Woof"

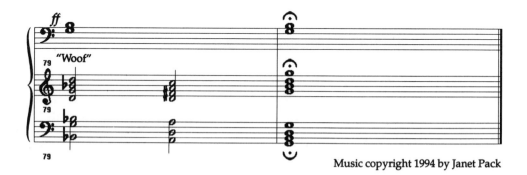

For Gary, my life-partner.
Thank you for all your love, confidence, and
encouragement.

PERFORMANCE NOTES FOR
"CLOSING THE SEVENTH GATE"

This piece begins with the synthesizer representing Chaos. It is a very pale portrait of the Chaos that existed. Use a setting (or a couple of them, if possible) that has a raw, wild sound in the bass and a keening in the treble.

There are several unusual symbols in the score. They are:

Asterisk (star)—A hit. Strike the keyboard sharply with your hand.

Square—"Walk" your hand from thumb to outer edge (or vice versa) up or down the keyboard as indicated.

X—A small cluster of notes created by leaning the side of your hand on the keyboard.

=—A glissando, or run of notes, done with the back of either your thumbnail or the nail of your second finger. Up or down the keyboard is shown by the raised or lowered right side of the sign.

Triangle—Lean heavily on the keyboard with your palm, holding it as long as indicated.

The first nine measures are designated "Ad lib." This is done to allow the accompanist to generate a more thorough feeling of Chaos. Chaos attempts to escape whatever tries to contain it, and usually succeeds. This begins to change after Alfred starts singing confidently. Chaos endeavors to return several times throughout the piece, such as in measures 38 and 39, also in measures 57 and 58. Alfred and Haplo, assisted by the Dog, manage to subdue Chaos each time it tries to overwhelm them.

The Dog's voice should have the deep chesty resonance of a larger canine (similar to a collie, a Labrador retriever, or a golden retriever). You might have a friend who barks well take the part of the Dog. However, if your friends refuse because of shyness or for other reasons, you can use a sample bark from a synthesizer library. If you don't have access to a synthesizer library with a decent dog bark, record a canine with an appropriate voice on tape.

Neither Alfred nor Haplo sing words. Because they are singing a special and rather specific magic, there is no way to accurately translate it into representative syllables. Sing their parts on "Ah" or any similar open vowel.

You may notice there is no key signature indicated in the music. Because Alfred and Haplo are so different, they are singing in two different (but related) keys. Alfred's part is in G major. Haplo's is in a G minor scale called a mode. Occasionally their voices hit a dissonance, just as their relationship does. They have, however, learned to work together despite their diverse natures; hence the fairly consistent harmonies they produce.

When Alfred begins singing in measure 10, he is unsure of himself. His voice is fairly quiet, barely heard through the wildness of Chaos. He has difficulty getting started. Persisting, he continues singing louder and more powerfully until his melody finally develops in measure 17.

But Alfred himself isn't strong enough to prevail against Chaos. Haplo begins helping in measure 22, and the Dog adds an occasional "Woof" to encourage the duet. Together, the three beings prevail over Chaos. The Seventh Gate itself is shut during the reprise, which starts in measure 60.

Those singing Alfred's part may want to exchange a few lower notes for the ones written in measures 26, 34, and 64. The substitutions are:

Measure 26: C,B,C,C;
Measure 34: C,A,C,C;
Measure 64: C,D,C,C.

Have fun!